The Reluctant Millionaire

Joseph Birchall

Acknowledgements

Thanks AGAIN to Jean Grainger for her continued
support and advice.

Thanks to my beta readers for correcting my grammatical mistakes:
Kay Birchall, Claire Whitty, Mary Cummins, Shane Kenny and
Brent Matthews

And thanks to my wife and best friend, Eileen.
You rock!

For Kai

1

Michael Irvine opened up the packet of disposable razor blades that his mother had bought for him earlier that day. He shoved one of them under the lukewarm water, removed his glasses and leaned forward into the mirror. Sliding the blade across the foamed parts of his face, he edged around the borders of his goatee.

Michael didn't mind the tepid water.

'One hour per day is more than enough time for the immersion to be on,' he had often heard his father telling his younger sister, Samantha, before she moved out ten years earlier.

Anyway, he normally only shaved once a day. But this evening was different. Today was his birthday. His thirty-third year.

'The same age Jesus died on the cross,' his mother had informed him when she woke him that morning with a cup of tea. Not being able to think up a suitable retort, he had sat up and sipped his tea until she had opened the curtains and left.

He cupped the water in the sink with his hands and splashed it onto his face. Then he put his glasses back on and checked for any remaining shaving foam.

He didn't regard himself as the handsomest of men, and he knew he wasn't alone in that conviction, but he wasn't exactly ugly either.

Indeed each facial appendage, if taken on its own merit, might even be regarded as anatomical perfection in itself. For example, his nose, he felt, could stand beside the nose of any modern movie star. He was certain it would not appear out of place nor deemed inferior in any way, and could even outshine many of its nasal contemporaries.

And the same could be said for any of his facial features; his mouth, his hazel coloured eyes, his chin, his ears and even his face's very shape. All were fine examples of human anatomy that performed their respective functions as required and when called upon to do so.

It was only when they were all seen as a group that a sense of mismatch and disproportion was somehow deemed. Unfortunately for Michael, how else could they be appraised except as a whole?

Michael had often heard his supervisor, Trevor Tiernan, being referred to by his female co-workers as a good looking man. This Michael found utterly perplexing given that Trevor's nose was nothing short of gargantuan, and that his right eye was at least thirty percent larger than its colleague, the left eye.

Hilary Byrne, the receptionist, often called Michael 'handsome Mike' when he arrived in work. Even though she was at least twenty years older than him, lived alone with seven cats and quite possibly wore a wig, it always brightened his morning.

The accessory, however, which Michael admittedly felt most let down by was his hair.

It was, according to his barber, 'unmanageable'. The scissors duly clipped noisily around his head as required, and clumps of curly fair hair could even be seen to fall apathetically to their death, but when he left the barber shop, it was a tough job to spot any difference whatsoever from when he had walked in.

Michael buttoned up the blue shirt his mother had ironed for him, and sprayed on some aftershave that his sister had bought for him last Christmas. He heard the shuffling feet and hushed whispers in the kitchen as he made his way downstairs. Operation 'Surprise Michael with a Birthday Cake' was in full swing for another year.

He pushed open the kitchen door and looked dutifully surprised as a chorus of 'Happy Birthday' broke out on cue. Although technically a solo by his mother, Rose, rather than a chorus, his father, Jack, did appear to hum along and nod approvingly.

His mother, to her credit, did sing with gusto, however a rendition of 'For He's a Jolly Good Fellow' was quickly abandoned when his father ducked back into the sitting room to watch the end of Crimewatch. Michael promptly extinguished all three candles.

'Don't forget to make a wish,' Rose urged him, then lowering her voice, 'maybe ask to meet a nice girl this year?'

He wanted to remind her that Jesus had also been a bachelor at that age, but an acute sense of humiliation prevented any response. Jesus, being the son of God and saviour to all mankind, while Michael's career aspirations having thus far reached the meteoritic height of an insurance claims handler for Irish Trust Insurance.

'Someone like Julie,' Rose urged. 'She was nice. I miss her.'

He had met Julie two years ago in a dark pub. He had almost convinced himself she hadn't only agreed to go out with him because he casually mentioned to her that he had won two backstage passes to the Kings of Leon in Marlay Park for the following evening. It had been a great gig. So much so, that he had stuck around for almost an hour even after he'd seen Julie being led by the bassist's hand into a tour bus.

Michael had asked her to meet him for their second and final date at his house just to prove to his parents that he wasn't gay. Not that he had anything against being gay. In fact, he often thought his life would be somehow a lot less complicated if he were attracted to men. He suspected though he would be seen as even less of a catch to the generally good looking gay community.

Embarrassingly he had feigned a prolonged phantom relationship with Julie, often leaving the house to attend the cinema alone or to read the newspaper in a quiet pub. Eventually they had 'broken up', and despite his mother's enquiries, he had insisted there 'was nothing to talk about'. A line that was ironically the only piece of truth in their entire six-month fantasy affair.

'Here, son, buy a drink for yourself,' Rose whispered, shoving a twenty euro note into his hand.

'Thanks, Mam,' Michael said slipping it into his pocket.

'Will you have a slice of cake before you go?'

'No, thanks, Mam. I'm grand.'

'Why don't you take it with you to the pub to share with your friends?'

'Em, I don't think so. Why not give some to Dad?'

'Okay then. Enjoy yourself tonight, Michael,' she said cutting a slice and popping it onto one of the small Mickey Mouse paper plates that were stacked beside the cake.

'Might shut him up for a while,' she added, licking the cream off the side of her finger, and carried it into him.

It was already dark when Michael reached Harry's pub, a short ten minutes' walk from his house. The pub was run by a bald-headed fifty-year-old called Harry Brennan. Or Hard Harry as everyone, including his mother, called him.

Michael pulled the heavy door open, allowing the light and the cacophony of chatter, clinking glasses and laughter to temporarily spew onto the street. Above the din, he heard the cackled laugh of Joey McGuinness, and instinctively moved to the opposite end of the bar.

Michael couldn't remember a time when he didn't know or didn't hate Joey McGuinness. From Junior Infants to present day, Joey had always been a part of his life, like a bad smell that just wouldn't go away.

'Wherever Joey is, that's where the party is,' he'd heard someone once say. 'Yeah, and the fight afterwards,' someone had added.

There were many reasons why Michael hated Joey. At age six, they had a fight in First Class in the school yard. Mrs. Connolly had caught them and made them shake hands, which they did, but as soon as she had turned her back and walked away, and while still shaking hands, Joey had punched Michael hard in the stomach with his six-year-old clenched left fist.

Then when Michael was twelve, he did something he swore he'd never do again and had kept that promise to this day; he volunteered. He liked the drama teacher, Mrs Kelly, perhaps even had a teenage crush on her. So when she asked for someone to read the welcoming monologue at the Christmas school play, Michael's hand had shot into the air.

He had voiced his concerns later on to Mrs Kelly, but she insisted he would get over his fears and it would be all right on the night. It wasn't. At first he froze in front of the two hundred seated parents in the large hall. He could hear Mrs Kelly's voice encouraging him to speak. He could hear the principal's voice threatening him to get off. He could do neither.

Next the giggles began. Barely suppressed sniggers from the audience. Shouts of 'get on with it' from some older students. He willed his body to move, but his feet stayed planted on the wooden stage.

And then the warmth. At first it was almost pleasant. He could feel the trickles down his left leg. The giggles turned to pointing and laughter. It probably only lasted twenty seconds before Mrs Kelly walked on stage and put her arm around him and walked him off, but it felt like twenty minutes.

Even today he sometimes woke to those hundreds of eyes looking at him and the laughter ringing in his ears. Joey McGuinness may not have come up with it initially, but it was from him that he first heard his name change from Michael Irvine to Michael Urine.

But as dreadful, at least at the time anyway, that these incidents were, they paled in comparison to the real reason that even Joey's voice made Michael nauseous, and Joey's proximity made Michael's skin crawl.

Joey McGuinness had done what Michael had never done, and as much as he fantasised about it even to this day, it was something that fate would assuredly deny him forever; he had dated the most beautiful, desirable and loveliest girl in the whole wide world - Lauren Fox.

The girl whom he had first noticed when she was just seventeen-years-old getting off a bus in a green school uniform. The girl whom he had painfully watched being chatted up by every bloke (except him) in Ace's nightclub every Saturday night. The girl who had unknowingly broken his heart when he had seen her kissing Joey McGuinness while lying on the grass on a sunny afternoon in Beckett's Park. And the girl whom he always thought of when he became bored and frustrated with his own bachelor life.

The same girl, now a bartender, who was walking towards him, her shiny jet black hair tied up in a bun and her sparkling green eyes smiling at him. The same girl, even after all these years, who still managed to set his heart racing at the mere sight of her.

'Hiya, Michael,' she said. 'You're looking very sharp tonight.'

'Thanks, Lauren. How's Max?'

'He's great, thanks. Don't forget it's his birthday next month. He'd love you to be there.'

'Of course I will.'

'And bring your two nieces if you like.'

'Great. I will. They love hanging out with Max. I think they like to mother him.'

'You're very good to him, Michael. So, what can I get you?'

Lauren Fox was perfection.

He never called her it, nor referred to her by that name, but he understood why most of the guys called her (at least behind her back) Luscious Lauren.

'The usual? Carlsberg shandy?' she asked.

'No thanks, Lauren. I feel like something different. It's my birthday.'

'Well, congratulations, Michael. What do you fancy?'

'How about, em… a Heineken shandy?'

'Really?' she asked, raising her eyebrows at him.

'Okay, then. How about one of them?' he said and pointed to the Bulmers cider tap across the bar.

'I think I can manage that,' Lauren said, smiled and grabbed a pint glass from the shelf.

He genuinely tried his utmost not to watch her walk away, but her curves to him were like the headlights of a car to the eyes of a small rodent scurrying across a country road at midnight. He stared at her for just a moment too long until he was forced to grab the side of the bar, such was the wallop he received from a clenched fist into his right arm.

'Are you checking out my girlfriend's arse, Urine?' said Joey McGuinness an inch or two from Michael's ear. Michael could feel wet spits of beer sprayed onto the side of his face. He tried to gain his composure even though the pain from the blow pulsed down his arm.

She's not your girlfriend, was all Michael could think to say, but of course didn't.

Joey rested his elbow against the bar. He wore the same faded blue denim jacket and plain white sweater he always wore. Where once the sweater was baggy and loose, it was now stretched to catered for years of excessive beers and late-night fast food. Michael often wondered was it the same jacket Joey had worn in school, or had he a continual supply of them in his wardrobe. His jeans were the same shade of blue, and his white trainers were stained with black flecks of oil.

He had a plain gold earring in his right ear that wobbled whenever he moved his head. His straight blonde hair was always a little long and scruffy, and his eyes were as blue and cold as the morning sky in winter. In the background, Michael could see Joey's black and white keffiyeh scarf thrown across his chair.

'I don't blame you looking though,' said Joey, and he put his arm around Michael and looked at Lauren. 'Would you just look at the body on her?'

Michael looked at Lauren and then turned away. The smell of nicotine from Joey was making him nauseous.

'Even though she's popped out a kid,' Joey continued, 'she's still a ride and a half. I don't know how she does it.'

Michael noted the use of the indefinite article, 'a' kid, and not the possessive adjective 'our' kid.

Some evenings, although it was all too rare, Joey and his boisterous friends would leave Harry's early, and head off to Ace's nightclub. The crowd would peter out, leaving Michael to sip on his pint and have Lauren almost to himself. They spoke about their jobs, their hopes and even their dreams.

One night after having a second glass of Zinfandel, she spoke about her son, Max. It had been an unplanned pregnancy, she confided, which then led to Joey insisting and then demanding a trip to the UK for a swift termination. He had even offered to pay half the bill. It was the first of many arguments through a difficult and painful pregnancy that ended in an emergency Caesarean section in the seventh month.

Max, born at just over three pounds, spent his first six weeks in ICU in Holles Street hospital. His diagnosis of Down syndrome was made within a few minutes of his birth. After crying hysterically for a full ten minutes, Lauren begged that Max be brought back down from ICU, which in fairness to the consultant, he did. Lauren sat up, as best she could, and wiped away the tears.

The doctor handed her her new baby, her new life and her new world. She held him close, kissed him on his lips as gently as she could and thought light was shining from his skin, such was his beauty to her. Max, for his part, happily took over every aspect of her life too.

During those initial six weeks, as she camped out at Max's bedside, she read and googled everything she could get her hands on about Down syndrome. So much so that after a few weeks she knew that to give Max everything he needed, she would have to quit her job in the pharmacy, give up her apartment in the village and move back in with her mother. Already a litany of appointments had been set up after Max's release; physiotherapist, cardiologist, audiologist. Many professions she had never even heard of before.

As often happens in life when the most unexpected of difficulties present themselves, true characters were revealed. Unfortunately, many of her close friends who only six months before she had linked arm-in-arm down Grafton Street at 4am singing a Katy Perry hit, now had lives too busy to visit her or even phone. Joey McGuinness was no exception.

At first, Lauren allowed and even forgave him his transgressions, his non-attendance of important meetings and appointments, his heavy drinking, his days of absence from her and Max's lives, his insistence on a blood test to prove that there was 'nothing wrong' with him.

Then there were the arguments that Lauren was spending 'far too much' time with Max and ignoring him. All were forgiven by Lauren on the assumed grounds of him being in shock or denial and for the sake of keeping their family together. It was only when he called over to her at her mother's house with plans for Max to be institutionalised, and declarations of his right as the father to have a say, and about what in his opinion was best for Max, had Lauren eventually kicked him hard in the nuts, dragged him out of her mother's house, and dumped him unceremoniously in the front garden.

Once he'd recovered to a vertical, if somewhat stooped, position, he didn't knock to be let back in. Lauren never actually uttered the crowd-pleasing phrase of 'it's over', but the outcome was nonetheless understood by all parties concerned.

'What do you want, Joey?' Lauren spat at him, as she placed the pint of Bulmers on the counter in front of Michael.

'Jesus. Do you hear that, Urine?' said Joey. 'Do any of your exes ever talk to you like that? Oh, sorry I forgot. You don't have any exes, do you?'

'Piss off, Joey,' said Lauren. 'Leave him alone.'

'Oh, listen to her,' said Joey, and then leaning back into Michael's ear, 'maybe she'll pop your cherry for you? Eh, Urine?'

'Whatever he's saying to you, Michael, ignore him. Here's your pint.'

'Bulmers?' said Joey, 'what happened to the shandy man?'

'Thanks, Lauren,' Michael said, reaching into his pocket for his wallet.

'That's okay. It's on me. It's your birthday pint.'

Michael's insides cringed, and his shoulders drooped forward. He had too much knowledge and had too much first-hand experience of the modus operandi of your average bully, and so understood the significance of sharing any personal information with them. Anything they could use as a weapon, or saw as a crack in their victims' armoury could prove to be disastrous.

But Joey ignored the comment.

'It's a long time since Lauren bought me a pint for my birthday,' Joey said. 'How come he's gets free gargle, and I don't?'

'Because Michael is a gentleman, and you,' said Lauren, 'are a prick.'

The slight twitch of annoyance and anger in Joey's left eye went unnoticed by Lauren. He knew better than to go head to head against her, especially in public. But Michael noticed it. He knew that twitch and how it would work its way through a bully's body until it eventually manifested itself as an eruption of gratuitous violence against an innocent passer-by. Being both an innocent and a passer-by, Michael waited for the expected blow as Joey dismounted his bar stool.

'Women. Eh, Mike,' said Joey going back to his friends. 'Can't live with them, and can't murder them and plead justifiable manslaughter.'

'Sorry about that, Michael,' said Lauren when he was gone, 'I shouldn't have said anything.'

'That's okay, Lauren. He's just being his usual self.'

It was only then that Michael realised that Lauren had placed her hand on his arm. He could feel her warmth through his shirt and it went through his entire body. Even though she had walked to the other end of the bar, he could still sense the weight of her arm on his, her perfumed smell, her bright green eyes looking into his.

It was most definitely because of those dreamlike sensations that at first he didn't even notice that everyone in the whole pub was looking at him, and that Joey was standing on top of a round table shouting something and pointing at him. But he was finally woken from his daydream when the entire pub broke into a chorus of...

Happy birthday to you,
Happy birthday to you,
Happy birthday dear Urrrrinnnne,

Happy birthday to you.
Then claps, cheers, whistles, and utter utter humiliation.

2

Saturday morning began for Michael as all Saturday mornings for him began.

It started with a light breakfast of porridge followed by a twenty-minute swim and ten minutes in the sauna on the lowest bench at his gym. (This thirty-minute session took two hours owing to the fact that Michael's gym was a thirty-minute drive from his house. There was a gym closer by, but the thoughts of bumping into a work colleague petrified him. He disliked small talk in general, but semi-naked small talk was unimaginable.)

Once, another gym member had approached Michael and asked him for some tips on having a physique similar to his. Michael's routine of porridge and swimming fell far short of the detailed workout session the gym member had hoped to receive.

Lunch consisted of a green apple and a can of Red Bull, followed by a three-hour visit to the library. Michael loved the library. He saw it as somewhat of a sanctuary. A silent womb of words away from the boorish Saturday afternoon shopping masses. Small talk with strangers was unnecessary, discouraged and disapproved of. In the library he rarely happened upon an inquisitive acquaintance of his, and everyone, including the staff, ignored him. As he ignored them.

Michael's literary interests varied greatly according to his whim. He could be seen leafing through magazines on car maintenance, photography and travel; buried behind a hefty classical novel by Dickens, Tolstoy or Bronte; contemporary works by Martin Amis,

Will Self, Zadie Smith and Rushdie; Scientific and medical journals; articles on art, technology and literature.

He belonged to the unfortunate group who possessed the worst type of intelligence - intelligent enough to read, understand and indeed enjoy everything, but not quite smart enough to create it.

On the first Saturday of every month, at around 2pm, Lauren and some other mothers of special needs children would come to the library, and Michael would read to them. Undeniably, this was to him, the highlight of his month. Max, Lauren's little boy, would sit in front of him on the floor, while his mother would sit beside him on the bench.

The only tarnish to the hour-long session, was one of the other mother's blatant and incessant attempts at seducing him. Michael found it extremely embarrassing. Lauren found it extremely entertaining. The woman, a divorced mother of three, was in no way bashful in letting Michael know of her intentions. She would flirt shamelessly with him and rub her hand up and down his arm, commenting on his 'well developed biceps'.

Later in the afternoons, Michael would end up in Starbucks, sipping an Americano. He always ordered a black coffee as the array of choices on offer frightened him a little. He was sure that if he tried to order one of the other concoctions with an 'o' at the end, he would undoubtedly make a mess of it, and only end up embarrassing himself. The barista misheard his name and scribbled 'Michelle' on the side of the cup.

For an hour he watched the busy café breathe in and out its clients. Young couples sharing their laughs, their touches, their plans, their futures. Busy looking men and women with open laptops and fashionable hair, and with things to do even in their free time. Elderly people chatting about elderly things, and with quite possibly more exciting futures than the thirty-three-year-old sitting in the corner, unnoticed and unnoticeable.

As much as he tried not to, he thought back to the previous evening in Harry's. The embarrassment of it still crawled beneath his skin. He had sat red faced for five minutes, taking giant gulps from his pint glass in order to hide his face. When Joey and some of his sidekicks went out the back for a cigarette, and while Lauren was at the other end of the bar, he casually got off his stool as if he were going to the bathroom, and walking by the front door, quickly slipped outside.

Where exactly had he gone wrong in his life? What turn had he unwittingly taken that had led him to now? To this. Had he not played by the rules? Their rules. He had studied at school, gone to college. Passed the interviews. Achieved the great and steady job. What crime, he thought, had he unknowingly committed to receive this life? This sentence. The crime of reliability and punctuality and banality? He had friends in his early twenties and they had all gone to the pubs and the nightclubs together, but one by one they had all settled down, leaving him unsettled. All his friends' wives liked him, he felt, but always there was a sense of sympathy and charity in their chat and conversation.

His only mistake in life was not having made any. Too few miscalculations had proven to be in fact an error in itself.

As he left Starbucks, a team of teenage girls with a shared Frappuccino between them, quickly took his place, erasing any indication of his having been there at all. The only evidence of his day so far was the name 'Michelle' written on the side of a cold coffee cup at the bottom of a black bin liner.

At 7pm, Michael got into his 2005 Ford Focus. Although it had four doors, only the driver's had ever been of any use to him. Its colour bordered somewhere between yellow and green, a non-descript blend that if stared at for too long would result in a frightful headache.

It had very low mileage even when Michael had bought it six years ago (its previous owner having sold it to pay for a trip to a London neurologist who she was advised could help her with her relentless migraines) and the short five-minute commute to and from his workplace had barely added to the odometer. The car salesman had been delighted to receive the full asking price, given that all other potential buyers, although initially enthusiastic, had left suddenly despondent and complaining of headaches. Not upgrading his car was not due to an absence of funds but rather an absence of imagination. Indeed, Michael had at that moment €182,463 in his Bank of Ireland account.

Having such a hefty sum was not as a result of any complicated savings or investment scheme. It was merely a matter of his meagre outgoings being far less than his incomings over an extended period. His net pay equated to €2,496 per month and apart from fifty euro a week, which he gave to his mother, gym membership, a few litres of petrol for his car and the odd pint, almost two thousand euro remained untouched in his bank account each month.

The car started each morning when he asked it to, and every evening it brought him home. What he could possibly have achieved with a newer or even different vehicle was simply beyond him.

He had promised Samantha, (or Sam as she preferred), his younger divorced sister, that he would babysit her two daughters; Emily, aged seven, and Katie, aged four and a half. Samantha was engaged to a stockbroker, Derek, and who, contrary to initial misgivings, Michael liked very much. His car was too black and too flashy and too big, but Michael assumed that financially he was doing quite well owing to the amount he must spend on hair gel each month. But none of that was Michael's business. Derek made Samantha happy and her two girls laugh.

Michael parked his Ford in front of his local shop, Boylan's, where its boisterous proprietor Bobby Boylan dispensed newspapers, confectionery and cigarettes for those who asked and paid, and imparted his wisdom and advice on both local and global issues to those who neither asked nor paid.

Unusually for Michael, he was a little behind schedule and didn't have the time nor the interest for Bobby's sermon. Although he never at any point had the interest. Fortunately, when Michael entered the shop, Bobby was preoccupied with a different customer who'd only popped in for a sliced pan and had already stood impatiently through,

1. The clandestine machinations of the Saudi royal family to buy vast swathes of County Kerry to exploit the secret gigantic lake of oil under the Gap of Dunloe and whose existence is known only to five families in the Middle East (and Bobby Boylan apparently)

2. How Manchester United's manager has zero knowledge about the game of football (despite the manager's fifteen years as a professional player and ten years' experience as a manager and a five million pound salary)

3. How if he had have stayed in San Francisco thirty years ago, where he worked as a part-time car mechanic, he'd be most definitely and without any shadow of a doubt be a multi-millionaire by now.

Bobby glanced up enthusiastically to watch his latest customer/victim walk into the shop, but seeing that it was Michael glanced away unenthusiastically.

'...and do you know why this current government doesn't give two shites about the working class man? I'll tell you why...'

Michael huddled up next to the other customer determined to order and promptly leave. A Kinder Surprise for Emily and a lollipop for Katie.

'Could I get...?' Michael called out, but Bobby was in full swing.

'...but who's even offering a half decent alternative to this government? Labour? Sinn Féin...'

'Would you mind if I get..?'

'...I'll tell you who. No one. They're all a shower of shites. Every last one of them only interested in what's in it for them, with one eye on their pension...'

'A Kinder Surprise and a lollipop please, Bobby,' Michael tried again, louder.

'...do you know who's running this country today? I'll tell you who. The criminals. The drug pushers. The gangsters. The...'

'Kinder Surprise and a lollipop please,' Michael practically shouted out.

Without taking his eyes off his audience or taking an extra breath, Bobby reached out for the Kinder Surprise and pressed a few buttons on his till.

'...but no matter how you look at it, it's always the common decent working man on the street, €5.20, who has to bend over and...'

Michael had a five euro note in his hand and was momentarily confused by the requested amount of €5.20. Never one to argue, but genuinely surprised by the sum demanded for a chocolate egg and a lollipop, he managed to stammer, 'how much?'

With potential fiscal matters in dispute, the current government and its degenerates were quickly sidelined.

'€5.20,' Bobby replied with conviction.

Almost to himself Michael mumbled, 'but all I asked for was a Kinder Surprise and a lolly please.'

'No,' Bobby informed him. 'You wanted a Kinder Surprise and a lottery plus.'

'Did I?' Michael asked, unsure now.

'Yes you did,' Bobby said as if speaking to a foreign student with only a minor grasp of the English language. 'It's the EuroMillions tonight and a ticket costs €4 and a Kinder Surprise is €1.20. Now correct me if I'm wrong, but when I went to school that equalled €5.20.'

Bobby threw a wry smile at his customer and his customer dutifully smiled back.

'Unless you, Paddy,' said Bobby handing his customer over the ticket, 'you'd like the ticket?'

'I'm grand,' said Paddy holding up his hands. 'I have mine already.'

'So have I,' said Bobby. 'So I guess that means this ticket must be yours.'

'But I've never bought a lottery ticket in my life,' Michael said.

'Well congratulations,' Bobby told him, handing him his Kinder Surprise, his lottery ticket and his receipt. 'There's a first time for everything.'

Michael obediently took the items and rummaged in his pocket for the extra twenty cents. By the time he had placed it on the counter, Bobby had returned to his tirade unfettered.

'And it's not my generation that'll suffer the most. It's today's,' he continued. 'Most of them don't know their arse from their elbow. No political conscience whatsoever.'

It took a moment for Michael to realise that their attention was now squarely back on him.

'Sorry, what?' he said.

'I asked you,' Bobby said, 'did you vote in the last election?'

'Was there an election?' Michael asked.

'Jesus, Mother of God,' said Bobby. 'Do you see what I mean, Paddy?'

'I must have missed it. Sorry,' Michael apologised.

'When did you last vote is what I'm asking you?' Bobby demanded.

'Me...' Michael started, 'I don't think I've ever voted.'

Bobby stared at Michael, and Michael unsure whether he'd said something right or wrong, stared back.

'You've never voted?' Bobby asked in a tone as if he'd just found out Michael had never in his life drank water.

'No,' Michael told him.

'And you've never played the lottery either?' Bobby asked.

'No,' said Michael, although he failed to see the connection between the two.

'Well, fuck me sideways and call me Joanna. Did you hear that, Paddy? Never voted. Ever.'

Michael shifted from one foot to the other.

'Don't you know that people have died to give you the right to vote?' Bobby asked.

'Yes,' said Michael, 'but they also died to give me the right not to vote, didn't they?'

'What the fuck does that mean? Are you being smart with me?'

Michael desperately wanted to leave now. He wasn't being smart with him. He'd never been smart about anything. He simply didn't understand how he'd not only purchased a lottery ticket by mistake, but was now involved in a civil rights debate with Bobby Boylan, neither of which he had asked for.

'A lot more people have died for my right to go to mass every week,' Michael said, 'and I don't do that either. Do you?'

They both stared at Michael until he felt that enough time had passed that he could leave.

'One Kinder Surprise between them?' Samantha asked, smiling at her brother. 'Are you sure you can afford this, Mike?'

Both Emily and Katie adored their uncle. Michael, for his part, although slightly embarrassed by their affection for him, thought the world of them too. For the last twenty minutes they had each sat at their mother's bay window, attempting to shove each other off the edge, as they waited for Michael's car to appear around the corner.

'How are you, Mike?' asked Derek, and put out his hand to be shaken.

Derek was a hand shaker. He shook hands to say hello, and he shook hands to say goodbye. Michael wasn't a hand shaker. He always felt that if someone wanted to shake his hand then they wanted to sell him something.

'Hi, Derek,' he said, awkwardly grabbing Derek's hand and then releasing it as soon as he could.

'Uncle Mike, can we stay up till ten o'clock?' asked Katie.

'I can,' said Emily, 'but you have to go to bed at nine. Isn't that right Uncle Mike?'

Michael looked up at Samantha for assistance, but she merely smiled and followed Derek who had already shaken Michael's hand goodbye and opened the front door.

'Thanks, Mike,' she called back. 'I owe you one.'

By the time they had returned after midnight, they found pyjama-clad Emily and Katie asleep on either side of Michael on the sofa. Despite offers to stay, he helped carry the girls to their beds, kissed his sister on the cheek, vigorously shook hands with Derek and left.

The streets were quiet for a Saturday night as Michael drove home in silence. He thought about his nieces and his sister and was happy that they all seemed happy. He suddenly felt consumed by a sense of loneliness and an inevitability that such was his lot. He found it difficult to accept that fate had no other path for him to follow, but he believed it nonetheless.

He was comfortable and had a lot to be thankful for and should have greater appreciation for it all. He knew all that. He lacked for nothing in his life except for someone to share that life with. What did it matter, he felt, how he now spent his time? To succeed or to fail. To be happy or not. All irrelevant when unshared. Without someone. Without a witness. A witness for who he is and for whom he once was. Proof that his existence mattered. At the very least for one other person.

As he slid into bed and turned out the light, he tried not to think about Lauren, but there she was. Forever his last thought. Forever his perpetual, foolish, adolescent and unrequited love. He wondered, as he always did, what she was doing at that moment. Wondered did she ever spare him a thought.

Foolish of him to think it. Even tortuous.

He had often wanted to speak to Sam about it, ask for her advice. But he knew what she'd say. 'Just ask her out for God's sake.'

It was his biggest fear that Lauren would say no. A rejection that would rock him to his core, but more importantly a rejection that would end his dreams of one day being with her. Without a definite no, there was always a possibility, a hope, a fantasy.

His second biggest fear was that she would say yes. What then? Who was he to go out with Lauren Fox? Somehow he just couldn't see himself walking down the street with her and daring to hold her hand. Sharing popcorn and sitting beside her at the movies. Across from her in a restaurant, her laughing at a joke he'd made.

He could continue to live with the reality that Lauren was not a part of his life, but could not live without the dream that one day she might be.

3

The next morning, Michael rose, showered and then made himself a breakfast of grilled bacon and poached eggs. Both his parents were still at ten-thirty mass so the house was calm and silent.

He had often thought about finding his own place, or even buying his own house, but the best mortgage rates and terms in the country were insufficient enticements against the dissuading powers of an Irish mother. Despite the seasoned medical skills and precise surgical instruments used by Dr. Richards thirty three years ago in Holles Street hospital, an umbilical cord, albeit a phantom one, was still very much in evidence between Michael and his mother.

No matter how hard Michael had tried in the past to free himself, the guilt-laden pain expressed by his mother had always put a halt to his moving out and sent him scurrying back to his own bedroom. The very same room where he had first slept as a baby. The same room where he had locked the door as a teenager. The same room where, miraculously, his laundry would be taken away, and magically reappear washed and ironed. And the very same room where, Monday to Friday, a cup of tea would be brought just before his alarm went off at seven-thirty each morning.

Michael switched on the radio and started to wash up. The bland voice of the RTÉ newscaster chattered in the background, drowned out intermittently by the clanking of dishes and pots in the sink.

...the government says that a decrease in levels of unemployment... a man was charged in connection with the murder of… there was only one winner of last night's EuroMillions lottery with a total sum of… the weather will be dry in most parts today with an outbreak of showers later in the west…

Michael switched off the radio. It was such a nice morning that he decided to walk rather than drive to Boylan's for his Sunday Times, Sunday Independent and Sunday Business Post. Michael was an avid fan of the Sunday papers, although in general, he wasn't a huge fan of Sundays. Sure, they had their uses, but they held too much of an uncertainty that needed to be filled. Like a blank canvas with too many paints and too little imagination. What to wear, what to do, what to eat? For that reason, Michael liked to stick to a premeditated plan that saw him carefully navigate the hours until the evening came and the whole silly business could be forgotten about. At least until the next weekend reared its head.

The first thing Michael noticed that was out of the ordinary was the amount of cars parked outside Boylan's shop. Inside was so full that there was a small crowd at the entrance looking in. Had Boylan finally got a preacher's licence and opened up a church in his shop? Michael thought to himself. Sunday papers and a Sunday sermon. He pictured Bobby standing behind a pulpit surrounded by chocolate bars and crisps delivering his eulogy and being interrupted every now and then to hand out change for a can of beans. Michael almost turned around and went home again, but curiosity got the better of him. Perhaps Bobby had collapsed? Even died?

He walked along the front and tried to look in. He couldn't see Bobby, but he could certainly hear him. He was even louder than his normal boisterous self. A flash of light. Someone had taken a picture.

Michael approached a neighbour whom he recognised. 'What's going on, Mr. Greene?'

'You haven't heard?'

'No. What?'

'The winning ticket for last night's lottery was sold here.'

'Wow,' said Michael. 'Who won?'

'They don't know yet.'

A champagne cork made a loud pop inside followed by more camera flashes and a big cheer.

'So why is Bobby celebrating?' asked Michael.

'Because he gets a twelve grand bonus,' Mr. Greene shouted

above the noise.

'Well someone's in for a surprise this morning,' Michael said.

'You can say that again,' replied Mr. Greene. He turned and looked up at Michael for the first time. 'Did you check your ticket yet?'

'No. No need,' said Michael, 'I never play the...'

A small drop of cold sweat suddenly formed at the back of Michael's neck. It hesitated ever so slightly and then rolled slowly down his back.

He knew roughly the odds of winning the lottery. Millions to one. That's not why he didn't play it though. He never played because if ever he had the misfortune of actually winning, he couldn't imagine what he'd possibly do with a million euro. He saw it only as a chore or a burden.

Michael began to breathe heavily beside Mr. Greene. Think logically, he told himself. Bobby probably sold hundreds of lottery tickets last night. The odds are still greatly in Michael's favour. Luckily, there was still every possibility of him being one of the losers.

He moved away from the crowd and started home. He could get the Sunday Times later. In another shop. As he reached the end of the block, a large white van passed him. It had a small satellite on the roof and the words 'RTÉ NEWS' written on the side.

Michael began to walk faster.

What would anyone do with that much money? Whenever he heard anyone in work talk about winning the lottery, it usually involved a bigger something or a better something. A car, a house, a holiday. For him, more money meant more problems. More possessions meant more responsibility. Exotic holidays meant sunburn and flesh eating insects.

'I'd give most of it away to friends and family,' he'd heard Lisa in accounts say. But if her dream was to win a large amount of money just to give it away, surely that made even less sense. Besides, he thought, it's not like I've even won the lottery. I don't even know what I did with the ticket.

But he did know. He knew exactly where it was. It was crunched up with a receipt for a Kinder Surprise in the ashtray of his car. As he walked by his parked car outside his house, like a woman who had once betrayed him, he ignored it and looked straight ahead. His parents hadn't returned from mass yet, and the house seemed even more quiet and empty. Michael switched on the kettle and then sat at the kitchen table. He imagined his parents coming in and telling him that Mrs. Browne down the road or Paddy Walsh had won the lottery last night. The water began to boil. Michael began to fidget.

He tried not to think of the lottery ticket curled up in his ashtray. Maybe he should check. Put his mind at rest. See that he hadn't won, and then get on with his day. But what if he had?

The kettle's water bubbled noisily in the kitchen. Michael tried to swallow, but his throat was too dry. Why were his parents taking so long to come home?

He looked at the clock, and then looked at the front door. Beyond the door was his car. In his car was the ticket. Waiting. Almost watching. Hiding in the dark but not going away. He stood up. He sat back down again.

The kettle climaxed in a crescendo of bubbling boiling water until it switched off with a loud POP.

As if the sound were a starter gun, Michael jumped up and ran out of the kitchen. He grabbed the car keys from the hall table, opened the front door and ran to his car. Shoving the key into the lock, and opening the driver's door, he dived inside and pulled open the ashtray. Without looking, he grabbed the ticket and receipt, then slammed the door shut and ran inside. He sat back down at the table, breathing heavily.

Opening his hand slowly, as if a butterfly were inside and would fly away, he looked at the ticket. He placed the receipt on the table and unfolded the lottery ticket. Not sure what he was expecting, he stared at it in his hand. It looked innocuous enough. Could this little piece of paper really be worth a million euro?

Again he reminded himself that it was probably a losing ticket, and this gave him comfort and he breathed easier. It was a random collection of numbers printed in black on a light yellow coloured piece of paper. He saw a thirteen. Then a seven. But the numbers didn't mean anything to him.

How do I know if it's worth all that money or if it's just a piece of paper for the bin? I need the numbers.

He took out his old laptop and opened up Google. He typed 'Lottery numbers Ireland', and Google, ever efficient, popped up seven numbers onto his screen.

He saw a seven and a thirteen and then quickly slammed the

laptop shut.

'Oh my God,' he said out loud, and began to have palpitations again.

Get a grip of yourself, he told himself and slowly opened the laptop again. He clicked on the Google page and the seven numbers reappeared on the screen. He spread out the lottery ticket on the table.

Like watching a tennis match, his eyes switched back and forth from the screen to the ticket.

When his parents finally arrived home they were full of excitement and chatter. Unusually, the focus from the congregation that Sunday had not been predominantly on the Holy Ghost, but rather on more earthly issues and whether or not a lottery millionaire sat amongst them.

Father Sean had mentioned on several occasions the dire conditions of the church windows and their need to be replaced. Mysteriously, or rather miraculously, Matthew 19:24 appeared as the second reading - 'It is easier for a camel to go through the eye of a needle than for a rich person to enter the Kingdom of God.'

His parents burst into the kitchen and saw Michael sitting motionless on his chair.

'Michael, Michael, did you hear?' they chimed in chorus, happy to be able to share the news with someone who didn't know yet. Whether or not he'd heard was irrelevant as they didn't wait for a reply. 'A local has won the EuroMillions.'

'Isn't it amazing?' his mother asked. 'RTÉ is down in Bobby's shop right now. Apparently TV3 is also… Michael, are you okay?'

Michael, ashen faced, stared at the floor.

'If that bollox next door has won, he'll stay where he is just to spite me,' said Michael's father.

'Jack, shut up,' said his mother. 'Michael, are you okay?'

Michael looked up at them both. His expression and complexion made them both utter an involuntary gasp.

'You look like you need a doctor,' said his mother.

Michael shook his head weakly.

'Is it your sister? Are the kids alright?' his father asked.

'Everyone's okay,' Michael said and slid the piece of paper on the table over to them. 'It's this.'

Jack reached down and picked up the paper.

There was silence, his lips moving quietly as he read.

'What is it?' asked his mother.

'I think Michael bought a Kinder Surprise,' said Jack.

'What?' asked Rose.

'Not that piece of paper,' Michael shouted at him. 'This.'

He handed his father the lottery ticket, and his father studied it.

'What is it? Jack?'

'It's a lottery ticket,' said Jack.

'It's not a lottery ticket,' said Michael.

'Well, it looks like a lottery ticket,' said Jack turning it in his hand.

'No, what I mean is, it's not a lottery ticket. It's the lottery ticket.'

'What lottery ticket?' asked Jack.

'Oh, sweet Jesus,' said Rose. 'Oh, sweet Jesus.'

'Are you saying?' asked Jack, dropping it back onto the table as if he had just received a small electrical shock from it.

Michael nodded solemnly.

'Where'd you get it?'

'Oh sweet Jesus,' said his mother again.

'Bobby's shop.'

'You found it?'

'No.'

'Who owns it then?'

'I do.'

'Oh sweet Jesus.'

'But you don't play the lottery.'

'I know,' said Michael shifting in his seat, 'I bought it by mistake.'

'Oh sweet...'

'Rose, will you shut up.'

'What am I going to do?' pleaded Michael.

'What do you mean?' Jack asked.

'The ticket,' said Michael, panicking. 'What am I going to do with the ticket?'

'I haven't a clue to be honest,' said Jack. 'I suppose you'll have to phone someone somewhere.'

Nobody moved as they all stared at the yellow ticket on the table. The wall clock ticked loudly as they all breathed in and out to its rhythm. Everyone unsure what to say or do next.

'I'll make some tea,' said Rose eventually.

'I don't want it.'

'That's okay. Would you rather a coffee?'

'No,' said Michael, 'I mean, I don't want the ticket. I don't want the money. I don't want any of it.'

'Are you mad?' asked Jack.

'You take it,' Michael told his father. 'Tell them that you bought it.'

'I don't want it.'

'I'll give it to Sam,' said Michael, suddenly pleased with his idea. 'Yeah, she can have it. She'll know what to do. She can get something for the kids or something.'

'But it's yours,' said Rose.

'Rose, put the kettle on,' said Jack.

Jack sat down across from Michael.

'What am I going to do, Dad?'

'Claim your money,' he said. 'What else can you do?'

'Do you think Sam would say it was hers?'

'I don't know, son. That's up to her.'

'So much money,' said Michael placing his head in his hands. 'What am I going to do with a million euro?'

It only took ten seconds before Michael noticed the silence around him. Rose was standing with the kettle in her hands. Jack looked up at her. Then both of them stared at Michael. Michael raised his head again.

'What?' he asked.

Both his parents looked at one another and then back to him.

'What is it?'

'Em,' started Jack. 'It wasn't...'

'It wasn't what?'

'It wasn't a million euro,' said Rose.

'It wasn't?' Michael asked.

'No,' said Jack. 'Not this week.'

'Okay then. At least that's something,' said Michael breathing a little easier. 'How much was it, then?'

More silence.

'Five hundred thousand?' Michael asked.

No answer.

'Less or more than that?'

26

'You see,' said Jack explaining slowly, 'the jackpot hasn't been won in a couple of months, Mike.'

'What does that mean?'

'It means that they add the jackpot every week that it's not won.'

'You mean that it's more than a million euro?' Michael asked flabbergasted. 'How much more?'

Jack gulped noisily. Rose put the kettle down slowly onto the counter.

'Oh, holy God,' said Michael looking from one parent to the other. 'How much was it? For God's sake, Mam, Dad, how much was it?

4

'Everything's okay,' Michael could hear his father saying as he began to come round. 'Drink some water.'

'What happened?' Michael asked, still feeling a little dizzy.

'You fainted,' his mother told him. 'Are you alright, Michael?'

'I fainted?' he asked.

'Yes,' said Rose. 'Just when we told you that you'd won one hundred and ninety million euro.'

Michael became light headed again, and the room started to spin.

'Jesus, Rose,' Jack said, 'are you trying to kill the boy?'

'I don't feel well,' Michael said.

'Will I call the doctor?' Rose asked.

'On a Sunday? Are you mad?' Jack said. 'He'll charge a fortune for coming out today.'

'This is awful,' whispered Michael rubbing his frontal lobe in a circular motion. 'What on earth am I going to do with that much? What could anyone do with that much?'

'Look, let's check the ticket together to be absolutely sure,' said Jack. 'Maybe you made a mistake. Hand me that ticket, Rose.'

The newspaper was duly laid out on the table and the ticket placed beside it. Both Jack and Rose fetched their reading glasses. Calm, at least temporarily, was restored.

'Okay, Rose, you call out the numbers from the ticket, and I'll check them from the paper.'

Rose leaned into the ticket and called out loudly, 'thirteen.'

'Jesus, will you keep your voice down. It's not a feckin' bingo hall we're running here,' said Jack. 'That's all we need. Next door coming in to see what all the noise is.'

Rose started again, and one by one called out all seven numbers.

'I'm afraid,' said Jack solemnly, after a few moments' silence had passed, 'it looks like you've won.'

'Wait a second,' said Rose with a flash of enthusiasm, 'this is the Sunday Mirror. Should I not check a more reputable newspaper? I'll go down to Bobby's and get the Sunday Times.'

'Don't go outside,' shouted Jack. 'We need to stay inside and decide what to do next.'

'Call Sam,' said Michael faintly.

Samantha was having a late breakfast with Derek and the girls when she received the call. Samantha, being a perpetual worrier, on hearing the strain in her father's voice immediately asked, 'what's wrong, Dad?'

'It's Michael,' her father replied.

She could hear Michael and her mother talking in the background, Michael sounding stressed.

'What's happened?' she asked, Derek and the girls hearing her tone and turning to her. 'Is everyone okay?'

'Everyone's fine,' her father assured her unsuccessfully. 'It's just there's something that Michael needs to tell…' More voices in the background. 'Look, it's best if Michael tells you himself.'

'Is he alright?'

'Yes, yes, he's fine,' he said.

'Well, is it bad news?'

'You'd better come over Sam.'

'Dad, if it's bad news, please tell me. Is Mam okay?'

She could hear him place his hand over the receiver and then her father's muffled voice, 'she wants to know if it's bad news.'

There was a moment's silence, and then her mother's voice, 'tell her no, but to come over straight away.'

'Your mother says no, but that you've to come over straight away.'

'Will I bring the kids? Why don't you just tell me?'

'No, just come on your own.'

'Okay. Derek will mind them. I'm coming.'

The line went dead as her father hung up the phone. She looked at her mobile phone for a few seconds before turning to Derek and the girls, who were all staring at her.

'What is it?' asked Derek.

'I think Mike...' said Samantha, almost to herself. 'I think Mike is coming out of the closet.'

'I knew it,' said Derek clapping his hands. 'I never wanted to say it to you, Sam, but I always knew it.'

'Why was Uncle Mike in a closet?' asked Emily.

'He wasn't in a closet. It's just an expression,' said Samantha.

'It means,' said Derek, 'that he likes boys not girls.'

'Uncle Mike doesn't like us anymore?' said Katie.

'Oh, Jesus Christ,' said Samantha, as both girls began to cry. 'I'll be back as soon as I can.'

Samantha drove the short distance to her parents' house as quickly as her Nissan Micra would allow. The closer she got to the house, the more it all made sense, and the happier she was for Michael that it was all finally out.

When her father's furrowed brow answered the door, she noticed him glancing up and down the street before closing the door firmly behind them. Michael was in the sitting room. He looked pensive and tired when Samantha walked in.

'Will you have a cup of tea, love?' asked Rose.

'No, no, I'm grand, Mam, thanks. I just had my breakfast.'

'Michael has some news he'd like to tell you,' said Jack. 'Perhaps you'd like to sit down.'

Michael rubbed the palms of his hands together, and looked up at Samantha before turning away again.

'Go on, son,' said Jack. 'You're amongst family.'

'It's okay, Mike,' said Samantha with a smile. 'I know already, and I'm delighted for you.'

They all looked at her in amazement.

'You know?' asked Michael.

'Who told you?' asked Jack.

'No one told me. It's obvious. I just put two and two together.'

'If Sam figured it out, who else will do the same?' said Jack.

'Sure who cares if the whole world knows?' said Samantha with a laugh.

'I do,' said Michael standing up.

'I think Samantha's right,' said Rose. 'We should tell people. There's nothing to be ashamed of. We should make an announcement.'

'There'll be no announcements,' Michael yelled.

'Maybe your mother's right, Michael,' said Jack. 'Sure everyone's going to find out sooner or later.'

'We don't have to tell anyone,' Michael said. 'I can keep it a secret if I want to.'

'Why would you want to keep it a secret?' asked Samantha.

'You'll have to give up your job now,' said Jack.

'No, he doesn't Dad,' said Samantha. 'That's ridiculous.'

'Oh God, will we have to move?' asked Rose.

'Of course not, Mam,' said Samantha. 'That's so old fashioned.'

'It's the law, Sam,' said Michael. 'I don't have to tell anyone if I don't want to. It's best that way. I can just carry on with my life as normal.'

'But why would you want to?' asked Samantha. 'You should be able to live any life you choose now.'

'It's different for other people. This is not something I chose. It was an accident.'

'It's not an accident,' said Samantha. 'Never say that. There's nothing to be ashamed of being gay.'

The room went silent. Both of Michael's parents looked at him.

'What?' said Michael.

'You're...' said Rose. 'You're gay?'

'Why didn't you tell us, son?' said Jack.

'It all makes sense now,' said Rose. 'You should have told us, Michael.'

'I'm not...' but the words got caught in his throat. 'I'm not...'

'This is all too much news in one day,' said Rose sitting down and putting her hand over her forehead.

'What's going on?' asked Samantha. 'Is there more news?'

'What's that supposed to mean, Mam?' asked Michael. '"It all makes sense now?"'

'What other news?' asked Samantha again.

'Oh, it's just that Michael,' said Jack, 'won last night's EuroMillions jackpot.'

'What exactly all makes sense now, Mam?' asked Michael. 'I'll have you know...'

But Michael was interrupted by Samantha's ear-piercing scream as she jumped up and down and stamped her feet. She rushed over to Michael and threw her arms around him. Then hugged her parents, lifting her father into the air. She went back to Michael and squeezed him again.

After about thirty seconds of this, Michael wrestled himself free from her grip and held her by the shoulders. 'Calm down, Sam. Take a few deep breaths.'

Samantha took a few deep breaths, and Michael released her.

Then she screamed again, jumped up and down, stamped her feet and threw her arms around Michael again.

Michael spent two hours walking through the Kilmashogue Forest in the Dublin Mountains. He realised that most of the population would be engaging in some form of celebration, or even a shopping spree, if they were in his shoes, but he really needed to just clear his head. The fresh mountain air of the Wicklow Way did help him a little.

He still, of course, felt utterly plagued by this so-called 'win', but he saw some minor advantages to suddenly possessing the sum of €190,000,000. Advantages for other people obviously, not for him.

A portion of the money could be used for Emily and Katie, ensuring a good education and some sort of trust fund for them both. Indeed Samantha might also find a use for some of the millions. He would offer her whatever she wanted, be in one hundred thousand or ten million. Although why on earth she would want ten million euro was beyond him.

This sudden sense of partial lightness, albeit short-lived, resulted in Michael parking his car outside Harry's Pub at about 6pm. He normally wouldn't have a drink on a Sunday, but today was no ordinary Sunday.

Sunday afternoons in most pubs were usually reserved for sports fans, and despite the territorial and testosterone driven chants for the different teams, Michael always felt a tinge of envy for them. The fans always looked so comfortable in front of the big screens, always with a full pint separating them and a green pitch. Often, he would even wish he were among them. Sharing in their camaraderie, their bonding, their single purpose and determination. But he wouldn't be, and he couldn't be.

He was banking on most of the crowd having retired for the day, and luckily it had. He sighed with relief at the quietness of the pub when he opened the door, then inhaled with excitement when he saw a flash of black hair behind the bar.

He quickly scanned the room for any signs of Joey McGuinness or his gang, then made his way to the bar. He sat up straight and waited for Lauren, like a puppy dog waiting at the door for his master to come home.

'Hi Michael,' said Lauren smiling when she saw him. 'What has you in here on a Sunday?'

'Oh, just passing, Lauren. How are you?'

'Wrecked, to be honest. Apart from the usual Sunday match crowd, we've had quite a few journalists and television crews in looking for the mystery lottery winner.'

Michael's heart skipped a beat.

'Why here?' Michael asked, trying not to sound too alarmed.

'Oh, not just here. They were in all the pubs in the area. They're looking for someone who might be celebrating.'

'Oh, I see,' said Michael.

'I told them if someone had nearly two hundred million euro, or whatever it was, in their pocket, this'd be the last place you'd find them.'

'I suppose,' Michael agreed.

'There'd be more chance they'd be walking around the Dublin Mountains than being in here,' Lauren laughed sarcastically. 'What can I get you?'

Michael forced himself to laugh. 'Em, just a Guinness, please.'

'Guinness? You're getting into the big league now,' Lauren said and grabbed a glass from behind her.

'I'm sorry about the other night,' she said.

'When?' he asked, having genuinely forgotten his humiliating experience. Friday night seemed like weeks ago.

'On Friday night. I shouldn't have told Joey it was your birthday. It was stupid of me.'

'That's okay, Lauren.'

'Well anyway, I felt like crap when I saw you were gone. You're probably the only normal and decent person I get to see all week.'

Michael looked up at her, his mood instantly lifted. 'Really?'

'Yeah, really. That's how pathetic my life is.'

Michael lowered his head again.

'No, sorry, Michael. I didn't mean it like that.'

Michael took a mouthful from his pint.

'Lauren,' someone called from the other end of the bar.

'Coming,' she called back. 'Sorry. Back in a sec.'

Well, thought Michael, at least she thinks I'm normal. I suppose that's a good thing. Although I could hardly be referred to as 'normal' anymore.

'How's your mam and dad, Michael?' Lauren asked when she came back.

'Grand, thanks. Both enjoying their retirement. They're just back from their holidays in Spain.'

'God, I'd love that. I don't think Max and I have ever been away on a proper holiday.'

'Why don't you then?'

'I'll tell you a secret. I was the one who won the lottery last night. I'm just working here for the craic and the intellectual stimulation.'

Lauren laughed out loud at her own joke.

Maybe, Michael thought, I could get Lauren and Max a holiday in Spain.

'What would you do with all that money if you'd won?' asked Michael.

'You know what, Michael? All day I'm listening to people tell me how they'd spend that money, and you're the first person to ask me what I'd do with it.'

Michael blushed and tried to hide it by taking a mouthful of his Guiness.

'One summer, Joey took me on a trip to the West Coast,' Lauren said. Michael shifted in his seat at the mention of his name, and Lauren noticed. 'Sorry Michael, I know he's an asshole to you. He wasn't always like that. He took Max's diagnosis pretty bad. I think he felt it was somehow a reflection on his manhood or something. God knows. Maybe that's why he acts more macho now. To prove something. Problem is, his piece of shit father used to beat up his mam, so I don't think he even knows what being a real man is.'

Michael took a mouthful from his glass. He had many weaknesses, he knew that, but he wasn't gullible enough to fall for that as an excuse for Joey's behaviour. She noticed his silence.

'He's still a prick though,' she smiled at him, and Michael laughed too.

'Go on, tell me about your holiday out to the Wild West.'

'Okay,' said Lauren, looking over her shoulder to check that none of her customers were looking to be served. 'There was nothing planned, of course, and we just drove to Westport and spent the night there. Anyway, we drove up to Achill Island and on one side of the island we stopped at this little pub by the sea. The beach was almost at the front door. There was a fire blazing on one side and the bar was on the other. We sat by the fire drinking the creamiest pints you could only imagine. Out the window behind us I could see the ocean and the waves and fluffy white clouds floating slowly across the blue sky. Then we walked around the village. A gorgeous little village with a couple of shops and a tiny school. There was a restaurant and we had fresh fish and baby potatoes with real golden butter melting off them.'

Lauren paused, breathed in and then sighed as if smelling the ocean again.

'I'd go there,' she began again, as if to herself. 'Or somewhere like that. Away from the grey of Dublin. Away from the stares from strangers. Take my beautiful little boy and just go. Buy a small pub and a white cottage for Max and me to live in. One with a real turf fire and Max could go to the local school and play in the fields with the kids and swim in the sea and he'd be the happiest little boy in the whole wide world.'

'Lauren, when you're ready please,' a voice called out behind her.

Michael watched her take a deep breath and compose herself. She looked down at him again. 'Sorry,' she said. 'I'm tired. I got a bit carried away.'

Michael wanted to say something, but he didn't know what.

'Anyway,' she said, 'back to reality.'

Michael finished his pint slowly. He could have sat there all night, but he had his car with him and knew he should get home. He waved to Lauren as he left, and she called out a goodbye to him.

Outside he suddenly felt hungry. He hadn't eaten anything since his breakfast. Across the road he saw the flashing lights of a fish and chip shop, crossed over and ordered a fresh cod and a bag of chips.

'And a can of coke, please,' he asked the lady at the till.

'I'm sorry, I only have the large bottles,' she said. 'They're an extra two euro. Is that okay?'

Michael smiled and assured her that it would be perfectly okay, and he drove home.

Forcing themselves not to jump up when they heard Michael coming through the front door, his mother called out in as casual a tone as she could muster, 'is that you, Michael?'

'Yes, Mam,' he called back.

'Are you alright, son?' Jack asked.

'I'm okay, thanks.'

Rose got up and came into the kitchen. 'Do you want something to eat?' she asked him.

'No, thanks. I got some chips on the way home.'

'I'll put the kettle on so,' said Rose, happy to have a reason to stay in the kitchen. 'You'll have a cup of tea.'

She took down some cups, and noisily made a pot of tea. Jack walked into the kitchen, his hands in his pockets.

'Do you fancy a few chips, Dad?' Michael asked.

'No thanks, son. We had our dinner earlier.' He sat down opposite him at the kitchen table. 'Well?'

'Well what?' Michael asked.

'Did you have a think about what you're going to do?'

'I don't know yet.'

'Maybe you should go to bed early and things'll seem better in the morning, Michael,' said Rose.

'Maybe,' said Michael.

'You just need a little time to get used to it, that's all. Let it all sink in. I'll say an extra prayer for you tonight.'

'Okay, thanks Mam.'

'I'll lock up,' said Rose.

'I'll do it,' said Michael. 'I still have to bring in the new Ferrari I bought into the driveway.'

'What?' asked Rose.

'You bought a Ferrari?' asked Jack getting up from his chair. 'What colour is it?'

He turned around, and they both looked at their son's face, then smiled at him.

Jack's eyes popped open and he felt instantly awake. He lay there in the darkness of the bedroom listening. Something had woken him, but he wasn't sure what. He sat up and looked at Rose sleeping soundly beside him. Beyond her the red digital numbers of her bedside clock shone on her face. It read 03:38.

He had always been a light sleeper but rarely woke without good reason. Perhaps the strain of the day had just put him on edge a little, he thought. Rose stirred slightly then fell back into a deep sleep. She always wore an eye mask, which, as he had often told her, made her look absolutely ridiculous. She had a small collection of them. This one was pink with 'Do Not Disturb' written on the front.

After another minute of not hearing anything, he allowed his head to sink back into the pillow and his body to relax. He closed his eyes and sighed deeply. But his sigh was interrupted by the sound of a chair scraping along the floor in the kitchen downstairs.

He held his breath. In one swift movement that belied his age, he pulled the duvet off him and was creeping out of the bedroom, leaving Rose undisturbed (according to her mask's wishes).

On the landing, he peered downstairs and saw a light coming from under the closed kitchen door. He looked in the direction of Michael's room, but it was in darkness. His bare feet tread softly on the carpet as he made his way downstairs, avoiding the creaky sixth step.

He froze at the bottom of the stairs when he heard a cupboard door closing. A shadow moved across the light under the door. He needed a weapon. With only a lamp on the hall table at his disposal, he slowly unplugged the lamp. With his right hand, he grabbed it by its heavy base.

Gripping the lamp hard above his head, he ran the remaining distance to the kitchen and burst open the door.

'Hold it there,' he shouted.

'Jesus Christ,' said Michael, the cup he was holding in his hand falling and smashing on the tiled floor.

'What the hell?' said Jack.

'What are you doing, Dad? You scared the crap out of me.' Michael bent down and picked up the pieces of the smashed mug, still shaken from being startled.

'I thought you were a burglar,' said Jack, breathing heavily. 'What are you doing up at this hour? I thought you were in bed.'

'I couldn't sleep,' he said, throwing the broken mug into the bin. 'Thought I'd have a cup of tea. Might help me relax.'

'Yeah, caffeine is a well-known sedative,' said Jack sitting down at the table.

'Well, either way,' said Michael, 'I'd rather be down here than in bed staring at the ceiling all night.'

'Have you thought what you might do with the lottery money?'

'Yeah. I've decided I'm going to ask Sam if she'll take it. That's the best thing to do. Derek, being a stockbroker and all that, they'll know what to do with it. Investments and bonds and equities and all that sort of thing.'

'If that's what you want, son, that's okay.'

Jack fell silent. Michael looked at him.

'Do you think I should keep it?'

'Whatever you decide to do, I just hope you don't regret it later,' Jack said, arranging the salt and pepper cellars so they lined up together.

They sat in silence for a few moments.

'Did I ever tell you about one of my pals from school, Charlie Byrne? We were the best of mates. I'm going back about forty years here. Anyway, Charlie had an uncle living in Boston. One summer, he came home to visit. We thought he was like a real John Wayne. He probably did too.'

'He said things like "cool" and "hi". We hung around him for a few weeks and he told us stories about Boston and places he visited in America, and about the pub he was going to open one day. Although he called it a "bar".'

'As he was leaving, he gave each of us a ten dollar bill and told us that if we wanted more of them, we could come work for him when he had his pub. Two years later, in fairness to him, Charlie's dad told him the uncle had opened up his own pub and had sent home word that there was a job waiting for Charlie and me.'

'Charlie barely hesitated. But by then I was going out with someone. Someone very special and very beautiful who I was convinced one day I was going to marry.'

'Mam?' said Michael smiling but slightly embarrassed.

'No, no. Audrey Redmond. Your mother was much later.'

Michael took a deep breath.

'What's your point, Dad?' he asked impatiently.

'I'm getting to it,' he said. 'Charlie was gone within a week. He tried to convince me and Audrey to go too, but we didn't. Charlie was braver than us. Less afraid of the unknown.'

'He did well for himself, Charlie did. Eventually, he saved up enough, moved out to California and opened up his own bar. San Diego, I think it was. No, San Francisco. Or maybe San Tropez.

San something anyway. He married an ex Miss Texas. Had two daughters, who I heard are even more beautiful than their mother. I think one of them is a doctor now.'

'My point is that Charlie took the opportunity with both hands and he ran with it. And I didn't. I still have that ten dollar bill, and it'll always be a reminder to me of 'what if'. Regret is terrible thing, son.'

Jack got up off his chair slowly, his feet cold on the kitchen floor.

'Where's Charlie now, Dad?' Michael asked. 'Do you ever hear from him?'

'No, not for years. He became an alcoholic and lost his bar. When his missus left him and moved back to Texas, she took the kids and they don't even talk to him anymore.'

Michael placed his elbows on the kitchen table and his head in his hands in exasperation, trying to figure out some moral or logic to his father's story.

'But he took the opportunity,' Jack said. 'I'll give him that, unlike Audrey or me.'

'Dad,' Michael called to him as he left, 'I know I'm going to regret asking this, but what happened to Audrey Redmond?'

'Oh, she stayed in Ireland. She was working in a chemist when we were going out, but I broke up with her as she was always working long hours. She ended up owning a chain of pharmacies, would you believe? Sold the lot for millions and retired in her forties. So, it just goes to show you.'

'Show me what? Charlie took the opportunity and lost his business and family, and Audrey stayed and became a millionaire.'

'Yeah, well,' said Jack. 'Hindsight is a wonderful thing.'

'Dad, I've no idea what you're talking about.'

'Regret, Mike. Regret,' Jack said stoically.

Michael sighed heavily. 'Goodnight, Dad.'

He listened to his father plugging back in the lamp in the hall, then climbing the stairs, pausing to avoid the sixth step. Michael remained sitting in the kitchen at more of a loss what to do than ever before. He got back up and turned on the kettle to make some more tea. He couldn't go back to bed now. It was going to be a long day.

5

'Yes, Mrs. O'Brien, I realise that,' Michael told her, 'but because you weren't insured during the time of the flood, then Ireland Trust has no obligation to cover the policy.'

Michael found this part of his job the most difficult. He loved to help people when they were covered under their insurance for the recent event or disaster in their lives, but when they are seventy-year-old ladies who didn't pay their insurance and won't get a penny, he wished he were anywhere else but there.

'But we've always been a customer of Ireland Trust, since we first bought our home forty years ago,' Mrs O'Brien told him again. 'How am I going to pay for all the damage? The water went everywhere. The whole of downstairs is destroyed. You see, it was my husband who took care of all these things when he was alive. He passed away last year, and there's so much paperwork, and I just don't...'

She didn't finish the sentence and Michael hoped she wasn't crying.

'But my manager has said the policy expired four months ago,' Michael told her. 'They have no obligation to pay, Mrs O'Brien.'

There was no answer at the other end of the phone, and Michael knew now she was crying.

'Mrs O'Brien? Are you there?'

Michael stood up in his cubicle and looked around the office.

'Mrs O'Brien, can you hear me?'

He heard her snuffle.

'Mrs O'Brien. Listen to me.'

'Yes,' her voice was weak.

'Do you have a pen?'

'Hold on,' she said, and he heard her fumbling.

Michael stood up again and looked around, then sat back down.

'Write this down,' he told her.

'I'm ready,' she said.

'You need to hang up and then call the same number you just dialled. This time ask for extension 332.'

'322.'

'No, 3-3-2.'

'332.'

'Then tell them you filed a B729 form, but it was never received. This happens all the time.'

'B789, yes,'

'No, Mrs O'Brien. B-7-2-9.'

'B729.'

'Perfect. Tell them you've been told your policy has expired, but since you filed a B729 form, that you'd like to avail of the six-month extension to your policy because of the death of the principal policyholder.'

'Principal policyholder. Okay,'

Michael could hear her writing it down.

'They will change it on their system. It takes about a day. Then tomorrow, call back up and tell them you'd like to make a fresh claim. When they check the system, they'll see you're insured and you shouldn't have any problems. You'll be covered for the flood damage.'

There was silence on the phone again.

'Mrs O'Brien?'

He could hear the faint sound of her crying.

'Mrs. O'Brien?'

'Thank you,' she said.

'You're welcome, Mrs. O'Brien. Goodbye,' Michael said and hung up the phone.

'And how was your weekend, Mike?' asked Trevor Tiernan, when Michael was pouring hot water into his cup, later that day. His arm moved slightly and boiling water spilled onto his hand.

Michael winced in pain.

Standing very close to him and with a height of six-foot three-inches, his supervisor towered above him.

'Grand, thanks,' said Michael.

'I'll tell you a good one,' Trevor said. 'A couple of the lads and myself were out on Saturday for a few. This bar maid, a real cracker, probably not more than about twenty-years-old and she...'

Normally, Michael would have stood there for as long as was necessary, braving a forced grin and inhaling Trevor's rancid breath, all the time with a sense as if he were being pushed back against a wall. He felt looser today though. Less burdened and certainly less compelled to stand and listen to this tirade. So he took a step back, turned and walked away.

Trevor was so confused by this, and not having experienced such behaviour from anyone before, he found himself for several seconds standing alone and talking to no one.

Michael most definitely felt, as he walked back to his cubicle, different today. There was less of a connection with his surroundings, and even a disconnection from his colleagues, which, although strange, he liked.

Aileen's unverified anecdotes of her neighbours' comings and goings in which she always had the last laugh seemed even more tedious than normal. Kevin's complaints at work about his unappreciative and lazy family members (which switched at home to complaints about his unappreciative and lazy work colleagues) seemed even less bearable that morning. And when Trevor, in front of two women, had asked Michael did he watch 'the match', knowing full well that he hadn't, Michael's right hand had formed into a fist.

Nothing, in fact, had changed at the office that morning. The only thing that had changed was Michael.

Unable to focus on his job, he decided to keep his promise to his mother and call the lottery head office to verify, at the very least, that he really was in possession of the winning ticket.

'National Lottery, this is Ella speaking. How may I help you?' said the cheerful voice coming from his mobile phone.

Michael sat, fully-dressed in the second cubicle of the third floor toilets. He cupped his hand around the mouthpiece of his phone and whispered into it.

'Hello,' he said, 'I need a check made on a ticket please. To see if I've won or not.'

'Well, sir,' said Ella, maintaining her alacrity, 'the easiest way is to go back to the retailer where you purchased the ticket, or any officially licensed lottery retailer, and they will be able to scan the ticket for you there and then. If the sum is under one hundred euro then they can pay you instantly.'

'Oh, I see,' said Michael.

'If the sum is more than that,' Ella continued, barely aware of the slight interruption, 'then you can post the ticket into us and we'll send you a cheque within five working days.'

'Okay. I'll do that so. Thanks.'

'Just don't forget to register your letter,' Ella added with a forced laugh. 'I'll give you the address to send the ticket to now. How much, may I ask, is the winning sum for? To the nearest one hundred euro is fine.'

'Oh, hold on. I have it written on my phone. I took a picture in case you asked me that.' Michael skimmed through the images on his phone. 'Here it is. I have the exact figure now if that'll help.'

'Great, thank you, sir. And the sum is?'

'€189,864,631,' said Michael matter-of-factly.

After a few seconds, Michael began to think that he'd lost the connection.

'Hello,' he called into the phone. 'Ella? Are you still there?'

'Please hold the line, sir,' said Ella, and then Michael heard holding music. The theme song from Chariots of Fire, he believed.

'Hello, Jackpot prize enquires. This is Claire speaking.'

'Hello, Claire. Em, I believe I have the winning ticket, and I just need to verify it please,' Michael told her.

'Okay, sir. If you can just look at the back of the ticket for me please. We've already had fourteen calls this morning to claim the prize, believe it or not, so if you could just call out those numbers to me.'

Michael did as he was asked, and he heard the tapping of a keyboard in the background. More silence.

'May I have your name, please, sir?' asked Claire.

'It's Michael Irvine.'

'Well, Mr. Irvine. At this point it appears that you are indeed in possession of the winning ticket. So firstly congratulations.'

'Oh, okay,' said Michael a little dejected. The last hope that this had all been a mistake and could go away left Michael's mind. He sighed.

'Well, Mr. Irvine,' came Claire's voice again, 'in the seven years I've worked here, I've never got that response before.'

'Oh, I'm sorry. I mean thank you, I suppose. So what happens now?'

'You can come in and collect your winnings any time that is convenient for you. We normally send a car to collect the winner though. You can even come in today if you like.'

'I'm not sure my supervisor will give me the time off,' said Michael.

Another silence.

'May I ask what you do for a living, Mr. Irvine?'

'I work for Ireland Trust.'

'What do your friends call you? Michael, Mick or Mike?' asked Claire, the formality of her voice waning a little.

'Mike,' answered Michael obediently.

'May I call you Mike?'

'Sure.'

'Look, Mike. While the National Lottery has your money, we're making interest on it. Now, I don't know your salary but as a rough estimate, every day that we keep your money, you're losing about the equivalent of at least a month's salary. That's just the interest, Mike. Do you understand?'

'Yes,' said Michael unconvincingly.

'Do you love your job that much?' Claire asked.

Michael genuinely thought about it. It was a question he had never asked himself before. The answer surprised him, if not Claire.

'No,' he admitted. 'No, I don't.'

'Well then, the chances of you ever working there again at this point in time are quite slim. So, Mike, why don't you inform your supervisor that you're taking the afternoon off work and quite possibly the rest of your life.'

'But I'd have to give him a month's notice,' Michael answered immediately.

More silence.

'Okay, then' Michael said, 'I'll go ask him.'

'No, Mike,' said Claire. 'You go tell him.'

As instructed, Michael duly sought and found Trevor. He was in the canteen sitting at a table with four other men. Michael stood a few feet away from him hoping he could catch him alone as he left the canteen and went back to work. There was a notice board hung on the wall and Michael spent his time mindlessly reading the ads and posters.

It wasn't until the third time Trevor had called his name that he heard him.

'Sorry, what?' he asked.

Everyone at the table was now looking at him, most in anticipation of some entertainment at someone else's expense.

'I said, are you looking for another job, Irvine?' Trevor repeated.

'No,' Michael told him.

'So why then are you reading the job notices? Thinking of going for a promotion, are we? Bettering ourselves?'

The man to his left sniggered.

'No, not at all,' Michael said, staring at all the faces now focused on him.

'So go on back to work then, there's a good fella,' Trevor told him, and then turned back around to the table.

Michael took a step closer. 'I need to take the afternoon off,' Michael said.

Trevor turned back around to face him.

'What?'

'I know it's short notice, but I need to take a few hours off. Sorry.'

'I don't think so, Mr Irvine. Unless there's been a death in the family or an emergency, then no, you cannot have the afternoon off. Has there been a death?'

'No,' Michael told him, lowering his head.

'Well, then, off you go. Back to your little cubicle.'

The man sitting across from Trevor raised his eyebrows indicating that Michael was still standing there. Trevor turned back around, saw Michael there and stood up. He walked over to where Michael was standing and looked down at him.

'It's just that...' Michael began. 'The lady... Claire. She said I have to go because of all the interest I'd be losing on the one hundred and ninety million I won yesterday. I can't remember the exact amount, but it seemed like a lot.'

'The what?' Trevor asked.

'The EuroMillions,' Michael told him. 'She said I should collect it today. Is it okay if I go for the afternoon? I'll be back tomorrow.'

The blood had drained from Trevor's face, and he took a step back.

'Is it okay then?' Michael asked him again, and Trevor took another step back as if he'd been punched in the chest.

'Is that true Mike?' someone at the table asked. 'You won the EuroMillions?'

'Yes, but I need to take a few hours off. Is it okay?'

Trevor fell back into his seat, but he continued to stare up at Michael.

'Trevor?' Michael asked.

'Mike,' the man said. 'Go. Just go.'

Michael nodded a thanks to him and turned to leave.

'And Mike,' the man called after him, smiling now. 'Congratulations.'

He first drove to his parents' house and told them he had arranged to meet Claire at 2pm and asked them if they would like to come with him.

'It shouldn't take too long,' he said. 'Just a formality, I suppose.'

'Should I wear something nice?' his mother asked, flustered.

'No, Mam, you're grand as you are. We'll be back in an hour or so.'

Parking his car in Temple Bar, they walked the short distance to Abbey Street where the lottery headquarters were located.

'Put your wallet in your front pocket, Michael,' advised Rose. 'Pickpockets are rampant these days. Let's just get the cheque and go home.'

'No, let's get a pint to celebrate when we're finished,' suggested Jack.

'I think,' said Rose, 'that the best thing to do is to just do what we have to do and go home. One of us will need to get the bus home anyway.'

Michael stopped. 'Why do we need to get the bus home?' he asked.

'Because,' she explained, 'you'll never get that big cheque into your small car.'

'Mam, they don't actually give you a massive cheque to...'

'Hang on,' said Jack, 'looks like trouble or there's been an accident ahead.'

A large crowd was gathered at the Abbey Street Luas stop. Gardaí were directing the crowds and two garda cars, their blue beacons flashing, were stopping cars from entering the street.

'I'm always saying those trams are a death trap,' said Rose.

Four or five men with large telescopic-lens cameras were huddled together, chatting and drinking coffee. Michael saw two large two video cameras on the ground between the legs of two other men. Three glamorously dressed women chatted among themselves, each holding a microphone at their sides.

'Don't say anything to anyone,' Michael instructed his parents, fully aware of what was happening. 'Now follow me, quickly.'

'What's going on?' Rose asked.

'Just move,' he told her.

'What's wrong?' asked Jack.

Keeping his head down, Michael approached the crowd as if they were trying to get through to the other side, then just as he passed the front door to the lottery offices, he turned swiftly and made straight for the door.

He pushed the glass door, but it was locked. He pulled at it. Nothing. He pulled and pushed again. A few of the men looked in his direction. There was an intercom at the side of the door, and he pressed the buzzer. A loud BUZZ rang out. The three women with the microphones stopped talking and looked over at the door. Michael was having trouble breathing. Why are they taking so long?

'Is that them?' he heard someone behind him ask.

Michael closed his eyes and wished he were somewhere else. He pressed the buzzer again. An elderly porter walked slowly over to the door.

The journalists started to crowd in, forcing Rose forward.

'Michael,' she called out. Jack put his arm around her and squeezed in tighter to the door.

'Michael,' one of the journalists called.

The porter arrived at the door. Michael pulled at it again. Harder this time. The porter pressed a button, and Michael heard his voice 'Yes?'

'Open, please, open,' was all that he could manage.

'Michael, are you the winner?' a woman's voice asked, shouting above the crowd.

Rose stumbled forward again, and Michael turned to catch her. As he turned he was forced forward and his back pressed up against the door, his parents on either side of him.

Suddenly their faces were lit up by overhead lights and a barrage of flashes.

'Michael, Michael,' they called out. 'How are you feeling today?'

The women with the microphones were in front of him now, and they shoved their microphones in front of his face.

'What's the first thing you're going to do?

'Do you have a girlfriend, Michael?'

'What does she think?'

'Are these your parents?'

Inside the building, a woman with a clipboard was passing through the lobby and saw the commotion.

'Do you have an appointment?' the porter's voice came out over the intercom.

The woman inside immediately rushed over, calling out to the porter as she ran, 'open the door, Kevin. Open the door. Come on. Hurry.'

With a thin buzzing sound and then a loud CLICK, the door opened inwards and Michael almost fell through the doorway. He grabbed both of his parents with each of his hands and pulled them after him. Kevin pushed the journalists back and as the door closed shut, so too did the noise and shouts of 'Michael', camera flashes and the city itself dwindled to a muffled din.

The woman who had instructed the door be opened stretched out her hand, 'Michael Irvine, is it?' she asked.

Michael, still a little dazed, shook her hand.

'I'm Aoife, and you must be his parents?' she said and firmly shook the hands of Jack and Rose. 'Congratulations to you all.'

The camera flashes continued to light up the reception, but the television camera men, disappointed with not getting an interview, or at the very least, a humorous soundbite, lowered their cameras and microphones.

'Come on,' said Aoife, 'let's find somewhere private, and I'll let Claire know you're here.'

By the time they had made their way to a more suitable room, Claire arrived slightly out of breath, and shook hands enthusiastically with everyone.

'So nice to meet you, Michael,' she said. 'You're our biggest winner so far. I'm so excited for you.'

'Okay, thanks,' said Michael.

'I must say, Michael, you don't seem to be that excited about it all. We've had winners of fifty thousand euro in here that were so jubilant you'd think they'd won the EuroMillions.'

'Sorry,' said Michael.

'Oh, no need to apologise. You're probably still a bit overwhelmed by it all.'

Michael glanced around the room. The chairs and the sofa were a little plusher looking than what you'd expect in an office building. There were photos on the walls of previous winners holding large cheques and wearing broad smiles. Whatever torment and stress all that money may have brought them later, Michael thought, at least on that day they were happy. He also noticed Claire in a few of them.

'So what happens now?' asked Jack.

'Well, we normally check the ticket, and then arrange for the money to be transferred directly into your bank account.'

'Of course, no problem,' said Michael reaching into his back pocket, finding nothing, and then quickly checking his front pocket. 'Oh my God, I've been pickpocketed.'

'Jesus, Mary and Joseph,' said Rose. 'Didn't I tell you to watch your wallet?'

Claire covered her face with both her hands.

'Only messing, Mam,' Michael said and took out his wallet.

'Fecking eejit, ye are,' Rose scolded him.

Claire laughed nervously. 'It's good you have a sense of humour, Mike. You're going to need it.'

Michael pulled out the ticket, and she took it from his hand and studied it briefly.

'Well, it certainly looks in order,' she said. 'I just need to bring it upstairs to have it officially verified. Is that okay with you?'

'Sure,' said Michael. 'In the meantime, Aoife can get you anything you need. Champagne perhaps? How about for you Mrs Irvine?'

'I've only ever had champagne one time before, I think. It was at Samantha's wedding. She's Michael's sister. She's two beautiful girls, Emily and Katie...'

'Mam,' said Michael sternly, interrupting her.

Rose turned and faced Claire. 'Just a cup of tea for me please, love.'

'No, problem, Mrs Irvine,' said Claire. 'Anyone else?'

'Three teas would be great, thanks,' said Michael.

By the time the teas had arrived, so too had Claire returned. This time she wasn't alone. Two men wearing dark suits, bright ties and an air of self-importance, which all three Irvines found a little intimidating, followed her into the room.

'Michael,' said Claire, 'this is Tony Murphy and Graham Jones. They're independent financial advisors who work in conjunction with the lottery, and they provide financial advice to all our lottery winners.'

More shaking of hands.

'We'd like to sit down with you, Michael, and go over some options available to you at this point,' Tony said opening a folder.

'Well, I, em,' said Michael taking a step backwards.

'What we're here to do,' interrupted Graham and speaking very slowly, 'is to assist someone like you, and provide them with the information needed to handle such a large sum of money.'

'Someone like me?' asked Michael.

'Yes,' agreed Tony. 'Someone from your background who perhaps wouldn't have the financial knowledge to fully exploit or appreciate the opportunities available to them at this time for efficient and effective wealth management.'

There were a few moments silence in the room as Michael looked at his parents, and they looked at him.

'Mike,' said Claire softly, 'the best thing to do is to take things easy at first. In fact, what you should really do now is nothing at all. You need some time to take all of this in. Process it and then make some decisions.'

'Do I have to do all this now?' he asked, looking at the two men.

'Of course not. Take their cards, and you can call them at a time that suits you.'

'Well, perhaps if we could sit down today for just ten minutes,' Tony burst in.

'Thank you, Tony. Thank you, Graham,' said Claire, and she directed them out of the room.

Michael relaxed a little. He liked her.

When the door was closed, Claire gave Michael a large brown

envelope.

'Here's a booklet and some other information that might help you over the first few days,' she said.

Michael looked down at it. 'What about keeping my winnings private?'

'Well,' said Claire, 'the media seems to know your first name already. Normally we'd send a car, and you'd come in a side entrance.'

'Are we free to go?'

'Of course,' said Claire laughing. 'I'll organise a car to take you home.'

'That's okay,' said Michael. 'We're parked in Temple Bar.'

'Then perhaps, you'd like to leave by the side entrance?'

'Yes, that'd be great, thanks.'

'The only thing I need now,' said Claire, 'is your bank account details, so we can transfer the money in. It'll probably take a few days. Expect an excited call from your bank manager.'

Michael laughed.

'The best advice I can give you, Michael, is to do nothing at all for at least a week. Either stay at home or go abroad for a while. Allow yourself time to just let it all sink in.'

'You should go for a few days to the Isle of Man, Michael,' suggested Rose, then turning to Claire. 'That's where Michael's father and I went on our honeymoon. It's a lovely place. We stayed in a wonderful B&B for a week.'

'That's a great idea,' laughed Claire, 'or you could go for a couple of weeks to a five star resort in the Caribbean or the Maldives and take all your family on a private jet. But that's up to you guys.'

Michael laughed.

'My number's on that info pack, Mike, so call me if you need anything, okay?'

'Thank you, Claire,' said Michael.

'You've been very helpful,' said Jack.

'Now,' said Claire, 'unless you'd like to give an impromptu press conference, I'll show you the secret way out.'

6

Zoe Simms watched as the side door opened onto Marlborough Street, and out stepped Michael and his parents into a warm Dublin evening. In the reflection of the window she was facing, she watched them look from side to side before quickly shuffling off towards the quays, away from the other journalists who were still gathered outside the front door. Zoe allowed them to walk away, and for a moment looked at herself in the shop window.

Sometimes, she thought to herself, before following them onto the quays, it's just too easy.

At Zoe's birth, at the exclusive three-thousand-euro-a-night Mount Carmel private hospital twenty eight years ago, Zoe's parents bestowed on her two things she would later come to despise. The first was from her father - her name. He thought, at the time anyway, it sounded contemporary and cute. Its owner, on the other hand thought it juvenile at best, and idiotic at worst.

The second was from her mother - her striking good looks (Miss Ireland 1979 and the second runner up for Miss Universe 1980).

When she was fourteen and everything about her was developing, so too did an apathy begin to develop about everything. As boys showed an increasing interest in her, she grew more and more indifferent towards them.

At secondary school, she was assumed by the boys to be a lesbian, and many girls had wished that too, but all to no avail. Her parents signed her up for various extracurricular activities -

swimming, tennis, guitar lessons. Although she feigned interest to the best of her ability, it soon became apparent to the teachers they were wasting their time. Three chords of a guitar, the basic keys of a piano, the opening moves on a chessboard, how to properly hold a camogie stick.

Her father, who was the only person she seemed to cherish in any way, suspected a form of autism. He sent her for several sessions of psychotherapy, only to be bitterly disappointed with a diagnosis of mild Paranoid Personality Disorder. 'But doesn't everyone,' the psychiatrist concluded when handing her father his report and his bill.

The psychiatrist also told her father that Zoe was smart. Very smart in fact. She was also physically healthy and very beautiful (although why that was in the report was questionable), and he felt, in his professional opinion, it was merely a teenage hormonal condition that would soon pass. His professional opinion proved to be wrong.

The day after her sixteenth birthday, her father sat her down to try, as best he could, to explain the reasons why he was leaving her mother. Zoe had purposefully ignored the recent escalation in her parents' arguments and the increased frequencies of door-slamming. As smart as she was, his leaving was incomprehensible to her. She saw his parting as his rejection of her and not of her mother. For her, having a dysfunctional and unhappy family was better than no family at all.

He was her first love, and was still, to her, the handsomest man in the whole world. The day after he left, the house felt empty, as if a large party had just ended. The reality of the big bad world came into her house and into her life that day, and nothing would ever be the same again.

He had promised weekend adventures together, daddy daughter dates and trips to concerts and the cinema. Instead she got long weekends with her reticent mother in a house that was suddenly way too big.

The years passed. Coming from a six-figure-income home, and doing well in her final exams, despite not studying for them, she had her choice of colleges. When presented with her options, she chose University College Dublin as it was only ten minutes from her house. She viewed the courses available to her - Health Science, Engineering, Agriculture, Arts. A seemingly endless list of banality.

She eventually chose the one that appeared the vaguest of interests to her - Business.

Wanting her to participate fully in college life, her mother arranged residency on the campus. 'To prevent her from constantly hiding up in her room and be forced, by close proximity to her fellow students, to improve her non-existent social skills,' was the general idea.

She shared a room with three other girls. An Arts student from California named Melanie, who was as effervescent as Minnie Mouse and rarely sober. A Human Sciences student from Manchester named Esmeralda who was almost pretty and rarely without the company of a male student or professor. And finally a South Korean named Hea Jung who was rarely in the room.

Melanie thought, because Zoe never laughed and didn't drink, that she was a recovering alcoholic. Esmeralda thought that since Zoe never slept with anyone, either male or female, student or professor, that she was frigid. And Hea Jung didn't even know Zoe's name.

Her father, now leading the life of a senior manager at KPMG with yet another new girlfriend called Tiffany or Sheryl, and her mother, the gin-fuelled former beauty queen in her fifties, felt they had done all they could for their daughter. On her nineteenth birthday, feeling somewhat guilty of their Pontius Pilate style parenting, they bought her an expensive car on top of her €1,000 a month allowance.

When college life became unbearably boring for Zoe, (which was pretty much from day one) she would drive into the city and sit in the cafes all day. Or sometimes she would make the short distance to her parents' house, where a true image of complete boredom would be presented by her mother.

It was in her second year in UCD that the miracle happened. Professor Gary Quinn was delivering his usual sleep inducing lecture Foundations of Management Thought, when for the first time that year, Zoe picked up her pen and began to write. For the next forty minutes, she wrote a one-thousand-word short story titled A Day in the Life of Ian Dennis about a fictitious student in UCD.

Not wishing to receive either credit or blame for the real life people she had parodied in her story, she signed the bottom Simon Simmers, and sent it off to the student magazine - UCD Today.

The short piece was published and became the talk of both the campus and the staff rooms for the next two weeks. Its effect on the college, however, shadowed the cathartic and cataclysmic consequence it had on its author. The article's notoriety created a spark that ignited a passion in Zoe, and for the first time she felt something she had never experienced before - enthusiasm.

She celebrated this new sensation by buying her first bottle of vodka and sleeping with the first guy who approached her at the student bar. Both experiences resulting in a feeling of slight nausea.

Not wishing to further aggravate her parents with yet another failed effort at something, Zoe sold her car to pay for an evening course to gain a journalist's degree in Griffith College. After her last class of the day at UCD (although invariably it was skipped), she took the bus to Griffith College and attended there from 6pm to 9pm, four evenings a week. She found the bus journey to and from Griffith gave her sufficient time to study for the two courses.

Her mother only once questioned the whereabouts of her 'lovely' car, and Zoe told her it was parked on the campus as she needed the exercise. It was never mentioned again.

And so, for four years, Zoe commuted from college to college, applying herself where needed, partaking in college life only when absolutely necessary and sleeping with boys, and the occasional girl, whenever it suited her. She began to use her body as a tool, just like her brain, and applied its use when necessary or beneficial. She was a voracious reader but could claim to have never read a work of fiction in her life. Facts and reality were, she felt, astonishing and dramatic enough.

For her graduation at UCD, she walked across the stage to receive her degree, clapped on by her father (before he needed to leave to take an important call) and by her mother (before leaving to see if the bar was open).

For her graduation at Griffith's College a week later, a perfunctory round of applause from those in attendance accompanied her across that stage. Apart from her lecturer and a girl she had sat beside, no one in the room knew who she was.

Her career in the world of journalism failed to take off like the rocket she had hoped for, despite her hard work. She tried freelancing for a while. Initially sending lengthy articles to the national papers, then smaller articles to more local papers, then even frivolous articles to several glossy magazines she would normally have thought of with disdain.

Then one evening, as she was about to send an email to the Irish Gazette, she paused and regarded her signature at the end - Zoe Simms. In a moment of inspiration, she reverted back to her male alter ego and signed it Simon Simmers.

The next day, Simon Simmers received an email of acceptance for her article from the editor, and with that her career was truly launched. Within a year, her (adopted) name became known and often feared by the upper and lower echelons of Dublin society. She exposed those who needed exposing and highlighted the imbecility of celebrities. She didn't care too much for the hardships of the poor, nor the responsibilities of the captains of industry. She cared only for the story.

Her looks and background granted her access to VIP parties where she overheard gossip, spied on politicians, and even slept with the odd personality - who were more often than not married. Anything to get the story was her internal motto.

After two years of anonymity as Simon Simmers, one of her 'victims' exposed her real identity as revenge for a career destroying article she'd written, and her work became more of a challenge. To gain access to her unscrupulous prey, she leaned more on her network of contacts, bribery and even the occasion disguise.

Now, with her infamous name and face known among the ever-corrupt and ever-vigilant throughout Ireland, Zoe Simms moved less easily in their world. What didn't change was her tremendous apathy for her victim or her tireless enthusiasm for her story. And Michael Irvine was definitely a story. Her story.

She watched them pay their parking fee and then drive out into Dame Street. Hailing a taxi, she jumped inside and, not for the first time, said, 'follow that car.'

'You taking the piss, darling?' asked the driver.

'Do you want me to get another taxi, or do you want to earn a fare?' she said opening the door.

'Alright, alright, keep your hair on,' he said. The taxi driver pulled out and caught up with Michael's car following it out of the city, a sudden headache slowly getting worse as he tried to stay focused on the car ahead.

As they opened the front door to their house, Michael heard his mobile phone ringing. He had left it on charge and forgotten to bring it with him, He didn't reach it in time to answer, but when he picked it up, he saw eighteen missed calls and thirty one text messages.

'Oh, God,' he said out loud.

One of the calls had been from Samantha, and he called her back.

'Sam? Is everything okay?'

'Michael. You're all over Facebook and Twitter.'

'But I'm not on Facebook or Twitter.'

'There are pictures of you outside the Lottery building saying "Biggest Irish Lottery Winner. But who is he?".'

'Oh God,' he said.

'There are video clips as well. You've gone viral, Mike.'

'What time is it?'

'Almost six.'

'I'm turning on the news.'

'I'm coming over,' Samantha said and hung up.

'What's going on Michael?' Rose asked him.

Michael went into the sitting room, his parents following, and turned on the television. The Six-One News was just starting.

The newscaster gave a summary of the headlines of the day – 'Further escalation in Afghanistan... Fianna Fáil minister apologises for calling the working class 'a burden on society'... 1950's actor Romero Atkins dies in Los Angeles today... And do you know this person?'

Michael and his parents stood open-mouthed as they watched themselves under a hail of flashes and questions struggling to open the glass doors of the Lottery building.

The newscaster continued... 'And the hunt goes on for the family who are the biggest lottery winners in the history of the State.'

Michael switched the television off. There was silence.

'It's true,' Rose said. 'Television does add ten pounds. You looked like you've put on a bit of weight there, Michael.'

By the time Samantha was letting herself into her parents' house, Michael's phone had rang another eight times, and the landline six times.

'Lottery or no lottery,' Samantha heard her father shouting, 'I want that spade back.'

'What's going on?' she asked.

'It's your father,' said Rose. 'He wants to go into Liam Flynn next door and get his spade back.'

'But your son's just won millions and millions, Dad,' Samantha said.

'Exactly,' he agreed, as if she'd just summed up his whole argument, 'and that's exactly what he'll say when he finds out. Then I'll never get it back.'

'It's just a shovel, Dad,' said Michael.

'It's a very good shovel,' said Jack.

'Sam,' said Michael, ignoring his father now, 'what's it saying on Facebook?'

'Nothing yet. It's just showing your face and asking if anyone knows you.'

She took out her phone, and they went into the kitchen. 'Here's a picture of you,' she said holding it out to him. 'It's on a social media news channel.'

'That is the worst photo I have ever seen of myself,' he said, scrolling down the phone. 'Eight hundred and fifteen comments?'

'I wouldn't even bother reading them,' said Samantha, reaching out for the phone, but Michael moved it out of her reach.

'"With a hundred and ninety million in his pocket, I'd probably ride him now…" "I wonder if he already has a girlfriend…" "No look at him, he's DEFINITELY single…" "He wouldn't be too bad if he got a proper haircut…"'

Michael handed her back the phone. 'These are brutal. I don't want to read any more.'

'What are you going to do now?' she asked.

'I don't know. I suppose I could go to some expensive barber. Maybe get some new gear to wear.'

'No, you idiot. I mean about the money.'

'Oh, I see. I think I'm going take the advice of that lady in the lottery headquarters and just do nothing for a while. I might even go into work tomorrow and…'

The doorbell rang, and everyone froze.

'Who's that?' asked Jack.

'How do I know?' said Michael.

'You answer it, Rose.'

'You answer it.'

Samantha walked passed them and looked through the spyhole

in the door.

'It's Liam Flynn next door. He has a spade with him.'

'Thank God,' said Jack, walking to the door.

'I'm only kidding. It's Uncle Jim.'

'Wouldn't you know it,' said Jack. 'The first sign of a few bob, and he's over.'

Samantha opened the door and in poured Jack's eldest brother, his wife, June, and their three children, Jim jr, little June, and Bobby.

'Is it true?' shouted Jim, holding out his hand to be shaken by someone.

'I'm delighted for you,' cried June, holding out her arms to be hugged by someone.

The doorbell rang again, and Samantha, still standing at the door, peeked through the spyhole again.

'It's Aunty Pat,' she called out.

'Wouldn't you know it,' said Uncle Jim. 'The first sign of a few bob and she's over.'

Within fifteen minutes the house was full of family, friends and neighbours. Michael's hand was sore from all the handshakes and his face dotted with lipstick. The kettle boiled constantly and all biscuits were quickly consumed. Uncle Jim tried to round up everyone for a celebratory march to Harry's pub.

'You'll pay for a few drinks, won't you, Mickey?' Uncle Jim said, nodding his head.

Michael looked at his father squashed up against the wall in the dining room.

'Okay,' he agreed.

'Come on, everyone,' Uncle Jim called out. 'We're off to Harry's. And Mike's buying.'

Everyone cheered, the front door opened and the house began to empty.

7

Like an invading army entering a peasant village, the Irvines arrived at Harry's just after seven o'clock.

Hard Harry had the night off and it took all of three minutes before the barman, Larry (or Lazy Larry as the customers called him), found himself 'unable to cope with the sudden rush', and he phoned Lauren to come in.

Even before Lauren had changed her clothes, asked her mother to mind Max and then driven the short distance to the pub, the singing had begun. She was thrilled for Michael and even gave him a big hug, which caused him to blush profusely.

'All the women will be hanging out of you now,' shouted Uncle Jim, forcing Lauren to quickly get back behind the bar.

Everyone seemed happy at Michael's news, so he allowed himself, if temporarily at least, to feel happy too. Well not exactly happy per se, less apprehensive anyway. Surely winning one hundred and ninety million euro, he thought to himself, can't be all bad news. Everyone else seemed to think so, anyway.

Michael saw a few of the regulars, who were sitting at the bar, grumbling to Lauren about something.

'Everything okay with them,' Michael asked her.

'Oh, they're fine,' she said. 'They're just not too happy with all the noise. Not their idea of a quiet pint.'

When Michael asked Lauren to include everyone on his tab, they soon failed to notice any further disturbance, even joining in with a couple of songs and tipping their drinks at Michael to wish him luck.

'What about them?' Lauren asked him, nodding towards a table at the back.

At the table sat Joey McGuinness and two of his friends. Michael had avoided making eye contact, although he had occasionally glanced in their direction. The three of them sat hunched over their pints on the table as if discussing a private matter. They never showed any jubilation whatsoever for Michael's good fortune. Again, this made Michael happy.

Feeling brave with most of his extended family in the pub, a massive pile of cash in his pocket and, if he had to be honest, the elated sensation he still felt from receiving a hug from Lauren, Michael made his way over to Joey's table.

'Hiya, lads,' said Michael.

'Alright,' replied Joey. The other two said nothing.

'Sorry if we're ruining your few quiet pints tonight,' Michael said nodding over in the direction of his family.

Two of his cousins, Mairead and Nancy, were linked together arm-in-arm and squealing out their rendition of 'Money Can't Buy You Love' (All songs sung so far had some form of currency in their title). One of his uncles was examining the labels close-up of two bottles of top-shelf whiskey, one in each hand, while Lauren waited patiently for him to choose. His cousin, Paul, who was wearing an Arsenal football shirt and who, previous to this evening, had said less than ten words to Michael, four of those words being 'Arsenal', was sitting with Michael's parents, crouched over the table as if oblivious to the party around him.

'Em, well done on your win,' Joey said, as if congratulating him on a five euro bet on a horse race.

'Cheers, Joey,' Michael said.

There was more than a momentary awkward silence before Michael thought of something else to say. 'Listen, I asked Lauren to look after you for a few pints.'

'Cheers,' Joey said, and raised his pint glass to him. The other two did likewise, raising their glasses off the table just enough to slide a beermat underneath.

'My cousin, Joanne, is talking about going somewhere later. Maybe into Style's Nightclub. Said she knows a bartender there. He'll keep a section for us. You never know, we might bump into someone famous. You're welcome to join us if you like.'

'Really?' said one of Joey's friends, both of them looking up from their pints for the first time.

'That kip?' said Joey. 'Rip off central. You wouldn't get much for a tenner in there.'

Both of Joey's friends lowered their heads again.

'Ah no, don't worry about that. It's my treat. It's all on me.'

'Seriously?' asked Joey's other friend, both of them raising their heads again.

'Yeah, apparently it is,' said Michael, looking over his shoulder at his family again.

'Cheers,' said Joey, 'but some of us still have to get up for work in the morning.'

Both of Joey's friends lowered their heads again into their pints.

'Oh, okay that's fine,' said Michael, pretending not to see the blatant animosity shown to him. 'Well, if you change your mind, we're going to order a few taxis later.'

More nods all round. Another awkward silence. Then, with a sense of saying goodbye to someone for the last time, Michael walked away.

Zoe took a sip from her diet coke and watched Michael walk away from Joey's table and sit beside his parents.

Well, that was interesting, she thought to herself.

No one had noticed her when she first came into the pub. She was wearing what she called her 'anonymous attire' – knee-high brown leather boots, black skinny jeans, crisp white shirt and a dark jacket.

It would allow her to sit unnoticed in any five-star hotel lobby in the city, or in the corner of any suburban pub in Dublin. Normally at this stage, her modus operandi would be to open up two buttons of her blouse, lean over the bar, play with the tip of her straw with her mouth, and then ply the barman for all the information she liked.

A female bartender was a little trickier however. If she were a lesbian, and from her experience most female bartenders were, it wouldn't be a problem. Two years ago while working on an article to prove that a councillor was skimming money out of the 'Help Victims of Drug Abuse' bank fund in order to feed his own cocaine habit, she had slept with the female bartender from the councillor's local pub, who also happened to be his white powder supplier.

This bartender however was not, in her opinion, of the lesbian persuasion. Contrary to all male fantasies, most lesbians did not look like this bartender.

Lauren, as she'd heard someone call her, was not only a very beautiful woman, but she had intelligent green eyes and an easy-going, attractive manner. Zoe wondered what terrible misfortune or mistake this girl had made in her life to find herself stuck behind a bar in this shit hole on a Monday night. An permanently ill parent? An unplanned kid? Single mother? And then Zoe stopped wondering, because she didn't care.

Unbuttoning the top button of her blouse, as one button would be more than sufficient for this job, she slid down from her stool and made her way to the other side of the bar.

She slipped up onto the stool nearest the table where Joey and his friends were seated. It appeared to her that Joey was the leader of their little gang, but she thought his dress sense was a little off. It was as if he were stuck in the eighties. His two companions, however, were much more contemporary in their style.

She took another sip from her Coke, and like a black widow spider, patiently waited for her prey.

It didn't take long.

'Lauren,' Joey called up from his table, 'give us three whiskeys. And since Urine is paying, make sure they're the good stuff. Twelve-year-olds at least.'

His two friends giggled like school children. Zoe saw Lauren reach up and take down a bottle of whiskey from the top shelf and put out three glasses.

'And make them doubles,' Joey called to her. More giggles.

Lauren scowled over at them. Zoe watched as Lauren took out another bottle of cheap whiskey whose label she didn't even recognise, and fill the three glasses with it.

'I'm only messing,' said Joey, his two friends in fits of laughter. 'I meant triples,' he told her, prompting him to burst into convulsions of laughter.

Like a fisherman casting his line out to sea, Zoe slowly turned her head in Joey's direction and caught his eye. The slightest of smiles to jab the hook in, then simply turned away to reel him in. The table fell silent, and Zoe heard muffled whispers at the table behind her.

Sometimes, she sighed to herself, it really is too easy.

Three large whiskeys were placed on the bar beside her. Zoe smelt the petrol and car fumes from Joey's clothes even before she saw his oil stained hands cupped around the glasses. After almost a minute of guessing to herself as to what his pick up line was going to be, Zoe suddenly realised that there wasn't going to be one. She wondered if this approach worked for him; park up next to the girl of his choosing and let the pungent aromas of body odour and diesel do the talking for him. He was a good looking guy, in that Tarzan holding a wrench sort of a way, but he wasn't that good looking.

'Are you going to drink all of them yourself?' she blurted out as he lifted the glasses off the table and was about to walk away.

With reassured aplomb, Joey placed his drinks back down on the counter and turned to her. It was never a good idea, Zoe reminded herself, for a woman to be the initiator in a relationship. It gives the man a false sense of superiority and confidence. And God knows the bastards have enough advantages over women to begin with.

'I might do,' Joey replied, then fell silent.

Looks like I'm going to have to do most of the work on this one, she thought.

'Is it true what they say about men who drink too much whiskey?' she asked him.

'What do they say?' asked Joey, leaning into her, his automotive aromas joined now by the smells of beer and nicotine.

'That they have trouble performing,' Zoe said, and pursed her lips around the tip of the straw. Joey said nothing.

'Whiskey dick, I believe it's called,' and she sucked up some coke from her glass.

'Not something I've ever had a problem with, honey,' said Joey.

'I guess I'll just have to take your word for it,' she replied, cringing at the baseness of it.

Silence.

'Do you fancy one so?' asked Joey.

'What?' she said, genuinely shocked by his hastiness at finishing the sexual innuendo section of the foreplay.

'Would you like one?' he asked again.

'Really?'

'Yeah, why not?'

'What? Here?' asked Zoe.

'If you like. Or we could go up the back way if you'd like something a bit more private.'

'I beg your pardon.'

'Come on, don't be shy,' said Joey. 'You look like you could do with one.'

'Well, it's a bit sudden,' said Zoe.

'You might as well. It's not every day I don't have to pay for it.'

As much as Zoe wanted Michael's story, she decided that this obnoxious brut wasn't going to be her gateway to him. She started to lift herself off the chair.

'Lauren,' Joey shouted, raising his whiskey in the air, 'give us another one of these, will ye?'

'A whiskey?' Zoe asked.

'Did you not want one?'

'You were talking about whiskey. Of course.' Zoe said to herself.

'How do you take it?'

'Straight up, I suppose,' she said relaxing back into her bar stool.

Before approaching Joey, Zoe had spent a few minutes working out an appropriate backstory as to why she was in Harry's and more importantly, who she was, or rather, wasn't. Fortunately, none of this proved necessary as Joey was far more interested in spewing out information about himself than seeking any information about her.

His monologues consisted mainly about himself being wrongly done by, either by his boss, a work colleague or a family member, and where he, the eventual and inevitable victor, came through it all triumphantly. Zoe found in fact, she didn't even need to use an alias or nom de guerre. Of course, there were many circles in Dublin where her name would have shut down all conversations within fifty yards, but this was not one of those circles.

'There was this other time when a customer says to me...' Joey began again, but Zoe felt that she'd listened to her fair share of anecdotes whose denouement would invariably see its anti-hero once again outwit his adversary.

'Tell me, Joey,' she interrupted him, 'what's going on over there?'

She noticed Joey's expression change from bravado to disdain. 'He only won the fucking EuroMillions, didn't he,' said Joey and finished off the remainder of the whiskey in one swift and aggressive gesture.

'Wow,' said Zoey, feigning surprise, 'that's amazing. How much did he win?'

'Too fucking much,' said Joey. 'Biggest fucking loser in Ireland, he is.'

'Biggest loser becomes biggest winner,' said Zoe out loud, visualising a headline.

Joey burst out laughing. 'That's a good one alright. I must tell the lads that one.'

'Do you know him?' she asked.

'Yeah, went to school with him. He still lives with his ma and da. Loser. He always fancied my ex-bird. She works behind the bar.'

'Who? Lauren?'

'Yeah, do you know her?'

'No, no. I heard you calling her name.'

'Yeah, we have a kid, but she doesn't let me see him much.'

So you are Lauren's fuck up, thought Zoe. She's probably chasing him for child maintenance and has to stand there watching him piss it away on drink every weekend on booze.

Almost two years ago, Zoe had researched and then written an article on negligent fathers. She had called it, 'the most socially acceptable crime of our generation'. It had won a lot of praise from various child protection agencies, but the article wasn't picked up by much of the mainstream media. Probably because, she had figured (and correctly as it happens) many of the newspaper owners and shareholders were themselves child maintenance dodgers.

'Where does he work?' asked Zoe. 'Or should I say, where did he work?'

'Not sure,' said Joey. 'Something clerical in an insurance company. He's worked there since he left school.'

'And he's not married?'

Joey exploded in laughter. 'Him? I've never even seen him with a bird. He's probably a queer.'

'But I thought you said he fancied Lauren?'

'Yeah, well. He'd probably take anything he can get.'

Zoe looked over at Michael and saw his group standing up and putting on their coats. 'They're leaving,' she said in a slight panic.

'Yeah, they're heading into Style's Nightclub.'

Zoe had to think fast. 'Oh, I'd love to go there. I heard it's always full of celebs.'

'It's an overrated kip,' said Joey.

'Have you been?'

'No.'

Zoe allowed a few seconds to pass, keeping one eye on the crowd loving towards the door.

'I should probably go home so,' she said, as casually as possible.

'No wait,' said Joey, 'I could get you into Style's if you want. I'll say it to Urin... Mike.'

'Wow, that'd be awesome,' she said, as eagerly as possible.

Joey was right though, she thought to herself. It is an overrated kip.

Luckily for Zoe, when they arrived in a stream of taxis to Style's, they went in as a group. Normally Zoe, who was recognisable and often barred by all the bouncers and managers of the top restaurants and clubs in the city, would have to use either a disguise or a bribe to get past them.

Joey, in fairness to him, while filled with equal measures of whiskey and lust (he had barely looked at Zoe's face half a dozen times, mesmerised as he was by her cleavage) had swallowed his pride and asked Michael if they could go to Styles.

Being a Monday night, the nightclub was reasonably quiet. Zoe already had her news story but instinctively couldn't resist scanning the room for a fresh scandal.

She noticed a Leeds football player who was married to a strawberry blonde romance novelist sitting beside a very brunette glamour model. A magician with his own magic show on TV3 coming out of the bathroom and rubbing his nostrils a little too avidly. And a junior government minister sitting alone at the bar. He wasn't necessarily doing anything wrong except that his sad expression never looked up from his whiskey, and it was most definitely way past his bedtime.

All stories worth further investigation, she thought. But not tonight.

She nodded at Ricky behind the bar. Just as some Irish men were almost a parody of the drink-loving stranger-friendly stereotype, so too was Ricky a clichéd blonde Australian bartender. She thought he laid his Aussie accent and persona on a bit thick sometimes, but that was probably just for the girls. He'd tipped her off on several occasions when there was some well-known personality in the nightclub doing something they would rather have remained unknown.

She'd also slept with him as a Thank You on a slow news day. She liked to tell herself that her visits to his bedroom were purely for business reasons, even if some pleasure was derived from the transaction. Sometimes, however, when she was dressing on a Sunday morning and Ricky was still sleeping and still naked lying across the white sheets of his bed, she often wondered how her life would be if she were to make some coffee and get back in beside him. How it might feel to spend the day with him, go for walks, eat lunch while swapping Sunday newspapers across the table, and all that other shit that normal people did so easily and so naturally.

Invariably though, she would kiss his dumb beautiful cheek, go back to her own apartment to change and would have ten kilometres clocked up on her Garmin GPS watch before Ricky even noticed she was gone.

Finally after an hour, Zoe saw the opportunity she'd been waiting for. Joey and his cronies were all at the bar, and with a free tab to abuse, were trying different shots with Ricky's assistance.

'Hi,' she said, sitting down in front of Michael so he could get a good look at her. 'I just wanted to thank you for a great night.'

Michael had first noticed Zoe bending her head down as she got into the taxi outside Harry's. She was the only one in the group whom he didn't know, but he knew she was with Joey. Joey was often known to bring a girl into Harry's, mostly, Michael guessed, to antagonise Lauren. Lauren, however, barely ever even noticed the other girl being there.

But that wasn't the only thing that had set off a cautious alarm bell in Michael's head. It was more to do with a combination of a few small things that didn't quite add up. He had had a good look at Zoe sitting at her table in Style's, the coloured lights bouncing effortlessly off her. She was far more comfortable in the lavish surroundings than either he or any of his crew were.

And with all due respect to the female clientele of Harry's, he had never seen anyone who looked like her do anything more than stick their heads through the doorway for three seconds before making a swift exit. (With the exception of Lauren, of course) He had also caught her giving a surreptitious nod to the bartender, who discreetly nodded a greeting back to her.

The final piece of suspicious evidence against her though was when he heard Joey calling her from the bar. It wasn't such an unusual name, but it certainly wasn't that common either, and there was only one Zoe he had ever heard of. Michael was, after all, an avid Sunday newspaper reader. So here he was, the best kept secret in Dublin, so far anyway, and here she was, the best teller of secrets in Dublin.

Michael didn't believe in coincidences.

'You're with Joey tonight?' asked Michael.

'Yeah,' she said putting out her hand. 'I'm Zoe.'

'You wouldn't be Zoe Simms by any chance?'

For several moments Zoe felt completely off guard. Normally if one of her interviewees suspected her of being a journalist, there would be a sudden avoidance from one of them. Zoe started to mumble something but fell silent.

'It's okay,' said Michael. 'Someone would have spilt the beans soon enough. I've gone viral apparently, even though I'm not 100% sure what exactly that means. I'm just surprised you were so fast, that's all.'

Initially, Zoe felt angry that a whole evening had been wasted. She looked over at Joey at the bar and shook her head in disappointment.

'How did you know?' she asked, Michael noticing her accent having suddenly changed to a slighter posher one.

'Does it matter?'

'No, not really.'

'So, what now?' asked Michael.

'I don't suppose you'd like to give me an exclusive interview, would you?'

'You suppose correctly.'

The man sitting in front of her was the polar opposite to the man she had assumed him to be. Although she only really had Joey's character assassination of him to go by.

'How about if you decide to give an interview later or in the coming days that it'll be with me?' she asked him.

Michael looked around at his quickly tiring entourage.

His Uncle Jim who had told him earlier in Harry's that 'the

night is still too young to go home', had failed to realise that although the night may indeed be too young, he certainly wasn't. He now sat in a red velvet sofa, his head tilted backwards, snoring like an asthmatic silver backed gorilla. Even the younger members of his newly formed faction were beginning to wilt and show fewer signs of their former ebullient selves.

Only Julie, the daughter of his next door neighbour Liam, appeared to have any steam left in her. She was barefoot on the dance floor still wearing her light brown supermarket cashier's uniform, her arms outstretched and swaying from side-to-side like a falling autumn leaf.

'I don't think I'll be giving interviews anytime soon,' Michael told her.

'Okay then, how about I interview a few of your few close friends?'

Michael gave a short laugh. 'I'm not so sure I have any close friends to be honest with you. Although I have a feeling in the coming days, there's going to be a lot of new ones coming out of the woodwork claiming undying camaraderie.'

'How about that nice girl from the pub. Lauren, wasn't it?' Zoe was fishing, but her instinct had rarely let her down. Michael's sudden change in expression let her know she'd hit a juicy target.

'She's nothing to me,' Michael said and turned away from her.

He's bluffing. 'Okay then,' she said, 'you won't mind so if I pop back tomorrow and have a chat with her.'

'Alright,' said Michael with resignation. He'd been outsmarted by her and they both knew it. 'I'll tell you what. If you leave her out of your article entirely and you don't bother her, then I'll promise in the unlikely case that I do give an interview in the future, I'll do it exclusively with you. Is that fair?'

For Zoe, it was a small price to pay. 'Fair enough,' she said, extending her hand for the second time to him.

He shook it.

How sweet, she thought, protecting a girl he has no relationship with. And how pathetic too.

'Now remember, I'm first. If any of the other amateurs come near you, you just say "I'm sorry, but I'm not in a position to give any interviews or answer any questions at this time". Okay?'

'Okay. Now I think I'll go home' said Michael.

'Better pay the bill first,' advised Zoe. 'I don't think your new found friends would let you out alive without paying their tab.'

Michael nodded and stood up.

Zoe saw a melancholic expression pass over his face. 'I hope it all works out for you, Mike,' she said, surprising both Michael and herself with her genuine sentiment.

'You just never know,' he said, 'nice to meet you, Zoe. We'll probably never meet again though.'

'You're right, Mike. You just never know, but one last piece of free advice for you,' she said.

'Yeah?'

Her expression changed to one of solemnity.

'Never trust anyone again.'

He forced a smiled at her and then left.

Zoe took a long look around the room. Her date for the night had his head resting on the bar, his two associates sitting either side of him, sipping on their pints of lager.

Ricky was wiping glasses and already starting to clean up. He stopped wiping when he saw her sitting alone. He smiled at her. A smile full of promises and pleasure, or perhaps promises of pleasure. But Zoe had work to do. She looked at her watch. There was still time to make the morning edition. She had already decided she would go easy on Michael.

She knew that as sure as Michael's world was about to implode and explode in a way he still hadn't quite come to terms with that she would see him again sometime soon. He didn't know anything about the world that she knew and once they came for him, he'd be back to her, looking for a way out at best or an explanation at least. She hoped they would let him keep some of who he was, or he'd be able at least to hang onto it himself.

She waved over to Ricky and didn't wait for him to wave back, the opening sentence in her article already forming in her head.

8

Michael woke but kept his eyes closed tight against the unusual morning brightness in the room. He felt disoriented, and he had a slight headache.

In a sudden panic with the thought that he was late for work, he forced open his eyes. What day was it? Then he remembered. The lottery.

There was a cup of tea beside his bed. He reached out for the cup. It was cold. He had forgotten to set the alarm on his phone and looking for it now, saw that it read 09:32.

It was only then he became aware of the noise below him. A bubbling chatter from the kitchen under his bedroom floor. Had it already been there as he awoke? Incoherent murmuring, doors closing, clinking cups. He couldn't distinguish any particular or familiar voices, but it filled him with dread.

Who was downstairs? Had all the neighbours come round again? This time looking for breakfast?

He pulled the duvet off himself and crawled slowly out of the bed, his body stiff and aching. He sat on the edge listening to the voices downstairs and looking at himself in the wardrobe mirrored doors. His hair stood up and out, like the top of a Christmas tree. He wasn't sure at what time he had gone to bed, but he mustn't have been that drunk as he had managed to properly dress himself in his blue Mr Men pyjamas.

He heard a car pull up outside his house, the engine stop and then the doors open and close, accompanied by more voices. More long lost family arriving? he wondered. Before getting dressed and venturing downstairs, he decided to take a peek outside from under the window blinds, just to see what or who he was up against. Hunching down at the window, he raised the blind slightly off the window sill and peered between the gap.

The road of his neighbourhood resembled a small carpark. There were jeeps with company logos on their doors, cars parked on the neighbours' grass verges, two vans with satellite dishes on their roofs. It was a similar scene to what he'd seen outside of the lottery headquarters yesterday.

An entrepreneurial ice cream man had parked his van outside Mr Flanagan's driveway and many of the waiting journalists were licking choc ices and ice cream cones. Just as he was about to pull the blinds back down, he saw the top of his mother's head as she walked out of the house carrying a tray of tea and cups, offering them to the reporters and photographers in his garden.

Michael had seen enough and made the easy decision of going back to bed for the day. He was only on series two of Game of Thrones on Netflix, and planned to use the entire day to catch up.

As he pulled down the roller blind by its cord, it clicked the release and sprang upwards with a swift whirling sound. Michael jumped up to catch the cord but by then a dozen cameras had spotted him at the window and flashed in rapid succession. Reporters called out his name as he fought with the cord for several seconds. The last thing he saw before pulling it back down was his mother as she had turned and waved up at his, balancing the tray of cups in one hand.

His heart racing, he sat on the floor and buried his head into his hands. Even Mr Happy on the pyjama sleeve looked thoroughly disconcerted.

Like a prisoner on death row unsuccessfully trying to postpone the inevitable, Michael slowly dressed himself. He opened the laptop in his room and searched to see if Zoe's article had been published. Even though he was half expecting it, he was still quite shocked to see images of himself appear on his computer. The main one appeared to have been taken in the nightclub. It was towards the end of the night and was taken at about two feet from him.

He had noticed her placing the large black handbag on the table as she had sat down, but he hadn't commented on it. Why would he? The secretive contents of a woman's handbag were far beyond the realm of Michael's knowledge, understanding or imagination.

The bag did appear too big to him at the time, but too big for what exactly, he wasn't quite sure. Obviously big enough for a camera, and, after reading his word-perfect conversation with Zoe transcribed in the article, plenty of room for a microphone as well.

He wouldn't have called the article unkind, but on the other hand it was certainly a few metaphors short of appearing sympathetic or even charitable towards him. She had though kept her promise of not mentioning Lauren, and for this he was grateful.

Before going downstairs, Michael shaved, brushed his teeth and used the toilet. He contemplated on how being a multi-millionaire had very little impact on his bodily functions and needs. At the top of the stairs, dressed and ready to face his congregation below, Michael paused and looked down.

He had no idea how many steps there were to the bottom. Perhaps fifteen. Each one would lead him closer to a new phase and a new place in his life from where there would be no coming back. He could choose to go back into his room. Choose to lock the door. Choose not to answer his phone. They would all eventually go away. Eventually leave him alone.

But where had all his choices lead him up to now? Had they been the right decisions? Did he want a life of afternoon coffees in a shopping centre alone forever? He never chose to win the lottery. In a way, it had chosen him.

Perhaps it was time to let go a little? To see what the world had to offer him. One thing was certain, it had a lot more to offer him now with almost two hundred million euro in his pocket.

Sure anyway, he finally thought to himself, if it doesn't work out, I can always come back and lock myself into my room.

And for that slight moment, as he descended the first step, Michael almost convinced himself that that was true.

'Ah, there you are now, Michael,' said his mother as she passed him in the hall carrying a tray with a fresh pot of tea, a pint of milk and a bowl of sugar. 'I was going to come up to you to see how you were.'

He saw two men and a woman in the kitchen crowded around the little table. Michael closed the door.

'Who are these people, Mam?' Michael asked.

'They're the people from the Lottery yesterday. The advisors. Don't worry, I know you're a little camera shy so I told all the journalists to stay outside.'

'What people from the Lottery?'

'The people who can help you with your new found wealth. Help with investments and assets and bonds and stuff like that. They're very nice, Michael.'

Michael sighed. 'Okay, Mam. I'll talk to them.'

When he opened the kitchen door, the two men and the woman stood up. He now recognised the two men from yesterday. They had on the same dark suits and bright ties. He shook hands with them and they called him 'Mr. Irvine'.

After listening to them for an attentive, although strenuous, seven minutes, Michael felt that any further financial consultation at this time would result in his brain silently imploding, and him collapsing on the floor in front of them.

'... and with competent fiscal planning right now,' Tony, the more senior of the three was concluding, 'within three to five years we could fully exploit that sum and help it grow exponentially, which given the global markets at the moment could easily double your investment.'

'With the right strategy,' Graham, the youngest of the group, added, 'we could guarantee you a seven percent increase per annum that could be compounded over ten years resulting in a gross dividend, minus tax, of...'

Michael watched him get more and more excited as he spoke about his money in an almost sexual-like frenzy.

'So what you're saying,' Michael said, unaware whether he was interrupting anyone or not, 'is that I can use the one hundred and ninety million to make a lot more money.'

There was an audible sigh of relief in the room.

'Exactly,' said Tony, delighted by the simplicity and inevitability of it all, and then as if summing up a classroom lesson, 'it's called leverage.' All three syllables were pronounced slowly and deliberately.

'But the thing is,' said Michael adopting the same leisurely tone, 'even if I live to be a hundred-years-old, I can't possibly imagine what I'll do with all the money I already have. Why do I need to worry about trying to make even more money?'

A silence fell in the kitchen as if blasphemy had been committed in front of the Pope. They all looked from one to the other, barely comprehending what Michael was saying.

'Well, it's not just about making more money,' said the woman, whose name Michael couldn't remember.

'No?' asked Michael.

'No, no, of course not,' she said, this time everyone looking at him, obviously as curious as Michael was. 'It's also about security. To know, Mr. Irvine, that your money is safe.'

Again there was much relief in the room.

'Are you saying,' asked Michael, and the three of them leaned forward, 'are you saying that my money's not safe in the Bank of Ireland?'

'No, no, no. Of course it's safe. What I mean is…'

'Look,' Michael said, raising his hands in the air as if in resignation. 'I really appreciate you all coming here this morning, albeit uninvited, but if you'd like to leave me your business cards, I'll get back to you when I have a bit more time. When everything settles down a bit. You understand?'

They all agreed, producing shiny white business cards out of thin air, firmly shaking Michael's hand and making solid eye contact with him before leaving. Michael sat in the kitchen for a few moments after they were all gone. He wasn't sure why, but somewhere in his solar plexus he felt a very real sense of triumphal achievement.

In the silence of the kitchen now, Michael heard chattering from the sitting room. His Uncle Jim, Aunt June, cousins and a few more from last night were sipping tea, eating Hobnob biscuits and chatting like relatives of the family at a wake.

'Morning, Mike,' they said, as if it were the most natural thing in the world that they were in his sitting room, and that this was something they did every morning.

'The reporters are stomping all over your mother's geraniums,' said Uncle Jim reaching for another Hobnob. 'Probably best to say something to them to clear off, Mike.'

As Michael went into the hall, his mother came in carrying another tray, this time with used cups.

'It's getting very busy out there, Michael,' she said. 'I'm just going to pop down to Bobby's to get some more tea and milk.'

'Where's dad, Mam?' Michael asked.

'He's upstairs last time I saw him. Said he was going to read the paper in peace.'

'I'll talk to them.'

'Who?'

'Them out there.'

'Are you sure?'

'Why, you don't think I can?'

'No, no, it's just, well, what are you going to say?'

'I've no idea.'

'What about the milk?'

'Forget the milk, Mam. Just… just… I don't know. Just wait here.'

'Do you want me to come with you?'

Michael was about to say yes but still fuelled with the morsel of confidence he received from telling all the suits to leave, he decided he'd like to try to figure this one out on his own. At least for now.

'No, I'll be grand. Thanks, Mam.'

Michael pulled the door towards him.

'Are you sure?' asked Rose, obviously unconvinced.

'Yes,' Michael said. 'I'm sure.'

When Michael opened the door, he wasn't expecting such a large amount of reporters and photographers to be waiting for him. It seemed a lot smaller crowd from his bird's eye view earlier.

There was a small frenzy of unfit bodies and heavy equipment as they awkwardly ran to the recognisable figure in the doorway. Shouts of 'Michael', 'Mike' and even 'Mr. Irvine' were yelled out to get him to look one way or another as camera flashes lit up his face.

There were obvious questions called out; 'Mr. Irvine, how does it feel to be a multimillionaire this morning?'; silly questions, 'Michael, do you think your life will change now?'; personal questions, 'Mike, do you have a girlfriend?'; blunt questions, 'Michael, are you going to share any of your winnings?; and just plain obnoxious questions, 'Mike, are you going to move to a nicer area now that you can afford to?'

Remembering his promise to Zoe, Michael kept it short. 'I'm sorry, but I'm not in a position to give any interviews or answer any questions at this time.'

As if he had asked for further questions, the reporters called out even louder and the camera flashes became more intense. Michael suddenly became frozen in the barrage of voices and bursts of light. He could hear the shouts and his name being called. He could see the flashes, each one causing him to blink. But he was unable to move.

Thoughts of his humiliation at school twenty years ago flooded into his mind and he looked down at his trousers. After what seemed like five minutes to him, he felt a heavy hand on his shoulder and his body being turned. An arm went around him, and he heard the front door closing behind him. The calls and flashes stopped. It was only when he was seated back at the kitchen table did all his senses fully return to him.

'Fancy a cup of tea, son?' asked Jack.

'Yeah, thanks, Dad,' said Michael. 'Sorry about out there. I sort of froze for a minute.'

'That's alright.'

Jack took down two mugs from the cupboard and switched on the kettle.

'And sorry you had to go upstairs to read your paper,' said Michael.

'That's okay, Mike. There's a lot of things we're going to have to get used to in the next few weeks.'

'Do you think we'll have to move?'

'No. Your mother will never move out of this house. You can probably afford any house in Dublin now, but she still wouldn't move.'

'I suppose.'

'But you might have to though.'

Michael thought about this as his father made them both a cup of tea.

'This money's going to give you a lot of opportunities you might never have thought possible, Mike. Some will be bad but most will be good.'

'And how am I supposed to know the good from the bad?'

'You won't know. At least not until you've done it.'

'Then what, Dad?'

'Learn from it, and for fuck sake, don't do it again.'

Michael lifted his cup to his mouth and sipped.

'Since when did you become so wise?' Michael asked him.

'I've always been. I just never get a chance to talk with your mother in the room.'

They both laughed as the doorbell rang.

'I'll go tell them to get stuffed,' Jack said standing up.

'No, Dad,' Michael said and stood up before him. 'I'll go. But thanks.'

When Michael opened the front door, he didn't recognise the man standing there, nor did he know what he wanted. He did know, however, that he was not a reporter. The man was about Michael's age and build, and a word popped into Michael's head that, to the best of his knowledge, he had never had cause to use before - dapper.

'Mr. Irvine?' the man asked.

'Yes?'

'My name's James Prestige from Prestige Motors.'

'Okay,' is all that Michael could think to say.

'I'm here to offer my services to you on behalf of Prestige Motors.'

'What service?'

'Prestige cars.'

'You sell cars?' Michael asked.

James Prestige gave a slight forced chuckle.

'Yes, we do. We've offered our services to all lottery winners for the past twenty years, and...'

'I'm sorry,' said Michael interrupting, 'did you say your name was Prestige from Prestige Motors?'

'Yes.'

'That's your real name?'

'Yes. My father is Peter Prestige,' said James Prestige.

'And you didn't change your name?'

'No, of course not.'

'Okay. So you want to sell me a car?'

'Well, it's more than that. As I said we offer our services to a very small number of clients in Ireland, and what we do is, we...'

At an almost innate level of consciousness, Michael stopped listening and started to turn away. As he moved to close the door, while trying to verbalise an excuse of some kind for closing it, he looked over James's shoulder.

Subconsciously, his lower jaw dropped a couple of centimetres. It wasn't intentional. Indeed, Michael wasn't even aware he had made the gesture. But James noticed.

'Nice, huh?' he asked.

'Sorry, what did you say?'

'I said, it's nice. Isn't it?'

'What is it?' Michael asked.

'A Lamborghini. A Lamborghini Gallardo LP560 to be precise.'

James had parked the Lamborghini at a forty five degree angle to the house, thereby showing off both the front and side of the car.

'Would you like to take it for a drive?'

Michael looked from the car to James, and then turned to see his father still sitting at the kitchen table. He thought about his father's advice. It would be so easy just to slowly close the door. To take James Prestige's business card and to say 'no thanks'.

He sneaked another look at the car. Black and shining in the early day's light, like a black panther patiently waiting and lying in the grass. He had never seen a car like that before. Not up close anyway. His own car was parked in the driveway. A poodle rather than a panther. A tired old poodle wishing not to be disturbed.

Michael suddenly felt the urge to sit in the Lamborghini. He wasn't going to drive it anywhere. He just wanted to sit in it for a minute or two. Just to see. Or rather, just to feel.

'Is it okay if I sit in it for a minute?' Michael asked.

'Absolutely,' said James, and held out a key for him to take.

Michael took the key and studied it. 'How much is it?' he asked.

'To sit in?' James said. 'Sitting is free.'

'That's not what I meant?'

'Why? Do you want to buy it?'

'No.'

'Then the price is irrelevant, isn't it?'

Normally Michael would have felt intimidated by James's very presence, but Michael liked him. He liked his confidence anyway. Michael didn't think he had ever felt that confident about anything in his life.

He walked up to the car but was unable to see where the door handle was. James anticipated this and to avoid any awkwardness on the part of his client, reached over casually and opened the driver's door for him. Michael thanked him and slid into the seat.

James closed the door and slowly, with all the patience of a true salesman, walked to the other side, allowing Michael time alone in his cocoon of luxury.

Michael looked around him, gripping the steering wheel with both hands. He thought about a summer he'd spent in an amusement arcade in Courtown, the days spent playing a Formula 1 game, and begging his parents for another fifty pence piece.

The leather seat enveloped him and felt as if it were hugging him. The road looked only a few inches below the seat. There were several dials that measured temperature and pressure, but he really didn't know what half of them were for.

The passenger door opened and James slid in beside him, then closed the door.

'It suits you,' he said.

Michael knew this was just sales flattery, but couldn't help taking the compliment. He squeezed the thick leather steering wheel and allowed himself a smile.

'Give it a start,' James suggested.

Michael took the key from his lap and placed it in the ignition. Forgetting all self-promises to just 'sit in it', he turned the key and the Lamborghini burst into life. He rested his foot too hard on the accelerator and the car's engine exploded with noise.

Michael's heart raced and he took a deep breath.

'Sorry about that,' he told James.

'That's okay,' James said. 'She's a little more sensitive than most cars. Press it again.'

Michael pushed his foot down, softer this time and the car responded instantly. It sounded angry. A no-nonsense sound full of assurance and testosterone.

'Drive it around the block,' James told him.

Michael looked around the cockpit of the car and, unable to find anything resembling a gear stick, asked, 'is it an automatic?'

'Sorry, yes,' James replied. 'Just press that forward.'

'I've never driven an automatic before.'

'You're going to be doing a lot of things you've never done before,' James said.

'That's what my dad told me.'

Michael clicked it into gear, and they moved forwards very slowly.

Michael's heart raced. He forced himself to stop smiling, but within a minute his face had returned its wide grin. He couldn't put words to his emotions, but he never felt like that before. As he continued to follow James's directions, he gained more confidence in the car and increased his speed slightly. He felt his body pushed back into the seat when he accelerated too much.

He drove by a school on a break and the children ran to the fence and pressed their faces to stare at him. Two men in suits carrying takeaway coffee cups stopped mid-sentence, their eyes following the car. A jogger stopped and quickly took out his camera to video the Lamborghini going by.

Michael felt his chest expanding as he watched the watchers. The car was exquisite, there was no doubting that, but it wasn't the car that made his blood, for possibly the first time, rush through his veins and give him such a heightened sense of awareness. Nor was it the power of the engine that he commanded. Nor was it the realisation that many more exciting and wonderful experiences were now available to him.

The reason he felt a little light-headed was that for the first time in his life, Michael was being noticed. Never before had anyone turned their head to look at him, and if they had done, they would quickly turn away again. Now their eyes followed him. Finally he had, albeit momentary, witnesses to his life. Witnesses to his very existence.

After a few more minutes of driving, Michael settled into the car. James watched him. He wanted to explain to him how exquisite the car was. He wanted to tell him that there were faster cars in the world, but none as exhilarating. To explain the power of the car. He wanted to tell him about the YouTube video with thirty million views of a young man picking up women off the street just by opening his Lamborghini's door and without saying a word.

But instead he fell silent. He had never seen anyone use so much effort to keep his emotions in check. He had taken this drive many times with other Lottery winners and most had simply screamed with the excitement of driving one of his cars and knowing that it could be theirs. Some had cried. Michael's stoic face however seemed almost contorted, as if he were having sex for the first time and in shock that he was indeed having sex.

'Just pull in here to the left, please, Michael,' James eventually asked him.

Michael obeyed. He left the engine running, its mechanical purr now the only noise they could hear. He panted slightly as if he'd been running.

'Well?' James asked.

Michael turned to him, as if unaware that James had even been there.

'How much is it?'

'Not as much as you think.'

Michael looked at the instruments around him. His hands were still gripped around the steering wheel.

'It doesn't have to be your only car,' James told him, as if he were answering a question that Michael had asked.

Michael released the steering wheel and stretched his fingers.

'See across the road?' James asked.

Michael looked and saw a car sales room with Prestige Motors written in large black letters across the side of the building.

'Today is Tuesday,' James continued, 'take the car till Sunday. Then you can simply hand me back the keys, or... buy it.'

No one had ever handed James back a set of keys.

'Have fun,' James told him as he shook his hand, and before he had a chance to say another word, he was gone.

Michael sat for a moment alone with the humming of the engine, then clicked it into gear and drove home.

9

For the third time in as many minutes, Samantha swore to herself for biting her nails. She moved her hand away from her face and gripped the steering wheel tighter. Why was she so nervous anyway? Michael had won millions of euros. This was a good thing after all. Wasn't it? She had barely slept the night before, waking Derek every hour with a financial question.

She turned into her parents' housing estate, taking the corner a little too sharply, and an ice cream van, coming in the opposite direction, blew his horn at her. She parked outside the house but didn't get out.

After she had dropped Emily and Kate to their school and crèche, she had gone home as usual. The house had felt even more silent than it normally did after the flurry of activity involved in getting the girls dressed, fed and into the car. It was as if she knew she had somewhere else to be but didn't know where. The two extra coffees that morning didn't help either.

Thirty minutes of mindless house chores later, and then realising she was sweeping the kitchen floor for the second time, she grabbed her car keys and headed to her parents' house, where she now sat outside, biting her nails and contemplating what this lottery win really meant for them all.

After her divorce, Samantha decided, as it was still her children's surname, not to change her name. Rather than revert back to a Irvine, she remained, despite her misgivings, a Shortbottom. Even after all these years, whenever she had to publicly declare her name or repeat it over the phone, a part of her would cringe at its divulgence.

'Samantha Shortbottom,' she would mumble to a doctor's receptionist.

'Please take a seat, Mrs. Shortbottom,' they would say, barely hiding their surreptitious smile. And when called upon, her full name was always pronounced that little bit louder than the other patients. And always twice.

However, having such an egregious ancestral name as Shortbottom, she was soon to discover, was the least of her ex-husband's shortcomings.

When nineteen-years-old and still a Samantha Irvine, her mother switched on the lights in the sitting room and found Samantha kissing her then boyfriend, Brian Delaney. Mrs. Irvine screamed. Samantha screamed. Brian Delaney screamed. Then all three watched Mr Delaney's manhood rapidly wilting between Samantha's pink nail polished hand, until she had the presence of mind to throw a cushion over it. Albeit a small cushion.

Brian was asked to leave, even as he was putting his coat on. Samantha stormed to her room. Mrs. Irvine put the kettle on before collapsing onto a kitchen chair. The cushion was never seen again.

Within a week, Samantha had moved out. The 'Brian Delaney Incident' was the eventual catalyst that had followed several months of heated debates with her parents about her treating the house like a hotel, returning home drunk in the morning when the neighbours were on their way to work, and why it was inconceivable that the immersion, used to heat the hot water, needed to be operational for longer than one hour per day. Surprisingly, she remained calm and mature when she informed her parents she was moving in with her friend, Maggie, who rented a two-bedroomed ground floor apartment on the north side of the city. Also surprisingly, and secretly disappointingly for Samantha, her parents had calmly conceded.

The apartment was small, bare and cold. The kitchen, Maggie told her with a laugh, wasn't designed for anything more culinary than beans on toast. Outside of her bedroom window ran a busy, narrow path, and beside that ran a busy, wide road. Whenever she opened her bedroom window, the passing pedestrians would have to step onto the road, to inevitable honks of car horns.

There was a calendar pinned above the sink that had to be filled out every time she or Maggie took a shower. This, they had hoped, would help deduce the mystery formula to determine the most likely times the shower would produce either very hot or very cold water.

She lay alone on her new bed on that first night, listening to the sounds of the city outside her window. Her few possessions were still packed in a haversack by the door, next to an artificial potted plant. She had enough money to pay Maggie for this month's rent, and another €200 her dad had shoved into her hand as she left home. She looked up at the shadows on her ceiling, moving in sync with the passing traffic, and realised she had never been happier in her life. Besides, she thought to herself, I love beans on toast.

Her efforts to find employment, having completed her one year legal secretary course two months previous, took on a more immediate urgency in her life. She accepted her first job offer; a small position in a large solicitors firm in the newly developed docklands.

The front of the building overlooked the River Liffey with sweeping views of Dublin Bay. Her desk at the back overlooked the staff car park and a bottle recycling plant. Each hour of her day was punctuated by the explosive sound of thousands of glass bottles being emptied into huge metal skips, except on Mondays when it increased to every half hour.

Her supervisor, Mr. Ganley, who smelt of onion soup, spent his entire day complaining to her about everyone in the firm who was higher up the food chain than he was, which, of course, included everyone except Samantha.

But the salary paid her rent. What was left was spent on long nights out with Maggie, bouncing between whatever pub would be popular that month, until it became so popular that it stopped being popular.

Food was deemed a necessity but a begrudging expenditure. Dinners often consisted of bowls of cereal, accompanied by copious cups of sweetened tea. As each month came to a close, a decision had to be made whether to fill their nights with music and laughter, or their stomachs with noodles and toast. The noodles never won. It was only then, on the mornings that followed, that Samantha found Mr. Ganley's odour somewhat pleasant.

After two years and four short-term boyfriends, the party came to a sudden end when Maggie's French boyfriend, Louis, had the audacity to propose. A wedding needed to be saved for, and overnight Maggie's financial obligations went from party dresses to wedding dresses. Louis decided that a place in suburbia would save them an extra €400 a month, and Maggie persuaded Samantha to move with them.

Waking at 8:30am to be in work for 9am became a thing of the past. Samantha's alarm clock was switched to 7am, and it would often be after 7pm before she arrived home in the evening; an evening that was often spent on the sofa watching Maggie and Louis cuddling up to yet another romantic comedy that invariably revolved around an absurd plot at a wedding.

Despite the commute, she refused for over a year to give up her job in the meagre hope of somehow returning to her former party life. She found herself harbouring secret desires that perhaps the happy couple would not remain so happy after all, and for these thoughts she was later remorseful. Of course.

It was Maggie who first spotted the ad placed by O'Gorman Solicitors & Co. in the local gazette. At that point in her life, Samantha didn't feel like the 'enthusiastic, energetic and self-motivated' legal secretary the ad was seeking to find. Her eventual decision to apply was more location driven than career driven.

It was at the interview for the job that she first met and shook hands with Simon Shortbottom. He was, to her, everything that a man should be. He had a nice smile that showed off his ivory white teeth. He was tall, and had a confident yet relaxed gaze. His nose was in proportion to his face, as too was his chin. His suit was sharp but not flashy.

Suspecting, and hoping, that it was for her benefit, he removed his jacket during the interview, revealing an upper torso that would require at least one hour per day in the gym to maintain. When he pronounced her name, (with emphasis on the 'tha' at the end) his voice gave her goose bumps, and she imagined him whispering it into her ear with her head sunk deeply into a pillow.

A week later, he called her and offered her the position, and she was so delighted that she dragged Maggie out for a night of visiting their old haunts. Mr Ganley looked genuinely sullen when she handed in her notice.

Having been such a small cog in a big wheel for years, she found her new role in a smaller firm a little challenging at first. But the alarm not demanding her attention until 8am and gaining almost two hours in the evening made up for the extra workload.

After working there for a little more than a week, O'Gorman Solicitors & Co. took on a big case that demanded everyone to work late. Not having had much opportunity to chat to or even see Simon during her first week, she now found herself teamed up with him on an almost constant basis.

As the case progressed, her skirts became a little shorter and her hair looser. She thought at first perhaps he wasn't as interested in her as she had first suspected, until she caught him in the reflection of the window staring at her black stockinged legs.

Not wanting to appear too easy, she finally accepted a lift home after the third time he offered. They sat in silence on the short drive, the radio talk show adding to the slight tension in the car.

'This is me on the right, thanks,' she said, and he parked the car outside her house.

When nothing was said for a whole ten seconds, she grabbed the door handle and opened the door.

'Right, then,' she said. 'I'll see you in...'

'I really like you,' he blurted out.

Another three seconds passed before she said, 'thanks,' and got out of the car.

Simon watched her walk up the driveway, and then he faced the road again, berating himself for acting so childishly around her. Why couldn't he just ask her out? What's the worst thing that...

The car door opened again. 'Ask me out, then,' Samantha said, her head bent forward into the car. 'And not just to a pub, please,' she said and closed the door.

Simon drove with the radio off, and although he realised it made him look like a complete twat, he smiled and allowed himself several deep sighs all the way home.

Over a glass of wine with Maggie, and after a successful, if sometimes awkward first date with Simon, Maggie suggested that Samantha wait until at least the fourth date before she slept with him. Samantha, wanting it to be more than just a sex-driven fling that would fizzle out after a few months, thought five dates or possibly six would be a more appropriate number.

Two days later, on their second date, Simon called over with two tickets booked for the 7pm showing of the latest George Clooney film. Maggie and Louis had gone to yet another wedding fair and wouldn't be back until the following day. Having the house to themselves, and with almost a sense that their parents were away, it only took a few sips from their wine glasses, and a guided tour of the house, which ended of course in Samantha's bedroom, before the temptation became too great.

An hour later, they lay naked under the sheets of her bed, their sweating skins pressed against each other. A short distance away, George Clooney stared down from a twenty-two foot screen at a packed movie theatre, with the exception of two empty seats on the back row.

Only on a rare occasion, within a few weeks of that first night together, would Samantha find herself going to bed alone. On those nights when she would stretch out in bed and not find him there, she would feel rebuked, and curl into a foetal position. After two months, she began to think, and indeed worry, that their relationship had become, as she had feared, based on sex alone. Great sex. Unbelievably great sex. But just sex nonetheless.

They had already confessed their love for each other, but always in the throes of passion or when panting immediately after. She tried to reassure herself that they didn't spend all of their time in bed, but also went out on proper dates to movies or to restaurants. But then she also had to admit that those occasions were either preceded and or concluded by sex. And sometimes both. She seemed to spend more time getting dressed or undressed than actual time on the date.

For just once she was determined for them not to sleep together before the actual date part, and she said this to him, and he agreed. Then he placed his open hand on her neck and kissed her on the mouth and she melted under his presence and pulled him into her.

Over dinner, on another evening, she told him she feared their relationship had become based on them making love whenever they were together. Both of them got so turned on by the conversation that they ended up having sex in his car in the restaurant's car park.

Then one night, having run out of condoms, and while searching through Samantha's wall cabinet like a junkie searching for family heirlooms to sell, Simon found a thin strip of pills with the days written along the side.

'Is this what I think it is?' he asked her, holding the foil strip in the air.

'Depends what you think it is,' she replied.

He scoffed at this. 'How long have you been on the pill?'

'About two months.'

'And when were you going to tell me?'

'Why should I tell you?' she said. 'It's none of your business.'

He thought about this for a couple of seconds, and then realised she was right.

'There aren't any condoms,' he declared, as if answering a question.

'Then you'll just have to entertain me with your witty conversational skills, won't you?'

'Samantha?' he said, crawling onto the bed like a cat. 'But you're on the pill.'

'It's not a hundred percent foolproof, and I don't want a kid at this stage of my life, thanks very much.'

'And what? You think I want some little brat ruining my sleep and puking on the back seats of my BMW?'

'You have a very strange perception of children, Simon.'

'Whatever. You know what I mean.'

They lay on the bed, side by side, staring at the ceiling.

'Have you ever made love without a condom?' he asked, breaking the silence.

She didn't reply.

'The pill is as safe as a condom, you know.'

She turned her head towards him, and looked into his eyes. He had the bluest eyes she had ever seen.

'So much for your conversational skills,' she said, and they both started to undress.

Drinking milk, and then tasting cream, or grape juice and then experiencing wine, were some of the metaphors that spun around in Samantha's head. Their love making intensified even further, and three months later, the same sex-based relationship questions began to pop up in her conversations with him.

One evening in his apartment, he surprised her with her favourite prawn salad and a bottle of chilled rosé. At 4am he woke to the sounds of projectile vomiting from his bathroom. When he tried to comfort her, she told him to go away. The next morning he left her sleeping in his bed and felt a little guilty when he checked the best before date on the prawns, disposing of the evidence in a neighbour's bin on his way to work.

'You must have a stomach bug,' he told her later that evening when he found her pale and shivering on his sofa.

She wrapped the duvet tighter around herself.

'Listen, babe,' he said opening a can of beer, 'any chance you could pop back to bed so I can watch the match? It's starting in a few minutes.'

The smell from the opened can filled the room and she burst out of the duvet like a frightened cat. Simon propped his feet onto the coffee table and clicked on the television, drowning out the sounds of Samantha dry retching into the toilet.

Within two days she was back in work, although on a diet of dry toast and black tea, and their lovemaking had resumed with a vengeance.

It was only a few weeks later, them both lying in bed on a Sunday evening when Simon turned to her and asked, 'shouldn't you have had your period by now?'

It was a question she had asked herself and hearing it from someone else and out loud, made the blood drain from her face.

In work the next morning, and as soon as she could sneak away, she ran to the pharmacy in the village and bought a pregnancy test. She waited until she was home before using it, partly because she was afraid how she might react while in work, and partly because in her heart she already knew what it would tell her.

Simon didn't take the news too well. He had a thinking-out-loud conversation with himself in front of Samantha that included the phrases, 'I'm screwed', 'I'm fucked', 'What am I going to do?', 'I'm trapped', and on and on.

Samantha, for her part, considered a termination, but by the next day when Simon also suggested it to her, the consideration had gone. Whenever a bathroom was within her proximity, she would lock herself inside and have as long a cry as possible. After seven days, she stopped crying. Simon, who had been drinking himself into a stupor every evening, was sat at her kitchen table.

'I'm telling my parents this weekend,' she told him.

'Okay, I'm going to hold off saying anything to my parents for a while,' he said.

'No you're not, Simon. You're going to tell them this weekend as well or I'll tell them for you.'

He looked at her and knew she wasn't bluffing.

Samantha's parents greeted her news with a congratulations that was laden with an inevitability. Their lack of shock and anger both shocked and angered her.

Simon's mother, on the other hand, made up for Samantha's parents' lack of disappointment. When he informed her of his news, she used sentences that centred on the word 'catastrophe', and enquired if Simon felt that the girl had 'duped' him in some way in order to 'trap' him. Simon said no, but secretly had pondered the thought himself.

After his initial silence, Simon's father suggested a way that Simon could 'use this to his advantage'. It was time for him to settle down anyway in order to further his career in law, and this girl would be as viable an option as any, despite her background.

By the time the baby had arrived, Simon and Samantha had furnished a four-bedroomed semi-detached house five minutes' walk from Simon's parents, kitted out an SUV that Samantha thought was 'way too big', and booked a hotel venue for a four-hundred guest wedding the following July.

It had all happened so fast that Samantha often sat in the silence of her IKEA designed kitchen feeling as if she had somehow stumbled into someone else's house and even someone else's life, and then berating herself for her ingratitude.

Then baby Emily would cry to be changed or to be fed or to be held, and Samantha would squeeze her tight and breathe in the smell from her skin and would be so overwhelmed with the love and the happiness for her daughter, that she would sink into her super-king sized bed. Also from IKEA.

On the morning of her wedding, Samantha stood in front of the mirror. Throughout the day, she would hear repeatedly how 'beautiful' and how 'lucky' she was. How beautiful Emily was, how beautiful her house was, how beautiful her life was and how lucky she was to have Simon.

So it was a surprise to her mother when Samantha sat in her wedding dress in the kitchen of her mother's home and told her she didn't want to go through with it. And how unhappy she was with her life and with Simon, and how she suspected he may even have cheated on her.

Her mother told her that it was just 'wedding nerves', and how 'beautiful' she looked and how 'lucky' she was to be marrying Simon. Besides, she told her, what about all the guests that had arrived? Samantha bowed her head, and then went to reapply her eye makeup for the fifth time.

During their two-week honeymoon in a five star resort in Thailand (Simon's suggestion), Samantha took every opportunity to be romantic and to dwell on her blessings, while Simon took every opportunity to get maniacally drunk and to dwell on the pretty Thai waitresses' asses.

She would spend the afternoons on Skype to Emily back at home, while Simon was playing a round of golf. She enjoyed her four hours alone and talking to Emily and then reading a novel by the pool so much, that she banished from her mind the fact that Simon had never shown the slightest interest in golf before their honeymoon.

They made love once. It was before Simon was too drunk to talk and on a day he hadn't played golf.

Back at home, they settled into a routine of Simon at work for most of the day, quiet dinners in the evenings except for the spine curling sound of knife and fork scraping the plate, and Sunday afternoon trips in the car to the park or by the sea. Samantha would push Emily in her pram, and then later hold her hand as she took her first steps. Simon would have his head buried in his phone, with only the model of his phone changing as the years went by.

But Emily kept Samantha busy with various appointments and Samantha delighted in watching her develop and grow. When she started in a local Montessori at three years of age, Samantha's morning hours became still, and filled with silence. She dreaded going home to the empty house and waiting for the hours to pass before she could collect Emily again. For several mornings she spent the entire four hours sitting in her car outside Emily's Montessori building.

On one such morning in her car, she had the idea that perhaps she could go back to work for the few hours while Emily was at school. Helping out with any paperwork or tidying up, she wouldn't mind whatever the job was. She was so excited at the prospect she even made Simon his favourite steak and chips dinner.

Simon slammed his cutlery down so hard onto the plate and roared his objection that for the first time, she became a little frightened of him physically.

'No,' he yelled at her. 'That is not going to happen.'

'But it would only be for...'

'I said no.'

'It's not only your decision, Simon. I can do whatever...'

'You're not going near my business. No fucking way. Do you hear me?'

When Emily burst into tears, Simon pushed back his chair and left the house. Samantha stroked her daughter's hair to soothe her as she listened to Simon's car starting up and then reversing out of their driveway.

The following week they attended the National Solicitors' Conference, which had become one of the rare annual night's out for just the two of them. While Emily had been in school that morning, Samantha had treated herself to two hours in her local beauty salon and then over an hour in the hairdressers. That evening she found she was able to fit into a long black evening dress, which she hadn't worn since her engagement party, and with her only pair of red Jimmy Choo shoes and the contrast of her blond hair, she couldn't help admiring herself in the mirror before leaving for the conference.

All the men's eyes followed her as she moved through the room that night, and none more so than her husband's. Simon even apologised for his overreaction to her job request. For at least a few hours she felt off-duty as a mother, and even allowed herself an extra glass of Chardonnay with her dinner. And then another. And another.

She was genuinely caught off-guard when Simon surreptitiously placed his hand on her bottom. Later when they danced, she couldn't help but feel excited as he kissed her neck and ran his hands down her back.

They made love that night as they once had; passionately, lovingly and carefree. It would be the last time they made love.

She knew before it was possible to know. But in her heart, she just knew. Then the morning sickness started. Her dread at the forthcoming pregnancy was shadowed by Simon's indifference. Only her parents showed any delight. Worried about her and Simon's relationship, they mistakenly saw the new baby as a sign of stability.

Five months into her pregnancy, she got a call from Maggie out of the blue. Louis, now her husband, had buggered off to his family in France for a week, and since she didn't fancy seven days sitting around not understanding a bloody word anyone was saying, would Samantha like to meet up for lunch at the new hotel that had opened up in the city centre?

Being the newest restaurant in town, it was quite busy, but they found a table near the entrance. Immediately, they began chatting as if they were back in their old apartment on the north side of the city.

'Wow, Sam,' said Maggie, digressing from her own long monologue about the annoying habits of her French in-laws. 'There's a girl sitting over there in reception that is the spitting image of you. Well, maybe you a few years ago. When we first met.'

'You mean,' said Samantha, 'when I was young?'

'No, no. I don't mean that. You're still young and beautiful. She's just younger, that's all.'

'I think there's a compliment there somewhere,' said Samantha laughing.

'She's your… what do you call it? Doppelgänger,' said Maggie. 'Have a look.'

Samantha turned in her chair, pushing herself out slightly to avoid hitting her stomach off the edge of the table. Even she could see the similarities, although she would never have regarded herself as quite that pretty.

'Told you so,' said Maggie as Samantha turned back to her.

'Well, I don't think I was ever that...'

'Oh my God, there's another one.'

'Another what?' said Samantha, turning uncomfortably in her chair again.

'Another doppelgänger. He's the image of Simon, don't you think?'

Samantha saw a man walking across the hotel's foyer and up to the reception.

'That's not Simon's doppelgänger,' Samantha told her.

'Well, he's very similar.'

'No, I mean, that is Simon.'

Samantha pushed the table away from her to go over to her husband. This took a little longer than normal. Long enough for her husband to take the room key from the receptionist, and stroll over to the pretty blonde, his face beaming as he approached her. Samantha had managed to stand up straight just in time to see

Simon kiss the woman on the lips, and sliding his arm around her waist, make their way to the large brass doors of the hotel lift.

The blood drained from Samantha's face, and she felt as if she might faint as they disappeared behind the lift's sliding doors.

Holding the back of the chair, Samantha lowered herself back down into it.

'I'm so sorry,' was all that Maggie could think to say.

'Well, then,' said Samantha behind a tight mouth, the white napkin which was still in her hand matching the colour of her clenched fist.

'Well, then,' she repeated, 'aren't I the big, fat, stupid, bloody, pregnant idiot?'

She slammed her fist onto the table hard enough for some of the diners to turn in her direction.

'No, Sam,' said Maggie. 'He's the idiot. He's the prick.'

Samantha looked up at her friend across from her and burst into tears. A couple of the waitresses were now looking over.

'Sam,' Maggie said, but Samantha's face was firmly buried into her hands. 'Sam,' she tried again.

Samantha sniffled and rubbed her eyes. She looked around for her bag and picked it up. Rummaging around inside, she pulled out her mobile phone.

'Don't do anything too rash,' Maggie warned her.

As if not hearing her, Samantha dialled her phone and then listened to it ring.

'Hello,' said a voice on the other end.

Samantha took a deep breath.

'Hello,' the voice said again. 'Sam? Is that you?'

'Hi Simon,' Samantha blurted out in as cheerful a voice as she could. 'Can I pop around to see you? I need to talk to you about something.'

There was a silence.

'It's important,' she added.

'Em… can't it wait?' Simon said. 'I'm just about to go into a meeting.'

Now it was Samantha's turn to be silent.

'Sam?'

'Yes, yes. Of course it can wait. I'll talk to you later.'

Simon was starting a sentence when she cut him off by closing her phone.

A flurry of emotions raged inside her; anger, humiliation, embarrassment, hatred, grief. But mostly it was anger.

'Wait here,' she told Maggie as she got up and walked out of the restaurant.

The receptionist smiled as Samantha approached her desk, and then dropped her smile as she got closer.

'May I help you?' she said.

'The man who you just gave a room key to. Can you tell me what room he's in?'

'I'm afraid I'm not in a position to disclose any of our guests' information, ma'am.'

Samantha looked towards the lift doors.

'I'll pay you,' she said, turning back to the receptionist.

The receptionist couldn't help but laugh. 'I'm sorry ma'am. That's not possible.'

Samantha could feel the anger rising in her again. The receptionist saw it as well.

'I'm afraid, ma'am that you'll...'

'You're married, aren't you?' Samantha asked her.

'I don't see what that has to do with...'

'Imagine if you saw your husband with another woman right now. Sure, you weren't the happiest of couples, but at least you had trust. And honesty. You had each other. And then you see him kiss a younger version of you. The father of the child you're carrying around inside of you. The man you once loved with all your heart. The man who kisses your children goodnight. The man who crawls into bed beside you. And then you discover that he's a prick. He's a prick like all the other pricks. And what makes it worse is that you always knew in your heart he was a prick. But he was your prick. Now imagine the rage. The anger. The humiliation. Embarrassment. The sheer...'

'Room 310.'

Samantha swallowed hard, and raised her hands to wipe her face.

'Now go get the prick,' the receptionist told her.

Samantha took a deep breath and nodded at the receptionist, then turned and walked towards the lifts.

The lift doors opened up on the third floor, and Samantha followed the room number signs and arrows on the walls. She wasn't surprised at how angry she was, but she was surprised at how in control she felt. Her breathing was deep and measured as she marched towards the door marked 310.

Like an angry neighbour complaining about the noise, she raised her fist to the door. And then she heard it. A giggle at first. But enough to freeze her hand mid-air. Then a voice. A male voice. She lowered her hand and pressed her ear to the door. Silence. Then such a shriek of laughter that she almost fell away from the door.

As she approached the room again, there was silence and then the faintest of moans. A girl's moan. Then louder. A man's moan. Moaning with pleasure. Simon's pleasure.

Samantha felt her insides recoil and her knees weaken. She allowed herself to slide down the door and then turned and rested her back against it.

She sat there on the floor, her knees up, clutching her unborn baby, and listened to her husband's pleasure only a few feet away from her, and did not move until Maggie found her and helped her up and carried her away.

Samantha switched off the radio in her car. There were a few more cars than were normally parked outside her parents' house. The curtains in Michael's room were pulled shut. She pictured him hiding under the covers of his bed, his door locked from the inside.

Of all the people in the world to win so much money, Michael was probably the last person she would have nominated to win it. God's wicked sense of humour, she supposed.

But perhaps, she hoped, it might help him to come out of his shell a little. Give him a little confidence. Show him, even slightly, that there's a whole world outside of the bubble he exists in. Make him realise...

The sound of a low bass growl of an engine, and her car vibrating from the noise woke her from her daydreaming. The lowest, longest and blackest car she had ever seen drove by her slowly and parked outside the house. The door opened, but not like a normal door. It opened upwards.

She felt her mouth open at the sight of it, but her chin dropped even further when she saw Michael step out, close the door and go into the house.

10

Michael found himself whistling as he walked up his driveway, but then stopped when he realised he didn't have a key to get back in. He rang the doorbell, and while waiting he saw a dent in the top right hand corner of the door.

How had he never noticed that before? It was as if he had grown a couple of inches since his drive in the Lamborghini. Perhaps, he thought, the low seats had stretched out his spine, as he had to admit he did feel a little taller.

As he walked in, Samantha came in behind him.

'Hey, Sam,' he said.

She was a little off put by his cheerful greeting, given how concerned she was, and thought he might still be drunk from the previous night.

'Hi Michael,' she said as they entered the sitting room. 'Did you have a good night last night?'

'Did we what?' replied Uncle Jim. 'It was certainly a night to remember, that's for sure.'

'Did you pay for everything, Mike?' Samantha asked in as hushed a voice as the small sitting room would allow.

'He did indeed,' said Uncle Jim. 'And why wouldn't he? Aren't we all family here? Sure he's more money than the Queen of England now.'

'Yes, that's true,' said Samantha. 'And it is nice to see you here again, Uncle Jim, rather than just the once a year at Christmas like we normally do.'

'Well, he's going to need his family around here now, Susan. People that really know him. People who are going to look out for his interests.'

'It's Samantha,' said Samantha.

'What?'

'You called me Susan. My name's Samantha.'

'So, who's Susan then? His other sister?'

'He doesn't have another sister?'

'Are you sure?'

'Positive, Uncle Jim.'

'So who's Susan then?' he called out, turning to his wife. 'June, what Susan am I thinking of?'

'Susan Flannery?' asked Aunt June.

'Who the fuck is Susan Flannery?' asked Uncle Jim.

'You remember Susan Flannery,' Aunt June assured him. 'She used to work with me in Tescos.'

'There are no other sisters, Uncle Jim. It's just me,' said Samantha.

'Well, that's good news. That means there's less people you have to share with so.'

'Jim,' said Rose interrupting. She always interrupted whenever voices were raised. 'Will you have another biscuit?'

'No, thanks, Rose. I'll turn into a fucking biscuit if I eat another one. Hey, Mike. How about we go into town for a bite to eat?'

'Uncle Jim,' said Samantha. 'I'd like to have a chat with Mike.'

'No problemo. But let's eat while you chat. What do you say, Mike?'

Michael hadn't been listening to their conversation. He was staring out of the front window at his new car. He had already decided that he wouldn't be giving it back. The sun glistened off its shiny black surface as if it were smiling at him. He wanted to drive it again. He wanted to see people turn and look at him go by, and to pretend not to notice them looking at him. What would they think of him if he pulled up to work in that car? He jumped slightly when he thought of pulling up alongside Lauren and offering her a lift. The two of them driving through the Dublin Mountains. The radio playing in the background. Her sudden and infectious laugh at a funny remark he'd just made. Reaching over and...

'Mike,' shouted Uncle Jim.

'Sorry, what?'

'You're away with the fairies.'

'Sorry.'

'We were saying about driving into town for something to eat?'

'Driving?' Michael asked. 'Yeah, let's go.'

He turned and saw Samantha glaring at him.

'What?' he asked her.

'I'll order the taxis,' said Uncle Jim taking out his phone. 'June, do you fancy a bit of steak?'

'Oh, I love a bit of steak.'

Uncle Jim began making arrangements on his phone as Samantha grabbed Michael by the arm and dragged him into the kitchen.

'What are you up to?' she asked.

'What do you mean? We're going for lunch.'

'But all of them too? What's their real motivation here, Mike? Have you thought about that?'

'Em... hunger?'

'Don't take the piss with me. They're only using you and you know it.'

'It's only lunch, Sam. Don't worry.'

'Lunch today. Drinks yesterday. So what'll be tomorrow?'

'Dinner?'

Samantha folded her arms.

'Look, Sam. It's okay. I know...'

Uncle Jim marched into the kitchen. 'Taxis will be here in five minutes. Sorry, Susan. I forgot about you. Are you coming as well?'

'No, Uncle Jim. I have to collect the girls from school.'

'Jesus. I forgot about my two kids. Sure we can collect them in the taxi on the way in and bring them with us.'

As a ten minute argument could not be resolved about who should or should not sit beside him in his new car, Michael found himself alone for the short drive into the city centre. This, if anyone had thought to ask his opinion, was his preferred choice anyway.

When he attempted to overtake a bicycle on the Crumlin Road, and pressed down on the accelerator, he was forced back into his seat so hard by the sudden propulsion forward that he thought he may had given himself whiplash. He didn't feel he had applied an enormous amount of pressure with his right foot, but it was as if someone had slammed their car into the back of his when the car leapt forward.

He now meandered with less bravado through the Dublin streets. He was also happy to give more of his fellow citizens the opportunity to turn and to admire and to take pleasure from his new found joy.

Uncle Jim had chosen the Shelbourne Hotel to have their lunch. Michael knew where it was and had even walked by it on several occasions but had never been inside. It was one of those places in the city where he always felt slightly intimidated by its apparent plushness and formality. A place where other people went but not him

As he approached the hotel, he saw his family climbing out of several taxis that had pulled up in front. He parked in behind the last taxi and watched them go in. He counted fifteen relatives in total, and that included the children, some of whom were still in their school uniforms.

His parents got out of the last taxi, his mother looking up at the grandeur of the hotel. A porter helped her out of the car, and he could hear her repeatedly thanking him. It had probably been some time, he thought, since a car door was held for his mother. His father waited for her on the footpath to join him.

The uncertainty of the near future scared him a little, even with the safety of the money to support him, but one certainty he knew was that his parents would never want for anything again.

The emptied taxis began to pull away, and he could see most of his family gathered together outside like tourists waiting for their tour guide, while Uncle Jim spoke to the maître d'. One of his nephews, who was dressed in a Manchester United tracksuit, was being scolded by his mother for pulling the petals off a large flower display that took up a whole corner of the entrance. Two other school-uniformed nephews were chasing each other in and out of the revolving doors, while a porter looked on with an expression under his tall black hat that barely disguised his desire to bash their heads together.

For a moment Michael considered driving away. Maybe up the coast road. Think about all these changes in his life and what choices he had now. He pressed his foot on the brake pedal, and shifted the car into first gear.

There was a tap on the window, and Michael turned to see a uniformed porter.

'Is your vehicle to be valeted, sir?' he asked, after Michael had rolled down the window.

'You mean you'll park it for me?' he asked.

'Yes, exactly.'

Michael sighed. 'Okay, thanks,' he said and climbed out.

The staff at the hotel had set a table for twenty people in a private room on the first floor overlooking St. Stephen's Green. Michael was unsure whether this was to preserve their privacy or to separate them from the other hotel guests. They had also asked to take Michael's credit card number before seating them. He wondered again whether this was standard practice or was he the exception.

They ordered drinks and read the menus while one of the children ran around the dining table with his arms stretched out and making loud airplane noises. Both staff and parents behaved as if he weren't even there.

'Excuse me,' Aunt Deirdre called out, raising her hand in the air as if she were in a classroom. One of the waiters walked over to her.

'Yes, madam.'

'Is there no steak? I really fancied a bit of steak,' she whispered.

Everyone turned to the waiter. It was the question they had all wanted to ask; the steak, of course, being the ultimate in dining extravagance.

'The filet mignon, Madame,' said the waiter, pointing his finger to it on the menu. 'It's the cut from the smaller end of the tenderloin.'

'Good, is it?' she asked.

'Yes. The best.'

'I'll have that, so,' said Aunt Deirdre handing him back the menu. 'And chips.'

'Chips?' the waiter asked.

'I'll have that as well,' Uncle Jim called out.

'Yeah, me too,' everyone concurred.

'Oh, and will you do some chicken nuggets for the kids, please?' asked Aunt Deirdre.

'And how would you like the steaks done?'

'Well done,' said Aunt Deirdre, and they all nodded approvingly.

'Very well,' said the waiter.

'I'll have mine raw,' said Uncle Pat, and leaned back in his chair, puffing out his chest.

They all looked at him

'Raw, sir?' the waiter asked.

'Yep. I like it nice and bloody.'

'Do you mean rare?'

'That's the one,' he said. 'And bring me a large bottle of Bulmers, please. And a pint glass of ice.'

There was a chorus of drinks called out, the waiter not bothering to write it down as all the men wanted Bulmers, the ladies vodka and 7up, and the kids ordering cokes. Michael would much rather have had an orange juice, but didn't want the waiter to have to go to any extra bother just for him.

He sat between his parents. His mother's only remarks during the meal were on how 'beautiful' and 'gorgeous' the room and everything in it was. His father spent the entire meal surreptitiously scowling across the table at his in-laws and elbowing Michael every time they ordered more drinks or food.

For Michael, the afternoon passed like most family gatherings; slow and agonising. He ate most of his steak and sipped on his Bulmers and waited on the time to pass. He thought about sitting outside the hotel earlier in his car and how he wished he had driven away.

He didn't even flinch when the waiter handed him a credit card receipt to sign for just over €2,000. He would have paid ten times that amount if they would just have all left him alone.

'Mickey,' Uncle Jim called over as he was getting up from the table. 'It's alright, isn't it, if we go downstairs for a couple of drinks and put it on your tab?'

'Sure, Uncle Jim,' said Michael, conjuring up the best fake smile anyone could muster after being in the room for over two hours with him.

'Nice one,' said Uncle Jim. 'We'll only have the one or two.'

Michael's mother touched his arm and he turned to her, but not before hearing Uncle Jim instructing someone to call 'some of the boys from the local' in order to help 'liven things up a bit.'

'I think your father and I are going to head home now, Michael, if that's okay with you,' his mother was saying. 'Thanks very much for the lunch. It's been a lovely afternoon, but it's probably best if we head off home and leave you lot to it.'

'Okay, mam,' said Michael. 'We'll do something with Sam and the kids and just us another time to celebrate, alright?'

'That's if Jim and his lot don't clean you out first,' said Jack.

Michael laughed, but the thought had already crossed his mind too. 'Get a taxi home. There are loads at the front door. I'll pay for it.'

Michael watched his parents shuffle out as the waiters zoomed past them carrying plates and cutlery as they cleared the table.

'Is this finished, sir?' a waiter asked him, pointing at his untouched slice of tiramisu cake.

'Yes, sorry. It was a little too much for me I'm afraid.'

'I feel the same to be honest,' said the waiter, lowering his voice. 'It's a little too rich. It's not always a good thing.'

Michael looked at the waiter taking his plate away, then stood up and walked to the large windows that were framed by heavy gold-coloured curtains and which overlooked St. Stephen's Green.

It was a beautiful day and the greenery of the park stood out like an oasis in the desert of buildings of grey and glass. He saw the heads of his parents coming out of the hotel, his father walking two feet in front of his mother. They passed the taxis and crossed the road. He knew where they were going - Chapel's Corner to catch the 547 bus home. It would be pointless trying to convince them to take a taxi. They were at an age where trying to change their minds would be as difficult as trying to change the weather. He wondered if he too was of that age and hoped that he wasn't.

'Excuse me, sir.'

Michael turned to the waiter, who looked a little flushed, as if he'd been running up the stairs.

'Yes.'

'There's a slight...' he searched for the word, '...discrepancy.'

'A discrepancy? A discrepancy where?' asked Michael.

'In the bar. In the bar downstairs.'

'What is it?'

'It's the Macallan, sir.'

'What's a Macallan?'

'It's a whisky. A rare forty-year-old single malt Scotch whisky. The bar manager refuses to serve it without the credit card owner's approval. I'm very sorry for the inconvenience, sir.'

'Will you please stop calling me sir? It makes me very uncomfortable.'

'Of course, sir. I mean, Mr. Irvine.'

'Mike. Just Mike is okay.'

'Yes, Mike.'

'Now, Tony,' said Mike, reading the waiter's name tag. 'I assume it's expensive is it?'

'Three hundred euro, I'm afraid, si… I mean Mike.'

'Three hundred euro for a bottle of whisky? Holy shit.'

'No. It's three hundred euro for a glass.'

Michael sighed. It was a deep sigh. He could see the waiter wanted to say something else, but he didn't.

'Okay, then, Tony. Let's go.'

The bar looked as Michael could have predicted it would look. Dark brown wood and ceiling-high paintings of scenes of Dublin through tourists' eyes. Brass fittings and crystal chandeliers that shone despite the sunlight pouring past the same thick gold curtains as were in the room upstairs. Parquet flooring, Michael thought, and then realised he wasn't sure exactly what parquet meant. It was a floor that would impress someone who knew about these things. In fact, he could say that about everything in the room.

He spotted his uncle sitting on a stool at a table a few feet from the bar. His arms were folded and resting on his protruding, blue-shirted stomach. Members of his family were sitting on tables surrounding him. No one was talking. Behind the bar, the barman stood rigid mirroring the uncle's defiant stance.

They both reminded Michael of his two nieces Kate and Emily when they were unwilling to share a new toy, and would rather it was taken away, than see the other derive any pleasure from it.

Michael walked straight up to the bar. The barman, keeping his posture, walked over to Michael, never taking his eyes off Uncle Jim.

'I'm really sorry about all of this,' Michael told him.

'He can't be talking to me like that,' the barman said.

'Look, I don't know what he said, but I apologise for whatever it was.'

The barman looked at Michael for the first time. 'Is it your credit card?' he asked.

'Yes.'

'No one can order drinks without the card holder's permission.'

'I understand.'

'Especially not the Macallan.'

'I know, I know. The hotel has my credit card, and I'll cover whatever he wants.'

'He can't be talking to me like that either.'

'Yes, I know. Again, I'm sorry. Look, have a Macallan yourself if you like. A little peace offering. What do you say?'

A couple of years ago, the barman remembered licking his fingers when he 'accidently' mis-poured some of the Macallan for an American drunk who was trying to show off to two girls half his age. He had wanted a proper glassful ever since. He lowered his arms.

'I know it's not your fault, sir,' said the barman, 'it's just they're the rules.'

'I know, it's fine,' said Michael holding out his hand. 'And again I apologise. My name's Mike.'

The barman shook it. 'Phil.'

'Thanks, Phil.'

Everyone looked at Michael as he approached the table, except Uncle Jim.

'I'm not apologising,' he said. 'It's the principle.'

Michael looked at his family. Everyone waited for his response. Even the children sensed that their fun might be over, and they were all going home. His feelings of resignation towards his family shifted slightly and were replaced by a sense of irritability.

'If you'd rather go back to Harry's, Uncle Jim, that's your choice.'

Everyone turned to Uncle Jim. 'I didn't say that. I just said I'm not saying sorry.'

'You don't have to. I apologised for you.'

Uncle Jim gave a slight chuckle. 'That's your choice, buddy. But I'll keep my principles if you don't mind.'

'And I'll keep my money if you don't mind.'

There was a collective intake of breath, and everyone, including Michael, looked at Uncle Jim in anticipation of what was next. The tension had even spread to the tables surrounding theirs.

'What the hell sort of a party is this?' Four men and two women approached them and one of the men slapped Uncle Jim on his back. 'You said there was a party with free drinks, but this place is dead.'

'Jim,' said Aunt June. 'Do you want another drink?'

Uncle Jim turned and looked at his wife, and as if released from his grip, Michael also turned away. Feeling a little flushed, he went into the bathroom and, avoiding looking at himself in the mirror, he splashed water onto his face.

He noticed his hands shaking a little. Michael couldn't remember ever being that confrontational with anyone before, and he wondered what had triggered it. By the time he had returned to the bar, his group of family and friends had returned to their celebrations, as two lounge girls carried trays of drinks to their tables.

Michael took a seat at the bar and ordered himself a Carlsberg shandy. He had his back to them, but he could hear the loud talking and bursts of laughter from Uncle Jim's tables. He sipped on his drink and began reading all of the different labels on the bottles behind the bar. A big cheer went up behind him and Michael turned towards the door to see Joey McGuinness and two others walking in. Michael's shoulders slouched a little more and he gripped his pint glass a little tighter.

After over an hour, Michael had managed to get halfway through his second pint, rip up three beer mats and walk in and out of the bathroom seven times. He recognised more and more faces from Harry's as the evening went on. Some of them nodded a greeting to him. The only text he received on his phone was from his parents to say they'd arrived home safely. After he'd been on the news, he thought he'd get a lot more texts from people but then realised that very few people had his number.

He thought about Lauren and pictured her behind the bar in an empty pub, since most of her customers were in here. An image popped into his head of him sitting in front of her, the two of them almost alone, chatting and laughing. He sat up with the excitement of the image.

What if I talk to the manager or Phil or Tony and tell him I'll approve any purchases in the bar, he thought. What if I give them my mobile number and they can contact me any time they like? He pulled his stool out and turned towards the foyer door.

Flash! He was blinded by the white light. Then another. He put his hand up to his face to protect his eyes. Three more flashes. Camera shutters clicking.

'Michael.' 'Look here, Michael.' His way was blocked by bodies. Shadows behind the flashes.

'How about one with the whole family?' Click, click, click.

'Michael, over here.'

Several reporters and photographers surrounded him. Michael tried to get up, but a microphone shoved into his face forced him back into his seat.

'Out, lads. Out now.' Phil had come out from behind the bar and was using his outstretched arms to give Michael some space. Two of the doormen came running into the bar and helped push them back.

'Just a couple of snaps,' one of the photographers called out.

'Hey, get your hands off me,' a female reporter shouted at one of the doormen.

Some of the photographers were leaving, their eyes already on the back of their cameras, scanning the shots they had. The rest allowed themselves to be guided out of the bar, through the lobby and out of the front doors of the hotel. Michael looked out at them. They formed a small pack at the entrance, discussing what their next move might be.

Michael's gaze moved from the group of reporters to his own group at their tables. Not one of them had moved to help him. His eyes rested on Joey McGuinness, who was staring back at him. A small smirk crossed his face and he turned away. Michael also turned back to the bar.

So this was hell, he thought. This was exactly how he had envisioned his life when he had first realised he had won the money. Trapped from leaving by paparazzi while he watched his so-called family and friends getting drunk on his winnings. The small triumph he had felt against Uncle Jim earlier had faded into the distant background. He lifted his pint glass, allowing the flat beer to barely touch his lips and then rested it back down on the bar.

'Hi, Mike.'

For a moment, the familiar female voice flashed an image of Lauren across his mind. He turned in its direction and saw Zoe sitting beside him.

'Expecting someone else?' she asked, reading his instant disappointment.

'No.'

'Hoping, then?'

'What do you want, Zoe?' he asked her.

'That's an unusual chat-up line. It's direct, I suppose. I'll give you that. Had much success with it?'

Michael turned away from her.

'How come they didn't throw you out with all the other reporters?' he asked her.

'There are two types of people in the world, Mike. Those who come in the front door and those who come in the back door.'

'Isn't that where they keep all the rubbish?'

'Ouch. So there is a bit of a spark to you after all. All you need to do is... what is my mother use to advise me? "To make more of an effort". That's it.'

'Did your mother mention anything about using other people's stories to make a living?'

'Wow, you really are on fire tonight. Is it because of that intellectual wit that you're thirty-three-years-old, have no girlfriend and still live at home with your mammy and daddy?'

Michael sipped on his drink.

'Oops. Did I go too far? You're not going to cry into your shandy now, are you?'

She raised her hand up to call the barman. 'A JD and coke, please, Phil,' she said when he arrived. 'And put it on Mike's tab. I might as well free-load off him like everyone else in the bar.'

'Like I said, what do you want, Zoe?'

'Can we not just have a drink at the bar like friends?'

'You're not my friend.'

'Oh, I'm sorry. So, where are your friends then, Mike? Is that them over there?' Zoe turned and pointed at Michael's family.

Michael didn't look over at them.

'They've been clamouring up so much to you to say thanks that I'm lucky to even get a seat beside you. With friends like them, Mike...'

Michael took a sip from his drink but didn't look at her. Phil placed Zoe's drink in front of her.

'So what would you like to toast to?' she asked him.

'Privacy.'

Zoe laughed. 'Good one, Mike,' she said. 'How about to new friendships?'

She raised her glass towards him. 'Come on. Don't leave a girl hanging.'

Michael lifted his glass from the bar, and she clinked her glass against his.

'To old friends and new,' she said and took a sip from her glass. 'Speaking of old friends, where's your girlfriend tonight? Lauren, wasn't it?'

'She's not my girlfriend.'

'Obviously she's not your girlfriend, Mike. I was being facetious. If she were your girlfriend, she'd be here and you'd be happy and confident and not the sad loser that you find yourself to be.'

Michael stood up.

'Hey, hey, sit down,' Zoe said, grabbing his arm. 'There's no need to take things so personally.'

'What's not personal about being called a loser?'

'Fair enough. I can see how that might cause offence to some people.'

Michael sat back down. Zoe stared at him for a minute, and he could feel her stare. He turned to look at her.

'You know, Mike,' she said, 'you're not such a bad looking fella. I mean obviously, you have no style, sophistication or sense of dress but your physique and basic bone structure aren't too bad.'

'Thanks. You're a real charmer, Zoe. Did anyone ever tell you that?'

'No, to be honest, I think you might be the first person, Mike,' she said raising her glass to him and smiling.

Michael smiled back at her.

'And you have a nice smile as well. I think that deserves a selfie with my favourite multi-millionaire,' she said and took out her phone.

Michael stared at her as she raised her phone in front of them.

'What are you doing?' he asked.

'I'm taking a selfie.'

Michael looked at her and then the phone. 'A what?'

'A selfie,' she said, lowering her phone.

He looked at her.

'You have heard of a selfie, haven't you?'

'No.'

'Jesus, what planet are you living on? How can you not know what that is?'

'I don't watch the news.'

Zoe let out a huge laugh.

'I don't think it's something they announce on the news,' she said.

'Well, I've never heard of it.'

'You're obviously not on Facebook.'

'No.'

'Twitter? LinkedIn? Instagram? Snapchat?'

Michael stared at her. 'I've heard of some of them.'

'A selfie,' she explained, 'is when you take a photo of yourself.'

'For what purpose?'

'To put on your social media site.'

'A photograph of yourself? And then you upload to show everyone?'

'Exactly.'

'That's the most narcissistic thing I've ever heard.'

Zoe looked at her phone in her hand. 'Actually,' she said, 'you're probably right.'

She put her phone on the bar. 'Do you even have a smartphone?'

'I can use my phone to talk to anyone in the world. I'd call that pretty smart.'

Zoe laughed again. Michael liked when she laughed at something he said.

'Can I see your phone?' she asked him.

He reached into his jeans pocket and pulled out his phone. She let out a huge laugh as soon as she saw it.

'Do they still even make those phones?'

'I don't know. It's a few years old.'

She looked at him holding his ancient phone in his hand, his flat shandy in front of him evaporating quicker than he was drinking it, and with enough money in his pocket to perhaps buy the whole building.

'I like you, Mike.'

'Thanks,' he said, trying not to show his pleasure at hearing that.

'Well, maybe not "like", probably more of a "feel sorry for" sort of a feeling,' she said taking a sip from her glass. 'They're quite similar emotions, you know.'

Michael sighed and turned away from her.

'Oh, come on,' Zoe said. 'Don't be like that. Let me buy you a drink.'

He looked at her and then over at his family. 'That'd be a first today.'

'You're going to have a lot of "firsts' in the next few months, Mike.'

'Yeah, that's what my dad said.'

'Well, he was right. What do you fancy?'

Michael opened his mouth to order a drink, but Zoe interrupted him. 'And I mean a proper drink. Not some shandy crap.'

Michael smiled. 'Okay, I'll try one of them,' he said nodding to her drinks.

'Excellent. Now we're talking.' Zoe raised her hand in the air. 'Two more of these please, Phil.'

'Someone else buying me a drink,' Michael said, 'now that deserves one of your Sophies.'

Zoe burst out laughing. Michael laughed too, although he wasn't exactly sure why.

'Yes, Mike,' said Zoe, picking up her phone. 'That certainly does deserve a Sophie.'

11

There were two things that Michael first noticed when he opened his eyes in the darkened room the next morning. The first was the unfamiliar and expensive-looking furniture surrounding the largest bed he had ever seen and had apparently slept in. The second was the noise of a running shower, which came from a partially opened door off the bedroom. The light from the gap cast a thin, yellow line over his bed, across the room and up onto the closed curtains.

Then there was a third thing he noticed - under the sheets he was completely naked.

The shower stopped running, and he listened to the opening and closing of the shower door and the shuffling of towels. He turned his head to look for his glasses and a pain, like he had never suffered before, exploded in his head. He placed his hand on his temple and pressed down gently.

He let out a loud moan.

'Good morning to you too,' a female voice said.

He removed his hand from his face to see the blurred outline of a woman wrapped in a white towel and drying herself with another. He didn't need his glasses to know her identity.

'Zoe?'

'Why do I always get the impression that whenever you say my name, you're expecting someone else?'

Moving as if the slightest false move would set off a bomb in his head, he fumbled on the bedside locker for his glasses, and put them on.

Still unsure where exactly he was, and not wanting to ask Zoe, he surveyed the room. It appeared to be a hotel room, although he couldn't see the front door. It was a bedroom inside of a hotel room and with enough space for a sofa. It must be a suite, he figured. He remembered being in the Shelbourne sitting at the bar, but everything after that was a blur.

Zoe was talking, but he didn't hear what she was saying.

'Sorry, what?'

'I said, I've ordered you some breakfast. I hope you're not a vegetarian,' she said, continuing to dry her hair.

'Breakfast? What time is it?'

'It's after nine. I don't think we got to bed till at least three.'

We? Bed? Does she mean the same bed?

Zoe stopped drying her hair and threw the damp towel onto the bed, and began to look through her clothes. She sniffed the armpits of her black shirt. 'Shit. It'll have to do.'

She straightened up, and with her back to him, allowed the second white towel to fall to the ground. Michael's eyes widened at the sight of her naked body and he turned away. She talked as she dressed and Michael turned his head back a few inches in her direction.

'We must have cleared them out of their stock of Jack Daniels last night,' she laughed. 'I can't remember the last time I...'

She stood with her back to him, the sunlight from the window behind her. She had her underwear on and she was clipping her bra shut. Both were black. Her damp, dark hair contrasted with her fair skin. She was lean, but not skinny, and her arms and legs were toned. She had a slight tan line over her bottom. The image was one of the most beautiful things Michael had ever seen. She turned around to face him. Now this image was the most beautiful thing he had ever seen.

'Are you even listening to me or am distracting you from staring at my tits?' she asked.

'What?' he blurted, turning away. 'No, I just...'

'It's okay,' she laughed and continued to get dressed. 'You certainly weren't that shy last night. And by the way, you should stop wearing such baggy clothes and show off your toned figure a bit more.'

Michael turned to her again, this time making every effort to only look at her face. 'Did we?... em... you know...' he mumbled, pointing his head towards the bed.

'Get drunk?' she said. 'Absolutely. We were shit-faced by

midnight. Then you ordered champagne...'

'No, I mean, did we..?'

'What?'

'Did we, you know?'

'Did we what, Mike?'

'Have... em... relations with one another?'

'Relations?' Zoe asked. 'Are you kidding me? You're asking did we fuck? Is that what you're asking me?'

Michael shifted in the bed. Zoe let the silence hang in the air between them for a minute, delighting in his awkwardness.

'You honestly don't remember?' she asked him.

'No. Sorry.'

'Well, I don't know how a girl's supposed to feel about not being remembered,' she said, feigning an offense against her reputation.

'No, no,' Mike blurted out, sitting up in the bed. 'I didn't mean it like that.'

'I suppose next you'll be telling me you don't even remember your big bust-up with your Uncle Jim.'

'What?' Mike shouted at her.

'Thank God the cops arrived when they did. I simply can't imagine what would have happened if they hadn't have pulled you off...'

'What? What did I do to Uncle Jim? Oh, my God. I'd better call my mam,' Mike said and reached for the phone.

'I'm joking, I'm joking,' Zoe laughed. 'Relax. Christ, you should see your face.'

'I should call home anyway. They're probably worried sick about me.'

He checked his phone and saw that he had three missed calls - one from his parents and two from Samantha. He glanced up at Zoe and watched her as she closed the last of the buttons on her shirt.

'Em, Zoe.'

'Yeah?' she asked, walking back into the bathroom.

'Were you joking about everything or just the Uncle Jim bit?'

'You mean about us?'

Michael nodded.

'You seriously don't remember?'

'No.'

'Well then, Mr. Irvine,' she said slowly and crawled onto the bed towards him, her face getting closer to his, 'if you don't remember, what difference does it make whether we fell into bed unconscious, or made passionate yet sweet, gentle love until we both climaxed in unison?'

Michael's phone rang on his lap. Zoe looked down at it.

'It's your mammy,' she said and jumped off the bed. She closed the bathroom door behind her. Michael stared at the door.

'Michael?'

He looked down at his phone.

'Michael? Is that you?'

'Mam?' he said, putting the phone to his ear.

'Michael, where are you?' asked Rose. 'Why didn't you call?'

'Sorry, sorry. I'm afraid I had a little too much to drink and got a room in the hotel.'

'You should have called us, Michael. We were very worried.'

'Yes, you're right.'

'Samantha called the hotel, but they wouldn't tell us if you were there or not.'

'I'm sorry.'

'We had to tell the reporters that you weren't here.'

'What reporters?'

'I told them you didn't come home last night, and they all left.'

'Oh, God,' Michael said.

'Should I not have told them?'

'No, it's okay, Mam. Sorry again. I'll call you later.'

'Hold on, your Uncle Jim wants to have a word.'

'Uncle Jim? Why is he there?'

'Hello, Mike,' said Uncle Jim's rough voice.

Michael let out a deep sigh.

'Are you there?' he asked.

'Yes.'

'What's going on? We've been waiting here for over an hour.'

'Waiting? Waiting for what?'

'We thought about giving the ladies a bit of a day out. Give them a treat. Clothes shopping, makeup stuff and things like that. The lads could have a few scoops while we're waiting on them.'

Michael held the phone away from him, as if the weight of it were too heavy to hold in his hand. He could still hear the gruff voice calling his name.

'Mike. What time do you reckon you'll be here at? Mike? Are you there?'

It took him a few seconds before he realised that the phone had been taken from his hand. Zoe ended the call and then turned the phone off.

'What are you doing?' Michael asked her.

'What am I doing? What the fuck are you doing, Mike?' she demanded.

'I was on the phone.'

'Do you owe this guy something?'

'Owe him?'

'Yes, owe him. Do you owe him money?'

'No.'

'Some big favour?'

'No.'

'Did he give you his kidney or a lung or some shit like that?'

'No.'

'Then why don't you tell him to fuck off?'

'I can't.'

'Why not?'

'He's my uncle.'

'He's a fucking bully, Mike.'

Michael lay back down on the bed. He wasn't used to this much confrontation. Especially not this early in the morning. Zoe walked over and sat on the bed beside him.

'Look, Mike. You've spent your whole life trying to please everyone except yourself. Now that you have so much, more people than ever want a piece of it, a piece of you, they'll tear you apart if you let them.'

'But they're my family.'

'So give them a few grand. Let them spend it or waste it or do whatever the fuck they want with it until it's gone.'

'And then what if they want more after that?'

'Then you can tell them to fuck off.'

Michael laughed. 'Okay, I'll do that.'

He looked into her eyes. 'Thank you, Zoe. Any more advice, oh wise one?'

'Yeah,' she said, the smile leaving her face. 'Don't trust anyone.'

'Except those very close to me.'

'No. Especially not them. Cause they're the ones who can really fuck you over.'

A look came into her eyes that he hadn't seen before. He wasn't sure if he should ask her about it, but then it was gone and she stood up.

'Anyway,' she was saying now, opening the curtains to reveal an elevated view of St. Stephen's Green and the surrounding buildings, 'that Uncle Jim of yours was right about one thing.'

'Really?' Michael said.

'Yeah, we should spend the day shopping.'

'Okay, if you want. But can I wait here while you're gone?'

'We're not going to be shopping for me.'

She walked over to him, and with both hands, rearranged his hair. Then she removed his glasses, stood back and looked at him as if contemplating a piece of modern art.

'I think maybe we should start with...'

There was a knock on the door.

'Breakfast,' said Zoe, and she left the bedroom.

As they descended the stairs, Zoe spotted a small group of reporters outside and to the left of the front door of the hotel. They had the appearance of any innocuous group of friends chatting among themselves, but Zoe recognised most of their faces. She told Michael to wait on the last step, and she glanced around the foyer of the hotel.

As one of the porters passed them, Zoe grabbed him by the arm.

'Excuse me,' she said, releasing his arm. 'For the price we're paying for a suite in your hotel, we'd very much appreciate it if a certain amount of privacy could be afforded while we're your guests.'

'Naturally, Madam,' the porter replied.

'So why is there a photographer from that rag paper, The Gazette, sitting in the foyer in anticipation of us leaving?'

The porter looked around the area but failed to rest his eyes on any single guilty individual.

'The cheap suit, brown shoes and ghastly white socks,' said Zoe. 'It's already quite a warm day, so I suspect the raincoat he has on his lap is there for the purpose of concealing a Nikon and Canon rather than the anticipation of morning showers.'

'Yes, Madam,' said the porter, 'I'll deal with it. Please accept our apologies.'

He began to walk towards the man, but Zoe grabbed his arm again.

'Perhaps an alternative exit for us would be more beneficial for the moment.'

'Yes, Madam. Of course,' said the porter, walking towards the restaurant. 'Please come this way.'

When the porter closed the exit door, a fifty euro note having slipped from his hand into his pocket, they found themselves in an ugly dark lane and surrounded by a stark odour of urine, which they could almost taste in their mouths. The lane was so narrow and the two buildings that flanked it so tall, that it was as if they had stepped into a tunnel with daylight on either end.

Various sized and coloured bins stretched its length. Michael thought of making a quip about Zoe entering and now leaving with the rubbish, but she was already ten feet in front and heading for the light.

Unusually for Dublin, it was another sunny day. The sun had shone every day since Michael had won the lottery, literally anyway, if not figuratively for him. The exceptional weather only added to Michael's sense of surrealism over the last few days.

Zoe walked about half a pace in front of him. She, at least, seemed to know where they were headed. He had a flashback to going clothes shopping with his mother when he was a boy, and being dragged against his will from shop to shop.

'Mike.' She had stopped in a doorway, her hand on a large brass door knob. 'In here,' she instructed.

He looked up at the sign above the door.

Newmont & Sons (Savile Row)

She gazed down at him from the top step of the entrance.

'What's wrong?' she asked him.

'Nothing.'

'So why do you have a face on you like you're about to walk into court?'

'That's my normal face.'

'Well then do yourself a favour and change it. Now tell me, what's my budget in here? Some of these suits can get pricey.'

'Well,' said Michael, biting his lip. 'After the Shelbourne yesterday and that room, I think there's still over one hundred and eighty nine million left.'

Zoe smiled at him.

'Okay. Well let's not go too crazy,' and then she turned the doorknob and walked in.

The shop was deceivingly larger on the inside than its modest facade belied. There was a sudden silence as if the clamour of the city was prohibited from entering. At first, it was as if he had stepped into someone's living room. There was an ornate yet unlit fireplace, several dark leather chairs that looked like no one had ever sat in, and hanging on the wall was a large oil painting of a suited man walking by a white sign on a black railing that read 'Savile Row W1'.

He followed Zoe deeper into the well-lit shop. His shoes clopped on the wooden floor, the noise echoing against the walls where different coloured suits hung on either side of the room. He breathed in the musk scented air, and was reminded of a school trip a long time ago to St. Bridget's church on Achill Island.

'Good morning.'

A tall and impeccably dressed woman approached them from the back of the shop, her hand stretched out in front of her as if her arm were being pulled by a rope. She shook Zoe's hand and then took three giant strides to stand in front of Michael. She squeezed Michael's hand so tight that he looked down at her thin bony hand expecting to see metallic robotic fingers squeezing him. He guessed her to be in her early sixties, but for Michael, he could no more guess a woman's age as guess the brand of perfume she was wearing.

'Morning,' Michael replied.

'I'm Jane. Jane Newmont,' she said, her posh English accent blending in well with the room. 'How may I be of service?'

'We're looking for something sharp,' said Zoe. 'Bright, but not too ostentatious. And not too old fashioned either. A contemporary cut.'

'That shouldn't be a problem,' said Jane, pointing to the racks against the wall. 'We have a large selection of...'

'No,' said Zoe. 'Sorry to interrupt, but it has to be tailored.'

'Okay. Again no problem. I'll get you measured up, sir.'

'And we need it by this evening.'

Jane laughed. 'Ah, well, then we do have a problem, I'm afraid. A suit like that would take two to three weeks to produce.'

'We'll pay twice the normal fee,' said Zoe.

'It's not about the money.'

'Three times.'

Jane Newmont was having a quiet month. Such a fee would look well on her books. But in one day? Perhaps if she called Simon. Offered him double pay to come in on his day off. Then start the preliminary cuttings herself.

'It would have to be of a material we had in stock,' Jane Newmont told them, her posh accent having noticeably waned somewhat.

'Fine,' said Zoe.

'Very well. I'll just make a quick call, and then I'll get you measured up.'

Without saying anything else, she marched back down towards the back of the shop.

Zoe stepped closer to Michael. 'Two things to remember for the future,' she said in an almost whisper. 'Most things that people think are impossible suddenly become possible when money is a motivating factor.'

Michael nodded. 'And the second thing?' he asked.

'When someone says, "it's not about the money," then you know for certain that it most definitely is all about the money.'

As Michael was measured, Zoe spent the time on her phone. Michael listened to her as she laughed with one caller but was serious with another. It was as if she were being a different person to each of the people on the other end of the phone. Michael found it a little unsettling to hear her switch her personality, and even her accent, with such ease. The changing character of a chameleon, Michael pondered to himself, and he was so proud of this little alliteration in his head, that it was several moments before he realised he was standing alone in the shop.

He walked outside and saw Zoe standing with her back to him and finishing another call.

'Okay, great. That's that,' she said to him, turning around to face him.

'What's next?' he asked.

She stared up at him, her eyes rising and then resting on the top of his head.

'It's gotta be the hair, Mike. It was always going to be the hair next.'

He reached up and combed his fingers through his hair, as if feeling he were suddenly naked in public.

'What's wrong with it?' he asked.

'The fact that you have to even ask, is the reason why I'm here.'

He flattened his hair down, and put his hands at his side. The people on the street walked around and between them as if they were two boulders in a flowing stream.

'What's this all about, Zoe?'

Her phone beeped, and she looked down at it.

'Zoe,' he said louder.

She looked up at him again.

'Am I some sort of Pygmalion project for you?'

She studied him and then took a step closer to him. 'No. Why? Do you want to be?'

'No,' he said.

'Look, Mike. I'm trying to help you out, that's all. I thought I could point you in the right direction on a couple of things, but if you're not into it, then fine. You can go back to the hotel.'

She closed her phone and put it in her pocket.

'But if I can give you one more piece of advice, though. Wear a hat when you walk by all those photographers later. No kidding. Your hair is a fucking mess.'

She turned and walked back up the street. Michael watched her leave, the crowd concealing her, and he felt as if he'd let his lifeline slip through his fingers. Before he realised what he was doing or had thought of something to say, he was running after her and calling her name.

When he caught up with her and turned to face her, she was smiling.

'There's nothing quite like having a man running after you on a crowded street, calling your name,' she told him.

'Why are you messing with me, Zoe?' he asked her.

'I'm not, Mike.'

'So what is this? Some sort of test?'

'No, I just want you to be a man who doesn't feel the need to run down the street after some offended girl whom he hardly knows.'

'But I need you to...'

'You don't need me, Mike. You don't need anyone.'

They stared at each other for a few moments.

'Well, can you at least take me to the places you were going to today?' he asked her.

'Sure,' she said, 'but on one condition.'

'What?'

'I get to call you Eliza Doolittle.'

He laughed. 'Okay, Professor, it's a deal.'

The hairdresser's salon's owner greeted Zoe with a hug, running his hands through her hair like a chef checking the firmness of his boiling spaghetti.

'You are such a bitch to your hair, Zoe,' he exclaimed.

'I'm not here for myself, Ronan,' she told him, pushing him away and turning him by the shoulders to where Michael stood at the entrance. 'This is Mike.'

Ronan let out an ear piercing shriek that caused the two seated customers in the waiting area to jump.

'Oh my God,' he yelled at Michael and charged towards him. Like a mating gorilla, he began to stroke Michael's hair, squeezing the strands between his fingertips.

As uncomfortable as this was, it was heightened, Michael felt, by the fact that Ronan was a forty-something-year-old, bald and pot-bellied man, and who was dressed more like a builder's labourer than a coiffeur artiste. He tugged downwards on Michael's goatee, causing Michael's mouth to droop open.

Turning to Zoe, he said, 'is he having a laugh, Zoe?'

And then staring into Michael's face and raising his voice slightly, demanded, 'are you having a fucking laugh?'

'Take it easy on him, Ronan,' Zoe said. 'Just do your magic. We've got a busy day ahead and need to be out of here in an hour.'

'An hour?' Ronan shrieked again. 'That's not magic you're asking for, darling. That's a fucking miracle. Look at these split ends. They look like a fisherman's rope that's been gnawed away by someone's teeth.'

Ronan opened and closed his mouth rapidly while making a loud chewing noise.

Michael's head and shoulders stooped like a child being scolded for not doing his homework.

'Go easy,' said Zoe, but couldn't suppress her smile.

'He has a nice face,' Ronan said, while still examining Michael like a museum piece. 'I'll give him that. Okay then. You go fuck off, Zoe, and do whatever it is you do. Come back in an hour. I'll put two of the girls on him straight away, then I'll work on him.'

'You're the best,' said Zoe, walking up to him and kissing him on the cheek.

Ronan ignored her, continuing to stare at Michael.

'Enjoy yourself,' she said to Michael as she walked out of the shop.

'Ignore her,' said Ronan, as two other male hairdressers approached him. 'One things for certain my little goatee-wearing badger - you're not going to enjoy this.'

12

Zoe spent the next hour, while waiting on Michael, in a coffee shop called 'The Family Bean'. It was just off Molesworth Street and, unfortunately for its owner, was also just off the tourists' path.

She had been there before and liked the variation of its clientele. Locals mostly, with the odd intrusion by a cackle of skinny, bearded twenty-five-year-olds dressed in fifty euro t-shirts and who couldn't decide whether the place was either upscale or downtrodden. It was neither, Zoe had decided. Just like her.

She paid the bill for her coffee and made her way back to Ronan's salon. She knew she was a little early but wanted to try and put a little pressure on Ronan to finish.

When she entered the shop she could see Michael sitting in a chair at the far end of the room. He had his back to her with a silk gown draped around him, but he wasn't facing a mirror. She stretched her head sideways to get a better look at him.

'Get her out of here,' Ronan shrieked from across the shop. 'I said an hour.'

A girl behind the counter with the largest and perkiest breasts Zoe had ever seen, shuffled her way to the entrance and using her assets to full advantage, gently pushed Zoe back through the open door and out into street.

Zoe turned and looked into the blue eyes of the girl. She had never regarded her bisexuality as a major part of her life. She was neither ashamed nor proud of the fact. It was a part of her, and it ran through her like the coloured lettering in a stick of rock. Zoe smiled at the receptionist, and she smiled back. A smile that made a connection and an understanding that there was more for them to explore at a later date.

Finding a quiet step, she sat on it and took out her cigarettes. She took long drags and, as often happened in her life, wondered how she managed to find herself in these situations. Then, as always, she dismissed those thoughts as sentimental, and then berated herself for having dwelt on them for even a few moments.

The door to Ronan's opened and she could see a head and two large breasts poke out onto the street. She turned from side to side searching for Zoe. Zoe stood up and the girl raised her arm to beckon her back in.

Michael was standing in the middle of the floor, his back to the entrance and with Ronan to his left. A small team, whom Zoe assumed had also been working on him and whom also wanted her praise, stood around him smiling.

With all the drama which she fully expected, Ronan twisted Michael's shoulders and exclaimed, so the whole salon could hear him, 'ta da.' He stood back from Michael, his arms outstretched and swaying up and down as if revealing the secret prize on a gameshow.

'Well, aren't you impressed?' Ronan asked Zoe, when she didn't jump with joy and squeal with approval.

But she was indeed impressed.

His hair had been cropped but was now a little spiky, and it made his face look longer and thinner. The goatee was gone, exposing a soft yet manly jawline. His hair appeared to be a little darker, perhaps dyed, she guessed but decided not to ask. Zoe thought he didn't look like a little boy anymore who was uncomfortable being a man.

'You don't like it,' Ronan hollered and stormed off, but not quite fast enough so that he couldn't be called back. 'What do you expect from me in an hour? It's not like I can...'

'You're a genius,' Zoe called to him. 'It's perfect. He's perfect.'

Ronan turned back around attempting to hide his delight, 'yes, I know,' he said. 'You hear that everyone? A genius. Now all of you back to work.'

The restaurant that Zoe chose for them to have lunch in was not a restaurant he would have chosen. Of course it wasn't.

Nothing he had experienced in the last couple of days had been anything he would have deliberately chosen.

'A booth, please,' Zoe asked the pretty hostess at the entrance.

'Yes, madam,' she replied and indicated for them to follow her.

'We're in a little bit of a hurry,' Zoe told her when they were seated. 'Would you mind asking someone to take our orders as soon as possible?'

'Of course,' the hostess said, smiling her best practised genuine smile. 'I'll have Cindy bring you menus immediately. Enjoy your meals.'

When they were alone again, Michael looked at Zoe, 'can I ask you something?'

Zoe nodded.

'I understand that you're trying to spruce me up, so it's sort of a question in that vein.'

'Why is your tone so apologetic?'

Michael smiled. 'Well, that's kind of what I wanted to ask you.'

Zoe stared at him but didn't say anything.

'It's a little embarrassing. Well, it's not really embarrassing. It's just that...'

'Hello, my name is Cindy. I'll be your waitress today,' said Cindy, handing them both menus.

Zoe put her menu down on the table. 'We'll both have the monkfish, with a side of potato gratin for him and a mixed salad for me, please. I'll have a gin and tonic with Gordon's, and Mike, what would you like to drink?'

Michael peered over from the top of his menu. Both Zoe and Cindy looked at him.

'Em... A coke, please? A diet coke. With no ice.'

'He'll have a gin and tonic as well,' Zoe told Cindy, who, without having written anything down, nodded and walked away.

'I don't really like fish,' he confessed to Zoe, leaning over the table at her. 'I hate the bones.'

'Have you ever eaten Monkfish with buttered spinach over a bouillabaisse sauce?' she asked him.

He didn't reply.

'Well, then.'

'And what's wrong with me ordering a coke?'

'Because you're not twelve, Mike. We're adults having lunch in a restaurant that doesn't give out free balloons to the kids. But I'm curious. Why did you want your coke with no ice?'

'Because,' he whispered, looking around to see if any of the staff was close by. 'Because they never give you as much coke if they put ice in it. It's a scam.'

Zoe looked across the table at him. 'Please tell me you're taking the piss.'

Michael lowered his gaze and then raising the menu, buried his head behind it. He continued to read the menu for a minute, then realising they had already ordered, placed it back down on the table.

'So what was the embarrassing thing you were going to ask me?' Zoe said.

'It doesn't matter now,' he said.

'What? Are you going to sulk?'

'No,' he said and made a pout that caused Zoe to laugh.

'Maybe,' she told him, 'we should see if they have any colouring pencils for you while we wait for our food.'

'Why are you making fun of me?'

'Because I've never seen a thirty-three-year-old man carry on the way you do. Look, you're a nice guy, Mike, that's obvious, but you've a bit of growing up to do. And fast.'

Michael lowered his stare. They sat in silence for a few moments.

'I'm sorry to give it to you so straight,' she said. 'It's only because you are such a nice guy that I'm saying this to you. There are a lot of beautiful girls out there who will eat you up and spit you out. And if you're not careful, Mike, within a year you'll be back home with your parents with no money and not even a shitty job to go back to.'

Michael looked at her as if trying to understand what she was saying to him.

'Here you go, guys,' Cindy said, placing their two drinks down in front of them. 'Enjoy.'

Zoe picked up her drink and sipped it. Michael did the same. He couldn't help raising his eyebrows in delight at its taste.

'So,' said Michael, a grin forming across his face as he took another mouthful from his glass. 'Where exactly would I find these girls?'

Zoe smiled back at him. 'Don't worry,' she told him. 'They'll find you.'

'And the monkfish for both of you,' Cindy said, laying plates on the table.

Zoe couldn't help noticing Michael stare at the meal in front of him with an expression on his face as if he were a vegan looking down at a mixed grill.

'Enjoy your meals,' Cindy said and walked away.

Michael picked up his fork and poked at the food as if looking for something hidden in it.

'Just try it,' Zoe told him.

He scooped up a morsel with his fork of what he deemed to be the most innocuous looking part on the plate and placed it in his mouth. Like a cow chewing its cud, the food bounced around in his mouth, his eyebrows furrowed in expectation of rejection. He swallowed.

'Not bad,' he volunteered.

'Try the fish,' Zoe encouraged him.

Feeling slightly more courageous, he ate a few more fragments before picking up his knife and putting whole forkfuls into his mouth.

'Now tell me,' Zoe asked him. 'What's the embarrassing question you were going to ask me?'

'It's okay. It doesn't really matter now,' he said.

'Why? Had it something to do with S-E-X?'

'No, no. Nothing like that,' he protested. 'It was just about the way you... Well... The way you...'

'The way I what?'

'The way you... I don't know how to put it... The way you talk to people.'

'The way I talk to people?'

'No, it's not just talk to them. It's the way you treat them. And it's the way they treat you.'

'What the fuck are you talking about, Mike?'

'It doesn't matter,' Michael said and put his focus back on his monkfish.

'Well, obviously it does matter. Am I supposed to be offended or something?'

'No, no, not at all. It's just. Well, that porter this morning. And then the tailor and the hairdresser and now the hostess and the waitress here.'

'And?'

'You talk to them as if you're above them. Not in a demeaning way or anything. It's as if everyone you talk to is your employee and when you ask them to do something, you just assume they will. And then they do.'

'But I'm paying them. At least you are anyway.'

'No, it's more than that. It's your confidence, I suppose. And the way you treat people.'

'And you'd like me to stop it?' Zoe asked him.

'No, no. I want you to show me how to be like that.'

Zoe put down her knife and fork. 'I'm sorry, Mike. I can fix your hair and your clothes, but I can't teach you to be something you're not. It's taken you thirty-three years to become the person you are, but not even Ronan the hairdresser or Mrs Tailor can change your personality.'

Michael lowered his head and played with his food a little.

Zoe sighed. 'Look, I'll point you in the right direction, okay?'

Michael looked up at her. 'What do you mean?'

'You just need to get out of your comfort zone a little, Mike. That's the only way anyone can change anything about themselves. Stepping outside what you consider to be normal. Pushing yourself a bit. Experiencing discomfort. At least that's the only way I know where any real growth can happen.'

Michael sat up in his chair. 'Okay, I'm listening.'

'That's it,' Zoe said and began eating her food again.

'That's it?'

Zoe, her mouth full, nodded at him.

'But I can do that. I think. I mean, it doesn't sound that hard.'

Zoe swallowed her food and took a sip from her gin and tonic. 'Our waitress is making her way over to us to ask how our meal is. Tell her it's fine, but you'd like a ten percent discount.'

'What?'

'Say, "Cindy, may I have ten percent off the bill, please?"'

'I can't say that.'

'Why not? What's the worst thing that could happen?'

'It's not that. It's just...'

'... Something you wouldn't consider to be normal?' Zoe interrupted him.

'No, of course not. But that's not...'

'How are we doing, guys?' Cindy interrupted him.

'It's excellent,' Zoe said, smiling. 'Mike? How's it for you?'

131

Michael stared up at Cindy like a school boy at his desk caught without his homework.

'Mike?' she asked again.

'Fine,' he said. Zoe raised her eyebrows at him.

'Great,' Cindy said and turned to leave.

'Excuse me,' Michael blurted out.

Cindy turned back to him. 'Yes?'

'Em, could I get ten... ten...,' he mumbled.

Cindy looked down at him. 'Ten?'

'Ten per... per...'

'Temper?'

'No, could I get ten...' Michael searched about the table as if the words he was looking for were there. He rubbed his hand across his forehead. His eyes fell on his gin and tonic. 'Could I... could I get another drink, please?'

Cindy looked at his full glass of gin and tonic, then looked at him. 'Sure,' she said and walked away.

Michael sat in his chair with his head bowed. His chest raced in and out as if he'd sprinted up and down the restaurant. Zoe couldn't help but smile at his distress.

Michael reached out his hand to pick up his drink, but then pulled it back when Cindy appeared at the table. She placed the second gin and tonic down beside the first one, and then left without saying anything.

Michael looked at the two identical drinks, side by side. He then looked across at Zoe, who had resumed eating her meal, smiling at him as she chewed.

13

Tears streamed down Michael's face. His eyes were red and puffed up. He used the white tissue he was handed to wipe his face. Zoe watched him from across the room, and Michael caught her gaze in the large mirror in front of him.

'I told you,' he blinked at her. 'I can't wear contact lenses.'

The optometrist washed her hands in the sink, as Michael turned back to the mirror and continued to blink at himself.

He sniffed again. 'Why can't I just get glasses? Some designer glasses even.'

'Because,' Zoe told him, stating the obvious, 'all glasses make people look either like geeks or weak.'

The optometrist, who made her living from selling glasses, and who also happened to be wearing a pair, stopped washing her hands and then turned off the taps.

'But lots of famous people wear glasses and they still look cool,' Michael pleaded with Zoe. 'Rodney Downey Jr. wears glasses and he's Ironman. Bono wears glasses and he's... Bono.'

'First of all it's Robert, not Rodney. And secondly, they look cool because they also happen to be Robert Downey Jr. and Bono. Brad Pitt could get a tattoo of a spider on his neck, and it'd look like the coolest fucking thing in the world. Because he's Brad Pitt. They look good in glasses because of who they are. Not because of the glasses. You are neither Rodney Downey Jr., or Bono or fucking Batman. You're Michael Irvine. And if you ever want a girl to sleep with you again then you can't wear glasses.'

Michael blinked at his reflection again. 'But they hurt,' he said, wiping the tears away with the white tissue.

'I don't care,' Zoe said, standing up. 'Clean up and I'll meet you outside. I need a cigarette.'

From across the street, Zoe watched Michael leaving the optician's. He shaded his eyes with his hand and blinked up and down in search of her. She couldn't help but smile at him. Putting out her cigarette, she crossed the road.

'Here,' she said handing him her sunglasses.

They were oval-shaped, with gold trimmings and covered most of his face.

'Thanks,' he said, and swivelled his head up and down, observing the world through his new contact lenses. The gold on the glasses glistened in the sun. Zoe smiled again at him, and when he turned to face her, he asked, 'what's so funny?'

'You are,' she told him.

'Thanks very much,'

'No, I mean that in a nice way.'

They stood looking at each other for a moment.

'The money's going to change you a lot over the next few months,' she told him. 'But try not to let it change you too much, Michael Irvine.'

He took off the sunglasses. 'They're not as sore now,' he said, handing them back to her. 'So, what's next?'

'Clothes maketh the man, they say.'

'But I already have a suit,' he protested.

'You can't wear the same fucking suit every day, Mike.'

'Okay,' he sighed. 'Let's go.'

The second floor of the men's department in Brown Thomas smelt of leather and wool. It was the time of day when the day shoppers had returned to their homes, and the evening shoppers had yet to leave theirs. The sales assistants too, expecting the lull, chatted among themselves and rearranged already perfectly displayed clothes.

Zoe was quick, however, to commandeer the services of one of them, a smartly-dressed but too thin twenty-year-old named Gary, who became Michael's personal shopping assistant for the next hour.

'Casual but very smart, is your remit,' she told him as she settled into a comfortable looking armchair opposite the changing rooms. 'We need at least five outfits.'

Both Michael and Gary stared at her, and then at each other. Gary looked Michael up and down.

'Okay,' he said, thinking out loud. 'Let's start with Ralph Lauren.'

Zoe checked her emails and messages, and replied to some, as a different Michael was presented to her every ten minutes for her approval. This she mostly gave, only criticising anything 'too nautical' or because 'he's not a seventy-year-old golfer' or once asking 'are you dressing him for a funeral?'

Once, when she was particularly rude to the sales assistant, (enquiring if part of the interview process for him working there had ever involved a test for colour blindness), she gave Michael a wink, and he bit back a laugh.

Three outfits and several thousand euro later, she stood up and told the sales assistant to send everything to their suite in the Shelbourne.

'I'll meet you upstairs,' she told Michael and wandered off.

Michael went into the dressing room, and seeing himself in the mirror, decided to leave the last shirt and trousers on.

He had stopped checking the price tags after he tried on a pair of Church's brogues and told the sales assistant that they were perhaps the most comfortable formal shoes he had ever worn and that really €80 wasn't that bad a price. When the sales assistant pointed out to him that he was missing a zero, Michael took off the shoes and promised himself only to wear them on a carpeted floor.

Ten minutes later, while making his way to meet Zoe, Michael found himself for the second time passing the same row of ladies' black and brown leather boots, and he forced himself to admit that he was lost. He decided to try the stairs instead of the elevator.

It was on the third step, when he had a higher view of the shop floor, that he saw her. At first he stopped. Then he bent down and hid behind the stairs banister. Why he was hiding he didn't know, but he felt as if he were witnessing a private moment not meant for anyone's eyes.

Zoe was coming out of a changing room. From that distance

and with a banister obstructing his view, he watched her find a mirror and perform almost a twirl in front of it. She had her back to him and was wearing a red dress that clung to her figure like the skin of an apple.

A passing sales assistant stopped and she seemed to be complimenting Zoe on her choice. Zoe turned from side to side in front of the mirror and the sales assistant pulled down on the hem of the dress before stepping back to admire it again. Then she said something that Michael couldn't hear and Zoe let out a loud laugh.

It was the first time Michael had heard her really laugh. He noticed that he too was smiling looking at her. He also noticed, much to his surprise, he felt something for her that bordered on affection. He cared for her. He wasn't quite sure when it had happened, but he saw a vulnerability in her that he was sure no one else saw. He wanted to protect her.

But the very thought of her needing his protection or even of her being vulnerable in any way was laughable. He shrugged off the idea as he watched Zoe hold out the price tag to the sales assistant. She said something and the sales assistant laughed as well.

Michael imagined him saying something to her, and Zoe laughing like that with him. He felt a sliver of pleasure run down his spine at the thought, and again, it caught him off-guard.

When he looked up again she was gone. He stood up and raced up the flight of stairs.

After visiting the perfume counters twice and rushing through the lingerie department, Michael saw the brightness from the glass doors and sighed with relief. Zoe was already there, and she shot him an impatient look.

'Sorry,' he mumbled to her. 'Got lost.'

She walked on ahead of him.

'Where to now?' he asked her.

'That's all for today, folks.'

'Really?'

'Yes, really. I've got some work to catch up on this evening.'

'But I thought…' Michael started, but then realised he wasn't sure what he thought. How exactly had he seen this day ending? And why did he feel so sombre at the thought of not being in her company?

He looked up at her and saw she was already a few feet ahead of him, her fingers and eyes passing over her phone's screen. He looked around at the people going by, making quick and busy strides in each direction. Zoe walked on and the further she walked ahead, the more vulnerable and alone he felt.

'Wait,' he called out to her, aware of the tone of desperation that betrayed him. 'Zoe. Zoe.'

She stopped and turned around.

To his left was a coffee shop and he ran inside. Zoe shook her head and checked the time on her phone. She wanted to get back to the hotel. She had two or three emails which she'd rather answer using her laptop.

One of the emails was from a source in a boutique hotel on Leeson Street who wanted to talk about payment before divulging the names of the couple who stayed at his hotel last night. But he had promised her it would be a big 'scoop'. She had laughed to herself at that one. 'Scoop'. Did he think he was in some sort of noir detective fiction novel?

Jesus, where the hell is Mike gone?

She looked down at her phone and when she looked up again, Michael was scampering towards her, balancing a plastic coffee cup in each hand and with a gratifying smile across his face. She wasn't sure why, but the image of a proud dog running to her with a bone in his mouth popped into her head.

'We don't have time for coffee, Mike,' she told him, as he shoved the cup to her.

'Taste it,' he told her.

'I don't want any coffee.'

'Just taste it.'

'But I don't want…'

'Taste it,' he shouted at her. Some of the passing crowds looked at him, but he didn't care.

She sighed and lifted the cup to her lips.

'Well?' he asked her while the cup was still at her mouth.

She swallowed it. 'Well what?'

'Notice anything?'

'You didn't put any sugar in it.'

'And?'

'I don't know. It's a little too hot to be honest. Look, Mike, I really just want to…'

'Are you sure it doesn't taste ten percent better?'

'What?'

'Ten percent. I did it.'

'You did what?'

'After I'd ordered the coffee, she says to me, the girl at the till, she says, "that'll be €4.80, please." So I say, "can I have ten percent off." And she just looks at me.'

'And?' Zoe said, smiling now at his enthusiasm and happiness, as if he'd just passed his driving test.

'And she says, "Okay,".'

'That's it?'

'That's it,' Mike confirmed. 'I mean, I pay her the money and I just walk out. I feel like… I don't know… I feel like…'

'Like you just won the lottery?' Zoe suggested.

'Yeah. I guess I do.'

'You're one crazy bastard,' Zoe told him. She stared at him for a few moments and the image of the dog came back into her head, only this time she saw the dog's innocence at pleasing its master. And his loyalty. She shivered at the thought.

'Tell you what?' she told him. 'How about we go for a celebratory dinner this evening.'

'Great, yeah.'

'Give you a chance to try out some of those new glad rags of yours.'

'Brilliant,' Michael said.

'Only on one condition,' Zoe said, as they both started to walk back to the hotel side-by-side. 'I'm paying for dinner.'

After Michael showered, he spent a little time attempting to style his hair the way the hairdresser had. Using the complementary tiny tube of hair gel and the miniature can of hairspray, he manipulated and cajoled his hair to the best of his ability. He felt a little strange spending so much time in front of a mirror, but he enjoyed it, and there was no one there anyway.

As soon as they had returned to the hotel, Michael had insisted on Zoe getting her own room, and luckily there was another suite available two doors away from his.

He came out of the bathroom and put the hotel's white bathrobe on. He felt its weight pushing down on his shoulders. The room had a large television and he would have been quite happy to lie on the bed and flick from channel to channel all night eating the macadamia nuts from the mini-bar, but he felt a need to impress Zoe. He wanted to make her smile and to hear her compliment him again.

The varied coloured miniature bottles clinked and glistened when he opened the mini-bar's door. He took a minute to study them, and then feeling brave, took out the dark Baileys bottle.

He found a wine glass and poured the bottle's full contents into it. He sniffed its contents and caught his reflection in the full length mirror. He adjusted his hair again with his right hand and then watched his reflection as he took a sip from his glass. Its taste surprised him. He had seen his mother drinking it, but he had never tried it. He took a fuller mouthful this time and savoured its milky texture.

Smacking his lips, he sat up on the bed and then lay back on the propped up pillows. He crossed his feet and rested the glass on his chest. He then only had to bend his neck slightly and tip the glass towards him to be able to sip on the Baileys. He began to wonder how the coming night was going to play out. He still wasn't sure exactly what had happened last night. He had wanted to ask Zoe all day but was afraid of her laughing at him.

Could they possibly end up together tonight? On this very bed? He stretched out his arm across the bed and imagined her lying beside him. Them kissing. Her hands reaching out to him. Her fingers undoing his bathrobe…

A rapid fire of knocks on his door caused him to jump so quickly that he forgot he was holding the glass. It leapt in the air spilling its remaining contents all over his bathrobe. The glass bounced out of his hand, onto the bed and then fell on the floor before coming to rest when it rolled into the mirror.

He jumped down off his bed and picked up the glass. Then another series of knocks.

'Coming,' he yelled, and went to the door. He fumbled with the lock while he tried to rub out some of the Baileys stain on his robe.

'Sorry,' he said opening the door.

Two porters stood in the hall surrounded by bags and boxes. One of them was so tall and the other so small that Michael thought they looked like the start of a comedy act.

'Sorry, I was just…' Michael said, pointing vaguely behind him, but the porters stood staring at him.

'A delivery for you, sir,' the tall one said.

'Oh, God, yes,' Michael told them. 'Of course, my clothes. Sorry, I forgot,' and he stood back to let them enter the room.

When all the bags were inside, Michael and the porters stood in a semi-circle and stared down at them.

'I'd no idea there were so many,' Michael said.

'Will that be everything, sir,' the tall porter said.

'Yes, thanks,' said Michael without looking up.

The two porters looked at one another. 'Well, then,' said the short one. 'We'll be heading off so.'

'Okay, then,' said the tall one a little louder this time.

Then they both nodded at one another and walked to the door.

'Oh, wait. Sorry,' Michael called after them.

They both smiled. 'Thank you, sir,' said the tall one, 'that's really not necessary…'

'Can you bring this to room number 403, please?' Michael asked, handing one of the bags to the short porter. 'It's just down the hall.'

'Yes, of course,' he said. 'No problem at all. Would you like us to open up all your bags for you as well? Help you put them away?'

'What? No, no,' said Michael. 'Thanks for the offer though.'

The tall porter pulled at his colleague's jacket's sleeve as Michael turned his attention back to the bags, which were now taking up a lot of the space in his room.

The doors of the lift made a loud PING as they opened in front of Michael. At the foyer desk, he saw one of the porters with a very tall and very thin man who reminded Michael of a character from an F. Scott Fitzgerald novel. Both men raised their heads and looked over at him.

Michael, for his part, had, for the briefest of moments, the sudden inclination to tap repeatedly on the floor buttons inside the lift. Instead, he embraced the 'new him' and stepped confidently into the foyer.

The tall man, who had been talking to the porter, began to make his way over to Michael, his long strides stretching like an insect's legs in front of him. Michael could see he was carrying a large black box under his arm, which he now placed in both of his hands.

'Michael Irvine?' he asked.

'Yes.'

'My name is Charles Poole. I represent the American Express Centurion Card here in Ireland.'

'Okay,' Michael said slowly, as if that was supposed to mean something to him.

'Do you know, Mr. Irvine, what the American Express Centurion Card is?'

Michael looked up at the man in front of him and then looked down at the shiny black box.

'No.'

Charles Poole paused for a moment and stared down at Michael. Not long enough that it became uncomfortable, but long enough for Michael to sense a slight disdain in his look.

'It is the most sought after, invitation-only, credit card in the world. It has a myriad of benefits for its holder, including but not limited to, first-class flight upgrades, car hire platinum services, access to all Priority Pass lounges around the world and privileges at leading hotels in all major cities.'

Another pause.

Charles Poole opened the box and pulled out a folder. It was also black.

'I have a sneaking suspicion that the card is going to be black,' Michael joked.

Charles Poole stared at him for a moment and then opened the folder.

He held it out for Michael to examine. Nestled in the middle of the black foam was a glossy black card. Michael raised his eyes up at Charles Poole, who gave a curt nod as if giving permission to take it out.

Despite himself, Michael couldn't help but be impressed with the rectangular piece of metal in his hand.

'It's made of titanium,' Charles Poole said, as if answering a question.

As Michael held the card, Charles Poole snapped shut the folder, removed an envelope from the inside pocket of his jacket and slid out a piece of paper folded in three. He unfolded the single page, and then, what appeared to Michael as a magic trick, a pen popped into his hand.

'Sign here, please,' Charles Poole ordered.

Michael hesitated, the card still in his hand.

'You'll never have to carry cash again. The card has no preset limit. Indeed, the card was recently used to purchase Amedeo Modigliani's painting of Nu couché at Christie's auction house.'

Michael shrugged apologetically.

'It cost $170 million,' Charles Poole told him.

Michael signed his name as if it were an inevitability. As soon as he had completed his name, the page and the pen were plucked from his hands, folded, and then disappeared inside Charles Poole's jacket again. Another curt nod, and he turned on his heel, the long strides moving quickly away from him.

Michael went into the bar and ordered himself a coke. He sat and looked at the black card as he twisted in his hand. No matter what happened tonight, he had decided, he was going to stay sober.

He was dressed in his tailored suit, although when he walked into the bar, he had expected everyone to turn and look at him. Not in an admiring way, rather as if they had noticed an imposter, and the clothes he wore were stolen.

He did notice, however, that the porter had held the door for him, whereas he hadn't last night. Also, Phil the barman had come straight over to him, when normally he would have to jostle for his attention.

Michael caught his own reflection in the mirror behind the bar and for a moment didn't recognise the figure staring back at him. He pulled the chair out a little and straightened his posture. Continuing to watch himself, he took a sip from his coke, then realising that Zoe would berate him for not having a 'proper drink', he raised his hand at the barman.

The barman, again, came down to him straight away and Michael ordered his drink.

'Tell me something,' Michael asked Phil as he poured. 'Is there really no difference in the amount you get whether there's ice in it or not?'

When Phil didn't reply, Michael looked up at him. He was holding the bottle mid-pour and his head was turned away and looking somewhere else. As Michael turned in his seat, he saw that the man seated next to him was also staring in that direction.

Michael followed their gaze and saw Zoe standing in the doorway. The image he saw, he was quite sure, was one he would always remember. Even as an old man.

She stood there, her eyes searching the room for him. The

doorman held the door for her, his eyes surveying the contours of her back. The red dress looked even more dazzling than it had done earlier. It was as if a spot light were shining on her.

She spotted him and waved over. Half the faces that were looking at her, now turned and looked at him. She took her time walking across the room to him, as if unaware the room had fallen silent as she walked.

Michael stepped down off his stool and pulled out the chair beside him. She approached him smiling and pressed into him, kissing him fully on the mouth. It was several moments before Michael realised she was sitting down and he was still standing up beside her.

Like a busy city centre's traffic that had paused to allow a wailing ambulance to pass through, so too did the room return to its din of murmuring and conversations.

'How did you know?' Zoe asked him when he was seated beside her.

'Know what?'

'The dress, of course.'

'Oh, I saw you trying it on.'

'You mean you were spying on me?' she asked.

'No, no. Nothing like that. I was only...'

'Relax, Mike. I'm only kidding you. I'm sure it was all perfectly innocent.'

'It was just to say thanks for today,' he said.

'A €2,480 dress is some way to say "thank you", but thank you anyway. It was very sweet of you.'

They had decided to eat in the restaurant in the hotel. Although they didn't admit it, neither of them felt like venturing back out onto the streets.

'Are you going to order for me again?' Michael asked Zoe when they were seated.

'No,' Zoe said. 'As long as you don't order the soup to start and the steak as your main.'

'But I like soup.'

'Only because you haven't tried any of the other dishes on the menu. Try to broaden your horizons, Mike. The saying is that variety is the spice of life. Not soup. In fact, I've never heard them mentioning anything about soup.'

'I never had you down, Zoe, for someone who ever listened to what "they" had to say.'

Zoe laughed. 'No, that's true. I'll give you that. But I know enough to know that a man standing in any non-gay bar in Ireland shouldn't be sipping on a glass of Baileys.'

'Well, then they should try it. It's a deliciously decadent beverage.'

Zoe laughed again and Michael smiled at the pleasure it gave him.

'At least,' she continued, 'you didn't ask for it without ice.'

'Now that you mention it, I did feel that the measure was a bit small.'

Michael's phone beeped in his pocket, and he slid it out and glanced at the screen.

'Sorry,' he said.' 'It's Sam, my sister. Again.'

'Everything okay?'

'Yeah, it's fine. My parents are just worried, that's all.'

'Why?'

'Cause I haven't been around.'

'You're thirty-three years old, Mike. It's time for them to cut the umbilical cord.'

Michael stiffened in his chair. 'It's not their fault,' he said, with more force than he'd intended. 'They've always been good to me. I'm not like you, Zoe.'

'Okay, Mike, okay. Calm down. I didn't mean anything by it.'

'I'm sorry,' Michael said. 'I just want to do what's right for them. Now with all the money and everything... it's just... I don't know...'

'What's wrong?'

Michael signed and relaxed in his chair again. 'It's my uncle. Well, it's not just him. It's other family as well. Sam says they've been hanging around the house all day, eating biscuits and ordering chicken curries and tikka masala. My dad's locked himself in his bedroom and is watching the portable telly. Mam's been running around the house making tea like Mrs fucking Doyle.'

Zoe put her hand to her mouth to hold back the laughter.

'I'm sorry,' she said. 'It's just I've never heard you swear before.'

'Sorry,' Michael said.

'No, it suits you. You should try it more often.'

A tall blonde waitress appeared at their table. They both strained their necks to look up at her.

'Are you ready to order, guys?' she asked.

Michael looked at his menu for the first time.

'Could you give us a few more minutes, please?' Zoe asked her.

'Sure, no problem,' she said and as silently as she had arrived, she disappeared. Michael studied his menu.

'Actually, the soup looks good,' he said.

'Put down your menu for a second, Mike.'

'But it's a French onion soup.'

'Forget the soup. I want to talk to you about tomorrow.'

Michael noticed Zoe's change in tone, and he closed the menu.

'Tomorrow?' he asked, happy there was going to even be a tomorrow with her.

'Call your sister and tell her to get all of your family members to meet at one o'clock in your house.'

'But that's a bit short notice.'

'Trust me. They'll come.'

'What'll I tell her it's for?'

'You don't.'

'And what is it for?'

Zoe closed her own menu and placed it on the table.

'By tomorrow, Mike,' she told him, 'I promise your parents will have their house back.'

14

'I'm afraid the manager isn't available at the moment,' the bank clerk said.

'How do you know he isn't available if you haven't even checked? Sheryl,' Zoe asked, pronouncing the name on her badge as if there were suspicions surrounding the authenticity of her true identity.

As Zoe had spotted two paparazzi photographers outside the hotel earlier that morning, a valet porter had driven Michael's car to the back door. They had barely spoken for the thirty minutes' drive to Michael's local bank. Zoe had tapped on her phone for the entire journey, and Michael had bitten on his nails and thought about the day ahead.

They now stood in front of a one-inch thick glass screen as Sheryl and Zoe stared at each other like two prizefighters at a press conference before a fight.

'Because you need an appointment to see him. Do you have an appointment?' Sheryl asked.

'No, we don't,' Zoe told her.

'Well then,' Sheryl said and looking over Zoe's shoulder called, 'next, please.'

The next person in line, a man in a suit, took one step forward, but when Zoe turned and looked at him, he took two steps back.

'We need to see the manager,' Zoe tried again.

Sheryl leaned her face closer to the glass, 'and I said he isn't available. Now please move away from the counter.'

Michael wanted to say something, but the short time he had known Zoe was enough to know that it really wasn't a good idea to interrupt her. Zoe leaned into the glass.

'Did you ever hear the joke, Sheryl, about the guy who goes into a bank and says to the bank clerk, "I want to open a fucking account." The bank clerk says, "You can't talk to me like that." And the guy says again, "I want to open up a fucking account." So the clerk goes off and gets the manager. The manager says to him, "what seems to be the problem?" "Look, it's simple," the guy explains, "I've just won one hundred and ninety million euro, and I want to open up a fucking account here." And the manager says, "Certainly, sir. And is this bitch giving you a hard time?"'

Sheryl stared out through the glass at Zoe, uncomprehending.

'You see, Sheryl,' Zoe said, pointing to Michael. 'In that story, he is the one who has won the EuroMillions, the bank manager is the manager whom you refuse to get, and the bitch of a bank clerk is... well, I'm sure you can figure out the rest.'

Sheryl looked over at Michael, who attempted a smile for her. She then looked one more time at Zoe before sliding off her chair and walking towards the offices.

There was nowhere to park outside his parents' house, so Michael had to drive two blocks away and walk back. The family members' cars were parked in every available free space on the road. Zoe said something about it showing their selfishness, but Michael's thoughts were on the meeting ahead.

'He's here,' he heard a voice call out before he had even opened the front door. He reached up to ring the doorbell before realising that technically this still was his home. As he began to search for the key in his pocket, the door opened.

'Mike, where in God's name have you been? Mam has been so worried. She... what happened to your face? And your hair? And your clothes?' Samantha asked then without waiting for a reply, stepped out and gave him a welcoming hug.

Releasing him, she turned and took in the woman standing next to him.

'Zoe, this is Sam my sister,' Michael said. 'And Sam, this is Zoe, my…'

'…friend,' Zoe filled in when Michael hesitated to search for a word.

Zoe stretched out her hand and Samantha shook it without saying anything.

'Well, you'd better both come in so,' Sam said. 'There's barely enough room to breathe in here with this lot. I hope you know what you're doing, Mike.'

Michael didn't reply, and they followed her into the house. The hall was filled with several people chatting loudly and drinking tea. There were even some people sitting on the steps of the stairs. They glanced up and nudged each other as he passed and then returned to their talking and their tea.

He spotted the back of his mother's head in the kitchen, the steam from a boiling kettle surrounding her. He manoeuvred his way towards her but was blocked at the entrance by a large stomach. His eyes gazed upwards to a flat chest and then a wide neck to where a balding head was perched.

'Ah, Michael,' it said, just before popping a whole Jacob's coconut cream into his mouth, the crumbs falling like snow and gathering on the summit of his protruding stomach. 'What's all this about then?'

But before Michael could reply he was shoved from behind by Zoe and forced into the kitchen.

'Hi Mam,' Michael said.

Rose turned around at the sound of his voice, a smile already on her face. She hugged him, then looked up at his face.

'You look good,' she told him. 'I never liked that little beard. Now, will you have a cup of tea?'

Michael was glad she never asked him where he had been or what this meeting was about.

'Thanks, mam. Let me introduce you to a friend of…'

'Mike,' a loud voice called out. 'What's going on? We're all waiting for you. What's this all about?'

'Hello, Uncle Jim,' Mike said, turning to face him.

'Go back inside, sir and take a seat,' Zoe told him.

'What? Who the fuck are you?' said Uncle Jim.

'It's okay, Uncle Jim. We'll all be inside in a minute.'

'It's not her house to be telling me what to fucking do.'

'It's not your house either. Now please go back inside,' Michael told him, and there was a moment's silence in the kitchen as they all stared at Uncle Jim.

'Fuck sake. We're out of tea, Rose,' Uncle Jim spluttered before turning around and walking back into the sitting room.

'Sorry about that, mam,' Michael told his mother.

'Come on, Mike. Let's get started,' Zoe said.

'Where's dad?' Michael asked Sam.

'The same place he's been for the last three days. In his room,' Sam told him.

'Can you go get him, please, Sam?' Michael asked. 'Come on into the sitting room, mam.'

'I'll just make another pot of tea first.'

'No. No more tea. Let's go.'

The conversation fell as quickly as the tension rose when Michael walked into the sitting room. He turned to Zoe, and they looked at each other. There was nothing else for her to say. He had practised his short speech a hundred times out loud and in his head a hundred times more.

He pushed his way through the crowd and stood in front of the hearth. As he was about to start, he saw his father's head crane around the door frame for a better view. Michael smiled and nodded at him and he returned both.

'Thank you all very much for coming here today at such short notice,' he began. 'I'll get straight to the reason for us being here. Ever since I've won all that money on Sunday, there's been a bit of a party atmosphere, and it's been great to see you all and to catch up. Especially with some relatives I haven't seen in years.'

Although not intentional, there was some uncomfortable feet shifting in the room.

'But what I'd really like now is to try and get back to as normal a life as possible. It's great that you've all helped me to celebrate my win, but I think it's time for all of our lives to return to where they were last week. I know mam and dad have loved having you visit, but I think you'll all agree it's time for them to have their house back.'

'I'd like to show my appreciation to you all by sharing my win with you. I'm also going to give a certain amount to various charities. Having said that, I can't keep writing cheques or picking up bills forever, no matter how much I'd like to. So this is a once-off payment. It's not like I won the EuroMillions.'

Here Michael paused and chuckled. In his head he had imagined everyone laughing at his joke but when all nonplussed faces peered back at him, he continued on.

'I went to the bank this morning and they kindly gave me some cheques. The cheques are all written to cash, so be careful not to lose them. They're for different amounts, and in order to be fair, I've given the aunts and uncles a bit more than the cousins or neighbours.'

Uncle Jim, who had been sitting in Michael's father's chair for the last few days, was seen to rub his hands together, and some cousins at the back of the room murmured to each other. Liam, from next door, squeezed his wife's hand and she smiled up at him. It hadn't been Michael's intention to build excitement in the room, and now that he's noticed it, he wanted to finish up as soon as possible.

'I hope you will use the money wisely and buy yourselves a few things you've always wanted, but I must stress again that this is a once-off. There's not enough to keep writing cheques all the time. Is that understood?'

Zoe had insisted he said this line and had told him to wait for acknowledgment from everyone. Only when a couple of people had said, 'okay,' and others had nodded, did Michael continue.

'Zoe has a list of names and cheques with her, which she'll hand out in the kitchen. If there's anyone not here, or someone I've forgotten, you can let me know later.'

All eyes looked at Zoe, and Zoe nodded confidently back at them, unsmiling.

'So that's it. Again thanks for coming and I hope…'

Michael's voice was drowned out by the noise of people standing up, chatting and shuffling their way towards the kitchen.

'What are you going to do with yourself now, Michael?' a voice asked.

It came from his Auntie Lily who was sitting on a kitchen chair by the window. She was a widow and lived alone in one of the cottages in the village. She always had a smile to share, and Michael remembered her slipping one pound notes into his hand when he was a boy. For that reason her cheque was the largest of them all.

Everyone stopped for a moment and looked back at Michael.

'Well, Auntie Lily, I'm not really sure to be honest. I really just don't know.'

There was another moment of silence, but when it was obvious that Michael had nothing further to add, they continued on their way into the kitchen.

The murmuring and whispering was now a crescendo of excited chatter as each person was handed an envelope with their name on it. Some compared the amount on the cheque with the person beside them. Others shoved the cheques straight into their pocket.

'That's very generous of you, son,' his mam said.

'I just want to try and get things back to as normal as possible,' Michael told her.

'Who's the girl?' Samantha asked him.

'She's a journalist. She's really nice.'

'Is she the one responsible for your makeover?' Samantha asked.

'Yes. What do you think? Too much?'

'No, not too much. Might take me a while to get used to, but you look well.'

'Thanks, Sam. How are the girls?'

'They're fine. Katie was asking me when were you going to…'

'I just noticed there, Mike,' Uncle Jim said, barging his way in front of Samantha, 'that Lily's cheque was a good bit bigger than the rest of ours. What's the story with that?'

Jim's wife stood behind him as did a few others, hoping to exploit the situation if Jim got an increase.

'It's not really fair, is it?' he said.

Zoe heard what had been said, and she too looked up at Michael from the kitchen. Michael just stared at Jim, and for a moment, it looked as if Michael was not going to say anything at all. Only his clenched fist gave any indication he had even heard what his uncle had said.

'I'm sorry, Uncle Jim. You're right. It's not fair,' he said.

Uncle Jim smiled and turned to his wife who smiled back at him.

'It's not fair,' Michael continued, 'just because I won some money that I have to give it away to the likes of you just so you'll leave me and my mam and dad alone. It's not fair you get a cheque for €50,000 for doing nothing and still complain that it's not enough. It's also not fair you bullied your way into the house because you think you're entitled to something that isn't yours.'

Michael's breathing became heavy, and he took a step towards

Uncle Jim, who in turn took a step back.

'It's okay, Michael,' Samantha said, putting her hand on his arm.

He turned to her.

'It's okay,' she repeated.

Michael let out a deep breath then looked back at Uncle Jim. 'If you don't want it, then give it back to me,' he told him and put out his hand.

The cheque that Uncle Jim had been holding in his hand was taken out of Michael's reach. 'Ah, now, Mike. There's no need to be like that,' he said and produced the best laugh he could manage. 'We were only saying. Weren't we, love?'

'Course we were,' said Aunt June, taking Michael's hand in both of hers and shaking it. 'You've been very generous, Michael. No doubt about that.'

'In fact,' Uncle Jim said, 'why don't we all go for a few pints in Harry's? A couple of quiet ones just to show our appreciation.'

'We'll even all buy our own drinks, won't we?' Aunt June said.

'Will we?' replied Uncle Jim.

'Yes, we will,' she told him, looking straight into her husband's eyes.

'Ah, of course we will,' said Uncle Jim. 'Sure we'll only have one or two.'

'No thanks,' Michael said.

'Ah, come on,' said Uncle Jim.

'Come on, Mike,' said one of the cousins.

'Yeah, Mike. That's a great idea,' said someone else.

Michael looked at his mam and his sister, then over at Zoe, who shrugged at him.

'Okay,' he said, and everyone either cheered or clapped.

'Order us a few taxis, Mike, will you?' said Uncle Jim.

'What?' Michael said, the anger returning to his face.

'I'm only joking you,' said Uncle Jim, laughing and slapping him on the back, as Michael reddened slightly.

Like a smoker who takes his first cigarette after having managed to quit for a few days, Michael felt a rush when he saw Lauren behind the bar.

'Wow, Michael. You look so different,' she told him when he walked up to buy a drink for himself and Zoe.

'Different good or different bad?' he asked her.

'No, different good. Definitely good. Really good, in fact.'

'Thanks, Lauren.'

'You'll have every girl in Ireland chasing you now. So what can I get you? The usual?'

'Ah, no thanks. Can I get a Baileys on ice, please?

'Sure. Is your mam here?' Lauren asked looking over his shoulder.

'No, it's for me.'

'Oh, okay.'

'Mam and dad said they're happy just to have their house back.'

'Fair enough.'

'And can I get a gin and tonic as well, please?'

'Sure,' Lauren said. 'Is that for your... friend over there?'

'Yeah, Zoe.'

'Grand so,' she said and turned away.

'Listen, Lauren,' Michael said calling her back and reaching into his pocket. 'I have something for you here.'

He pulled out a folded cheque from his pocket, then unfolded it and looked at it before he handed it to her.

'What's this?' Lauren asked.

'It's just something to help you with Max and all that.'

Lauren opened the cheque and read it, then took a deep breath in and put her hand to her mouth. 'Michael. What's this?' she asked. 'What's this for? I don't understand.'

'It's for you. It's for Max. It's for whatever you want, Lauren.'

'I can't accept this,' Lauren said folding the cheque back up.

'Of course you can. You can get something for Max with it.'

'I'm sorry. I just can't take it, Michael,' she said handing him back the cheque. 'It's too much.'

'Of course you can take it. I've given a load of cheques to people today and to different charities.'

'I'm not a charity.'

'I know that, Lauren. It's for Max.'

'Max is not charity either.'

'Sorry, I didn't mean it like that.'

Lauren placed the cheque on the bar. 'Thank you, but I just can't take it. Max and I are doing fine.'

'Please, Lauren. I didn't mean...'

'I know you didn't, but I can't take it. Thank you though,

Michael. It's very thoughtful of you. Now, let me get you those drinks.'

Michael stood at the bar for a few moments before reaching out and picking the cheque up. He fumbled as he placed it back into his pocket.

'A Baileys on ice and a gin and tonic,' Lauren said, putting the drinks down in front of him.

Michael looked up, and reached in to take his wallet.

'That's okay. They're on me,' Lauren said and walked over to another customer calling to her.

Michael took the drinks and made his way back to Zoe.

Most of the crowd in the house had followed him to Harry's. The rest had gone straight to the bank to cash their cheques.

Michael raised his glass to her and said, 'cheers,' then took a sip.

'You're really going to stick with the whole Baileys thing are you?' she asked.

'What's wrong with it?'

'Nothing. I guess that's one of the perks to having that much money in your pocket. You can do, say and even drink whatever the fuck you like.'

They watched his family, friends and neighbours as they celebrated their good fortune and chatted about how they planned on spending it. Now that Michael wasn't footing their drinking bill, everyone appeared to be drinking their normal drinks at a normal pace.

Michael heard Zoe say something to him. 'Sorry, what did you say?' he asked her.

'You haven't been listening to anything I've said, have you?' Zoe asked him.

'I am. I'm sorry. I was just…'

'You were just ogling your girlfriend behind the bar.'

'What? No.'

'And here's me thinking you had the hots for me. Rejected again,' Zoe sighed.

'I am. I do. Well, I…'

'It's okay. I'm only teasing you. I'm not your type, and I don't do monogamy very well anyway.'

Michael took a mouthful of Baileys and then looked up at Zoe.

'I just wish I could be more like you,' he told her.

'What do you mean? Manipulative, shrewd, foxy, astute,

decep…'

'No, I mean your confidence. I wish I could be as sure about things as you are. I feel different because of all the changes you've done on me, and I know I look better and I appreciate all that, really I do, but it's not going to change who I really am. Inside, I mean. When I come in here, and yes you're right, when I see Lauren, I still go back to that meek and stammering teenager who doesn't know his arse from his elbow.'

Michael stared over at Lauren for a moment and then back at Zoe. 'Maybe not more like you, but I'd like to be at least a little bit less like me.'

Zoe leaned forward on the table. 'You seemed to have handled Uncle Jim fairly well,' she said.

'Yes, but I think that's because of you. I knew you were there and just you being there gave me the confidence.'

'Well, I can't stick around forever.'

'I know that.' Michael raised his glass to drink it but put it back down on the table. His head bowed and his shoulders stooped.

'Jesus Christ. Stop being a victim, Mike.'

'Sorry,' Mike mumbled. 'I should probably just head home.'

'For fuck's sake,' Zoe said. 'I think you'll need to spend a large portion of your winnings on psychotherapy and find out exactly why you're such a wuss.'

Michael glanced up at her, his eyes accepting this judgement on him.

'Maybe,' he said.

Zoe exhaled. 'Look. As far as I know, there's only one way to gain confidence and to grow in any way.'

'Really?' Michael asked. 'What's that?'

'Like I've told you already, you do something you're uncomfortable doing. You push yourself. Then when you discover your worst nightmare, or your worst case scenario, is not so bad and you were able to deal with it, then something changes in you. And, for want of a better word, you become "different". More sure of yourself. More in control. Not of the world, of course, you can never control what shit the world is going to throw at you. But just knowing that whatever happens, you'll manage because you've been up to your neck in shit before, and you survived. And even thrived.'

Michael stared across at Zoe. He felt that a protective layer had lifted from her, and he was seeing the real Zoe.

'Yeah,' he said sitting up. 'That's what I want. How do I get that?'

'I told you,' she said. 'By doing stuff that takes you out of your comfort zone.'

'Like what?' he asked.

'That's up to you. What do you not like doing? What scares you?'

'Lots of stuff,' Michael said and laughed.

'Alright then, but you need to get specific,' Zoe said and opened up her bag. She took out a notebook and ripped out two pages. She placed the two pages in front of him and handed him a pen. 'On this page I want you to write down a list of things you'd rather not do. Things that would give you butterflies in your stomach at the mere thought of having to do them. That sort of thing.'

'And on the second page?' Michael asked.

'Well, I don't want to force you to do something you absolutely can't do. Let's keep it real. So just write a couple of things that are complete no-go areas for you on that page, okay?'

Michael leaned over the page and began to write. Zoe took a big mouthful from her gin and tonic and looked around the pub.

People drank and people chatted. Some laughed and some, despite their recent monetary gains, still had sadness in their eyes. They were normal people leading normal lives. She wondered why she always felt different than people like that. Like she didn't fit in.

Sometimes in college, she'd be at a party and the students would be getting drunk or getting high or getting laid, and she would always feel like an observer. Like a foreigner in her own country. She had always felt like an outsider, and when she did try to participate, she felt like a fake. She used to wish she could join in, be one of the gang, but she knew she was acting like a fraud. And the crowd always knew it too.

Now though, she embraced that difference and took comfort from being outside the circle. She'd be the first to admit she had done questionable things and that her morals had a certain elasticity and that even her definition of trust was somewhat borderless, but she knew who she was. There weren't a lot of people, she felt, who could say that about themselves.

'Okay, I'm finished,' Michael said, handing Zoe the sheet of paper like a schoolboy who was keen to show off his homework to a teacher.

She took it from him and glanced at the list of the ten or so items written on it. She saw, "run a marathon", "swim in the sea", "ride a motorbike" and a few other similar challenges.

'That's really good, Mike,' she said smiling, then crumbled up the sheet of paper into a ball and dropped it onto the floor.

Without saying anything, she grabbed the second sheet from him and began to read.

'No, wait,' Michael protested, but she silenced him with an abrupt gesture of her hand and continued to read.

There were only three lines written on this list.

"Anything to do with heights."

"Anything to do with talking in public."

"Anything to do with Lauren."

Michael's enthusiasm deflated like a penknife plunged into the side of a tyre. His head dropped, and he looked up at her.

'You know, Mike,' she said, 'I'm sure those puppy dog brown eyes of yours have worked wonders on your mother for years to get you out of doing shit, but I'm not your mother. So, suck it up. The next few days might just be the making of you.'

15

Michael eased the Lamborghini into the middle lane of the motorway. An upbeat song from the 80s, whose lyrics he vaguely remembered and now attempted to sing, came on the radio, and he raised the volume.

He was beginning to get a real feel for the car, and enjoy its sublime mechanical perfection. If he decided to keep it, he told himself, it certainly wasn't for any vanity reasons or for the fact that everywhere he went with it, he saw envy and even awe in people's faces. It was a beautiful car to drive, that's all. Nothing to do with ego. Or vanity. Nothing at all.

The night before, Zoe had left him to return to the hotel alone. He had wanted to just go home, but she convinced him that the hotel was a better option to keep the media away from his parents for a while longer.

Earlier that morning, she had woken him with a phone call and told him to meet her at Westin Airport at 1pm. Westin was a small private airport about 30 minutes' drive from the hotel, which gave him plenty of time to do something else he had not had time to do yesterday.

Michael had called his parents and then Samantha as he had left the hotel, and they were all now in his parents' sitting room.

'You should have just come home last night, Michael,' his mother told him.

'I wanted to mam, but it's probably best if I stay in the hotel for a while. It'll keep the reporters away from you.'

'Who's that girl you were with yesterday?' Samantha asked.

'With all due respect, Sam,' Derek, Samantha's boyfriend said, 'that's none of your business.'

'I'm looking out for my brother,' Sam told him. 'So it is my business.'

'Look, I have to be somewhere at 1pm,' Michael told them, 'so if we could just get on with the reason we're here.'

'But what is the reason we're all here, Mike?' his dad asked.

Michael cleared his throat. 'Yesterday I shared some of my winnings with all the relatives and...'

'I think you were mad to give that lot so much money,' Samantha blurted out. 'They've probably spent half of it by now.'

'And if they have, good luck to them,' Michael told her. 'But at least mam and dad have their house back, and I was very clear with them that it was a once off payment.'

Samantha folded her arms and sat back in her chair.

'Now, can I continue?' Michael asked.

All four faces stared at him in silence.

'Yesterday I shared some of my winnings with all the relatives,' Michael began again looking at Samantha, 'and today I'd like to share some of it with you.'

'Ah, Michael, that's not necessary,' his mother protested.

'Of course it's necessary, Mam,' Samantha said.

'To be honest, son,' Jack said, 'I can't think of anything I'd want to do with that sort of money.'

'Then you're not thinking hard enough, Dad,' Michael told him.

His parents looked at each other. 'What about giving up your job for a start?' Michael asked him.

'I've a few years yet to retire,' Jack said. 'Besides, I don't mind the job that much.'

'Dad,' Samantha said, 'you're always talking about your retirement, and how you'd love to spend a few of the winter months in Spain.'

'Ah, that's just talk, love. Everyone says that.'

'Look, here's the way I see it,' Michael told him. 'You have about ten years before you retire, so what I'll do is write a cheque for what you'll be paid over the next ten years and then you can decide tomorrow morning whether you really want to go to work or not.'

Rose reached out and took her husband's hand. 'It would be

nice to have you around the house a bit more, Jack,' she said.

'I'm not so sure,' Jack said. 'You'll drive me demented with all the little jobs you'll have me doing,' but then he looked at his wife and then at his family. 'Thanks, Michael. I'll think about it. But thanks.'

'And just to be fair and in the interest of equality,' Michael said, 'I'm going to double that amount so that you Mam can officially retire too.'

'Oh my,' his mother said. 'I don't think I can retire being a mother, Michael.'

'Well then,' Michael said and handed his father the cheque, 'you can hire a maid or a cleaner to take some of your work load.'

'Oh, God, I'd never take advantage of someone like that.'

'You'd be paying them, Mam,' Michael told her.

'Jesus, son,' his father yelled looking at the cheque. 'How much do you think I get paid? What am I going to do with all this money? It's way too much,'

'How about a nice kitchen extension, Mam?' Samantha suggested. 'You're always saying you'd like to add a sunroom.'

'Yeah,' Derek added, 'and it'd be a great place to relax and read the paper in the morning, Jack. Especially when you retire.'

'Jaysus, that'd really annoy Liam next door. Him looking over the wall at me sprawled out in the morning and him off to work,' Jack said. 'Even if I had the best job in the world, I'd do it just to see the look on his face.'

'And you'd finally have a bit of time to clear out that shed like I've been asking you to do for years,' Rose said. 'And you said you'd paint the bedroom as well,'

'Ah here,' Jack said handing Michael back the cheque. 'I think I'll stay in work for a while longer.'

'Well then, I'll just have to get someone in to do it for you,' Rose said and snapped the cheque out of her husband's hand.

'Fair play to you, Mam,' Samantha laughed.

'That's the way to do it, Mrs Irvine,' Derek said.

Jack smiled as Rose folded the cheque in two and put it in her pocket.

'And now Samantha and Derek,' Michael said turning to them.

'Please don't give us any ridiculous amount, Michael,' Samantha said. 'We're doing okay financially. Honestly.'

'Well, then,' Michael said, handing her a cheque, 'it's something for the girls.'

Samantha looked down at the cheque, and then looked up at Michael.

'I don't understand,' she said. 'There's nothing written on it.'

'It's a blank cheque,' Derek told her.

'I know what it is, dummy,' she said to Derek, 'I just don't understand why it's a blank cheque.'

'Because you can have whatever you like,' Michael told her. 'I can't decide what's best for you and the girls, so whatever you think you need, just write down a figure, and it's yours.'

Samantha looked from Derek to her mother to her father and then at Michael.

'You could have the wedding you've always wanted,' Rose suggested.

'We've saved for that, Mam,' Samantha said.

'Or the honeymoon,' Derek said, nudging her with his elbow.

'I told you we're not leaving the girls for more than a few days,' Samantha said.

'Something for the girls' future then,' Jack told her.

Samantha sighed. 'Well, what I'd really like, Michael, and tell me if this is too much. I don't want you to think I'm taking advantage, or anything but I think I would like, or rather, we would like... At least it would help us and the girls, for their future…'

'For Jaysus sake, will you just say it,' Jack interrupted her.

'It's okay, Sam,' Michael said. 'Anything you think is best.'

Samantha looked at Derek, and then took his hand. 'I think if we had our mortgage paid then it would give us a lot more freedom. It would also mean I wouldn't have to take any more money off that waste of space of an ex-husband.'

'Great,' Michael said, pointing to the cheque. 'Just write down the amount in the box there.'

Samantha smiled and wrote down the amount. She looked up at Derek again, and they both smiled at each other.

'Now, I just need to sign it,' Michael said.

'Thank you, Michael,' Samantha said, handing him back the cheque. 'That's really very generous of you.'

Michael scribbled on the cheque and handed it back to her. Samantha glanced at it as she folded it in two. Then she looked down at the folded piece of paper and opened it again.

'But,' she began and looked down at the cheque. 'But I…'

161

Derek looked over her shoulder and at the cheque, then looked up at Michael. 'But she only wrote €200,000.'

'Yes,' Michael agreed, smiling. 'And I only added two zeros to the end.'

'But that's...' Samantha tried to say again. 'But that's...'

'How much is that?' Rose asked.

'It's twenty million euro,' Derek said. 'You could buy forty of our houses.'

'You could buy two of them,' Jack said. 'One for each of the girls.'

'You know, Jack, that's not a bad idea,' Derek told him.

'Michael, how could I ever...' Samantha began again but Michael was already standing up.

'There's no need to, Sam,' he said. 'It's nothing you wouldn't have given me.'

'I'm not so sure about that, Mike,' Derek said, and Samantha slapped him on his arm.

'Where are you off to?' Rose asked him.

'I have an appointment with someone,' he told her.

'I bet it's that girl,' Samantha said, her composure returning to her.

'Derek, do you mind if we have a word before I go?' Michael asked him.

'Sure, Mike,' Derek said and stood up.

Michael turned to his parents and hugged them, then his sister stood up and they embraced.

'Take care of yourself, Mike,' she said.

'I will,' he told her. 'I'm not as naive and gullible as you might think I am.'

'I know. But you're still my little brother. You have to be careful about who you can trust.'

'You're beginning to sound like Zoe now,' Michael hold her.

Derek opened the front door, and the two men stepped outside. 'What's up, Mike?' he asked

Michael handed him another cheque. Derek looked down at it.

'Ten million euro? What's this for?' he asked.

'It's a bit of security,' Michael said. 'I'd like you to invest that for me in stocks. Who knows what lies ahead?'

'I don't think you can call the stock market a secure option for your money, to be honest, Mike.'

'Yeah. I know but nothing is one hundred percent. Not even cash.'

'Okay, if you're sure.'

'I am.'

'How do you want it broken down?'

'What do you mean?' Michael asked him.

'I mean, do you want stocks, bonds, commodities? Stocks with dividends? ETFs?'

'Hold on,' Michael told him and took out a piece of paper from his back pocket. He unfolded it and read, 'fifty percent blue chip, forty percent funds and ten percent risky. Does that make any sense to you?'

'Yes. Pretty good advice who's ever giving it to you. Let me guess. The famous, or should I say, infamous Zoe.'

'Might be,' Michael smiled and put the piece of paper into his back pocket.'

Derek put out his hand and Michael took it. 'Best of luck, mate,' he said. Michael shook it and walked towards his car.

'It was the only option available to me, Joe,' the caller on the radio said. 'I'm a single mother with three kids. I just had to get them Christmas presents somehow.'

Michael was approaching Westin Airport but slowed so he could listen to the end of the conversation on the radio talk show.

'And did the money lender not make you aware of the extortionate interest rates when you borrowed the money, Mary?' Joe, the radio host asked her.

'I don't know. I was so desperate at the time. I just took the €500 and got the presents and the turkey and the ham for the Christmas dinner,' Mary told him.

'And did he not explain to you how exactly you owe him €900 now?' Joe asked.

'No,' she replied and began to sob. 'But he says that I've to pay him now or he'll…'

Her crying became louder, and the presenter tried to console her.

Michael steered the car into the airport's car park and found a spot near the entrance. He turned off the engine and took out his phone.

'The Joe Duffy Show,' the cheery voice on the phone said.

'Hello. Em... Is it okay if I don't give my name?' Michael asked her.

'Yes, of course. What's this in connection with?'

'I'd like to give... I mean, to donate the money... The €900 I mean,' he said.

'The €900 for what, sir?' she asked.

'To the lady on the radio. The one who the money lenders are after.'

There was a silence on the phone for a few moments.

'Hello?' Michael said again, unsure if they had hung up on him.

'Just stay on the line for a moment please, sir,' she said and then there was silence again.

'Well, Mary,' Michael heard Joe say on the radio as he hung up the phone a few minutes later. 'It may not be Christmas, but I think you have a secret Santa out there somewhere, because we've just received a donation for the full amount of €900.'

'What?' Mary asked. 'I don't believe it, Joe.'

'It's true. We've had a call from a listener just now who'd like to remain anonymous but he or she said they would donate the full amount. So you'll be able to get your life back on track. What do you say to that, Mary?'

There was more sobbing as Michael reached over and turned the radio off and got out of the car. He beeped the alarm on and reached out and ran his hand along its roof.

He looked up at the clear blue sky and, still filled with a sense of goodness for having helped the lady on the radio, allowed himself to breathe in the air and smile. Perhaps this whole lottery thing might turn out to be okay after all? He had already been able to help so many of his family and the thought that Samantha's girls would benefit when they grew up filled him with pride. Why not have a little fun now himself?

He once had some childish dreams as a boy about visiting the United States. Driving along Route 66 in a red Mustang. A poster's image from his bedroom wall twenty years ago flashed into his mind. He'd be able to do that now, couldn't he? The endless desert roads. Sun setting on the Rocky Mountains. Staying at motels, although he wasn't quite sure what exactly a motel was. But he would find out. Eating in diners. Everyone saying "hi" and "awesome" as he ate his blueberry pie.

A plane's wheels bounced off the runway, and their screech along the tarmac woke him for his thoughts. He looked over at it and then remembered why he was here.

He had written "heights" on his list of things he wouldn't do and here he was at an airport. He had tried not to think too much about it but now images flashed before him of the real possibility of him soon being on a plane thousands of feet in the air, the door being opened and him having to jump from it. He just hoped it was one of those where the person is strapped to a professional. Tandem, he thought it was called.

'Hey aren't you the guy who won the lottery?' a voice said behind him.

He turned and saw Zoe walking towards him. He looked from her, to the runway, to the sky, and then back to her.

'I'm having second thoughts about this, Zoe,' he told her.

'Second thoughts?' she asked him. 'How can you have second thoughts when you haven't even had first thoughts yet?'

Another plane landed and he jumped.

'I don't think I can do this,' he said.

'Do what?' she asked, trying and failing to hide her pleasure at his discomfort.

'You know what. A parachute jump. I don't think there's any reason that I can bring myself to jump out of a fully functioning airplane. Is it one of those tandem ones?'

Zoe laughed. 'Come on inside, Mike. And don't worry. You're not going to be jumping out of a plane today.'

They both started to walk towards the entrance.

'Really? It's just that I thought…'

'There you go again. You've too many thoughts.'

'So why are we here?'

'You'll see.'

When she'd fully pulled opened the hangar door, which they'd spent ten minutes walking to, Michael just stared at the plane inside. Zoe watched his face for his reaction. A big part of her thought he'd just turn and run back to his car.

'What's…?' Michael began and took a few steps forward to get a better view.

Zoe watched him. He stopped. After a few moments of complete stillness, he turned around to face her. She was genuinely shocked at the pale complexion on his face.

'No,' he said. 'No, Zoe. No. No way.'

'You'll be a hundred percent safe,' she assured him.

'No. I'm not doing that.'

'But you said…'

'I don't care. Forget about it,' he said and began to walk off.

'That's it?' she called after him.

'Yep. That's it. Can't do it. Won't do it.'

'Are you fucking kidding me?'

'No. Good luck to you. Not happening.'

'Yeah, that's what she thought you'd say,' Zoe said, almost under her breath.

He stopped and turned to face her. 'What? It's what who thought I'd say?'

'Doesn't matter,' she said and walked away from him.

'Hold on a second. Who are you talking about?'

'Who do you think?'

'My mam?'

'Don't be ridiculous.'

'Sam?'

Zoe didn't reply and just looked at him.

'Lauren?'

She stared at him.

'What did Lauren say?'

'Not much. She just said there's no way you'd do it.'

'When did she say that?'

'Last night at the pub when I told her what I had in mind.'

'You're bullshitting me.'

'Okay,' Zoe shrugged again. 'Whatever you say. I guess that'll always be the difference between you and Joey McGuinness.'

'What are you talking about?'

'That's why good guys always finish last, Mike.'

'What?'

'That's why Joey McGuinness will always have the last laugh with you. That's why he didn't spend the last ten years living at home with his mam wiping his arse for him. That's why you'll always be his little bitch. Mickey Irvine. Joey McGuinness's little bitch. And that's why he was the one out humping the love of your life while you were at home alone jerking off about her.'

'What do you know? You don't know what you're talking about,' Michael screamed at her.

'I know exactly what I'm talking about. I'm talking about you, Mike.'

Michael turned away from her.

'I'm talking about you grabbing the bull by the horns for once in your fucking life,' she continued. 'About taking a chance. Being a man, whatever the fuck that means. I'm talking about you not being such a pussy.'

'I'm not being a pu... whatever,' he shouted at her. 'I'm just afraid to do some stuff, that's all.'

He walked a few steps and then stopped. He took a few deep breaths.

'I'm not like you, Zoe. I thought I could be, but I can't. I thought I could be more confident and stuff like that, but it's not me. I'm sorry.'

'The only difference between me and you is that I try. I fail. I fail a lot. But I never stop trying.'

Michael turned and looked at her. Then he looked over at the hangar.

'Can I not just do a parachute jump?' he asked her.

She smiled at him but said nothing.

Michael walked back towards the plane. Zoe made a fist and punched the air as she followed him into the hangar.

'I'm swearing a lot more than I used to,' Michael told her. 'I seem to be picking that up off you easily enough.'

Zoe didn't reply as she walked up to the plane. Michael stared up at it.

'Did Lauren really say that about me?' he asked her.

She rubbed the side of the plane's nose as it were a horse's head she was petting.

'No,' she replied. 'Of course not.'

As the plane lifted its wheels off the runway, Michael let out such a loud scream that despite the front propeller engine being at full throttle, the pilot was still able to hear him. A large grin appeared across the pilot's face. It was still the part of his job he most enjoyed.

The bright red 1934 Boeing Stearman Model 75 aircraft lifted its nose into the sky. From the open cockpit, the pilot raised his head and looked all around him. A final instinctive check before climbing too high. Everything looked as normal, so he turned his head back in Michael's direction.

The six-foot carbon fibre platform that was attached to the upper wing in front of him looked secure. He did think it unusual, however, that despite having been in the air for several minutes now, Michael, who was standing attached to the structure on the wing, was continuing to scream.

The same thought always came to the pilot at this stage, why was it called 'wing walking' when the person doesn't actually do any walking?

He decided to level the plane in the hope that his client would stop screaming. Of course at this height his screams were mostly drowned out by the one hundred miles per hour winds and the rotating propeller blades, but he felt it wasn't good for his business to have an unsatisfied customer. He had only had one client who had crapped himself, and it was a most unpleasant experience as he remembered.

His client tried to turn his head around. They always did that. He didn't know why though. What was there to see back there? Although the pilot did notice, despite goggles covering most of his face, how pale he looked.

The pilot looked at his watch. He was supposed to stay up here for fifteen minutes, but he decided to start to head back down after ten. It was his turn to collect his youngest daughter from the crèche, and he didn't think this client would be complaining of it being too short.

Still, you had to give them their money's worth, so he released the fake smoke and it sent a trail behind the plane that stretched out like a grey ribbon in the sky. Now a quick nose dive for ten seconds and then level up. He checked his watch again. That should just about do it, he thought. The finale and back to the runway.

He checked around him again to ensure clear skies, then pulled back hard on the throttle. The nose pushed forwards and up. It was an old aircraft, so he had to use quite a bit of effort to hold the throttle back towards his chest as the plane became vertical for a few moments. He eased off as they became parallel with the ground in an upside down position.

He was making good time now, he thought, as he pushed the throttle to the left and straightened the plane. He hadn't been paying much attention to his client, but he noticed now he had gone very silent. A part of him felt a little insulted. They were supposed to be exhilarated.

He decided his daughter could wait a few minutes. He was going to do one final manoeuvre that was always a crowd pleaser.

He pointed the plane in the direction of the runway, and then just as he saw his client's head raise in expectation of his ordeal ending, he jacked the throttle back and did a loop the loop in the sky. The smoke poured out from the plane's undercarriage and formed a large circle.

The pilot smiled in self-satisfaction as he heard the swearing and screaming.

Now that's true job satisfaction, he thought to himself.

16

As Michael stretched out his hand to put the key in the ignition of his car, he noticed how much his hand was still shaking. He shoved the key in quickly. Zoe, who was sitting beside him, spotted it too.

'You okay to drive?' she asked him.

He nodded and took a deep breath.

He was still embarrassed from the pilot having to climb up onto the plane and carry him off the wing. He also felt it had been unnecessary for the pilot to tell them it was the first time he had ever had to do that. Nor laugh so profusely as he carried Michael.

'You haven't said anything since getting off the plane,' she told him. 'You should say something.'

He turned his head towards her, but she couldn't decipher his look.

'I think I ate about a hundred flies,' he said.

She smiled at him. 'Why didn't you close your mouth?'

'I couldn't close my mouth, Zoe, because I was screaming my fucking head off.'

She turned her head towards the window so he wouldn't see her stifle her laugh.

'Also my brain is still trying to figure out,' he told her, 'whether that was the stupidest or the most amazing thing I've ever done.'

She turned back to him. 'Both. Stupidity and amazing sometimes come as a pair.'

He placed his fingers in front of his face to check if they were still shaking, and he took another deep breath.

'How's your fear of heights now?' she asked him.

'I don't know,' he said. 'To be honest, I spent more time trying to deal with my fear of falling rather than my fear of heights.'

'You sure you're okay?'

'Yeah, I'm sure. I did do it though, didn't I?'

'Yes, you did. No matter what, you climbed up onto that plane yourself. Although in fairness, you did have to be carried back...'

'Okay, okay,' he interrupted her. 'We don't have to go over that bit.'

There were a few moments silence in the car while they both sat staring out at the runway.

'You did great, Mike. It was brilliant.'

'It was, wasn't it?' he said, a large smile growing across his face.

'Yes, you were brilliant,' she told him, mirroring his smile.

'Now what?'

'I think we could both use a drink, don't you?'

Michael started the engine.

'And I know just the right place,' she told him as he shifted the car into gear.

Harry's pub was noisy and already full of after-work drinkers, savouring their pints as they drank with a sense of deservedness. Zoe and Michael had sneaked in with a large group and had found a table near the back that was hidden away from the crowd. Lauren was busy serving drinks and hadn't seen them come into the pub.

'Why couldn't we just have gone back to the hotel?' Michael asked Zoe. 'After the buzz of the flight, this place is a bit of a downer.'

'Because Lauren doesn't work in the hotel,' she told him.

'Lauren?' he asked her. 'What's Lauren got to do with anything?'

'Because today, Michael, after years of torment, is the day you ask Lauren out on a date.'

'No, it's not.'

Zoe was surprised at how quickly he had replied with a refusal. It wasn't as if he had figured things out in his head and then had come up with reasons why her proposed course of action wasn't possible. It was more as if her suggestion had bounced off a wall. A wall, Zoe knew, that he had unconsciously build up in his own head over years of imagined rejections.

'You can do this,' she told him.

'No, I can't. I think doing the plane walking was easier, to be honest.'

'Don't be ridiculous.'

'I'm not. Besides, after all this time of not going out with me, it'll look like she's only saying yes now because I have all this money. We should just get out of here.'

'Let me give you a couple of reasons why that won't happen, and if you're still not happy about it then we'll leave. Is that fair?'

Michael sat back in his chair and folded his arms, but said nothing.

'Firstly, she likes you. I noticed that the first time I saw both of you together. There's chemistry there. Secondly, she hasn't refused you for years, and is now saying yes because of the money because you've never asked her out before. That's all in your head, Mike.'

Michael unfolded his arms and leaned forward slightly.

'What do you mean, she likes me?'

'Of course she likes you. Isn't that obvious?'

'No.'

'Well, it's pretty obvious to me.'

'Obvious how?'

'It's nothing specific.'

'Be specific.'

'Why is it always a problem for men to know when a girl likes them? You're really just well-dressed cave men, aren't you?'

'Obvious how?' Michael asked her again.

Zoe sighed. 'The way she looks at you. The way she smiles at you. The way she talks to you.'

Michael looked over at Lauren as she poured drinks and chatted to her customers.

'The way she flicks her hair when she's looking at you. The way she touches your hand when she laughs at your jokes. The way she brightens up when she sees you.'

Michael continued to watch her as she worked.

'I never knew,' he finally said.

'Of course you didn't,' Zoe told him. 'Men rarely do, until we hit them across the head with a club.'

'So why didn't she ask me out?' Michael asked, turning back to Zoe.

'Because nice normal girls don't ask guys out. It's one of the many unwritten rules. Although cunning nice girls usually get the man of their choice to ask them out, and even let the man think he made the first move.'

'You would ask someone out.'

'I'm neither nice nor normal, Mike. And I don't play by their rules.'

Michael looked over at Lauren again and then back to Zoe. He sat up a little in his chair.

'Okay then. What do I say to her?'

'As usual, it's not what you say, it's how you say it. The main thing is that you've got to keep it casual. Try not to think of it as asking her out and then waiting for a yes or no. You're merely suggesting that you both get together.'

Michael stared at her for several moments.

'So what do I say?' he asked.

'Jesus, Mike. What do you want? A word-for-word script?'

'Yes.'

Zoe sighed.

'Order your drinks from her and then do your regular small talk bullshit.'

'Okay.'

'Then you say something like, "Why don't we go get a coffee next time you're off". Keep it very casual and light.'

Michael cleared his throat. 'Like this? "Why don't we go get a bite to eat when you're off?"'

'What the fuck was that?' Zoe asked.

'What do you mean?'

'You sounded like Marlon Brando in The Godfather.'

'I was trying to sound casual.'

'What? Mafia casual? Putting a hit on her casual? Also, I didn't say "get a bite to eat". I said, "Get a coffee". You think a girl wants to sit and let you watch her stuff her face on a first date?'

'Then a movie?'

'Great. Two hours of silence in the dark. That'll work. Besides, you said she has a kid. She doesn't have two extra hours to waste. And what were you doing with your arm? Waving it about like that.'

'It's a casual gesture of the hand. Like a carefree expression,' Michael said looking over at Lauren. He didn't notice Zoe shaking her head.

'I don't know,' he said. 'What if she says "no"?'

'Then you quickly turn and run straight out of the door and never come back.'

Michael scoffed at her.

'And what if she says "yes"?' Zoe asked him. 'What if you have to sit down in front of her for two or three hours? What are you going to say then?'

Michael stayed seated and began to rub both of his hands up and down his trouser legs.

'Mike.'

'Yeah,' Mike replied without looking at her.

'Please, stop doing that. It looks like you're having a wank under the table.'

Michael looked down at his hands and stopped.

'Now go over there and ask her out. And then let's get the fuck out of here.'

'Okay. I can do this,' Michael said and took a few sharp breaths in and out, like a boxer about to enter the ring.

'Michael,' Lauren said as he approached the bar. 'What a nice surprise to see you.'

'Yeah, it is. I mean not for you to see me. For us. I mean, for me. It's nice, yeah.'

'Alright. Are you okay, Michael?'

'Yeah, I'm grand thanks. A few too many late nights.'

'Oh, I see,' said Lauren, unconsciously looking over in Zoe's direction. 'I see you're with your… em…girlfr…,'

'No, no. She's not my girlfriend. Zoe. God, no way. She's just a friend. An advisor. There's nothing, like… between us or anything.'

'Oh, I see. So what can I get you?' she asked. 'For the man who has everything?'

'A gin and tonic, please. And I'll have a Baileys.'

'No probs,' Lauren said and turned to take a glass from the shelf, then poured a measure of gin into it.

'Em, I was just wondering,' Michael said to her back. 'I mean, I was just saying to Zoe there. I was wondering if you wouldn't mind. Could I? Or I mean, could you… '

'Yes?' she said and turned back around to face him.

Michael made eye contact with her. 'If you wouldn't mind, em… putting some ice in the Baileys.'

'Absolutely. Baileys on the rocks it is.'

Michael cast a furtive look over at Zoe. He saw her raise her eyes to heaven then pointed at her watch.

'I was wondering, Lauren.'

'Yeah?'

'I was wondering, if you didn't mind. If you're free at all some time that maybe...'

Michael swung his hand casually to the right and hit the pint glass in front of the man who was seated beside him. The glass made a loud clink as it hit the wooden surface of the bar and the remaining third pint of Guinness flowed out and caused a temporary black waterfall as it descended off the edge.

'Oh, Jesus,' said Michael and grabbed the glass.

Lauren took a cloth and began to mop up the remaining dregs.

'Sorry about that,' Michael said then turned to the previous owner of the spillage, 'sorry. Sorry. I'm really sorry about that.'

'It's okay, Michael,' Lauren said. 'No harm done.'

'Jesus, sorry about that, Mister,' Michael said.

'You're alright, son,' said the man. 'Sure it was nearly gone anyway.'

'Let me get you another one,' said Michael.

'Another full one?' the man asked, sitting up.

'Of course, of course. Lauren?'

'I'll put you on another one, Danny,' Lauren assured him as she mopped up the remaining wet pools.

'Grand so,' said the man.

Michael looked over at Zoe. She had her face down and the palms of her hands covering her face. He reached out to grab the cloth in front of him to help clean up, and his hand landed on Lauren's hand. He kept it there for a few moments. Lauren stopped moving the cloth and she looked up at him. They looked into each other's eyes and Michael felt all the noise and commotion of the room fade into the background.

Zoe raised her head and she heard the two drinks being placed on the table. When she saw Michael's expression, she smiled. 'You did it?' she asked.

He nodded.

'And she said yes?'

Michael nodded again. 'Yep. Tonight. She finishes at ten. I said I'd meet her in town afterwards.'

Unusually for her, Zoe felt like jumping up and giving him a hug. 'Fair fucking play to you, Mike. I didn't think you had the balls to be honest.'

She took a sip from her gin and tonic. Michael watched her and then did the same with his own.

'The girl can make a mean gin and tonic as well,' she said, putting the glass down. 'Now let's get the fuck out of here.'

When she saw the expression on Michael's face change so quickly, she instinctively turned to see where he was looking.

Joey McGuinness stood in the door frame, two of his friends standing like bodyguards on either side of him. He had a look in his eyes as if he were searching for trouble.

'Let's just leave now,' Zoe said as she turned back around to face Michael. Michael had his head lowered and out of sight. 'Jesus, Mike. There's no need to be afraid of that little prick.'

Michael half sat back up. 'Let's just wait till he sits down and then we'll leave, okay?'

They both watched as the three men went to the bar. Joey spoke to Lauren, and it was clear he wasn't just ordering drinks. He pointed his finger at her and she took a step back and folded her arms. Hard Harry, who was standing a few feet away, looked over in their direction. His eyes unconsciously glanced at the wooden truncheon resting within reach.

The man whose pint Michael had knocked over said something to Joey. Joey bent down to hear him. Then he straightened up and searched around the bar. His eyes rested on Michael and Zoe, and his mouth formed a half smile.

Michael didn't look up, even when he knew Joey and his two buddies were standing beside his table. He stared down at the floor looking at Joey's White trainers, which were splattered with black oil like a Joseph Pollock painting.

'Here, Urine,' Joey began. 'I hear you're taking my bird out on a date tonight. Is that true?'

Michael didn't answer.

'Did you fucking hear what I said, Urine?'

'Piss off, Joey,' Zoe told him.

Joey lowered his head to Zoe. 'If I want your fucking opinion, cunt-face, I'll ask for it.'

Zoe was about to reply when she heard Michael say something. Joey turned his head to him, 'what did you just fucking say?'

'I said,' Michael repeated, looking up. 'She's not your bird.'

Joey stood up straight and looked down at Michael.

'Oh, listen to the big man now, lads,' Joey said turning to his two buddies. 'Thinks cause he has a few quid in his pocket he can answer back.'

'Come on, Joey,' one of his friends said, and put his hand on Joey's shoulder. 'Let's leave him.'

'Get your fuckin' hand off me,' Joey told him.

The people at the surrounding tables stopped talking and turned towards the commotion. His friend removed his hand.

'And whose bird is she then, Urine?' Joey said, turning back to Michael and stabbing his finger into Michael's shoulder. 'Yours?'

'Leave him alone,' Lauren called from behind the bar.

Joey turned to her, 'shut the fuck up, you.'

'Ignore him, Mike,' Zoe said. 'He's not worth it.'

'All the women defending you now,' Joey said. 'One sniff of all that money, and they're all out to ride you.'

'Come on, Joey. Let's go,' his other friend said to him.

'You shut the fuck up as well.'

Michael sat in silence staring at the door. Joey turned to him again and grabbed Michael by his jacket.

'That's it? You've nothing to say? Well then let me tell you something. Even if you had all the money in the world, you little prick, you'd still be a nothing but a fucking coward who lives with his ma and da.'

Joey released his jacket.

'Please Joey,' Lauren pleaded.

'You know she's only interested in you now because of your money,' Joey said to Michael. 'You know what they call that, don't you? Prostitution.'

Michael turned his head and stared up at him.

'You're right, Urine. She's not my bird anymore. She's your whore.'

The chair made a loud scraping sound as it was shoved backwards when Michael stood up.

Joey started to laugh.

'Don't think all your money is going to stop me from knockin' the fuckin' head off ye.'

'Come on, Joey,' said his friend behind him and pulled as his shirt. 'Not now.'

Joey swung his arm free. 'Let fucking go of me.'

There was silence as Joey stood and stared at Michael. Zoe braced herself for the punch, but Michael's expression didn't change. He continued to make eye contact with Joey.

A smile formed on Joey's face. He turned and looked at Lauren.

'Now that I think about it, you both deserve each other. Two sad losers.'

Michael looked over at Lauren.

'You can fucking have her,' Joey said turning back to Michael. 'Her and her little retard.'

The silence in the bar was broken by an audible gasp. Both of Lauren's hands went to her face. Zoe stared up at Joey in disbelief. Joey turned around to the crowd with a smile awaiting recognition for his funny remark.

Michael didn't move. A surge of anger swelled up in his heart and spread out through the blood in his body, collected in his hands and they formed into fists.

As Joey turned back to face him, having realised the crowd wasn't laughing at what he'd said, Michael took a step forward and swung his arm, aiming to erase that smirk across his face. The fist collided with Joey's jaw just as it straightened and make a cracking sound like two blocks of wood hitting each other.

Joey's head was forced back in the direction it came and his body had no option but to follow it. It twisted backwards towards his two stooges, who were still standing like goal posts behind him. Both of them took a step to the side and allowed him to fall between them.

For a few moments Joey appeared to be running backwards, his arms swaying in circles as if he were falling off a roof. Eventually, he forced his torso sideways but then his feet began to slip. Four people, who were seated at a round table near the door, saw he was heading in their direction and jumped up out of their seats.

The first thing that hit the table was Joey's arm. That in itself was enough to topple it, so by the time he hit the floor, the full and half-full drinks slid down and crashed into him.

A pint of Guinness missed his face but its contents spewed out and landed on top of his head. When all the noise of crashing glass and liquids had settled, only Joey's oil stained white trainers remained dry.

Everyone looked down at him and then at Michael, who stood

ramrod straight, anger still in his eyes. Joey turned his head to the side and saw two women laughing at him. All the faces in the pub were turned towards him. Some tried to hide their grins and jeering smiles. Others didn't.

Rage soared through him. He wiped the drinks off his face and stood up.

'I'm going to fucking kill him,' he said, more to himself than anyone else, as he stood up.

The impact of the truncheon across Joey's back made a loud BOOM in the pub. Joey, at first anyway, was more stunned than in pain. The pain came with a surge as soon as the second blow hit him.

He lifted his arms and tried to turn to protect himself from the attack when the third blow whacked him across his raised hand. The pain shot through him like an electric shock.

'GET OUT,' Lauren screamed at him, lifting the truncheon again. 'Get out. Get out. Get you, you fuuuuu…'

Joey fell to the floor, and she hit him again.

'You fucker. You fucker. Don't you ever call my son…' but her words were incoherent from her rage.

Everyone seemed to react at the same time, but Michael got to her first.

He grabbed the truncheon from her, but her fists continued to hit Joey, who was on his knees now. Michael grabbed Lauren and held her tight, her legs kicking out in Joey's direction.

Joey stood up quickly. He looked a little dazed.

'Out.' Hard Harry shouted at Joey. 'Now.'

Joey stood still and looked at him.

He spat some of the Guinness out from his mouth and onto the floor, and looked down at his clothes.

Raising his hand, he pointed a finger at Michael. 'Watch your back, Irvine,' he told him.

His voice sounded croaky and worn. 'You hear me?'

'He hears you,' Hard Harry said. 'Now get the fuck out.'

'One of these days,' Joey continued, pointing his finger.

'Alright,' Hard Harry said, 'less talking and more walking.'

Joey spat on the floor again. 'This place is a shit-hole anyway.'

'Really? Then don't bother coming back. You're barred. For life.'

'Fuck you.'

Hard Harry began to walk out from behind the bar, and Joey took a step back. He looked at his two friends.

'Let's get out of this kip,' he told them, and then turned to leave.

When he realised they weren't following him, he faced them again. 'I said, let's go.'

Both of his friends looked at each other, but neither of them moved.

'Then fuck you two as well. Pair of faggots.'

'Out,' Hard Harry screamed at him.

Joey spat again and without saying another word, pushed open the door and was gone.

Michael realised he was still holding Lauren. He let her go.

'You okay?' he asked her.

She nodded and walked back behind the bar.

'Lauren,' Hard Harry said, filling the silence of the room.

Lauren looked at him.

'I'll clean up the mess and you get everyone some fresh drinks,' he told her.

'Yes, Harry,' she said.

'Nice punch, Mike,' one of Joey's friends told Michael, smacking him on the shoulder.

'He's not Mike. He's Iron Mike,' said the other one, and they both laughed.

Someone picked up the table and somebody else started to pick up the glasses.

Zoe touched Michael's arm, and he turned his attention to her.

'So, can we go now, Iron Mike?' she asked him, and she saw his shoulders relax. He nodded. She slid her arm under his and walked him towards the door.

'Wait,' he said. 'What if he's still outside?'

'It's okay,' she told him. 'You'll protect me.'

He paused briefly as he left and then turned and made eye contact with Lauren.

She smiled at him.

He was basking in her smile as the door closed behind him.

17

The Lamborghini glided through the streets. Zoe had never heard Michael talk so much. Or seen his confidence so high. She had attempted to interrupt him several times already, but he had always brought the conversation off in another direction.

'Mike, listen,' she tried again.

'I hope Lauren doesn't think I have this aggressive streak in me now,' he said.

'Mike.'

'Although she might find that attractive. You know, in a manly way.'

'Mike,' Zoe screamed, her voice filling the small cockpit of the car.

Michael jumped and missed a gear as he went around a corner, grinding it into position.

'Are you alright?' he asked her.

'I'm sorry. I needed to get your attention.'

'Okay, well you have it now. What's wrong?'

'I need to tell you a couple of things,' she told him.

'Do you mean a couple as in a few or as in two specific things?'

'Okay, I need to tell you two things. We need to get back on track here.'

'You mean the third challenge?' he asked her.

'Yes. That and something else.'

'I'm all ears, Zoe. This one is talking in front of people. And you know what? I think I could talk now in front of a crowd. A small crowd,' he joked, slowing the car down a little so he could focus on her.

He found the car behaved like a bold child, and if he wasn't paying attention to it, it would get ahead of him, and he would need to rein it in a bit.

'Okay,' Zoe said. 'But I don't think you're going to like this one.'

'Well, I didn't like the last two, and they worked out pretty well.'

'Yeah, but I think this one, I may have overstretched a little.'

Michael was silent for a few moments, and he listened to the roar of the engine behind him.

'So tell me,' he said.

'After we get back to the hotel, we're going to change our clothes, and you're going to dress yourself up a bit sharper,' she began.

'And then?'

'Then a car is going to arrive and take us away.'

'Okay. Am I supposed to ask, where to?'

'If you like.'

'Where is the car going to take us, Zoe?'

'The RTÉ television studios.'

Michael thought for a minute. 'I'm going to be on the telly?'

'Yes.'

'Doing what?'

Zoe didn't reply. She could see he was trying to figure it out as he drove.

His face quickly changed from pensive to startled and then the car stopped suddenly. Zoe lurched forward in her seat, the safety belt preventing her from knocking her head against the dash. Cars horns beeped behind them.

She looked at Michael. His hands gripped the steering wheel and he stared ahead.

Slowly, he turned his head towards her. 'Not the Late Late Show?' he said.

She nodded at him.

'Surprise,' she said, but the car horns behind them drowned out her attempt at a cheerful tone.

It was only when the car was parked and they were walking through the lobby of the hotel that Michael remembered there had been two things Zoe had to tell him.

'I think I'll wait until after the show before I explain it to you,' she told him.

'Is it bad?' he asked.

'It is what it is.'

'That makes no sense.'

'I know. Let's go to our rooms and change. I'll meet you in the bar in thirty minutes. Okay?'

They rode the lift in silence, with only a curt 'see you later' as they separated.

Michael's suite was in pristine condition again and smelt of lavender. Everything had been rearranged and tidied. Lying across the bed was a black suit bag inscribed with the Armani logo in white. He unzipped it to find a three-piece navy blue suit.

He realised that it would probably be the only time he would ever be on television and hadn't given the slightest thought to what he was going to wear.

But Zoe had. Because Zoe thought of everything.

He showered and dressed. Putting the shirt and suit on, he felt them slide against his skin in a perfect fit. He figured that Zoe must have had it tailored for him. He made himself an espresso from the Nespresso machine and drank it as he looked out along the treetops of Stephen's Green.

The sun was setting, and its light spread a soft glow on the city's buildings and inhabitants. Michael breathed in the scene before him and he sipped his coffee. He caught sight of himself in the full-length mirrored wardrobe and he couldn't help but admire how he looked in his new suit.

He didn't mind so much now going on the television. Nor talking in front of all those people. His only thought was of afterwards. When Lauren would be meeting him and how smart he would look for her. Almost worthy of her. He would have plenty to talk about after the show with her. Beside her.

He allowed himself, if only for the briefest of moments, to imagine a world in which he always lived like this. Then realising there was no reason why he couldn't and that indeed this was life, it frightened him a little, and he quickly cast the thought from his mind, and hurried out of the room.

The lounge downstairs was busy and noisy, but he found two empty chairs against the bar. Michael shouted out his order, getting a gin and tonic for Zoe in case there was time, and the drinks arrived even before he had time to take out his wallet.

He sipped his Baileys and studied the various bottles behind the bar. He noticed the expensive bottle of Scotch whisky on the top shelf. He thought back to when he was here with his family and how they had tried to use him and that if it hadn't been for Zoe, maybe they would be still here. If there was time, perhaps he could try a glass of that whisky. Spoil himself.

He picked up the Baileys and became self-conscious that perhaps it was after all a bit of a silly drink for a man to order. He turned towards the door but there was still no sign of Zoe. A bit of Dutch courage before the show, he told himself and slid the Baileys to the side.

As he raised his hand to ask for the whisky, a man sat in the chair beside him.

'I'm sorry, that's taken,' he told him. 'My friend is on the way.'

'That's alright. Zoe's always late,' the man said and flashed him a smile.

At the mention of Zoe's name, Michael gave him more of his attention.

He was young, perhaps mid-twenties, but was probably younger than he looked. Michael didn't know a lot of black men and he found it difficult to guess his age. His clothes were beige and green, and seemed to give off a sort of military demeanour with various sized pockets and zips. At his feet was a large gym bag with two black straps poking out the top.

'Do you know Zoe?' Michael asked him.

'Everybody knows Zoe,' he replied.

'And do you know me?'

'No, but I feel like I do. I guess that's what happens when you follow someone around for a few days,' the man said and took a sip out of Zoe's glass.

Michael just stared at him not sure what to say. Or do.

'Follow?' he asked. 'Follow me? You've been following me?'

'Sure have,' he said smacking his lips with the taste of the gin and tonic. 'Day and night, my friend.'

'Why?'

The man looked perplexed at such an illogical question. 'Because it's my job, of course.'

Now it was Michael's turned to look perplexed. The man put down the drink.

'What? You really didn't know? I'm genuinely surprised, Mike. I mean, of course at first how would you know, but you look smart. I thought you had figured it out and were just playing us along.'

'Look,' Michael began and stood up. 'I don't know what you're talking about and if this is some kind of joke, then…'

'Relax, Mike,' the man said and put his hand up in defence. 'Sit down. I'm sorry, I honestly thought you knew, man. Zoe said you didn't but I didn't believe her. I mean, who believes anything that comes out of that girl's mouth, right? If she told me I had a black cock, I'd probably have to take a quick look at it to make sure she wasn't lying.'

The man burst into laughter at his own joke, and then took another large mouthful from Zoe's drink as he settled himself down again.

'Anyway, here's the deal, Mike. I've been busting my balls off for the last few days, while you and Zoe get to drive around in that nice car and stay in this place. I was in your room, by the way. Very nice. So, we had this deal, Zoe and me, that she'd take you here and there, splash the cash a bit, while I photographed some nice shots of you in the tailors, and you in the Lamborghini and stuff like that. She knocks together a one-thousand-word article to go with them and we sell it to some tabloid newspaper for 10 Gs. Everyone's a winner, right?'

Michael stared at the man. His head began to spin, and he held on to the back of the chair.

'I… I…,' Michael began. 'I don't believe you.'

The man looked straight at Michael. 'What don't you believe, Mike?' he asked him. 'Which part?'

'Every part. It can't be true.'

'Of course it's true. Why would I lie to you?' the man said.

He then reached down and pulled a camera out of the bag at his feet. Switching it on, he handed it to Michael.

'Here, flick through some of these,' he told him.

Michael looked at the images. Every picture had him in it. In Harry's. In the tailor's with Zoe. On the plane. Even a series of photos of Joey McGuinness falling onto the table.

'Why?' Michael asked.

'Why?' the man repeated. 'I told you why. Five grand each. I know that's not a lot of money for you, but five thousand euro for me is…'

'No,' Michael interrupted him. 'I mean, why are you telling me this. Why now?'

'Oh, I see. Here's the thing. I think it'd be real good to get a few shots of you on The Late Late Show tonight but Zoe says no. I want to go with you to the studio. It would really make the article even better. A perfect conclusion to the whole thing. What do you think?'

Michael put the camera down on the bar. He felt like he was going to throw up, so he stood up and took a couple of deep breaths.

'You look really pale, Mike,' the man said. 'You okay, man?'

Michael looked around the room. He only now realised how noisy it was. People talking too loudly. Laughing and smiling. A man looked over at him. Was he laughing at me? Michael thought. A woman looked at him, her face covered in a mocking grin.

The man beside him said something but Michael couldn't understand what he said. He needed to get out of the room. He needed some fresh air. He needed to… No. He needed to find Zoe. Zoe. A feeling of rage burst inside him. Zoe. As he walked towards the door, the anger got stronger.

He pressed the button on the lift. He pressed again. And again. He saw the stairs and ran to them, taking them three steps at a time. His heart was pounding by the time he got to the fifth floor. He stopped running and instead strode down the corridor. He paused for a moment when he reached the door and stood staring at it.

Then he knocked at it. There was no reply after two seconds so he knocked again. Harder this time.

'Zoe,' he called out and pressed down on the handle, but it was locked.

He knocked again.

'Zoe,' he shouted, his voice echoing through the corridor.

He heard a soft click and the door opened.

'Mike? I thought we were meeting downstairs,' Zoe said, but she turned back on him and walked into the room. She was dressed in a white bathrobe.

'Anyway, it's good you're here,' she continued. 'I can't seem to decide what to wear. Not that I'm the one who's going to be on television but there's no harm in making a good impression. You never know, perhaps…'

She turned to face him for the first time. 'Mike, what's wrong? What's happened?'

'Is it true?'

'Is what true?'

'Is it true, Zoe? Tell me the truth.'

'I don't know what you're talking…'

'Tell me the truth,' he shouted at her, the anger in his voice surprising him as much as her.

Zoe opened her mouth to argue but then closed it again and sighed.

She walked over to the makeup table, which was strewn with her cosmetics, and sat on the chair in front of it. 'How did you…?'

'The man in the bar,' he told her.

She looked up at him. 'What man?'

'The photographer.'

She nodded. 'Jake? That fucker.'

'So it's all true?'

'What did he tell you?'

'That you're a liar and a user, and that you don't give a shit about anyone but yourself,' he spat at her.

'It's not like that, Mike.'

'It's exactly like that.'

'So then why do you think he told you? What's his reason? Have you thought about that? I'll tell you why. It's because I told him that I wanted to scrap the article about you.'

'You're lying,' Michael shouted at her.

'I'm not, Mike. I told him you weren't who I thought you were. I told him you were one of the good guys, and that I wasn't going to write anything about you.'

Michael stared at her. He had allowed himself to lean so much on her over the last few days, and now he felt that without her he would fall. That everything would come crashing down on him.

'He's only telling you because he wants you to do exactly what you're doing now. I was going to tell you today but I decided to wait until after the show. I didn't want to upset you. I wasn't sure how you'd react.'

'How the fuck did you think I'd react?'

'I don't know. Either way, it's the truth. Honestly.'

'Honestly? You don't even know what that word means.'

They both stared at each other until Michael realised he had nothing else to say. He turned and walked towards the door.

He heard Zoe speak, but he didn't turn around.

'I did warn you, Mike,' she said quietly.

Michael placed his hand on the door handle.

'I told you when we first met that you shouldn't trust anyone. That's still true today.'

He opened the door.

'Hey, Michael,' she called to him. He turned to face her, and she was taken aback when she saw the anger and hurt in his eyes.

'For what it's worth, I'm sorry. I didn't mean for you to get hurt.'

'Yes, you did, Zoe. That's your job. To hurt people. To hurt people and then to write about it. That's all you do. Take and use. That's all you are. A... a... a parasite.'

He didn't touch the door as he left, and it closed slowly by itself. It clicked as it locked. Zoe stared at the closed door for five minutes. That was how long it took for her gather the courage to turn and face the image she was afraid to; her own face in the mirror.

18

Michael heard Zoe's door closing behind him. The anger fell away from him at its sound and his shoulders drooped. For the briefest of moments he wished he would hear the door open and hear her calling his name, but he didn't want that either. He just wanted to be alone.

As he pressed the button on the lift, he remembered the Late Late Show. He stepped into the lift when commanded to do so by its PING. When the door opened to a busy and noisy foyer, he felt panic as if he were about to fall off a cliff. He pressed the buttons again for the door to close. For the lift to rise. For something to happen.

'Mr. Irvine, Mr. Irvine,' a voice called out.

The hotel guests separated and the uniformed concierge ran through the break in the crowd.

'There you are,' he said, happy with his discovery.

The doors of the lift began to slide shut, but the concierge stretched out the finely pressed arm of his jacket, and the doors shot back open.

'There's a car and driver waiting outside to take you to RTÉ, Mr. Irvine,' he said. 'Shall I escort you to it?'

'I need to get something from my room,' Michael told him, pressing the buttons harder.

The concierge's arm remained in the door. 'He did mention that you were on a tight schedule,' he said. 'You don't want to keep Mr. Tubridy waiting, do you?'

Michael put his arm down and stepped out into the foyer. The concierge marched ahead of him, excusing people out of the way.

As they passed the bar, Michael slowed down to see if the photographer was still there, but he couldn't see him. The concierge had reached the front door and was waiting for him. Michael raised a finger to him to indicate that he would only be one minute. The concierge didn't try to hide his impatience.

'A Macallan,' Michael asked the barman.

'Certainly, sir,' he told him and ignoring all the other calls for drinks, reached up for the bottle. He poured a measure into a heavy whiskey glass and presented it to Michael as is if it were a secret recipe elixir.

'Ice?' the barman asked.

'No.'

Michael held it and was surprised how little was in the glass given its price. He smelt it and its odour reminded him of his grandfather, who passed away when Michael was seven-years-old. Rather than sip it, given its small quantity and lack of time, he tilted the glass and poured its entire contents down his throat.

Michael fell forward, his right hand slamming the glass onto the bar, and his left hand gripping the empty stool beside him. He felt as if his entire insides were on fire, but once the shock had passed, it left him with a mellow glow and his head became untangled and sharper.

He looked around the room, and although his anger was still there, he felt more focused and clear. The barman had been watching him, and he smiled at Michael and Michael returned the smile and nodded.

The concierge was standing at the door, and he too forced a smile at Michael.

'Shall we?' he asked him.

'Yes, we shall,' Michael replied.

There was a large black Mercedes waiting for him, its driver standing at the back door. He felt himself begin to hyperventilate again, so he turned around and ran back into the bar for another whisky. He heard the concierge swear behind him.

From where he was standing backstage, Michael felt as if he were already in front of the cameras. Only a thin partition separated him from the joke-cracking host, Ryan Tubridy, and the over-excited laughter of the audience.

A production assistant with a clip board held tight against her chest and a pair of headphones around her neck, was holding her hand up to him as if she were a Garda stopping traffic.

'What a great performance. Their new album "From There to Here" is out next week. Great stuff, guys. Thanks for coming in and playing for us. Now, our next guest had something happen to him last week that not only everyone in the audience wishes would happen to them, but quite possibly the entire world - he won the lottery. And not just any lottery, folks. He won the largest amount ever won by anyone in Europe. Here tonight to talk about his win, how he's spent his first week as Ireland's newest multi-millionaire and more importantly what his plans are for the future, ladies and gentlemen, please welcome the luckiest man in Ireland, Michael Irvine.'

With the sound of the applause, Michael saw the assistant's hand drop and indicate him to move forward. When Michael didn't move, she snapped her head around.

'Go,' she noiselessly said to him.

Michael didn't move. He stared at her as if he wasn't even sure who she was.

There had been a guest a year before who had also frozen like this. She remembered him: a writer who'd had huge success with his debut novel and who hadn't been heard of since. She stepped forward and did the exact same thing she had done to him. She pinched him hard on his arm. Michael grabbed his arm in pain and for the moment he was distracted, she pushed her clipboard into his back and shoved him hard from behind.

She then said the code words 'Ice cube' twice into the microphone on her headset. This informed Ryan that Michael had frozen backstage and Ryan came out from behind his desk and went straight over to Michael.

Michael emerged from behind the partition rubbing his arm and with an expression of an escaped prisoner caught in the spotlight.

'Michael, welcome, welcome,' Ryan said and shaking his hand, pulled him towards him and over to the desk and the chairs onstage.

Ryan could hear the assistant's voice in his earpiece again as he walked back to his chair, 'I could smell the whiskey off this one,' she whispered. 'Proceed with caution, Ryan.'

'Thanks for coming on tonight, Michael. Or is it Mick or Mike you're known by?'

Michael looked around him and into the camera lens that had a red glowing light on top of it. He could make out the silhouettes of hundreds of faces behind the cameras and the lights shining in his face.

'I think Michael is still in shock from his massive win, folks,' Ryan said. 'Let's give him a little encouragement.'

The audience burst into applause again and Michael snapped out of his daze.

'Mike, Mick, Michael,' Ryan called to him. 'It's okay buddy. Look at me. We're just having a chat here. No big deal at all.'

Michael turned back to him. There was a microphone on the desk in front of him. He leaned forward and spoke into it, 'most people call me Mike,' he said.

'Thank God,' a voice said in Ryan's ear.

'That's great, Mike,' Ryan said. 'Now tell me about how you heard the news of your win.'

Michael sat forward again to speak into the microphone.

'That's okay, Mike. You don't have to speak into that. We can hear you.'

Michael looked at it. 'So what's it there for?' he asked.

Ripples of laughter ran through the audience. Michael turned to them again.

'You know what, Mike? You're right. I have no idea why that's there. Nobody's ever asked that question before.'

Ryan grabbed the microphone off the desk and threw it onto the floor behind him. The audience burst into laughter.

'That's okay, folks. He can afford to get me a new one.'

The audience applauded again.

'Seriously though, Mike. How have you been spending your time over the last week?'

'Well, at first I was given a new car to try out for a while.'

'You didn't have to pay for it?'

'No, not yet I haven't.'

'Typical. As soon as you have the money, they start giving you stuff for free. What kind of car is it, Mike?'

'A Lamborghini.'

The audience gasped and a few people whistled.

Michael turned to them. 'I still have my old car just in case.'

They laughed and Michael sat up a little straighter.

'What else have you been up to?' Ryan asked him.

'Em, I had a small party for my family and friends.'

'I hope you picked up the bill for that one.'

'Of course I did, but then when I stopped paying, they all left.'

'They left? Why?'

'Cause they're a bunch of spongers. Most of them anyway. Not my parents or my sister or… well, that's pretty much it.'

'Okay. And did you do anything special for just your immediate family?'

'Of course,' Mike said shocked by the question. 'I told them they could take as many millions as they wanted.'

Some of the audience laughed and some applauded.

'Good for you, Mike. So when you heard the news were you alone or with someone. A girlfriend, perhaps?'

'No, I don't have a girlfriend.'

'You hear that ladies? Your very own bachelor millionaire.'

Michael blushed.

'So who have you been spending all of your time with now that, as you call them, the "spongers" have all been given the boot?'

'I was with Zoe… I mean she was… I… I….'

'Zoe? Is she a friend?'

'No.'

'Advisor?'

'No.'

'Pick it up, Ryan. You're losing him,' said the voice in Ryan's earpiece.

'Well, I'm sure there are many lovely ladies here tonight who'd be happy to have a drink with you.'

The audience applauded and laughed.

Michael turned to them. He could make out the faces of three women sitting in the front row. They were laughing and fixing their hair.

'No. I don't think so,' Michael said.

'Ah, come on, Mike. Don't be so harsh. There are plenty of ladies here whom I'm sure would be interested in you just for you as a person.'

'Really? Then where were they last week when I was a nobody?'

His tone came out angrier than he had intended and the audience went a little silent.

'I was on my own last week,' he continued. 'Nobody bothered me. Now everyone wants something from me.'

'Not everyone, Mike. Most people just want you to enjoy your win.'

'Exactly. Most people are all about the money. I never asked to win this.'

'Then, why did you buy a ticket?'

Laughter from the audience.

'I didn't. I... it doesn't matter.'

'Let's get back to this mysterious Zoe. What have you two been up to for the last week? And there's no need to give us too much information.'

More laughter from the audience.

'We... I mean she... she tricked me. I trusted her, and she lied to me.'

'Change the subject, Ryan.'

'Let's talk about your parents, Mike. Are you going to buy them a big house?'

'I thought that things were going to work out okay.'

'Sorry? What was going to work out okay? You're not going to buy them a house?'

'It's my own fault really. Who did I think I was? All the fancy suits and the car. Thinking I was so lucky she was around. People were probably laughing at me behind my back.'

Michael sniffled and wiped his nose.

'Is he crying? Oh, for fuck's sake.'

'Come on, Mike. You're making us think winning the lottery was a bad thing. What about all that money?'

Michael looked up at him. 'All that money? All that money just brings out the bad in people. Turns them into users.'

'Ryan, you need to wrap this up quick. This is brutal.'

'Not everyone, Mike. There's still a lot of good in most people.'

'You're not the fucking Dalai Lama, Ryan. Finish it up and go to commercial.'

'You don't have to think that way. It'll work out, Mike. Trust me.'

'Ryan, what the fuck! Cue band. We're going to commercial.'

'I only wanted… I mean, I thought…' Michael began but the band began to play and drowned out his voice.

A man walked in front of the audience holding up a sign that said APPLAUSE and the audience obeyed.

Ryan said something else to Michael but he couldn't hear him, so he stood up and walked back to where he had entered.

The band continued to play and the audience continued to clap as he disappeared behind the partition.

The driver didn't speak to Michael as he drove him back to his hotel. He'd driven hundreds of celebrities from their hotels to the studio over the last fifteen years, and one of the most important things he'd learned was when he should and shouldn't talk.

When they reached the Shelbourne, he stepped out and walked around to open Michael's door. Michael had been staring into the darkness of the back of the car for the entire journey, but was now awakened by the light pouring into the back seat. He looked up at the driver with an expression of not being sure exactly where he was.

'Your hotel, sir,' the driver informed him.

'Oh,' Michael said. 'Oh, right.'

He swung his legs around and climbed out of the car. He stood beside the driver and there were a few moments silence between them.

'Are you okay?' the driver asked him.

'Yeah. Thanks.'

Michael looked up at the hotel. It was an expanse of red bricks and orange lights.

'A long day, sir?' the driver asked him.

'What? Oh, yes. A very long day.'

'Well, then, perhaps a late nightcap or two before you hit the hay. Goodnight, sir.'

The driver closed the door and walked back to his seat. He had just closed the door and started the engine when he heard rapid knocking at his window. He turned to see Michael with a frantic look on his face.

'Forget something?' he asked rolling down the window.

'A late nightcap or two,' Michael told him.

'That's very generous of you, sir, but I should really…'

'No. It's Lauren. Can you drive me somewhere?'

'Listen, mate. I'd like to help you out, but I've got to get back to the studio.'

'Fuck.'

'Just get a taxi,' the driver said and put the car in gear. 'Sorry, mate.'

Michael looked around the street as the car pulled away. There were dozens of taxis driving by. He walked out into the road and held his hand up but after two minutes not one had stopped for him. He cursed again into the night air, and a couple of pedestrians looked over at him.

He saw one of the porters come out of the hotel and call a taxi for a guest. He put his hand into his jacket pocket to find the key to his hotel room so he could ask the porter to get him a taxi too, but his hand pulled out the key to the Lamborghini instead.

It was still parked in the underground car park whose entrance was just around the corner. He looked at his watch. He was already late for Lauren. Grabbing the keys tighter in his fist, he ran across the road and down into the carpark.

He spotted Lauren as soon as he opened the door to Le Roman Bar and Restaurant. He had spent ten minutes searching for a free spot to park his car, and then another five minutes running from the car to the restaurant. He looked at his watch. Forty-five minutes late. He used the sleeve of his jacket to wipe the sweat off his forehead and walked over to her.

'Sorry I'm late,' he told her.

She brightened up when she saw him. 'That's okay. I knew you might have to stay longer than you thought. Now that you're a big TV star and all that.'

He flopped himself down into the chair in front of her and took off his jacket. She smiled at him and he smiled awkwardly back. They sat in silence for a while, both looking at the surroundings of the restaurant.

'Nice place,' Michael eventually said.

'Yes, isn't it?' she replied, then they fell into silence again.

Lauren reached for her drink and sipped it. 'Oh,' she said, as if having just remembered something. 'I saw you on the show tonight.'

'God, it was a disaster, wasn't it?'

'It wasn't that bad,' she assured him.

'So it was bad though?'

'Well…'

'Do you think many people saw it?'

'Maybe. It is the most watched programme in Ireland so I'd imagine so.'

Michael leaned forward and rested his face into his hands.

After a minute's silence, Lauren asked, 'Michael, are you okay?'

He raised his head, rubbing his face hard with his hands as he did.

'I shouldn't have even done the show. I don't know what I was thinking. It wasn't even my idea. Fucking Zoe.'

'No, I don't mean about the show. I meant, are you okay?'

Michael leaned forward to her. 'I… I'm just so…' he began.

'Can I get you a drink?' the waiter said, almost appearing out of nowhere.

'What?' Michael asked, annoyed by the interruption.

'A drink?'

'Yes, em… okay. I'll have a Baileys with… no, I'll have a Macallan.'

The waiter looked down at him. 'Are you sure?'

'Am I sure?' Michael asked him.

'It's just that it's a very expensive drink?'

'And what? You think I can't afford it?'

'No, it's not that. I just wanted to make sure. It's my job to…'

'Do you know what your job is, Gary?' Michael told him, looking at his name tag. 'Your job is to get me a drink. And the drink I want is a Macallan. Is that okay with you… Gary?'

The waiter shuffled away towards the bar.

'What the fuck?' Michael said looking at Lauren.

Lauren stared back at him. 'Are you okay, Michael?'

'Am I okay? Yes, I'm okay. Why do you keep asking me that?' he said, still annoyed. 'Is he okay, you should be asking. He's the one being an arsehole.'

'I don't think he was exactly.'

'Great. So you're on his side. That's fantastic, Lauren. So I'm the arsehole?'

'I didn't say that. I just…'

They were interrupted again by the waiter wordlessly putting his drink on the table in front of Michael.

Michael lifted it and took a sip from it. He smacked his lips with pleasure as the whisky flowed down his throat and through his body. He raised the glass, and looked at it, then put it against his lips and knocked it back. He sat up in his chair, looking for the waiter again and spotting him, indicated to him with the empty whisky glass that he wanted another one.

Lauren opened her mouth to say something but instead sat in silence. When the waiter had given him another one, Michael drank half of it in one go.

Lauren leaned across the table at him. 'Did something happen, Michael?'

'Did something happen? Of course something happened. I won a shit load of money and then I get fooled by everyone. You don't get it, Lauren. It's all about the money for everyone. You wouldn't understand.'

'Why? Because I don't have any?' she said trying to make a joke. 'That's a problem I wouldn't mind having.'

Michael looked at her.

'Is that why you're here?' he asked her.

'What?'

'Why are you here, Lauren?'

'I'm here because you asked me to be here.'

'Yeah, I know but why now?'

'Because you never asked me before? I don't like the way you're questioning me, Michael.'

The waiter walked by and Michael grabbed his arm. 'One more, please, Gary. If you're not too busy, mate.'

He pulled his arm away from Michael and walked back to the bar.

'Don't you think you've had enough?' Lauren asked him.

'You're not my mother, Lauren. I'm allowed to drink.'

'Well, you're being a bit rude. I think we should go.'

'I'm not going anywhere. I'm having my drink.'

'Then perhaps I should go,' she said, picking up her purse. 'This is not how I imagined the evening would go.'

'Really? How did you imagine it? Me staring at you from across the table like some dumb puppy? Yes, Lauren. No, Lauren. Three bags full Lauren. You're so wonderful, Lauren.'

'Good night, Michael,' she said and pushed her way out from the chair and stood up. 'I hope you're very happy. Just you with your money.'

'Go then,' he said. 'You're just like all the rest of them. It's all about the money.'

'You're wrong,' she said putting on her coat.

'Am I?' he said, as the waiter approached with Michael's drink on a tray.

'Yes, you're so wrong.'

'Well maybe I'm not. Maybe I'm right. Maybe Joey was right about you all along.'

Lauren froze for a moment, her eyes piercing into him. The waiter had stopped and was looking from one to the other until Lauren walked off.

As the waiter placed the drink down on the table, Lauren's hand took it off him and in one movement poured its entire contents over Michael's head. Michael jumped from the shock and the ice.

By the time he stood up and turned around, he saw Lauren's coat flapping out of the door.

'Let's go back to the station, Frank,' Detective Garda Ciaran Butler said to his colleague seated next to him. 'There's nothing happening here.'

The two Gardaí had been sitting in their unmarked car for the last two hours, acting on a tip that there would be an attempted break-in at the jewellery shop three hundred meters from where they were parked.

Detective Garda Frank Mahon started the engine. 'I told you we were wasting our time. I'm going to kill that little fucker. I bet you anything he knew when we were...'

'Hold on a second,' Ciaran interrupted him. 'Look at this.'

Both Gardaí watched as a man leaned unsteadily against his car while he searched in his pocket for his keys. Finding them he beeped the car open then dropped them onto the ground. He screamed into the air in anger and kicked the side of his car.

'That is one nice fucking car,' Frank said.

'It'd be shame to have some drunk smash it into a wall,' Ciaran replied.

'A crying shame,' Frank agreed.

'I'll tell you what. I'll fill out the paperwork for the arrest if I get to drive the car back to the station.'

'Fair enough. But give him a second to find his keys and put them into the ignition.'

Both Gardaí sat in silence as they watched Michael on his hands and knees rummaging on the ground around his car.

19

Jack Irvine opened his eyes and looked up into the darkness of his bedroom ceiling. He was a light sleeper anyway, but since his son's lottery win he'd found it harder to sleep through the whole night without waking up at least a few times. That evening, because of Michael's performance on the Late Late Show, he was surprised he had managed to get any sleep at all.

He turned his head to look at his wife. She had a pink eye shade covering half her face that said 'Beauty Sleep in Progress' written across it. He yawned and turned onto his side and tried to settle his mind to go back to sleep.

The sound of something heavy falling onto the carpeted floor of the dining room downstairs forced his eyes open again. He listened but heard nothing. He was just about to close his eyes when he heard the cutlery rattle as a drawer was opened in the kitchen.

The first thought that came to his head was 'Michael'. He had tried to call him after the show but his phone was switched off. Had he driven around for the last couple of hours unsure where to go? Then finally realised that his home was his only real sanctuary. The best thing his son needed now was a cup of tea and some fatherly advice.

He crept out of bed without disturbing Rose, then made his way downstairs. He avoided the creaky sixth step, deciding to surprise or even frighten his son with a sudden entrance. He placed his hand on the kitchen door's handle and paused before opening it. He listened and could hear a cupboard door being opened.

'Don't be stealing your mother's biscuits,' he said loudly as he pushed open the door.

The figure standing with the cupboard door in his hand was dressed all in black. He turned his head and Jack saw two blue eyes staring at him through two holes in a full-face balaclava. The back door opened and another man, slightly smaller in stature and also wearing a balaclava, walked in carrying a hammer.

'I found this dad,' he said. 'This'll open it.'

Both Jack and the man at the cupboard turned to look at him.

Jack felt his entire insides churn and although he opened his mouth and tried to call, only the tiniest squeak came out. He continued to stare at the two men and they continued to stare at him until he heard a foot step behind him. As he turned, everything went dark as a black cloth bag was shoved over his head.

Both of his arms were grabbed and his hands were tied together with what felt and sounded like a cable-tie. He was dragged backwards and thrown onto the sofa in the sitting room.

'Don't make a fucking sound,' a voice warned, so close to him that he could feel the man's breath through the bag.

'What now?' asked another man.

'Get the wife,' he was instructed.

Jack's heart skipped a beat at this command and breathing in deeply he found his voice and let out a cry, 'Rose'.

'I told you to shut the fuck up,' the man said. Jack felt a blow, like a concrete block, hitting the side of his face. His head shot sideways and he lay there as the pain pulsed through his body.

In the darkness of the hood, Jack listened to footsteps running up the stairs, then after a moment, his wife scream in terror.

Jack tried to call out again but when he opened his mouth, his jaw throbbed with intense pain, so that all he could muster was a whimper of agony.

'Boil the kettle,' a voice ordered. 'I'll pour it on the wife first. There's cash in this house, and they're going to tell us where the fuck it is.'

Rose let out another scream as she was pushed down the stairs. The man standing above Jack let out a short satisfied chuckle.

Jack shut his eyes tight, but the tears forced themselves out through the sides as he lay there listening to his wife being dragged down the hall.

'Jesus Christ, you stink of whisky, mate. You'd think someone poured the stuff over you,' Frank told Michael, as he drove back to the Garda Station.

He looked in his rear view mirror. 'Are you supposed to be famous or something?' he asked.

Michael sat in the back seat with his head lowered. He leaned forwards slightly to try and make the handcuffs less comfortable. In the rear-view mirror, Frank could see the Lamborghini following them as they drove through the city.

Michael raised his head. 'No.'

'Are your parents?'

Michael chuckled at the thought.

'So what's with the fancy car?' Frank asked him.

Michael didn't answer.

'What did you say your name was again?'

'Michael Irvine.'

'Michael Irvine,' Frank repeated, his detective's mind searching through its files. 'Michael Irvine... Michael Irvine... Michael... Michael's millions! You're that Euro lottery guy, aren't you?'

Michael lowered his head again.

'Do you know what I'd do with all that money if I were you?'

'Oh God,' Michael said and sunk deeper into the seat.

'Firstly, I'd get a nice little…'

His suggestion was cut off by the squawk of the radio. 'Control to all units. Intruder on premises. All units respond.'

'Shit,' Frank said, looking over his shoulder at the Lamborghini behind him.

He picked up the radio.

'This is 206 responding. Go with address, Control,' he said. His previous light-hearted demeanour shifted to one of firm professionalism.

'Roger that, 206. Address is 176 Glenbay Road.'

Before Frank had time to respond, Michael had shot up in his seat and was leaning into the front.

'Sit back in your seat,' Frank yelled at him and switched on his sirens. The surrounding buildings were lit up by the blue lights from the car as it bolted forward to overtake the car in front.

'That's my address,' Michael told him.

'Sit the fuck down,' he commanded

'But it's…'

'Nobody drives a Lamborghini and lives in Glenbay Estate.'

'It's my parents' house,' Michael shouted at him, trying to be heard above the wail of the siren.

Frank looked at him. He saw the Lamborghini overtake several cars behind him.

'Okay,' he said. 'Sit down.'

Michael did as he was told. His heart was racing as the car roared ahead. He heard the detective tell his station he was two minutes away.

'When we get there,' Frank told him, 'don't get out of the car.'

Michael nodded.

'I fucking mean it.'

Michael's familiar road came into view. Both the detective's car and the Lamborghini drove at speed past the houses.

As they got closer, Michael saw two men come charging out of the house. Both were wearing balaclavas. One of the men was holding a hammer in his hand.

Frank slammed on the brakes of the car when he saw the men, but he was too late. His car slammed into the side of Michael's old car in the driveway. Michael lunged forward and smashed his head off the headrest.

The detective threw open his door and jumped out. His right hand pulled up his jacket and he withdrew his sidearm. Michael groaned with the pain.

The second detective, Ciaran, was driving too close behind and misjudged how quickly his partner's car had come to a stop. He crashed the Lamborghini into the back of the detective's car and Michael flew back and then forward again into the headrest.

Ciaran jumped out and ran into the house. Michael sat up but his head was spinning. He felt as if he were about to faint but the sight of his parents' open front door frightened him. With his hands still handcuffed, he tried to manoeuvre his body like a snake between the two front seats.

He succeeded, his head resting on the driver's seat. Kicking his way out, he managed to get his head and upper torso protruding out of the door. He could hear shouting and approaching sirens howling in the distance.

He wriggled until he landed his whole body onto the road, and then pushed himself up onto his knees. The sound of the sirens got louder as another Garda car turned onto the street.

He screamed more out of shock than pain when something started banging onto his head and back. He fell back down onto the road and caught sight of an umbrella as it smashed into him repeatedly.

'Stop, stop it,' he yelled.

'Stay down there you little scumbag,' said the lady's voice, as she aimed her umbrella.

He twisted from side to side until he saw the angry face of his next door neighbour Mrs. Flynn.

'Mrs. Flynn, stop it. For God's sake. Stop hitting me.'

Thrown by the sound of her name, Mrs Flynn obeyed and looked closer at her victim's face.

'Michael?' she said.

'Help me up,' he yelled at her, but as soon as she leaned down to him she was picked up and removed by a uniformed Garda.

'This way please, madam,' he told her.

A second Garda, also in uniform, grabbed Michael by the clothes on his back and shoved him up against the detective's car.

'Thought you'd make a quick run for it?' he sneered at him. 'Didn't ya, you little fucker.'

Michael let out a cry of pain as his head was forced onto the bonnet of the car. The Garda raised him up and dragged him over to the back door of the detective's car. He opened the door and shoved Michael in, then slammed the door shut.

Michael groaned in misery and pain. He thought of his parents and what had happened. He allowed his body to lie still as he listened to all the excited voices and noises around him. He shut his eyes tight.

The car door opened again and he heard Frank's voice. He was panting and out of breath. 'They got away,' he said. 'You'd better come in.'

He reached in and lifted Michael out. With his back to him, Frank took off his handcuffs. Then he turned him around.

'What the fuck happened to you?' he asked when he saw Michael's face. 'You look like you've had the shit kicked out of you.'

Michael rubbed his hands. 'Where's my mam and dad?'

'They're inside. They're okay. A bit shaken. Not as much as you though. Or your fancy car.'

Michael ran into his house, pushing anyone aside who blocked his way.

'Mam. Dad,' he cried out.

He found them in the sitting room. They were seated on the sofa with two guards standing in front of them. Detective Frank followed Michael into the room. Rose who had seemed calm up to then, burst into tears as they embraced each other. Michael then hugged his dad, and sat down between them.

'What happened?' he asked.

'Is was frightening, son,' said Rose. 'My God, Michael. What happened to you? And you stink of whiskey.'

'I'm okay. I'll tell you later, mam.'

Michael looked up at the detective.

'What did the men want?'

'Well, we're trying to determine at the moment whether it was a simple break-in or something a bit more sinister,' Frank told him.

'More sinister?' Michael asked.

'A possible kidnapping. We're not sure.'

'Jesus,' Michael said.

'Thank goodness Mrs Flynn saw one of them coming in the back door,' Rose said. 'It was her who called the police.'

'Michael,' Frank said. 'Where can your parents go tonight?'

'Go? Go where?' Jack asked.

'It's probably best if you spend the rest of the night with family or friends,' Frank told them. 'Forensics are on the way.'

'This is all my fault,' Michael said.

'No, son. Don't be silly,' Jack said.

'It is,' Michael told them. 'It's all my fault. If it wasn't for the money none of this would have happened.'

There was a moment's silence as they recognised this as the truth.

'I'm so sorry, Mam. I'm sorry, Dad.'

'You've nothing to be sorry for,' Rose said.

'You can't blame yourself for the actions of others,' Frank told him. 'Now let me just ask one or two more questions, and you can head off.'

The second detective, Ciaran Butler, came into the room.

'I told you,' Jack said. 'We didn't see anything. I had a hood over my head the entire time, and they were wearing balaclavas.'

'What about their voices?' Ciaran asked him. 'What kind of

accents did they have?'

'Dublin accents,' Jack said.

'There was a tall one and a shorter one. I didn't see the third one. He came behind me and put a hood over my head. But I think he was the one in charge, because he sent the others up to get Rose.'

Rose squeezed Jack's hand at the memory of it.

'Please,' Michael asked. 'Can I just bring them to my sister's house, and we can do this tomorrow.'

'Yes, of course,' Frank said. 'We'll have one. or two more questions...'

'Wait a second,' Ciaran said. 'How do you know he was the one in charge if you couldn't see them?'

'Because of his voice,' Jack said.

'Yes, that's good. But how do you know then who left the room?'

They all stood in silence looking at Jack. He thought for a few moments.

'Because of their shoes,' he finally said.

'But you said you had a hood on,' Frank told him.

'Yes, but I could see the ground. So I could see their shoes. The one with the big black boots was giving the orders. The other two had dirty shoes on. The tall one's were black. The shorter man's were white. White trainers.'

'Anything else?' Frank asked.

'No.'

'Dirty how?' Ciaran asked him.

'Just dirty.'

'With muck?'

'No. Oil,' Jack told him. 'Black oil spots all over them.'

Michael stared down at his father. 'White trainers, Dad?' he asked him. 'With black oil spots? Are you sure?'

'Of course, I'm sure.'

They were all now looking at Michael.

'Does that mean something to you, Michael?' Frank asked him.

'Em... no. Probably not,' Michael told him.

'Okay, let's wrap this up,' Ciaran informed them. 'Mr and Mrs Irvine, you've both been very helpful. We'll be in touch tomorrow, but for now how about we get you out of here. You said you have a daughter?'

'Yes, Samantha,' Rose said. 'But it's very late to be calling her now. They'll all be asleep. She has two children. Two girls. Here let me show you a photo of them.'

'He doesn't want to see photos of the girls, Rose,' Jack said.

'Of course he does, don't you?' Rose said, looking up at the detective.

'Absolutely,' Ciaran told her and escorted them out.

Just as he left, he looked over at Frank, and nodded at him to go to Michael. Frank nodded back.

Michael stood with his head down as the detective approached him.

'You know who it was. The white trainers with oil spots.'

Michael looked up at him.

'Don't you, Michael?'

Michael nodded.

'Good,' Frank said, a smile forming on his face. 'Very good.'

A few minutes later, Frank and Michael walked out of the house. Ciaran was examining his unmarked garda car, which was still sandwiched between Michael's original car and the Lamborghini.

'What are we going to do about this mess?' Ciaran asked, when Michael and Frank joined him.

Michael remained silent.

'You know, you could still be charged with drink driving,' Frank, told him. 'Unless of course…'

'I pay for the damages?' Michael suggested.

He looked over at his parents. They were both getting into a Garda car.

'That would be entirely up to you,' Ciaran said, putting his hands up in the air.

'Alright,' he told them. 'That's fair.'

They all shook each other's hands in agreement, and Michael made his way over to his parents. The two detectives remained looking at the cars.

'I don't know where it came from, Frank, but I'm starting to get a blinding headache.'

'Me too, mate. Me too.'

20

When Michael woke the next morning, the first thing he noticed was his headache. He put his hands to his head to block out the light in the room and winced when he touched his bruised face. He tried to swallow but his throat was too dry. The inside of his mouth had a metallic taste, which he guessed was blood.

Thoughts and memories from the previous night materialised behind his closed eyes - his parents; the TV show; Zoe; the guards; the chase; the Lamborghini; Lauren.

He thought of Lauren and winced in pain again.

There was a knock on the door, and it opened gently. Michael could hear the faint but excited voices of Katie and Emily downstairs.

'Michael?' his sister said. 'Are you awake?'

She came into the room and closed the door behind her.

'I was upstairs and I thought I heard you. How are you feeling?'

Michael put both his arms over his head.

'That bad, huh?' she asked.

'Sorry,' he said. His voice was raspy, and he tried to swallow again.

'Here,' she said. 'Drink this,' and she held out a glass of water to him.

He put his arms down and sat up in the bed. He took the glass from her and sipped it at first, then drank it all in a few gulps.

'How are you feeling?' she asked.

'How do I look?'

'Well, I hope you feel better than you look,' she smiled. 'You should get a doctor to look at those marks.'

'How's Mam and Dad?' he asked.

'They're okay. Considering.'

'Considering, it's all my fault.'

'No, it's not, Mike. Don't say that.'

'If Mrs Flynn hadn't alerted the guards then those men would have…' He cringed at his own thoughts.

'It's okay, it's okay,' she tried to assure him. 'The fact is that nothing happened. Well, at least nothing that's irreversible. They're safe.'

'They'll have to move.'

Sam scoffed at this. 'Are you kidding me? The Gardaí called to say they'll be finished with the house by twelve and mam's already said she's going home then. Dad's says he knows a man who can fit an alarm for €500.'

Michael attempted to laugh, but his face was too sore.

'There's something else,' she said. 'They've arrested two of the men from last night. You're not going to believe this. It was Joey McGuinness and his dad.'

Michael nodded.

'Did you hear what I said?'

'Yes.'

She looked at him. 'You knew already?'

He didn't try to deny it.

'How did you…?'

Michael turned away from her.

'Okay. I won't ask,' she said and walked over to the window. She looked down onto her street. 'What are you going to do now?'

'I have no fucking idea.'

She turned around to him and laughed.

'What's so funny?'

'I never heard you swear before.'

'Sorry.'

'What about your new friend? That girl, Zoe. Where's she?'

Michael didn't answer.

'Fair enough. But you can't stay in bed forever.'

'Why not?'

'I'll let you rest some more if you want,' she said walking to the door. 'Call me if you need anything. I'll try to keep the girls away as long as I can. When you decide to get up, help yourself to some of Derek's clothes. They should fit.'

'Sam,' he called to her. 'Can you call some security alarm company and get them to fit out Mam and Dad's house? Ten, twenty grand whatever it costs. Tell them I'll pay them double if they start today.'

'Alright. I'll call someone.'

'And Sam. You might want to get them to do the same with your house.'

She nodded.

'I'm sorry.'

She opened the door but turned to him first.

'Take some time, Mike,' she told him. 'Try to be normal today. Go for a swim. Or one of your walks. It's all going to be okay.'

She closed the door and he lay back down on the bed. The sky was blue again today. A single bird circled above, and he followed its path around and around. He wondered what it was doing. Looking for food. Looking for a mate. Showing off. Maybe it just wanted to be on its own. Free in the sky to roam. To be away from everything. And everyone. Never wanting to land again.

Michael waited until his parents had left before he got up. He wasn't sure why. Rose had knocked and had come into his room, but he had pretended to be asleep. He listened to them talking outside as they left - car doors closing and Katie and Emily cheering them on their way.

He showered and, wrapped in a towel, picked the least flashy clothes he could find in Derek's wardrobe. He surveyed the finished result in the full length mirror. The blue shirt was a bit tight (there was no way he could fasten the top button) but apart from the visible bruises, he thought he looked somewhat presentable.

'I said I don't know where he is,' Sam was saying into the hall phone. 'Please stop calling here.'

'Who was that?' Michael asked as he came down the stairs.

'I don't know. Journalist. Television. They all sound the same.'

'They're looking for me?'

'Anyone who'll confirm what did or didn't happen last night. I'm sure they'd be ecstatic to talk to you.'

'No thanks.'

'Where are you off to?'

'I think I'll take your advice and go for a walk.'

'Uncle Mike. Uncle Mike,' the two girls screamed as they ran into the hall.

They threw their arms around him and despite the physical pain, he felt better all over.

'Can you read us a story, Uncle Mike?' Katie asked.

'No. I want him to do a jigsaw with me,' Emily said.

'I asked him first.'

'Girls, girls,' Michael said trying to calm them. 'I'm afraid I have to go out for a while.'

They moaned in unison. 'I'll be back later. I promise.'

'Go back into the kitchen girls,' their mother instructed them. 'I'll be in soon.'

Samantha opened a drawer in the hall and took out a bunch of keys. She handed them to Michael.

'Here, you'll need these.'

'Why?'

'Last I heard both your cars were smashed up.'

'Shit, I forgot about that.'

'You're really getting into the habit of swearing now, aren't you?'

He took the keys from her, and they looked at each other for a few moments.

'What?' Michael asked.

'Nothing,' she said. 'You just seem different from last week.'

'Richer maybe.'

'Yes, of course. But different too. Older.'

'Jesus. Thanks a lot.'

'Be careful, Mike,' she said and leaned into him, giving him a deep hug. 'Just remember, there's always a simple solution to every problem.'

'Okay, Oprah,' he smiled as he opened the front door.

Michael's mind jumped from one thought to another as he drove around. Despite himself, he missed Zoe. He missed her no-nonsense advice, but he also missed her company. He knew his dream of being with Lauren was over but it was just one more thing that had changed forever in his life this week. His darkest thoughts always came back to his parents. What if they hadn't arrived when they did? And what if it happens again?

He was stopped at a red traffic light when he saw a coffee shop on the corner. It was one of the many cafés that had popped up around the city. This one had the word 'bean' in the title. He parked the car across the road and walked over.

It was only half full, so he decided to order a coffee and sit at the window looking out for a while. Maybe if he allowed his mind to wander, he'd be able to just figure things out for himself. He breathed in the aroma of the coffee and the fresh pastries and sandwiches. Maybe he could even open up a coffee shop of his own? Or a restaurant? Or a bar? He could employ Lauren and she would... Then again, maybe not.

His mind was drifting so much that he hadn't noticed he'd been standing in the queue for more than a few minutes. He also hadn't noticed that the chatter of small talk and the clanging of cups and spoons had stopped.

When he looked up at the barista, she wasn't looking at him. She was staring at him. When he made eye contact with her, she turned her head away in embarrassment.

'Can I get an Americano, please?' he asked her.

She nodded and picked up a cup.

His gaze fell onto the counter where several free copies of The Irish Times were laid out for customers to take with their coffees. On the bottom half of the page, a grainy picture of a man sitting on sofa caught his attention. At first the face looked familiar to him, but two seconds later he realised it was a picture of himself from the Late Late Show last night.

He stared at the oddity of it. He picked up the paper and looked closer. He began to read the article under his image.

Ireland's latest EuroMillions winner and richest bachelor, Michael Irvine, was seen to make somewhat of a spectacle of himself last night. The former insurance worker made quite a splash with his debut television performance when he...

Michael's heart sank. He picked up all of the newspapers in the pile and glanced through them in the maddening thought that somehow they'd be different. When he reached the last newspaper, there was a fresh pile of papers. This time it was the Irish Independent.

In big, black, bold lettering across the front he read KIDNAP ATTEMPT OF EUROMILLIONS PARENTS. Under it was another photo of himself. Beside that there was a photograph of his Lamborghini smashed into the back of the detective's car and the detective's car smashed into his old car. He tried to read the article but the words blurred and he felt weak.

It was only then he looked up and noticed the silence in the café. He turned to see every face looking at him. He could see his image on almost every table in the place. Some faces looked out from behind newspapers. Newspapers with his face on them.

He took a step back and walked into the counter. He looked around and saw the door. Without another word he walked as fast as he could towards the door. Eyes followed him, as he almost knocked an old lady down when he pushed open the door and rushed outside.

'Hey, watch it,' someone yelled at him, but he didn't look back.

While driving his sister's car, he reached into his pocket and pulled out his phone. It had been turned off since the TV show. He pulled the car into the side of the road and switched it on. There were eighty-seven SMS messages and one hundred and forty-three missed calls.

It rang.

'Hello?' he answered.

'Michael, it's Eamon Molloy here from The Herald. I'd just like to ask you a couple of questions regarding…'

Michael threw the phone out of his hand. It fell between his feet. He could still hear the tinny voice of the reporter calling his name.

He picked it up and ended the call.

It rang again. A different number.

Michael switched it back off again. He looked around him and saw a small corner shop up the road to his right.

'Hey buddy, be careful about parking there,' a man who was passing by while walking his dog warned him. 'They're always giving out tickets along here.'

'Thanks,' Michael told him but walked on.

'Hey,' the man said again, grabbing his arm. 'Aren't you that lottery bloke?'

Michael released his arm and walked back to his car as if he were being chased.

'It is you, isn't it?' the man called after him.

Michael started the engine and drove away.

He looked from side to side as he drove. He wiped the sweat off his forehead with his hand. A woman, who was holding a rolled-up newspaper, looked in at him as he was waiting at a traffic light. Michael locked all the doors in the car.

He soon spotted another shop and pulled in beside it. He looked into the back seat of the car and saw a pink haversack with some Disney character on it. Emptying its contents, Katie's school books and pencil case fell onto the passenger seat. At the bottom of the bag he found a pink Disney princess scarf and hat.

He wrapped the scarf around his face so that only his eyes were exposed. He then stuck the pink woolly hat onto his head, stretching it first. He checked his appearance in the rear view mirror and half-smiled with satisfaction. Although he couldn't see the smile.

Even with his disguise, he still kept his head low when he went into the shop. He bought a copy of every magazine and newspaper on the self, and a takeaway coffee.

'What about your change?' the cashier called after him holding up the two fifty euro notes.

He drove around until he found a secluded car park and parked in the furthest corner from the entrance. He was the main article on every paper. Most of them had pictures of him on the Late Late Show. Some had pictures of his house, the crashed Lamborghini, some very old photos from his school. There was an interview with Trevor Tiernan from where he used to work.

That bastard, Michael thought to himself.

He threw all of the papers into the passenger seat and looked at the magazines. He wasn't in any of them except for The People. That magazine, however, had enough photos of him to make up for the lack of photos in the others.

Roughly one third of its glossy pages were dedicated to him. At every turn of its pages, he felt more nauseous. He looked at photos of himself in the Shelbourne, outside the tailors, having lunch with Zoe, getting into the Lamborghini, getting out of the Lamborghini, at the airport, climbing up onto the plane's wing. One of the shots was of him hitting Joey in Harry's and of Joey sprawled out on the floor.

He laid his head back on the headrest and allowed the magazine

215

to fall from his hands. How could everything have gone so wrong, so quickly, he thought? And how was he going to untangle this mess of a life he had now? He felt trapped. Trapped in this life. Trapped in this car. He tried not to, but he thought of Lauren and wondered, as he had done thousands of times before, what she was doing at that moment. If he could just make things right with her. Be friends again. Share each other's thoughts and worries. She could be the one stable connection, outside of his family, that could bring him back to his old life. Or at least help him to find a small part of it.

Sam's words came back to him - there's always a simple solution to every problem. He seemed too far from any possible solution. His future looked so bleak. So dark and clouded.

He put his hand to his face. A volcano of pensive and dour emotions boiled up inside of him, and he shook with their force. Then tears began to seep through his eyelids. He felt them falling down his face and through his fingers as if they were something beyond his control. He had the strange thought that he couldn't remember the last time he had cried. Not since school.

His coffee went cold and untouched in the cup holder of his sister's car as the afternoon light grew darker.

It was without any definitive conscious decision on his part, that later that evening he found himself parked outside of Harry's Pub. He didn't know why he was there. He had no reason to be but then he felt he had no reason to be anywhere. Or for any reason.

For perhaps the first time, however, he had no nervousness in pushing open the door to the pub. He had always only gone to see Lauren. For years he had risked seeing and having to deal with Joey McGuinness just to have a few moments with Lauren. Today, both these apprehensions were absent in his life.

He would be lucky if Lauren would even talk to him. As for Joey McGuinness, he assumed he was in a cell somewhere with iron bars as doors. Or maybe that's just in the movies.

All he wanted from Harry's was a drink, and he knew it was probably the only place in Ireland where he could go and no one would bother him.

'I'm not talking to you Michael Irvine,' Lauren told him as soon as he sat down at the bar.

'Yeah, I guessed that, Lauren,' Michael said. 'And I don't blame you either.'

She stood looking at him with her arms folded. 'I'd like to have you barred but Harry would overrule me.'

Michael looked around the pub. He recognised most of the faces and those he made eye contact gave him a courteous nod.

'You look like shit, by the way,' Lauren said when he turned back to face her. She unfolded her arms and took a step closer to him. 'The newspapers and reporters have been in and out of here all day looking for you. I told them I'm not your damn secretary and to leave us in peace. You should call your mam as well. She phoned looking for you. All that money doesn't give you the right to treat everyone the way you like.'

'For someone who isn't talking to me, you certainly have a lot to say.'

'Don't be so cheeky.'

'I'm sorry Lauren.'

'I'm only passing on a message to you. If you don't want...'

'No, I don't mean I'm sorry for being cheeky. I'm sorry for last night.'

She folded her arms again.

'You know I didn't mean anything I said last night,' he told her. 'That wasn't me. I fucked up. I fucked up with a lot of things this week. But hurting you is my biggest regret. I'm truly sorry, Lauren.'

'Well,' she said. 'I appreciate that. It was still very hurtful.'

'I know.'

She unfolded her arms. 'I suppose I should forgive you since it was your first time to piss me off. But listen to me Michael Irvine. I don't take that shit from anybody. Anybody. And the next time you do or say anything to upset me or Max, you don't get to talk to me ever again. Ever.'

'I understand. And I never will,' he told her, and he knew he never would.

'Now, what do you want? Whiskey?'

'I think I'll stick to what I know best; a Heineken shandy, please.'

She smiled at him for the first time and picked up a pint glass. 'That's probably a good idea.'

His gaze wandered to the end of the bar where a pile of opened newspapers lay. He looked at them for a few moments. Lauren followed his stare.

'You're quite the celebrity now,' she said.

'It's nothing but a curse, Lauren.'

'What? Being a celebrity?'

'No, the money.'

She put the drink down in front of him.

'I feel so trapped by it. And it's not just me, it's Mam and Dad. Who knows what some psycho will do next. Or maybe next time it'll be Sam. Or the girls. I don't know what I'd do if…'

'Hey, don't think like that. You can buy your parents a house anywhere they want. You could buy them a castle down the country.'

Michael laughed at that. 'I could just see them. Lord and Lady of the manor. She'd spend twelve hours a day going around cleaning the place. Dad would probably have a heart attack cutting all the grass because he'd be too cheap to buy a proper lawn mower.'

Lauren laughed at him.

'It's funny. There are so many people in the world who need just a small bit of money to help them out, and here I am with more than I'll ever need.'

'Lauren,' somebody called her.

'Coming,' she called over her shoulder then turned back to Michael. 'Well there's a simple solution to that isn't there?'

'Is there?'

'Yes,' she joked. 'You could just give it all away.'

Lauren served the customer and tidied up the old newspapers. When she came back to Michael he was staring at the bottles behind the bar.

'Michael, is everything okay?'

'Everything's perfect,' he told her. 'You're right. I'm going to do exactly what you said. I'm going to give it away.'

'I was only joking, Michael. I didn't mean for you to just…'

'It makes so much sense. Why didn't I think of it myself? A simple solution. Sam was right. '

'Wow, Michael. That'd be very generous of you. How much are you thinking?'

'All of it.'

'But how much will you keep?'

He looked up at her. He had a slight manic look in his eyes.
'Not one penny.'

An hour later, Michael's Heineken shandy sat flat and untouched on the bar. It had been pushed to the side to make room for sheets of pages that Michael was now frantically scribbling on.

At first, Lauren had tried to persuade him that giving away €190,000,000 was not the greatest of ideas in the world, but she soon got caught up in his enthusiasm and focus as he began to write down all the immense good he could do with the money.

'The Simon Community,' Lauren suggested and he wrote it down. 'They do great work with the homeless. They could buy a building and make it into a sort of free hostel.'

'Irish Guide Dogs Society. You have to give them something.'

Michael sat up and bit the end of the pen. 'No, that's no good.'

'What?' Lauren asked him. 'You don't like dogs?'

'They're all great charities, and I know they need the money and we will give them all something but…'

'What?'

'Well… what about everyone else?'

'Like who?'

'Like them,' Michael said and pointed in the direction of the people in the pub.

'You want to buy them a round?'

'No. Not them specifically. I mean, people. Ordinary people. The granny who can't afford her heating bill this month. The woman whose husband has drank all his wages and she can't get enough food for her kids. The man who works abroad and wants to come home to visit his family. The kid who wants a pair of new trendy Nikes so that he's not the odd one out in school. Just regular people with regular problems that a few hundred euro would mean the world to them.'

Lauren smiled at him. She felt so proud of him but didn't know why.

'You're right.'

'So how do we do that?'

'I know. You go on TV and you…'

'I'm not going on television again, Lauren. No way…'

'Okay, okay, relax. Radio then. You go on the radio. A chat show. Em... Joe Duffy. Yeah, that's it. You go on the Joe Duffy Show tomorrow afternoon and you tell everyone your idea. You give them an address. A PO Box and an email address. I'll set one up for you tonight. Then they write to you and you send them cheques for whatever you decide. €1000, €10,000 or even €100. You'd get hundreds, maybe thousands of letters and emails and you sit and you choose which... why are you looking at me like that?'

Michael had a broad smile across his face as he looked at her.

'You can help me.'

'No, Michael. I can't.'

'Why not? I can't do this on my own. It'll take me forever to read through everything.'

'I can't just take a few days off. Harry would sack me.'

'Perfect.'

'What?'

'Listen Lauren, and hear me out.'

Lauren stood away from the bar and folded her arms

'Remember you told me about that little cottage? The one you dream about for you and Max? If you help me for the next few days or for how long it takes, then I'll buy it for you. I'll set you up wherever you like. The school, the beach. All of that. Your dream, Lauren. Can you help me?'

Lauren unfolded her arms and swallowed.

'I can't, Michael. Thank you so much, but I can't take your money. I know you're a good man, but I don't want to owe anybody anything.'

'You won't. It's a job offer. You work and you get paid. That's it.'

'But how am I going to get from there to work every day?'

Michael laughed. 'We can buy you a pub there.'

'No thanks.'

'Then a café. A bookshop. I got it – a Bed and Breakfast.'

'I'm sorry, Michael. That sounds lovely, but I can't.'

Michael sat back in his chair. He looked at all of the charities written down in front of him. He picked up one of them and looked at it.

'What about if I set up a trust fund to help out every family who has a child born with special needs? You're always saying how Max doesn't get the support he deserves because of cut backs. We can make sure that every child gets some help. You can do that.'

Lauren looked at him as she tried to hold back her tears. She wiped one away quickly as it fell down her cheek.

'You missed your calling as a salesman,' she said and laughed.

Michael didn't say anything. He breathed in the air in the pub as if it were morning air from the Dublin Mountains and felt the tension float away from him like evaporating rain.

21

'1850 815 915. Hello, good afternoon, and you're very welcome to Liveline.'

Lauren looked over at Michael as the theme music to the radio talk show played. The headphones looked huge over his ears. She thought his face had a nervousness under the illumination of the red light with the words ON AIR written on it. But when he looked up he smiled at her, and she smiled back.

'A very good afternoon, folks,' the presenter, Joe Duffy, said into his microphone. 'We have a slightly unusual show for you this afternoon. Sitting across from me is someone most of you will know at this stage. His name is Michael Irvine and he's certainly had his fair share of media attention over the last few days. Last Saturday night, as most of you will be aware, he was the sole recipient of the largest win ever in the EuroMillions. "The Luckiest Man in Ireland" he's been called and indeed some would say in the world.'

'I have no idea why he's here but when a man with €190,000,000 in his pocket says he has something important to say then it piques our interest here at Liveline. So, Michael it's over to you.'

Michael sat looking at the microphone in front of him for a few moments. The dead air in the studio only added further to the tension in the room. He cleared his throat and he could hear the sound of his cough in his headphones. He and Lauren had spent the morning writing out a one-page statement in his room in the Shelbourne. For four hours they had structured each word in each sentence until both of them were happy with the wording. The page now sat in front of Michael. He picked it up.

'Dead air, dead air,' a voice said into his headphone. 'Joe, he's frozen. You're back on.'

Michael saw a man in a black turtleneck sweater on the opposite side of the glass wall waving a clipboard in the air.

'It's okay, Mike,' Joe said. 'Go ahead. In your own time.'

Michael picked up the sheet of paper and leaned into the microphone.

'Hello,' he began. 'I would like, first of all, to thank the host for affording me this time in order to convey my message here today. Circumstances over the last week have lead me to arrive at the conclusion that my financial win has not been as beneficial to me as some of you would believe it has been.'

He heard his voice in the headphones, and he shifted in his seat. It sounded mechanical and vacuous. He looked down at the page in his hand. The weight of the headphones pressed down on his head. There was more dead air and the presenter looked over at Lauren.

Michael put the page down on the table and then reached up and took his headphones off. He sat up straighter in his chair and leaned into the microphone.

'Look, I'm just like most of you listening to this. Before the EuroMillions, I was an ordinary bloke, happy and content and living an ordinary life. Well, that's not exactly true. I was never happy and content. But that wasn't because of money.'

'I've only had all this money for a week, and what I wish most of all is that everyone listening to this could win that amount too. I'm sure you're all wishing the same thing. But there'd be a catch - you could only have the money for a week. And that'd be enough. Because then you'd see that all that money can buy anything but is worth nothing. The things that are the most valuable don't cost anything. It might be a walk by the sea or in the mountains. Or it might be watching your kids and realising that they're the most precious things and you wouldn't exchange a hair on their heads for all the money in the world. And I know that all sounds very hippy-dippy, but it's true.'

'Because all that money changes everything. But mostly it changes those around you. It acts as a magnet that draws out a sort of poison in your family and friends. Like a cancer. People who had no connection with you before suddenly think they have this claim over you. Snapping at you like, I don't know, like vultures on a piece of meat.'

Michael looked over at Lauren.

'But for those who had only goodness in them. Who only had your best interests at heart, it brings out a light. No, it doesn't bring it out because it was always there. It heightens the light. It makes their brightness brighter. And knowing that and learning that was worth €190,000,000.'

'So, I don't need it any more. I've decided to give it all away. Every penny. Well, minus a few hundred thousand that I'll need to pay for a crashed Lamborghini and my hotel bill in the Shelbourne.'

'Most of it will go to charities and various organisations that we're going to decide on over the next few days. But I'd also like to give some of it to individuals who need it. Ordinary people, just like me. After this statement, Joe is going to read out an email address and a postal address and you can send your requests there. Please also include an address where I can send a cheque to, or your bank details so I can transfer the money directly.'

'I promise that every letter and email will be read and considered whether it's for ten euro or a million euro. I'm not looking for investment opportunities and these aren't loans. They're once-off payments. I'm not looking for anything in return.'

'I know that when this is all over, I can't go back to where I was. I can't pick up where I left off. I'll have no job, and I'll be back living with my parents. And of course, I'll have no money. What life has in store for me then or what happens next, I've no idea, but I'm looking forward to finding out.'

'Thanks for your time and thanks for listening.'

Michael looked over at Lauren again. She smiled at him and nodded. They both looked across at Joe Duffy. He sat with his mouth open staring at Michael. The man in the turtleneck sweater and clipboard was frozen like an extra in a wax museum.

Michael pushed the paper with the new email address and the PO Box details across the table. He stood up and Lauren stood up too. Joe looked down at the paper and opened his mouth but no words came out.

Michael waved at the producer then bent down to the microphone.

'Dead air,' he said and then turned and walked out.

Michael rolled the window down a little and breathed in the air as Lauren drove them back to the Shelbourne. He wondered what it would be like to live in the city and to explore its streets. There was always something new at every turn and at every corner.

'Are you sure you're doing the right thing?' she asked.

'We'll find out soon enough,' he told her.

'It seems a bit like in Superman when he gave up his powers for Lois Lane. Only for you there'll be no going back.'

Michael laughed at the thought of being compared to Superman. 'And who's Lois?' he asked.

'No, I didn't mean me,' she said and blushed.

They drove in silence for a while.

'It's more like,' Michael began, startling her from her thoughts. 'It's like a hot air balloon and the money's weighing me down like those bags of sand on the side. The more money I give away, the higher I can fly again. Does that make sense?'

'Yeah, but where do you plan on flying to, Michael?'

'I don't know. I can't think that far ahead yet. Maybe get a small apartment here in the city.'

'So would you not just...' she hesitated.

'What?'

'You know. Keep some of it. Maybe just a million. Do you hear me? Just a million. As if that's a small amount,' she laughed.

'No, Lauren. I want the world to know that it's all gone. Besides, I'm not even sure what I'd do with a million euro.'

'Maybe you could...'

Lauren swung the steering wheel, and her car lunged into the side of the street. A car blasted its horn behind her.

'What is it?' Michael asked, looking at her face.

'Look,' she said and pointed out through the windscreen.

At the end of the road, the majestic red brick building of the Shelbourne hotel stretched into the sky. At its base, like screaming fans in front of a rock concert stage, a large crowd was gathered on the street.

Two Gardaí wearing high-viz jackets tried in a futile effort to push them back onto the path, but there was nowhere for them to go.

'Shit,' Michael said.

'Do you think they're there because…'

'Quick, drive down that road,' Michael instructed Lauren.

After a few lefts and rights, he told her to drive up to a dark green metal door off one of the side streets. It had a NO PARKING sign screwed onto it but apart from that it was as innocuous looking as any door.

'What's this?' she asked.

'Wait,' he said.

After about ten seconds a tall man in a security uniform appeared out of another door. He looked expressionless at Lauren in the driver seat.

Michael rolled down his window and stuck his head out.

'Charlie. It's me,' he called out.

Charlie's face broke into a smile of recognition and, giving a half salute, disappeared again behind the door.

The green shutter door opened upwards, and Lauren drove in. It was a large carpark and Lauren stopped as the shutters went back down behind them.

'I was keeping an eye out for you, Mike,' the man said. 'It's mayhem out there. Tommy's on duty at the front door today and he's doing his nut.'

He didn't sound as if he had much sympathy for Tommy.

'Thanks, Charlie.'

'No worries, lads,' he said, and Lauren drove on.

They took the staff lift up to Michael's suite. Lauren spent ten minutes saying 'wow, look at this,' and picking up everything to admire it closer. As she looked out of the window, Michael ordered some food for them.

'I think the crowd is getting bigger by the minute,' she said.

Michael walked over to her and looked down.

'Holy moly,' he said and then turned to look at her.

The lace curtain was swaying in the breeze and caressing her dark hair like a wedding veil. His heart began to race by being so close to her, and he admired the perfection of her face.

She turned her head towards him and they made eye contact. Michael stepped back and steered his attention back to the room.

He cleared his throat. 'Right then, we should get to work,' he said, clapping his hands together, then feeling ridiculous at the gesture.

'Yes, we should,' she agreed.

'There's a laptop in the other room. We can look up charities and groups and then make a list of how much is going to each. Does that sound good?'

'Yeah, but I can think of loads right off the top of my head.'

'Alright, let me write it down,' he said. 'What about Max?'

'Michael, he's not a charity. I hate the way…'

'I meant is someone minding him,' he interrupted her. 'Do you need to get home to him?'

Lauren lowered her head and turned away. 'My mam is,' she mumbled.

Michael stood looking at her. 'It's none of my business, Lauren but…'

'But what?'

'Well, sometimes you don't have to be so defensive of him. Or protective.'

'I know. I know I can be over-sensitive about him. But if I don't, then who will?'

'He will, Lauren.'

Lauren scoffed at this. 'But he's just a boy. He can't.'

'No, he can't. You're right. But he'll never learn how to if you always do it for him. And you can't. You're not always going to be there for him. Trust him. He'll do fine.'

She stood looking at him, but she didn't reply.

'Come on,' he said. 'Let's get to work.'

They spent the next hour writing a list with two columns. On the left-hand-side of the page they wrote the name of a charity and on the right-hand-side the amount they would donate. The larger charities got the larger amounts, but they took time to find small volunteer organisations where even €1,000 would be a huge sum for them.

'How much have we given away now?' Michael asked Lauren.

'I'll check.'

Michael stood up to stretch his legs while she added it all up. He peeked out of the window and saw the crowd had grown to twice its size.

'Just over ten million euro.'

'This is going to take longer than I thought,' he said. 'Why can't we just give it all to one charity?'

'Because you said you wanted the money to have a good effect on as many people as possible.'

'I suppose, but if we just gave the money to all the people outside, that'd save us a lot of time,' he said.

'Yeah, but that's not what you promised. You said you'd only answer letters and emails.'

'Did you check them yet?'

'Check what?'

'The emails.'

'No, but I'll have a look now if you like.'

She logged into the new Gmail account she had set up that morning.

'Oh my God,' she said.

'How many?'

'4,310 and dozens more are coming in.'

'Shit. We're going to need someone to read all of them.'

'I can make a start.'

'Yeah, but that could be ten thousand emails by tomorrow and then we'll have the post to go through. Shit. I didn't really think this through.'

'It's okay, Michael. We'll just need to get some help, that's all.'

Michael ran his hand through his hair and paced up and down the room.

'Em, I do know someone who'd be able to manage everything,' Lauren said.

'Really, who?'

'You mightn't like it at first, but she'd be perfect.'

'She?' Michael asked, then realised who she was talking about. 'No way, Lauren. I don't even want to talk to her.'

'Come on, Michael. You said yourself that you didn't give her a proper chance to explain. She could take control of everything and hire some people. She'd also have loads of contacts.'

'I can't trust her, Lauren.'

'Then get someone to work with her. I'll be there as well. And what about Sam? She'd love to do something like this. I'm surprised you haven't asked her to help already.'

'I not sure to be honest, Lauren. Sam, yes, but Zoe?'

'You know she'd be great at it.'

Michael walked back over to the window and looked down.

'By the way,' Lauren said. 'There's another two hundred emails in since I last checked.'

He shook his head. He had imagined that this would be a fun process and that giving away millions of euro and seeing how it would make people happy would give him enormous satisfaction.

'And I thought having all that money was stressful. Who'd have thought that getting rid of it would be more stressful?'

'It's still a good thing you're doing, Michael. I'm very proud of you.'

He felt elated at her compliment but then felt embarrassed as it showed in his face.

'Okay,' he said. 'I'll call Sam and ask her if she can help. Can you call Zoe and ask her to meet us in the room?'

'How will she get through all the crowd and security?'

'Trust me. That won't pose too much of a difficulty for her.'

He looked for his phone and was surprised how cheerful he suddenly felt at the thoughts of seeing her again.

'Here,' he said giving her his phone. 'Call her on this. Her number's in it.'

'Wow. Do these things still work?' she asked him while examining his phone. 'I think I had one like this when I was in school.'

They both laughed but then froze on hearing a loud knock on the door.

22

There was a second louder knock on the door before either of them moved. When Michael opened the door he found the hotel concierge standing there in full uniform and about to knock again.

'Mr Irvine,' he said with a sigh, as if saying his name was the answer to all of his problems. His face looked like he had been running.

'Mike. Please call me Mike.'

'Mr Irvine,' he said again, but it was more of a statement than a question so Michael stood looking at him, unsure of what to say next.

'May I please have a word?'

'Of course,' Michael said. 'Come in.'

He took one foot inside the door and this apparently was sufficient. He adjusted his name tag on his chest as if it were a rose on his lapel. It read THOMAS. Michael also took one step back.

'May I just begin by saying what an honour it is for us to have you staying here with us?'

His words were long and his sentences drawn out as if he were trying to fill the time with as few words as possible.

'Thank you,' Michael said. 'It's a beautiful hotel.'

Nodding in acknowledgment, he took another step forward and Michael took another step back.

'It appears that a…' he paused to search for the word, '… a situation has emerged since you left the hotel this morning. An unacceptable situation I'm afraid to say.'

'You're referring to the crowd outside?'

'Yes, Mr Irvine. I am indeed referring to the crowd outside. It is simply not in the interests of the hotel and in particular her guests to have such a rowdy gathering at our doorsteps. You must see that, don't you, Mr Irvine?'

'Yes, I do.'

'Excellent. Well, I'm delighted we're in agreement.'

'But I'm just not sure what I can do about it.'

'You can talk to them, Mr Irvine. Ask them go away. Disperse.'

'Talk to them?'

'Yes, talk to them. Tell them to go.'

'Go where?'

'Go anywhere.'

'Do you think they would, Tommy?'

'I think… it's Thomas, by the way, not Tommy.'

'Sorry. Do you think they'd listen to me? Thomas.'

'I'm not one hundred percent sure to be honest, but something has to be done so we need to at least try.'

'And what should I say to them?'

'Tell them to go home. Tell them they are a public nuisance and are interfering irrevocably with the reputation of the hotel. Tell them, Mr Irvine to bugger off.'

Michael looked over at Lauren. She shrugged.

'We enjoy having you stay with us, but these people are here because of you and if they can't be moved on then…' Tommy let the sentence hang in the air.

'Alright, I'll try,' Michael conceded. 'But I'm not sure what good it's going to do.'

'Thank you, Mr. Irvine. Thank you.'

They stood in the lift in silence as it descended the five floors. Michael was surprised at the noise when the lift doors opened. It sounded like the crowd at a football match. When he didn't make a move to leave the lift, Tommy took him by the elbow and escorted him out and into the foyer.

'What… What am I supposed to say to them?' Michael asked as he was lead towards the door.

'To go home. Just tell them to go home. Now.'

It was even louder when the hotel door opened in front of him. He stood like a calf that had wandered mistakenly into a slaughter house.

A middle-aged woman at the front was the first to recognise him. Her face lit up as if she'd spotted a long-lost friend. He saw her word his name, but with all the noise, Michael couldn't hear his name. The man standing next to her did hear her. He turned and looked at Michael, and his face lit up too as if he'd seen his missing child in a shopping centre.

The same thing happened over two hundred times until everyone was staring at him and he was staring at them. From the raised steps of the entrance he could see above all of their heads, right to the back.

Silence fell on the street and nobody moved. He looked at all of their faces. They were ordinary people living ordinary lives with one thing in common; desperation. He could see it in their eyes, and it frightened him.

Some had their children with them, some were alone. Some held banners saying things like 'Help Me' or 'I only need €500' or 'Save Me, Michael'. He saw banner that said 'We Love You, Michael.' One long grey haired woman was swaying back and forth with a sign that said 'Saint Michael - Heal Me'.

Then, like a crashing wave on rocks, the crowd erupted in shouts and cries, and in unison they surged forward towards him. Michael fell backwards in panic, his hands searching for the door behind him.

Two quick-minded porters stepped in front of him and pushed him through the door and into the foyer. Their tall black hats were knocked onto the ground just as one arm broke through and a hand grabbed Michael's shirt. Michael heard the tear and he winced in pain as the hand's nails cut into his skin.

Other staff ran to his assistance and managed to close the door. The two hatless porters escorted Michael to the lift and stayed with him until he was safely back in his room.

'We'd better go back down and help control things,' one of the porters said, as they helped him into a chair.

'Of course,' Lauren told them. 'Thank you.'

Lauren walked over to the window when the porters had left. Like a school of circling sharks having tasted blood, the crowd had become a frenzy of chanting and shouting. Lauren closed the window and went to the wet bar in the corner. She poured Michael a whiskey and then placed it in his hand.

He looked down at the glass as if unsure what it was or where it had come from.

'Drink that,' she told him.

He sipped it in an effort to appease her rather than wanting it and then again stared at it in his hand. There was a sharp knock on the door. He jumped.

'Tell them to go away,' Michael said. 'If it's Tommy, I don't want to talk to him.'

Lauren walked into the small hall and Michael could hear her opening the door. He raised the glass to his lips again but didn't taste it.

'Well at least you're off the Baileys,' a voice said in front of him.

He looked up.

'Zoe,' he said.

'Hi Mike,' she said. 'Sorry to hear about what happened with your parents.'

Michael nodded at her.

'And I'm sorry for everything else. I didn't realise you were one of the good guys until it was too late. I know that doesn't matter now, but I wish things hadn't worked out the way they did.'

'I believe you,' he said. 'That's why you're here.'

'How did you get here so fast?' Lauren asked in an attempt to break up the tension.

'I still have my suite down the corridor,' she said. 'I figured that since Michael was paying for it then why leave?'

'What?' Michael said.

'I'm kidding,' Zoe told them. 'I was outside. You're the biggest story in town. Where else would I be?'

'So you know about my plan?'

'Everybody knows your plan. Personally, I think it's fucked up and that you'll spend the rest of your life regretting it. But hey, maybe that's just me.'

Lauren couldn't help laughing at her honesty.

'What do you want from me, Mike?' she asked.

When Michael didn't answer, Lauren spoke. 'We need help. It turns out giving away all this money isn't as straightforward as we thought.'

'Go figure.'

'And we need someone to sort of project manage it. Or at least to point us in the right direction.'

'I'll pay you for your time,' Michael told her.

'That's okay. This one's on the house,' Zoe said. 'As long as I can write about it afterwards.'

'That's one of the reasons I asked you,' Michael said. 'So that you'll write about how we gave it all away. I want everyone to know when all the money's gone.'

Zoe looked at him. 'So what? You're using me now? And here's me thinking you only wanted me for my organisational skills.'

'Well, like someone once told me, you shouldn't trust anyone.'

Zoe smiled at him and despite himself, Michael couldn't help but smile back.

For the next few hours, Michael and Lauren went back to checking charities and allocating sums of money to each one. Even Zoe had been shocked when she saw the amount of emails pouring in. She set to work on her phone and they could hear her in the next room making phone call after phone call.

At each passing hour, outside their window, they saw the crowd grow bigger. Torches were produced as the night fell and even several tents were assembled by some of the more resourceful. Camera crews and reporters interviewed the attendees and opportunistic fast food vendors appeared along the street.

When it got late, Lauren said she had to go home to Max. She agreed a time with Zoe to be back tomorrow morning and waved goodbye to Michael.

'Try to get some sleep,' she told him as she left.

As soon as she was gone, Zoe looked up from the computer. 'What's the story with you two?' she asked.

'No story. Not now anyway. I screwed up. Turns out she doesn't like obnoxious drunks who make personal accusations against her.'

'I suppose everyone has their type,' Zoe smiled.

'Yep. And I'm not it.'

'So why is she here?'

'She agreed to help.'

'But if she didn't care then why is she helping?'

'Because I'm paying her. A lot.'

'That usually works.'

Michael stood up to stretch his legs.

'How are you feeling?'

'Believe it or not, I feel good. Really tired but also like a weight has been lifted off my shoulders. Or at least is starting to.'

'Why don't you get some rest?' Zoe suggested to him.

'Maybe.'

'I still have a few phone calls to make. I'll let myself out.'

'Okay then. Goodnight, Zoe. And thanks.'

She didn't reply and when he turned around to look at her, she was calling another number on her phone again. He fell asleep almost straight away to the sound of her voice in the next room.

The sound of movement in the room also woke him the next morning. He heard the rattle of cups on a tray and when the curtains were drawn back, the light came in. In his half-sleep he had the sense he was back at home in his own bedroom and that everything had been a bad dream.

'Mam?' he whispered.

'Michael, are you awake?'

His eyes adjusted to the light and only then did he see the figure who was placing a cup of tea beside his bed.

'Lauren?'

'Good morning,' she said. 'If it can still be called the morning.'

'What time is it?'

'Almost twelve.'

'Noon?' he asked sitting up in the bed. 'Why didn't anyone wake me?'

'Zoe said to let you rest. She said you'd need it today.'

'Where is she?'

'She's unbelievable, Michael. I've never seen anyone like her.'

'Yeah,' he agreed.

'You know, I'm positive she could become the next leader of the country if she put her mind to it.'

'The next leader of ISIS, you mean. Where is she?' he asked again.

'She's still setting up the press conference. She'll be over soon.'

'There's a press conference?'

'Yeah. Almost every news channel is here. The BBC, Sky News, Euro News. I've also heard some of the reporters speaking in German and French.'

'Wait. Do I need to be there?'

'Of course, Michael,' Lauren said almost laughing. 'You're giving the press conference.'

Michael dressed while trying to call Zoe on her phone, but she didn't answer. There's was a knock on the door.

'That's probably her now,' Michael said, as Lauren went to

answer it.

Two porters, each dragging a large grey sack along the floor behind them, walked into the room.

'Sorry to disturb you, folks,' the first one said. 'These arrived for you this morning.'

They placed the two sacks just inside the door, and then left before they had a chance to be questioned.

'What is it?' Michael asked.

'How should I know?'

'Open one.'

'You open one,' she said.

Michael, as if expecting a dead body to fall out, undid the string holding the top of the first sack closed. He peeked inside.

'Oh my God,' he said, and then looked at Lauren.

Lauren took a step forward as Michael put his hand into the bag. When he took it out, he was holding a fistful of letters. Lauren looked inside and then shoved both of her hands in.

'They're all addressed to me, care of the Shelbourne,' she said. 'There must be hundreds of letters here.'

'Here's Zoe now,' Michael said when there was another sharp tap on the door.

When he opened it, the two porters were there again. Each porter dragged another bag of mail into the room and quietly left.

Ten minutes later, Lauren was showing Michael the way to the hall that Zoe had hired to hold the press conference. It was a large ornate room with a long table on one end. There were about a hundred chairs facing the table. Camera crews were setting up their equipment and some hotel staff were testing the microphones on the long table.

Everybody was too busy to recognise him as his eyes searched the room. It took him a second or two looking at the woman arranging the chairs behind the table to realise that it was his sister.

'Sam? What are you doing here?'

'Hi, Mike,' she said and gave him a hug. 'Zoe asked me to help out. This is so exciting. I'm so excited. Everyone is talking about it. The whole country is buzzing.'

'And what are most people saying?' he asked.

'That you're crazy and that you'll regret it for the rest of your life.'

Michael's head dropped. 'And what do you say, Sam?'

'That it is crazy. And wonderful. And the most extraordinary and generous thing that only the most extraordinary and generous person in the whole world could do. My brother. I've very proud of you, Mike.'

She reached over and gave him another hug.

'Now, I've got to get on with my jobs,' she told him, wiping her eyes. 'That Zoe is a slave driver.'

He heard Zoe's voice lobbing out orders on the other side of the room and he made his way over to her.

'What's going on, Zoe?' he asked her.

She seemed surprised to see him and took him by the arm and led him into a small room behind the table.

'Zoe,' he said again. 'What's going on?'

'If we're going to do this, Mike,' she said, 'then we're going to do it right. We've got to get the word out quickly, and we're going to need help.'

'Help? Help from who? We don't need any help.'

'Are you kidding me? You and Lauren spent about six hours yesterday going through your list of charities and how much have you given away?'

Michael mumbled a figure.

'How much?' she asked again.

'About ten million euro.'

'And how many emails have you opened?'

He didn't answer that one.

'Have you checked how many there are this morning?'

Again no answer.

'Exactly. And that's why we need help,' she told him.

'But I don't want other people to be responsible for it. I don't trust anyone else to not give it to their friends and family and for it turn into a big mess.'

Zoe smiled when he said he didn't trust anyone, but she ignored it.

'You are going to be the one to give it away,' she told him. 'And you are going to be the one to sign the cheques and have the final say, but how can you possibly open up all of the emails on your own?'

Michael let out a big sigh.

'Do you really want this to drag on for the next six months? Or a year?'

Michael shuddered at the thought.

'Okay, Zoe. I suppose. And there's all those letters as well.'

'What letters?' she asked him.

'I'll show you later.'

'Look, it's going to be a quick conference. I've been to a hundred of these. They just want a sound bite. A minute or two of video or a few hundred words to keep their editors happy.'

'Okay, so what I am supposed to do? What should I say to them?'

She smiled at him. 'Just be yourself; Michael Irvine. And then you'll do great. Trust me.'

23

The room was fuller but more settled by the time Zoe and Michael walked back in. Zoe walked over to one of the microphones and tapped it.

'We're going to make a start soon,' she said into it, and like obedient school children, everyone took their seats. The camera crews put their heads behind their cameras, and the photographers aimed theirs at the top table. Zoe indicted for Michael to sit beside her. Michael waved over at Lauren to sit beside him, but she shook her head.

'Thank you to everyone for coming today at such short notice,' she began. 'I know most of you in the room, and I can confirm to you that it's much easier to be on your side of this table.'

She paused while they laughed.

'But today isn't about me, it's about the man sitting next to me. I met Michael about a week ago and can honestly say that he is one of the most original and kind-hearted individuals I've ever met. That may say a lot about the company I keep, including all of you, but when I heard him on the radio promising to give away all of his EuroMillions, I wasn't as shocked as perhaps the rest of Ireland was.'

'He's promised to answer a few of your questions in a minute but the main reason for this press conference is to ask for volunteers to assist us in taking on this big task ahead of us. As exciting and rewarding as it's going to be, it's also going to take a lot of work.'

'I say volunteer because despite the end goal of our mission, you will not receive any payment. Except perhaps all the free fast food and coffee you can consume. Any other reward you do receive will be purely altruistic. There are a bunch of emails already to read through, and I'm told one or two letters to open as well.'

'The number to call is 087 555 4635. We have two volunteers already, Samantha and Lauren, and they'll give you all the details and where you should go.'

'And now, the person you really want to talk to - Michael Irvine.'

The reporters began to yell Michael's name, ignoring everything that Zoe had said. Michael froze as they all roared at him. Zoe looked over at Sam and Lauren and they had concern on their faces.

Zoe leaned forward again into the microphone, 'okay, okay. Not all at once please. Why don't we start with em... you, Johnny?'

Johnny stood up.

'Michael,' he began as the others fell silent, 'we've heard rumours that there are ulterior motives behind this cash giveaway. What can you say about them?'

Michael looked at him. Zoe put her hand on his back and pushed him forward.

'Motives? What motives? I'm sorry, I don't know what you're talking about,' Michael said into the microphone. His voice boomed around the hall.

'That the real reason you're giving away the money is political.'

'Political? How?'

'Wasn't your father once a member of the Labour Party? Do you still have ties with them? Is this a way of buying votes?'

Michael leaned into the microphone again as everyone listened.

'Are there any... real questions?' he asked.

There were chuckles among the reporters, and Johnny sat back in his seat.

'Michael,' another reporter shouted. 'Sarah from Newstalk. Why are you giving it all away? Is it because of what happened to your parents?'

'Yes.'

Everyone in the room waited for more until they realised that was his complete answer.

Sarah was still standing so she continued. 'Em... Can you

elaborate a little please?'

'Yes,' Michael said again. 'Yes, it is the reason.'

Another reporter stood up.

'Michael. John Kelleher, TV3. What about your family?'

'What about them?' Michael asked.

'Well, do they not want it?'

'You obviously haven't met my parents.'

'Your girlfriend?'

'I don't have a girlfriend.'

'And what about all your friends?'

'I don't have any.'

'Your work colleagues.'

'I'm unemployed.'

'Doesn't your extended family, cousins and uncles deserve to share it rather than strangers?'

'Deserve? Who deserves anything?'

'Michael. Stephen Doyle, The Sun. How does it feel to be trending on Twitter for the fifth day in a run?'

'I'm sorry. I have no idea what that means.'

More reporters started shouting out questions to him in rapid fire.

'Will you at least buy yourself a house? Maybe with a swimming pool?'

'No. I'm afraid I'm not a very good swimmer.'

'You're honestly going to move back into your old room?'

'Unless my parents have rented it out, yes.'

'Someone said you don't have a smartphone. Would you consider yourself a Luddite?'

'No. I'm Catholic. Although I don't go to mass.'

'Who will you favour when giving your money away?'

'No one. Anyone can ask for anything. Unless it's a big house with a swimming pool.'

'What's the most someone can ask for?'

'I hadn't thought of that. Most of the ones I've seen so far are low sums.'

'What kind of things have you been asked for so far?'

'I'm sorry, all requests will be treated and answered in confidence.'

'And when will it all end, Michael?'

'I think when the money runs out. Don't you?'

There were more giggles among the reporters, and Zoe took it as an opportunity to end the questions.

'Thank you, everyone,' she said into the microphone. 'I think we're going to end it there.'

There were groans, but people began to pack their things away.

Zoe switched off the microphone. 'That was great. You did well,' she told him.

'Did I?' he asked.

'You'll be a professional by the time this is all over.'

'How long do you think it will all take?' he asked her.

'I don't know. It depends on how many volunteers we get. I've hired an office space not too far from here. It's basic but has everything we need; computers, tables, chairs, a small canteen.'

Lauren and Sam approached the table.

'Sam,' Zoe said, sliding a mobile phone across the table to her. 'You man the phone first. Give them the address of our new offices and tell them they can start straight away. I'm going around there now.'

'What'd you want me to do?' Michael asked.

'You and Lauren need to go back to the bank. I've set up an appointment for you and they're going to issue you with a ton of cheque books. Every cheque is going to have to be signed by you I'm afraid. We'll do transfers for anyone who gives us their bank details. By the time you get back, Michael, Sam and I will have an initial list for you to approve or disapprove. That's all you'll have to do. Write a tick beside each request or a cross. The volunteers will open the post and the emails. We'll do the rest. Is that okay?'

'Okay, Zoe,' Michael said, and then looked up as Tommy approached the table. 'Hi Tomm... Thomas.'

'Hello, Mr Irvine,' he replied. His uniform seemed even sharper than normal. 'I'm afraid I've some bad news for you. The management has requested that you vacate your room. The situation outside has become intolerable for our guests and untenable for us.'

Michael looked around at the faces on the table. 'That's fair enough. I completely understand. I'll be gone by this afternoon. Can you organise my bill for me, please?'

'Well, I must say, you are being very reasonable about it,' Tommy said, relaxing a little. He reached inside his jacket pocket and produced an envelope. He handed it to Michael. 'It was really nice having you stay with us, sir.'

Michael opened up the envelope and read a one-page itemised bill. The sum at the end said €117,483. Zoe looked over his shoulder and whistled.

'I notice you waited until the press had left before you kicked him out. That was very astute of you, Tommy,' Zoe told him.

Tommy gave a slight snort and turning on his heels, walked away.

'Where am I going to stay now?' Michael asked.

'Just go home,' Sam told him.

'No, not until this is over,' Michael said. 'I can just see mam spending the entire day making trays of tea for the crowd that would follow me there.'

'What about another hotel?' she asked.

'No,' Zoe said. 'They'd just follow you there. It has to be somewhere they don't know about.'

'My house?' Sam suggested.

'No, not with the girls there,' Michael said.

'You could stay at my place,' Lauren offered.

They all looked at her.

'There's a bed in the box room, and nobody knows who I am or where I live.'

'Are you sure, Lauren?' Michael asked.

'That's a great idea,' Sam butted in.

'Okay,' Zoe agreed. 'But first go to the bank and get the cheques. You can move your stuff later. You'll also need to sign a few things there but Sean Walsh, the manager, will show you what you need.'

'My car's parked downstairs,' Lauren said, and Michael followed her without another word.

'"That's a great idea",' Zoe mocked Samantha. 'Could you be any less subtle?'

'You're the one who suggested she drives him to the bank,' Samantha laughed.

'What is it about sisters? They always hate to see their brothers single.'

'Yep. That's because there's only one thing better than being a mother; an adored aunt.'

'No. An idolised granny trumps that.'

'I'm a bit too young for that yet,' Samantha protested.

Zoe raised her eyebrows but said nothing. Samantha gasped in mock horror as Zoe stood up to go.

'Bitch,' Samantha called after her, laughing as she walked out.

In the hotel lobby, Michael signed papers for Tommy and paid his bill. He didn't dare go near the front door, but the noise from outside was enough to tell him that the crowd had grown overnight.

'Michael Irvine?' a voice said behind him.

Michael turned and saw a face he recognised but couldn't place. 'Yes?'

'Charles Poole, American Express. I'm afraid I'll require you return your Centurion card immediately.'

Michael sighed, reached into his back pocket and pulled out his wallet.

'Last week, everyone was telling me they "had the pleasure" to do this or that for me,' Michael said taking out the black card and handing it to the man.

'Now, everyone says, "I'm afraid I have to". When you have money everything is a pleasure, but when you've none, everyone's afraid. Is that how it is?'

From his jacket pocket, Charles Poole produced a pair of scissors (which of course was black) and sliced the card in two. And then again into smaller pieces. He placed the pieces in his pocket and turned to leave.

'By the way,' he said over his shoulder, 'I think it's crazy what you're doing and if you ask me...'

'Well, I didn't ask you,' Michael shut him up, and then watched him leave.

A camera flash lit up Michael's face, and he turned to see Zoe's photographer, Jake.

'Who's this, Mike?' Jake asked nodding towards Lauren. 'Is she your girlfriend?'

He snapped another picture of Lauren and then one of the two of them together. Tommy raised his arm and called two porters over. They ran up to the photographer, but before they could grab him, Michael stopped them.

'No, wait,' he said. He smiled at him. 'Jake, isn't it?'

'Yeah, Mike. That's right.'

'He's only trying to do his job,' Michael told the porters. 'How about a few photos outside with the crowd, Jake. I should really say hello to them.'

'No, Michael, don't,' Lauren told him.

'It's okay,' he told her.

'Super stuff,' Jake said. 'Look, I'm real sorry about the other day, Mike, and the article and all that. I'm just doing my job. You know how it is?'

'Sure. I understand,' Michael told him as they both walked towards the door.

The crowd cheered and yelled when Michael came out. Jake stood beside him and started to take photos of him and the crowd.

Michael raised his hand in the air. 'Hello,' he shouted to them and they quietened down with hushes. 'Like everyone else, I'm afraid I have to leave the hotel.'

The crowd gave a collective groan.

'It seems my cheque has bounced,' he joked, and they all laughed. 'I am going to ask the hotel to bring you out tea and sandwiches before we all have to leave. My treat.'

They all cheered.

'And I just want to remind you all that if you have any requests for the lottery money then you need to send a letter or an email. I promise you that each of them will be read.'

Jake continued to take photographs of everyone. Michael looked at him now.

'This is Jake,' Michael said pointing at him. 'Remember to send in your requests by email or letter, but if you have any special demands in the meantime, then can you make sure you pass them on to him now? He will help decide who gets the money. Thank you all and see you later.'

With that, Michael stepped inside the door and closed it shut. It took Jake a few seconds to realise what had happened before the first wave of the mob descended on him. He tried to run but was pushed up against the glass door, his camera falling onto the ground and smashing as people collapsed onto him.

An image of an old zombie film that Michael had seen years before came to mind as he took Lauren by the arm and they made their way to her car.

The meeting with the bank manager took longer than he thought. Not due to all of the paperwork but because everyone in the bank wanted to shake his hand or get his autograph or have a selfie taken with him.

They drove by the front of the Shelbourne on the way back and the crowd was gone. There were still a few abandoned and sunken tents attached to the fence around St Stephen's Green, but there was a crew of cleaners removing any last remnants of their vigil.

Lauren parked outside and the porters welcomed them back. She decided to have tea in the lounge while she waited for him. In his suite, Michael packed away his clothes and any other personal possessions. Despite himself, he felt a hint of sentimentality for the room.

He took one last look outside and wondered would he ever see that view again. He thought of how he had first woken in the room and how, almost, it was like thinking of himself as a different person back then.

The phone rang waking him from his thoughts.

'Hi Zoe,' he said.

'Mike, where are you now?'

'Just packing up at the hotel. I was thinking about that time when we first got to the Shelbourne.'

'Yeah, yeah. Haven't got much time for nostalgia at the moment, Mike. Listen, can you get over here ASAP?'

'Over where?'

'The offices. There's about a hundred people here already going through the post and the email. I need to start sending out those cheques, and I also need your signature on a few things.'

'Okay, I'm on my way.'

'Great. I'll text you the address.'

Michael's eyes drifted out across the treetops of the park, along the grey buildings of the city and up into the Dublin Mountains.

'And Mike?' Zoe said.

'Yeah?'

'The hotel has been there for a couple of hundred years. You can go back anytime,' Zoe told him and hung up.

Michael put his phone in his pocket, picked up his bags and left.

'We have to get over to the new offices,' he told Lauren when he found her.

'I'm ready.'

'Michael,' a voice said behind him.

He turned around to see Tommy standing there.

'What happened the "Mr Irvine"?' Michael asked him.

'Well, technically you're not a guest any more since you've paid your bill, so perhaps a little informality can be permitted.'

'Does that mean I can call you Tommy?'

'No. No, it doesn't.'

Michael laughed and so did Tommy.

'Anyway, I just wanted to say goodbye and I hope we'll have the pleasure of your company again,' Tommy said putting out his hand. 'Although maybe next time without your congregation, I hope.'

Michael shook it, then reached into his inside jacket pocket. He pulled out an envelope and handed it to him.

'What this?' Tommy asked.

'Would you mind dividing that among the staff? There should be enough for everyone to get at least a few hundred euro. It's for all their extra work.'

'That's very generous of you, Mike.'

Lauren stood up and grabbed one of Michael's bags. They both walked towards the front door and Michael shook hands with a couple of the staff.

As they reached the front door, they heard someone clapping their hands. Then another. Then more. They turned and saw the staff looking at them and all of them were clapping their hands. Many of the customers stood and clapped along.

Michael nodded a thank you, and then felt silly as tears came to his eyes. He shook them off, bowed to them all and left.

The offices that Zoe had rented were hidden behind a modern glass building off the quays. He buzzed the intercom and Samantha answered and let him in. They could hear the activity even before they had reached the room.

Even though Zoe had told him what to expect, Michael was still shocked when he opened the door. It was a large room with over a hundred people inside. Most sat at their desks staring into computer screens. Others sat opening envelopes and reading letters. There was a large monitor at the top of the room with the figure €148,957,351 written across it in red.

As he made his way through the tables, the volunteers stood up and shook his hand. Some hugged him and others patted him on his back. Again a round of applause broke out and everyone stood and cheered him.

'I could get use to this,' he whispered into Lauren's ear.

Samantha also gave him a big hug when he reached the top of the room.

'Okay,' said Zoe when he finally got to her. 'Now that you're finished playing the messiah, you can get to work.'

She looked over at everyone who was still standing. 'And that goes for all of you,' she shouted at them.

Michael and Lauren sat at a table, and Zoe went over everything with him.

She told them that the screen at the top of the room was a website, and it counted down the amount left. Everyone in the world could log on and see it. She asked him for the cheques and handed him some forms to sign.

'Now at the moment, everything is on track. What I need you to do, Mike, is to simply approve or disapprove a request that's been handed to you. The volunteers already have a bunch for you to start with. They're sifting through them all and taking out the mad hatters or the ones that are trying to get you to invest in some whacky business idea.'

'Great,' Michael said. 'Thanks, Zoe. I can see you've been very busy.'

'And also, very important, Mike,' Zoe told him. 'You need to call Sam's partner now and instruct him to sell your shares. That won't take him long, but it needs to be done and then the amount transferred back into your account.'

'Okay, I'll do that first.'

'Michael?' Lauren asked. 'Is it okay if I get back to Max?'

'Of course,' he said. 'I'm going to be here for a while anyway.'

'Should I wait up for you?' she asked.

Samantha and Zoe exchanged glances, which were ignored by Michael.

'No, it's okay. I had a lie-in this morning so I want to stay here as long as possible. I'll text you when I'm on the way. Thanks again.'

'No problem,' Lauren said and stood up. 'I'll see you in the morning,' she told Zoe and Samantha and left.

'Alright then,' Michael said to Zoe and Samantha as he stood up. 'These millions aren't going to give themselves away. Let's get to work.'

24

Lauren stayed up till 1am waiting for Michael. It was only when her mother came down to her that she eventually went to bed. The next morning she knocked on the spare room's door and, hearing no answer, gently opened the door.

The bed was just as she had left it. With her mother and Max still asleep, she crept out of the house and drove to the offices.

There were two small offices at the top of the big room and because of the cacophony of computers buzzing and people chatting, Michael had found it hard to concentrate on the requests, so had planted himself in one of them. It was there that Lauren found him.

On his desk were hundreds of opened letters and printed emails. Michael sat, hunched over, reading one of the letters. In the main room there were about twenty people still working but more were coming in carrying disposable coffee cups. There was a glass wall between the two offices and Lauren could see Zoe asleep in the other room. She looked around the room but couldn't see Samantha.

'Why didn't you come home last night?' she asked him.

He looked up at her. His eyes were slightly bloodshot, and he attempted a smile through the sombre expression on his face.

'I'm sorry,' he said. 'I just… I just got lost in the letters. All of these requests for help. People's misfortunes. Their stories. Their hardships. Sorry, I should have called.'

'No, it's okay, but are you okay, Michael?' she asked him.

'Yeah,' he said, straightening up in his chair and stretching. 'What time is it?'

'It's just gone seven. Have you been reading all night?'

'I think this is going to take longer than I thought. Where's Zoe?'

Lauren pointed into the next room.

'Let's go get some breakfast. Get out of here for a while,' Lauren suggested.

'No, it's okay. Zoe has ordered a caterer for 8am. I'll get something then.'

'Do you want me to get you some tea?' she asked him.

'Yes, please. Here, I'm finished with all of these,' he told her and handed her a pile of sheets. 'Can you give these to Zoe to process, please? I'll carry on here.'

As promised, the caterers arrived and set up an array of food. More volunteers shuffled in, and after her kids were taken care of, Samantha also arrived just after nine. Soon the room was a din of activity again.

Michael, except for short breaks, stayed in his room reading and reading. His approved sheets were carried into Zoe, and she wrote out the cheques or transferred the money into the various accounts. Samantha assisted the volunteers with any help they needed and Lauren, for the most part, stayed with Michael, helping him in any way she could.

And so, for the next four days, a routine of sorts was established. Every night, Michael would collapse onto the bed in Lauren's spare room and then early the next morning, he would make his way back to his little room and read.

Some of the letters made him smile but most of them he found arduous and painful to read. Some of the requests were for small amounts, others for hundreds of thousands.

An engaged couple, who'd lost their wedding fund when the hotel they had booked had gone into liquidation - €10,000

An old woman who couldn't pay her heating bill and the electricity company was threatening to cut her off - €500

A man who was struggling to pay for his children's school uniforms and books this year - €1000

A woman who said she had low self-esteem and blamed it on her nose and asked to pay for plastic surgery - €8,000

A married couple who were losing their home after failing to pay their mortgage because the husband had been out of work for a year - €200,000

A four-year-old-girl who needed specialised corrective heart surgery that was only available in the United States - €600,000

A woman, whose alcoholic husband had left their family with no home or savings - €250,000

A six-year-old boy asking for a new bicycle because every year he was told that Santa couldn't afford it again - €500

A mother, whose eighteen-year-old son was killed in a motorcycle accident and had borrowed to pay for his funeral but could not repay the loan - €8,000

A newly married couple who couldn't afford a honeymoon - €5,000

A woman whose autistic son needed a service dog to help him to regulate himself and to be calm in crowds - €10,000

A little girl who was constantly teased in school for her government grant glasses and who wanted to buy a designer pair - €350

A new mother of twins who had no energy and who asked for a cleaner to spend the day cleaning her house - €150

A new car for a factory worker who had to take two buses to work and two buses home and as a result never got to spend any time with his children - €20,000

And on and on it went. Michael reading and approving, and never judging. Zoe transferred the money and wrote the cheques and never questioned Michael's decisions. Lauren went online and researched other charities that needed emergency funds. So many had lost funding over the years with the economy's downturn that the list proved to be endless. She felt a little guilty asking Michael to donate to services that she had personally been affected by; physiotherapy, speech and language professionals, occupational therapy.

The figures on the large monitor clocked backwards. Sometimes slowly. Sometimes in big jumps. After two days, it dipped below the one hundred million mark. Two days later it rolled under fifty million.

Samantha brought them daily reports from mainstream media

and social media networks but soon they too were losing interest. Other events had pushed Michael's activities into the lower pages of the newspapers.

It was sometime in the afternoon of the fourth day when Lauren, Zoe and Samantha all came into Michael's office. Behind them stood a man in a dark suit and a silk red tie. At first, he reminded Michael of an actor from an American gangster film, but when he spoke, his accent was pure Dublin.

'Em, Michael?' Samantha said. 'This man wants to see you. He says you're being sued.'

Michael looked up from the letter he was reading. It was from a single mother of two who had no idea where her next month's rent was going to come from. He remained seated.

'Yes?' he said.

'Michael Irvine,' the man said, placing his black leather briefcase on the table on top of all the letters and emails. He snapped the gold catches open. 'I am acting on behalf of certain members of your family. They are named here in this letter.'

He took an envelope out of the briefcase and handed it to Michael. Michael held it in his hand but didn't look at it.

'These family members are suing you for defamation of character for a comment you made on television recently calling them...' here he read from another page, '"a bunch of spongers".' It is also the belief of my clients that they have a legal right to one million euro each, promised by you to them on June 14th of this year. You are advised to seek legal representation. Do yourself a favour, Mr. Irvine. It's time to lawyer up.'

With that he snapped his briefcase shut and took it off the table. He nodded at the three women and turned to leave.

'Excuse me,' Michael called after him.

The man stopped and looked at Michael.

'Firstly, all those accusations are false and I can produce witnesses to back them up. Secondly...'

'Well, my clients can also produce...'

'Ah, ah, ah' Michael interrupted, silencing him with the closed envelope which he still held in his hand.

'Secondly,' Michael continued, but louder this time. 'I can probably guess what names are written here in this envelope and that they haven't paid you upfront for your legal fees. In fact, I guess they haven't even paid you enough funds to buy the fuel for that BMW you used to drive over here today. So I'm guessing you're on a contingency fee basis.'

'How I am paid is of no concern to yours, Mr. Irvine.'

'You see that big monitor out there with the numbers on it going down all the time?' Michael asked him, pointing to it with the envelope. 'Do you know what that is?'

'Of course.'

'Well, in the next forty-eight hours that's going to say "zero". That means that in two days, I'll be broke. It's been awhile since I've been to school but even if you're on a twenty or thirty or possibly forty percent contingency fee, well, forty percent of zero is still zero. So if they do win, which is highly unlikely, you're going to be paid a big fat zero. Do yourself a favour and don't waste your time.'

The lawyer stood and looked down at Michael, then stared at the envelope in his hand, then over at the television screen and then back to Michael. Michael stretched his arm out further and the lawyer snapped the envelope out of his hand and marched towards the door.

'By the way,' Michael called after him, causing him to pause in the doorway. 'You should read John Grisham novels instead of watching the movies. Nobody says "lawyer up' in real life.'

Zoè, Lauren and Samantha looked at one another with expressions of shock mixed with elation and pride as the lawyer stormed through the sea of volunteers.

'Can we all get back to work now?' Michael asked them, his attention already back on the letter in his hand.

Zoe's military hand salute was missed by Michael as all three went back to their desks.

On the fifth morning, as usual, Michael had got into the office ahead of Lauren.

'Good morning,' she said, as she entered the room.

Michael grunted and turned his head away.

'Michael? Is everything alright?'

He nodded his head but didn't reply.

She went over to him and put her hand on his shoulder. His head was pointed away from her, but she could see the tears streaming down his face.

'Michael, what's wrong?'

He took a deep breath and wiped his face. 'There's not enough,

Lauren.'

'Enough what?'

'Money. There's not enough money.'

'There's still almost ten million euro left,' she told him.

'But look at all of these,' he said pointing to the piles and piles of pages on the table in front of him. 'What about these? What about the ones still coming in? How are we going to help them all?'

'We can't, Michael. We were never going to be able to. Not even if you had a hundred hundred million euro. Whatever that is.'

'Then what was it all for?' he asked. He buried his head into his hands. Lauren poured him a glass of water and then sat down beside him.

'I heard this story once,' she said, 'about a man on a beach, and he sees this little boy throwing things into the sea. He asks him what he's doing and the boy tells him that he's throwing the starfish back in, because the tide is going out and the sun is coming up. The man laughs at him and tells him that there are thousands of starfish and miles of beach. What difference will saving a few make? The boy picks one up and throws it in and tells him, "well, it makes a difference for this one".'

Michael raised his head up and smiled at her. 'When did you become so smart?'

Lauren laughed. 'Hey, just cause I work in a bar, doesn't mean I don't have a brain.'

Michael stood up and took some deep breaths.

'You need a break, Michael.'

'No, we're almost finished.'

'Just for a few hours. We can handle things here.'

She tapped on the glass wall to Zoe's office and waved for her to come in.

'No, really, Lauren. I'm fine.'

Michael saw Zoe stand up from her desk. He wiped his face with his hands.

'What's wrong?' Zoe asked.

'Nothing's wrong,' Lauren told her. 'I just think Michael needs a break. To go for a walk around the city for a while.'

'Okay, fine,' Zoe said.

'I'll be alright,' Michael said.

'You need to clear your head, Michael,' Lauren told him. 'All these requests are affecting your health.'

'Why don't you go with him?' Zoe suggested. 'Go get lunch somewhere?'

'I can't,' Lauren said. 'I've to collect Max at 12.'

Zoe looked from her to Michael and then back to her. 'I'll tell you what. Go get Max now and come back here.'

'For what?' Lauren asked.

'You'll see. We'll meet you outside at the entrance in an hour.'

Lauren looked at Michael, and he shrugged at her.

'You know,' Michael told Zoe as they both watched Lauren walking through the volunteers. 'I know what you're doing.'

'What do you mean?'

'You and Sam. Trying to get Lauren and me together. It's not going to work. She's not interested.'

'I've no idea what you're talking about. Now, I've a couple of phone calls to make.'

'Calls to who?' he asked.

'You'll see. I hope we've cured you of your fear of heights,' she told him and went back into her office.

25

As Michael stood outside the building waiting for Lauren and Max, he realised that he hadn't seen daylight in four days. He took a deep breath in and exhaled.

'So, what's your idea?' he asked Zoe again for the tenth time.

They heard a car beep and saw Lauren park her car.

'Ah, saved by the bell,' Zoe told him, and they both walked over to her.

Lauren helped Max out of the car seat and then introduced him to Zoe. Max stretched out his hand and she shook it.

'Pleased to meet you, Max. I've heard a lot about you. I'm Zoe.'

'I'm Max,' he said. 'You have a funny name.'

'Max,' Lauren scolded him.

'You're right,' Zoe said. 'Everyone thinks that. But you're the first person to actually say it.'

'I think you've finally met your match,' Michael told her.

'Looks like it,' Zoe said.

'So now, will you tell us what this is all about?' Michael asked her.

Zoe ignored him. 'Fancy going on a bit of an adventure today, Max?'

'Sure,' he said.

'Okay, let's go,' she said and put out her hand for him. He took it and she led him back into the building.

Michael made a face to Lauren to let her know he had no idea what she was up to.

They got into the lift and Zoe asked Max to press the highest number of the buttons. When the doors closed, Zoe got down on her haunches and looked at Max.

'Now, Max,' she began. 'Mike here has...'

'Michael,' Max interrupted her. 'His name is Michael.'

'Sorry,' she said. 'Michael here has promised your mum something, do you know what it is?'

Max shook his head.

'That she can try to find a nice house near the sea in a little village. Somewhere for you play. Isn't that amazing?'

'I love the sea,' Max told her.

'Today you're going to help her to find that house.'

'What?' both Michael and Lauren said.

'And do you know the best way to look for a house like that?' Zoe asked Max, continuing to ignore Michael and Lauren.

'What?' Max asked.

The lift made a loud BING and the doors opened to a hall with a metal stairs.

'This way,' Zoe said and started to climb the stairs with Max still holding her hand.

There was a wide metal door at the top of the steps and Zoe pushed it open. The bright daylight flooded in and they stepped out onto the roof of the building. Max put his hands to his ears at the sound of the blue helicopter that sat with its propellers rotating.

'What the fuck?' Michael said. 'What's this?'

'It's a helicopter,' Max screamed above the noise of the engines. 'Mammy, Mammy, look it's a helicopter. Can we go in it?'

The wind whirled around them as they stepped away from the door.

'Tomorrow, you're probably not going to be a millionaire,' Zoe shouted at Michael. 'So this is your last chance to live like one.'

Lauren looked at Michael trying to hide her excitement.

'It's yours for the day. Go look for that village by the sea with Lauren and Max.'

Michael looked at Lauren, and she nodded her agreement.

'What about the requests? All the emails?' Michael asked.

'Sam and I will continue with them,' Zoe told him.

'But how will you know whether I'd approve them or not?'

'Michael,' she said and touched his face. 'You approve them all.'

Michael looked at Lauren and Max again, and couldn't help but smile back at their excited faces.

'Okay, then, let's go,' he said and the three of them walked towards the helicopter.

The pilot got out and helped them to get seated and then put large headphones over their ears. Then within minutes, they felt themselves rise above the building. Lauren squeezed Max's hand, and they all watched Zoe get smaller as she waved them out of sight.

The pilot took them up over Dublin City, along the River Liffey and then up towards the Dublin Mountains. He watched their faces as they stared in awe out of the windows, nudging each other to look at something else they'd spotted.

'Okay, folks,' a voice said into their headphones. 'My name's Greg and I'll be your pilot for today. And no, there's nothing wrong with your headphones. I am in fact an Australian and we all talk this funny. You seemed to be enjoying the view too much for me to interrupt you, but now we can get down to business. How are you doing, little fella?'

Max gave him a thumbs up.

'Those headphones you're wearing have a little mic attached so you can speak freely amongst yourselves.'

'We're doing great,' Lauren said and, they all laughed at hearing her voice.

'My name's Max,' Max said.

'Hello Max,' Greg replied. 'So, I'm told the schedule today is to find a nice little village near the beach. Is that right?'

'Yes, thank you,' Lauren said.

'Okay then. So just sit back and relax and we'll find some place nice. I'll head down the coast towards Wicklow and we'll see what happens. Max, look out to your right. That's the Sugar Loaf Mountain. I'll go in a little closer and you can wave to all the folks out there.'

The helicopter leaned to the right, and they could make out the faces of the hikers on the side of the mountain. Max waved at them and most of them waved back. Lauren knew Max was a happy child but the expression of sheer joy on his face at that moment filled her with elation, and she fought back the tears.

They flew low along the coast passing the white beaches of Brittas Bay and then past the town of Arklow. After about twenty minutes in the air, they heard Greg's voice again.

'What do you folks reckon on that place over there?'

They all leaned out of their seats and saw a village with about fifty houses, and the steeple of a church pointing up at them. There was an open square at the centre of the village where they could make out a few shops, a cafe, two pubs and a school.

Lauren tapped Michael's jacket and pointed out to their left. He saw a row of ten or fifteen houses just outside the village. Each house was different but they all had long green back gardens that bordered onto the beach.

Michael smiled and nodded.

'Can we land near there, please?' Lauren asked Greg.

Greg looked over to where she was pointing to. 'No worries,' he replied and the helicopter swooped down to the right.

It took him a couple of fly-overs before he spotted a safe place for them to land. They waited until the engine was turned off and the propellers had stopped moving before they got out.

'I better wait here with the chopper,' Greg told them. 'Just in case some farmer or bull comes out to investigate. Take your time though. Have a couple of bevvies if you like. The village is back that way about ten minutes' walk.'

'Thanks, Greg,' Michael said, and the three of them set off.

After only a few minutes Max began to lag behind so Michael lifted him onto his shoulders. They walked until they reached the town's square, then followed the road out towards the sea. A single pier stretched out from the harbour like a crooked finger pointing out to the horizon.

Without anyone suggesting it, they walked along its century old bricks until they reached the very end, then turned and strolled back. Max walked between them holding their hands, swinging back and forth like a pendulum. The sea was calm, and the boats that sat upon it cast their reflection on the water and barely moved, so that every view out to sea was like a painting on a wall.

Lauren and Michael spoke, as they always did, of happy things; their hopes, their wishes, their dreams. Lauren asked Michael what his plans were after all the money was gone, and he told her he hadn't given it too much thought and she believed him.

Lauren confessed, now that Michael had transferred the money into her account, of having already looked online for a suitable home. She told him Galway was looking a strong possibility and Michael promised her that he would come visit them when they were settled. She told him she would look forward to that.

Before they even realised it, they were back in the village. They chose the pub with the thatched roof and ordered tea and sandwiches. Although it wasn't a cold day, the fire was lighting and the smell of burning turf filled the room. They ate and drank without feeling the need to talk, and only the sound of the fire and the clink of cups on saucers broke the silence.

Afterwards, they walked in the direction where they had seen a beach. All along the road they could hear the waves but couldn't find any access. When they had passed the third house, Michael jumped over a small wall and ducked under a thick line of bushes. He disappeared for a few minutes before he re-emerged smiling.

'Come on. This way,' he told them, and Lauren grabbed Max and lifted him over the wall and into Michael's arms.

They poked their way through the bushes and climbed a small hill to be rewarded with a beach that stretched white and wide and ran for miles in both directions.

'Yippee,' Max cried and ran down the sandy bank.

'Be careful, Max,' she called after him, but didn't want to stop the exhilaration she saw in his face. Michael too got carried away by Max's pure delight and he ran after him, catching up and then grabbing him, and then both of them tumbling around in the sand like puppy dogs.

Michael brushed himself off and came back to Lauren. They walked as Max ran in and out of them, the sound of the crashing waves interweaving with Max's laughter.

'Michael, I know I've said it already, but I just want to tell you properly how much that money means to me. To us, Max and me,' Lauren said.

'If it gets you that house and new business you dream about, and it gets Max a new school then it'll make the last couple of weeks and everything else worth it.'

'It's not just about the school though. Or the house. It's about Max's future.'

'His future?' Michael asked her.

'There's so many things going on in his life right now, his speech and language, his physiotherapy, his constant yearly tests on every part of him. But you know what keeps me awake at night?'

Michael stopped walking and looked at her. 'What?'

'It's what's going to happen twenty years from now? Or forty?

Or fifty?'

Michael laughed. 'You don't have to think that far ahead, Lauren. No parent has to think like that.'

'But I do. Who's going to care for him when I'm gone? And even if that person is around, then who's going to pay for it? I know you gave me the money for a house and a B&B to buy and all that, and I hope you don't mind, but I've put nearly all of it into a trust fund for Max's future. We still have enough to start again somewhere else down the country but not enough for all the other stuff. I'm sorry, but it was important to me. Is that okay?'

'Lauren, it's your money. You can do whatever you want with it.'

'Thank you, Michael. I just wanted to tell you. I felt I was being a little dishonest with you by not using it for the reason you gave it to me.'

'But you should have said. There's still enough so that you can have both. Why don't we, when we get back…'

'No, Michael.'

'No what?'

'I know what you're going to say, and that's why I waited until the money was gone before I told you. You've already given us enough. I couldn't take anymore.'

'But it's not all gone yet.'

Lauren reached into her jacket pocket and took out her phone. She pressed some buttons and handed it to him. 'Yes it is,' she said.

Michael looked down at the screen of the phone and read the opened message.

Can't get through to Mike. Please let him know that mission accomplished. Bank account just hit zero. Zoe. PS Please try to bring the helicopter back in one piece as we've no funds to pay for a crash!

Michael looked up at her. 'It's over?' he asked.

'I guess so,' she said.

He let out a deep sigh. He turned to look at Max zigzagging his way along the beach, screaming and waving a stick in the air like a knight battling dragons. The sky was darkening where it fell into the sea and threatened the air with rain. Summer was coming to an end.

'Looks like a downpour is on the way,' she told him.

'I was right,' he said, more to himself than to her.

'You were right about what?'

'That nothing has changed. Everything is still as beautiful, and life goes on. With or without all that money.'

Max had made his way up to them by now. 'Please, Mam, can I go into the water?'

'Absolutely not,' she told him.

'But please. Just my feet. I'll take off my shoes and socks. I promise. Please.'

'No, Max.'

'I don't mind going in with him,' Michael told her, smiling. 'I promise to take my shoes and socks off too.'

Lauren shook her head. 'Okay, then. But if both of you have a cold tomorrow, don't blame me.'

'Thank you, thank you,' Max said, then reached up and pulled Michael by his hand. 'Come on, Michael. Let's go.'

He allowed himself to be pulled away from Lauren as they both ran towards the edge of the sea. Lauren watched them sit together on the sand, and Michael help Max to remove his shoes.

Perhaps, she thought to herself, looking out at the horizon. Perhaps, it wasn't going to rain after all.

After only ten minutes flying in the helicopter, Max fell asleep. Michael placed his jacket over him, and he and Lauren sat in silence, each of them gazing out at the passing world, lost in their own thoughts.

Zoe was on the roof to meet them as they landed. They both hugged Zoe and thanked her, but there was nothing much else to say. Michael lifted Max out of his seat and carried him down in the lift. He asked Lauren how it was possible he could sleep through the noise of a helicopter, and she suggested it was all the sea air.

As Michael leaned over him to strap him into the car seat, his almond-shaped eyes opened for a moment, and they looked at each other. Then his eyelids closed again and his head fell to the side and into a deep sleep.

Michael was overcome with sadness but didn't know why. He suddenly felt lonelier than he had ever felt before; as if he had just glimpsed the most beautiful thing in the world, and it had passed him by.

His parting with Lauren was brief. She thanked him again, and he shrugged it off. Then she hugged Zoe and told her she hoped they would meet again, neither of them believing that they ever would.

Michael and Zoe stood together waving until her car was out of sight. Only then did they turn and walk back into the building. Everyone had gone, and the room seemed bigger than it had before.

'Where's Sam?' Michael asked her.

'She left earlier. Said she'd call you tomorrow.'

'Who's going to clean up this place?'

'We paid them enough. They can do it themselves.'

'I had wanted to give the volunteers something before they left.'

'I did. I divided up the petty cash between them. About €500 each.'

'Thanks.'

The large monitor had a flashing red zero on it and it pulsed like a heart beat in the room. Michael became agitated by it and unplugged it. He went into his office and Zoe went into hers, and they began to pack away their things.

'Here, I got you something as a thank you,' Michael told her when he was finished. He threw a piece of paper on her table.

'I told you I didn't want anything,' she insisted.

'Then you can give it away.'

'What is it?' she asked.

'Look at it yourself.'

She picked up the page and read.

'Are you fucking kidding me?' she said. 'Mike, what the fuck is this?'

'A three-bedroomed townhouse in the heart of the city. You were always complaining about your other place.'

'But this must have cost... How much did it cost?'

'Too much in my opinion.'

She shook her head in disbelief reading the page.

'All you have to do is sign that bottom line and it's yours.'

'I don't know what to say, Mike.'

'Sometimes, Zoe, there is nothing to say.'

She picked up a pen and signed her name, then sniffled and wiped her nose.

'Are you crying?' he mocked her.

'No,' she said wiping her eyes. 'And don't go telling anyone that

I was either. Or I won't let you come visit me in my new place.'

'Okay, fair enough. It's a deal. Come on, let's get out of here.'

'Wait,' Zoe said, 'I got something for you too.'

She opened the drawer of her desk and took out a box wrapped in red paper. It had a white bow attached to the top.

'What's this?' Michael asked, genuinely surprised.

'A little something to say thanks,' she said and handed it to him.

He took it from her and ripped off the paper.

'An iPhone?' he said.

'The latest one,' she told him. 'With no money and a smart phone, it'll help you blend in with the rest of us.'

'Thanks, Zoe,' he said, and walked over to her and hugged her.

They walked through the empty desks. Zoe switched off the lights. It was starting to get dark when they were back outside.

'I thought you and Lauren would…,' Zoe said.

'Nah,' Michael told her. 'I guess some things just aren't meant to be.'

'So what now?'

'She'll probably move somewhere with Max. She's not too sure where yet.'

'No, I meant what now with you? What are your plans?'

He was silent then, and he looked up and down the street. A couple was walking towards them arm in arm.

'I don't really know, Zoe,' he told her. 'I really don't.'

'You'll figure it out. I'm not worried about you.'

'No, I'm not worried about me either.'

They both took a step backwards to allow the couple to pass.

'What about you?' he asked her, but when she didn't reply he looked at her.

'Zoe? You okay?'

'You know who that was?'

'Where? Who?'

'That man that just went by. Did you see who it was?'

'No. Who?'

'Martin Fitzsimmons.'

'Who?'

'The Chief Financial Officer for Myers International Bank.'

'So?'

'And you know that wasn't with him? Mrs Fitzsimmons.'

She buttoned up her jacket.

'Mike, I got to go. This could be big. I'll call you. And hey,' she said as she walked away holding up the paper he had given her, 'thanks for this.'

'Call me when you have your housewarming,' he shouted after her.

'Do you really think I do housewarmings?' she yelled back, smiling at him and then disappeared around a corner in the same direction as the couple had gone.

Michael stood alone in the street. He put his hands into his pockets and found his phone. He took it out. There were no missed calls.

He thought about calling Lauren but then quickly pushed the idea out of his head. He then thought about going to Harry's but then decided against that too.

He pressed some numbers on the phone and held it to his ear.

'Hello?' said the voice on the other end.

'Hello, Mam,' he said.

'Michael, your father and I were only talking about you. Where are you?'

'I'm in town.'

'I'm just putting the dinner on now. Would you like me to put some on for you?'

'Yeah, that'd be great thanks.'

'Alright, son. See you soon.'

Michael hung up, and put the phone away. A taxi went by and he took out his wallet and looked inside. There was only a single ten euro note inside. He smiled to himself.

'Looks like you're getting the bus home,' he told himself, and then zipped up his jacket and walked towards the quays.

JOSEPH BIRCHALL

ONE WEEK LATER

26

Michael stopped running and checked the jogging app on his iPhone. He smiled in satisfaction between gulps of air, then spent a minute stretching out the muscles in his legs.

'Been running again, have you?' Bobby Boylan asked, as Michael entered his shop.

'Did you used to be a detective?' Michael asked him.

'No,' Bobby replied.

Mrs Farrell, who had only popped in for a sliced pan, but who was still waiting twenty minutes later with the money in her hand having listened to exactly what Bobby would do about the refugee crisis, smiled.

Michael grabbed a bottle of water from the fridge.

'Hello, Michael,' Mrs Farrell said.

'Hello, Mrs Farrell. How are you keeping?'

'Grand. I hear they're making a film about you and the lottery and all that.'

'So they say, but sure who knows? They're only talking about it at the moment.'

'They'll probably get someone like Colin Farrell to play me,' Bobby added.

'Colm Meaney more like,' Mrs Farrell said, and Michael laughed.

'Whatever,' Bobby said. 'I heard they're going to call it "The Shop Keeper's Lucky Ticket".'

'I doubt it,' Michael told him.

'I heard it's called "The Millionaire",' Mrs Farrell said.

'Maybe,' Michael told her. 'A reluctant one though.'

He put his two euro coin onto the counter in front of Bobby.

'Do you want to know what I'd have done with all that money?' Bobby asked, turning his full attention towards Michael.

'No, Bobby. I don't,' Michael told him as he left the shop. 'Goodbye, Mrs Farrell.'

Michael jogged the remaining short distance to his house. A couple of cars beeped hello at him, and he waved back. A man called his name from across the street, and Michael gave him the thumbs up sign.

He showered and changed and went into the kitchen, where he found his mother.

'Hi Mam,' he said.

'How was your run?' she asked.

'Great thanks. Although it's getting colder in the mornings.'

'You know, I really wish you would shave that beard off,' she told him. 'You'll never get a job with a beard.'

'But I'm not looking for a job, Mam.'

'Why don't you just take your old job back? They've asked you enough times.'

'Because I'd rather go live with Uncle Jim than go back to that place,' he told her.

'Alright then. I won't mention it again.'

'Thank you.'

'Samantha's coming over with the kids. She has the brochure for her new house. I'll ask her to have a word with you.'

Michael shook his head and put the kettle on. The doorbell rang.

'That must be her now,' Rose said and rushed to the door.

Michael looked out into the back garden. His father had a lawnmower disassembled on a large table, and he was standing over it and picking up each piece like he had no idea what it was.

'Hello, love,' Michael could hear his mother at the front door, but he couldn't hear his sister's voice.

'He's in the kitchen.'

The kitchen opened behind him. 'I really have to get my own place ASAP,' he said without turning around. 'Maybe I'll move into your old place when you move out.'

'Okay, but my mother will still be there.'

Michael spun around.

'Lauren. I thought you were… someone else.'

'Hi, Michael. How are you?'

'I'm grand. How are you? How's Max?'

'We're good, thanks.'

They stood in silence for a few moments.

'I like your beard,' she said.

'It's a bit scruffy at the moment, but it'll grow.'

'It suits you.'

More silence.

'So,' Michael said. 'Do you fancy a cup of tea?'

'No thanks. Max is in the car. Your mam's minding him. We're leaving for Galway. The car's all packed.'

'Oh, I see.'

'What have you been up to?' she asked him.

'I've been very busy. Different things. I hardly get a minute, to be honest.'

'That's good.'

'So this is exciting. You moving. I'm happy for you.'

'Well, we're going to stay in a hotel for a week or so, and from there check out a few places around Galway.'

'And how's Max taking it all?'

'Actually, he talks about you a lot. He's always asking if he can visit Michael and his helicopter.'

They both laughed.

'I'm afraid all I can offer him at the moment is a disassembled lawnmower in the back garden.'

'He misses you.'

Michael tried to say something, but the words seemed to stick in his throat.

'And I miss you too, Michael.'

He heard her words but didn't believe his ears.

'What?'

'I said, I miss you. I miss us.'

'But, I thought…'

'I see how you are with Max, and I love the thought of us as a family, but I had to make sure that it wasn't just because Max loves you and that you love Max. I had to make sure that I loved you too.'

Michael stared at her.

'And I do, Michael. I do love you,' Lauren told him. 'Will you come with me to Galway? With us? Help us find a new home? Together?'

Michael said nothing.

'Unless of course, you've got too much going on here. I mean, if you have plans and you're...'

'No,' Michael told her. 'I'm not doing anything. And I can't think of anything else I'd rather do.'

Lauren walked towards him, and they embraced. Then they tilted their heads back and looked into each other's eyes and kissed.

After a few moments, they pulled away, both of them laughing.

'Give me five minutes to throw a few things into a bag,' he told her.

'Okay. I'll wait outside.'

He watched her walk away, and she turned and looked at him before opening the kitchen door and leaving.

As soon as the door was closed, Michael made a fist and jumped up and down into the air. He raised both his arms upwards as if passing the finishing line of a race. He took a few deep breaths and ran up the stairs to his room. He grabbed a bag and opened his wardrobe.

The phone in his pocket began to ring, but he ignored it. He went into the bathroom and grabbed his toothbrush. The phone rang again.

He took it out and looked at the screen. He didn't recognise the number.

'Hello,' he said, as he took a pair of jeans out of the drawer.

'Michael?' a voice replied.

'Yes? Who's this?'

'It's Derek.'

'Hi Derek. I heard Sam is on her way over. Were you looking for her?'

'No, Michael. I was looking for you. I'm afraid I've a bit of bad news.'

Michael's heart sank.

'What is it? Is there something wrong with Sam?'

'No, no. Everything's fine. It's just I've been meaning to call you for a while.'

Michael stopped packing. He looked out of his window and saw Rose talking to Lauren beside her car.

'It's one of the accounts that you had asked me to invest in,' Derek continued. 'I had, as instructed, placed ten percent into an aggressive fund, which could also be deemed as high risk. You were right not to put everything into blue chips or bonds given the market's liquidity and your own net worth at the time.'

Michael had no idea what he was talking about but just listened.

'Anyway, when I sold all of your stocks and bonds and funds, I was prevented from getting rid of one stock, Diazon, as trading had stopped due to a possible takeover bid after the release of their Zanac drug was proven to be so effective. There was also talk of a possible MBO or even an IPO. Then the SEC suspected some insider trading, so of course everything was put on hold.'

'Derek, can you speak in English please?'

'Sorry, Michael. What it boils down to is that everything has been sorted and the takeover went ahead.'

'And?'

'Well, that's the thing. I'm afraid that I've only now been able to access those funds again, and to take back control of that initial invested sum of €100,000.'

Michael saw they had taken Max out of the car, and his dad had come out to the front of the house as well.

'So, I still have €100,000 in my account?' Michael said.

'Well, no. Not exactly. You now have two shares of the parent company for every one of the old stock. Plus there was a split announced this morning.'

'You're losing me again.'

'Hold on,' Derek said and Michael could hear him tapping on his computer. 'At present market value if you sold everything, you're looking at about 1.4 to 1.5. Give or take a few euro.'

'So you're saying that I still have about €150,000 in my account?'

'No, Michael. I'm saying you still have 1.5 million euro still in your account. Look, I know that's quite a bit, and I also know how much effort you went to get rid of it all. I should have told you before, but it's only this morning the whole saga has finally settled down, and I said I'll call you straight away.'

Michael watched as his dad threw Max a ball on the road and then threw it back to his dad. Lauren and his mam were talking and laughing and leaning against the car.

'Michael? Michael, are you still there?'

'Sorry,' Michael said into the phone.

'So, what do you think?'

'About what?'

'About the million and a half, of course. Should I sell or hold? If you want I could have the money transferred into your bank account by this afternoon.'

'Does anyone else know about this?' Michael asked him.

'No, of course not, Michael. I'd never discuss this stuff with anyone. Not even Sam.'

'Okay, thanks. Yeah, do that, please. Sell it all.'

'And what are you going to do with it?'

Lauren spotted Michael looking down at them and she waved up at him and beckoned him down to her. He nodded and smiled back.

'Oh, I can think of a few things.'

'Okay, consider it done.'

'Thanks, Derek. I have to go.'

'Okay, Michael. I'll text you later when it's all done and dusted.'

'Okay thanks,' Michael said and hung up the phone.

Max ran to Michael when he saw him coming out of his house.

'Are you coming on holiday with us as well?' he asked Michael.

'Yes, I am, Max.'

'This is going to be the best holiday ever,' Max yelled. 'And are you coming? And you?' he asked Jack and Rose.

'No they're not,' Michael said, and realising he may have said it a little too quickly added, 'maybe some other time.'

'Are you ready?' Lauren asked him.

'Yep,' he said, holding up his bag.

'Throw it in the back with the rest of our junk,' she told him.

Lauren helped Max into his car seat, embraced Rose and Jack and got into the driver's seat.

Michael walked towards the passenger door then stopped. He turned around and went over to his parents and hugged both of them.

'Goodbye,' he told them. 'I'll call when we get there.'

Rose wiped away a tear.

'I'm only going away for a week, Mam,' Michael assured her.

She nodded but didn't say anything.

Michael climbed in beside Lauren. She turned around to Max.

'Are you ready to help us find a new home, Max?'

'Yes, Mammy. And can we go to the sea?'

'Of course,' she told him.

'And maybe,' Michael suggested, 'we can have a look out for that little pub you once told me about? We could buy it, and you could run it, and I could be your lounge boy? Or even just a little B&B by the sea.'

'I told you, Michael,' Lauren said. 'I don't think we have the money for that.'

'Maybe we do.'

'How? Did you win the lottery again?' Lauren laughed as she started the car.

Michael looked back at Max and then at Lauren.

'Yes,' he told her. 'I think I did.'

Rose and Jack stayed on the road waving as they watched the three of them drive up the street and turn the corner.

THE END

ABOUT THE AUTHOR

www.josephbirchall.com

Made in the USA
Middletown, DE
20 March 2018